The
Paris
Inheritance

BOOKS BY NATALIE MEG EVANS

The Dress Thief
The Milliner's Secret
A Gown of Thorns
The Wardrobe Mistress
The Secret Vow
The Paris Girl
Into the Burning Dawn
The Italian Girl's Secret
The Girl with the Yellow Star
The Locket

The
Paris
Inheritance

NATALIE MEG EVANS

bookouture

Published by Bookouture in 2024

An imprint of Storyfire Ltd.
Carmelite House
50 Victoria Embankment
London EC4Y 0DZ

www.bookouture.com

Storyfire Ltd's authorised representative in the EEA is Hachette Ireland
8 Castlecourt Centre
Castleknock Road
Castleknock
Dublin 15, D15 YF6A
Ireland

ISBN: 978-1-83525-561-2
eBook ISBN: 978-1-83525-560-5

For my mother, who first took me to Paris

PROLOGUE

'It's a boy?' She holds out her arms for the tiny, naked form wrapped in a strip of towel. This human miracle writhes inside its cocoon, eyes tight shut from the sudden contact with daylight.

Emotion pours into her, warm syrup straight into her veins. 'Of all days to enter this world, why this one?' When the minute-old focus fixes on her as if she were the light, she knows she will do anything to protect this life. She drops the lightest kiss on a wrinkled brow that smells vaguely of the sea. The eyes are the colour of water under a shaded sky.

When the Catholic sister who has attended the birth asks what name is to be given, she hesitates. The doctor, who came late, also awaits her reply. When she puts forward the one she's chosen, they look horrified. Such a name is impossible, they won't permit it! The sister says sternly, 'We must also agree what's to be done for the baby's care. This is no time for self-indulgence.'

'It's already decided,' she says, breathlessly. 'I will keep him.' No hesitation in her reply this time. Nothing will separate them. Her war baby, her winter miracle, born into a perilous existence. She will do anything – *anything* – to keep this precious gift safe from every conceivable harm.

When the time comes for her to leave, he goes with her, carried on her back. All her possessions fit into one bag. Pinned to the front of her coat is his inheritance: a silver brooch shaped like a dove in flight. It has only modest value but in a world at war, it represents faith in better times and most important of all, indelible proof of who he is.

_____

HOPE

LAZURAC, THE GERS REGION, SOUTH-WEST
FRANCE, THURSDAY 12 JUNE 2014

It was the planter that first caught her eye.

Vintage planks, artfully distressed with 'Oranges d'Espagne'
stencilled on the side. Exactly what she was looking for, except
it was full of art prints, the kind you find on the walls of chain-
motel bedrooms. She rifled through, wondering if she could buy
the box and leave the pictures. Where was Ash? Her partner
was better than her when it came to asking for what he wanted.
Not that she should be wanting this box at all. They'd agreed,
no unnecessary spending until their income started rolling in.

Only, she'd spent the last month up a ladder, painting
window frames to save employing a professional. A small
reward was not unreasonable... and the box would look perfect
on the terrace where their guests would sip their evening drinks.
If Ash agreed, she'd make the stallholder an offer.

Ah, there he was, pressed into the shadows of a stone fountain. His phone was jammed to his ear and he looked agitated,
though Hope put this down to the angle of the sun. Lazurac's

Thursday flea market had moved to its summertime schedule, mid-afternoon until late, and the day was drifting to its close. The stallholders would be packing up soon. After waiting in vain for Ash to finish his call, she continued to sort through the pictures, aware that she, in her turn, was being watched.

The stall's owner came to stand beside her.

'Can I help?' It was asked in French, with a local Gascon accent. Hope met dark eyes, heavy with eyeliner. Not overly friendly. 'They're all one price,' the stallholder added. She was mid-forties, more than a decade Hope's senior, but dressed younger in layered, multi-coloured grunge. 'I'll do three for the price of two,' she offered.

'OK...' Hope could offer to take a couple, if the crate was thrown in as well. Only, she couldn't sneak them home without Ash noticing and he'd made such a big thing about them reining in their spending.

How long was he going to be on that call? One sandalled foot was resting on the lip of the fountain, and he was grinding the stone in a stressed way. Hope felt a chilly apprehension. Late last night as they'd drunk peppermint tea on their candle-lit terrace, his phone had lit up.

She'd asked, 'Who's that at this hour?'

He'd swooped on it, saying, 'Nobody,' and turned the phone face down. But not quick enough. Who was DeeCee?

More curtly than she intended, she told the stallholder she'd carry on looking. The woman shrugged and left her to it. Hope rifled through the prints until her fingers encountered a textured surface. Intrigued, she lifted it out. Her breath caught.

It was an unframed portrait in oils of a young woman, but it was no chocolate-box image. Beneath savagely cropped hair, green eyes screamed out untranslatable emotion. Hope held it at arm's length, bizarrely fearful that the woman's pain might jump across. The face was sensitively done but the rest, the clothes and the background, was painted in a loose, Impressionist style. The subject wore a print summer dress with a turned-down collar and squared shoulders.

1940s? The style shouted 'wartime'. Hope's interest was piqued. As a former art student, a studier of technique, she'd been particularly drawn to mid-twentieth-century art. When her eye fell on an object on the lower right-hand side of the picture, critical detachment evaporated.

'Oh, my God.'

Hope could not accept what she was seeing.

It was a brooch, pinned below the second button of the dress. A bird in profile, its wings raised in flight. Hope felt a sensation like a balloon expanding inside her chest. Expanding then bursting. Disbelief flooded to her fingertips as she searched around for Ash. She urgently needed a second opinion – a calm, flat, dampening voice telling her she was seeing things. But Ash was no longer by the fountain.

'You like this?' The stallholder was back and must be hoping for a last-minute sale. A sweet, musky scent seeped from the woman's clothes which Hope realised, with her newly sharpened awareness, were all restored vintage.

'I'm not sure.' She wasn't hedging her bets or trying to haggle as the woman's irritated *tsst* implied. No. She wanted this painting with animal intensity. At the same time, she didn't want it. It was too... she grasped for the right words... too ardent. Too unhinged. With her own supposedly stable world showing its first faint cracks, it felt too much.

'It's a local artist, dead now,' the stallholder was saying. 'I'll give it you for twenty euros, Madame.' No attempt at coaxing. Clearly, she just wanted to go home. 'So?'

Later, Hope didn't remember taking out the money or saying no, she didn't need it wrapped. Thank you. A binbag would be fine. She must have done and said it all while completely forgetting about the orange box that she'd marked down as a perfect outdoor planter.

She hurried away with the picture, terrified that someone would tell her it hadn't been for sale, that she must hand it back.

She spotted Ash just then on the far side of the market. She shouted and waved, but he seemed to be moving further away. That's when she heard someone calling, 'Madame? Madame, please, wait.'

A man with rope-coloured dreadlocks was bearing down on her. He had a rugby player's build and stubble a shade darker than the dreads. 'Madame!' He looked wild and sounded frantic.

She knew intuitively that he wanted the picture and so she ran, flat shoes and low-waisted linen trousers helping her getaway. Her car was parked on a side street and she was driving away – heart hammering – when she saw the same man in her driver's mirror. He looked furious.

God. It was only an old picture!

A minicab pulled out in front of her, making her jam on her brakes. Jeez, that was close! Woah – was that Ash in the back? She waved frantically, sounded her horn.

It brought his head up and their eyes met. It might have been the layers of window glass between them causing distortion, but to Hope, his expression was of controlled blankness. He turned his head away.

At the next junction, she lost sight of him.

Drawing up outside their house on Rue du Cathédrale, expecting to catch up with Ash paying off his taxi, she found an empty cobbled parking bay. Reversing her Renault into its space, she grabbed the binbag with the picture inside. Going through the side gate and around the back of the house, she kicked aside a mat, revealing the kitchen door key. Calling Ash's name as she entered, assuming he'd beaten her home, she went upstairs, taking them two at a time. 'Ash?'

Her voice echoed. In the bedroom, she liberated the portrait, propping it against the pillows of their bed. She stared at it, taking a moment to renew her acquaintance with those tortured eyes, then pulled out a drawer. Socks, tights, silk scarves, an empty perfume bottle, became a tangled mass as she searched for what she wanted. She forgot Ash temporarily, and the near-miss with the cab.

Got it.

'It' was a small box that had once held staples. Opening it, she extracted something from a bed of cotton wool, holding it between finger and thumb. A brooch, a dove captured in flight. Throwing the window shutters wide to let in as much light as possible, she took it over to the bed. Removed from the glare of sunlight, the painting showed new detail. The stricken eyes had looked intensely green in the market but actually, they were composed from tiny dashes of black, grey and yellow ochre. The painting style was loose to the point of carelessness. In places, the canvas peered through but nothing about this portrait suggested detachment. Somebody's heart and soul had poured into it.

Sitting on the bed to get closer, Hope held the brooch from the box against the painted one on the portrait.

There was no doubting it, they were the same. A dove in profile, wings raised, facing left. Its single eye was a disc of pewter-grey enamel. The end of its beak was broken, both on the picture and in reality, in exactly the same place. She wasn't imagining it. The only discrepancy was that on the painting, the eye was rimmed with gold, but Hope could trace a circular groove on hers where the gilding had been lost. The bird's upraised wings, body and tail feathers were silver, inset with bright-coloured enamel. Her father had given it to her a few months before he died.

She recalled his words as he passed it to her: 'It's called "the Grey Eyed Dove" and it was my mother's. It's all I have of her because we were separated in the war.'

Was she looking at a portrait of her grandmother? There could not be two such brooches in the world, but how could she be seeing it on a portrait bought at a flea market for twenty euros? And why had that apparition with the dreadlocks pounded after her? Her lungs still ached from sprinting away from him, just as her heart still knocked from the emergency stop at the junction.

Ash... the look he'd thrown her. What was taking him so long? He'd be fascinated by this picture when he got over his irritation. He had a sister and two brothers, and both sets of grandparents were alive and present in his life. He found it astonishing that Hope had no family. No siblings, parents, grandparents, aunts, uncles or cousins. That she knew of.

She unwound her legs and got off the bed, thinking, I need to call him. A thudding at the front door told her she'd missed the moment. He was back, and not happy.

Putting the portrait in the wardrobe and slipping the brooch into her pocket, she went downstairs thinking that her first question ought to be – who were you calling for such a big, fat lump of time?

Or she could apologise, take the flak, so they wouldn't end up having a rotten evening. Hope pulled open the solid front door and her planned words evaporated on her lips. It was the man from the market.

He was out of breath, his face set in fierce indignation, eyes alive with anxiety. His dreadlocks spilled onto his shoulders and, close up, she could see they were the real deal, not braided extensions. He was built for manual labour and the chest hair nestling in the sweaty V of his olive-coloured tee-shirt was cider-gold.

'We have to talk,' he said gruffly. The fact that English came out of his mouth threw her. He looked beyond her, into the house. 'That picture – I need it – it shouldn't have been sold.'

She asked how he'd found her.

'I tracked you down.' A booted foot encroached on the threshold, implying he might force his way in. Thoroughly spooked, Hope yelled '*Dégage!*' and slammed the door, forcing him to whip back his foot. As the wood shuddered, she heard him swear, in French.

'And screw you too,' she muttered, shocked. Why did he want the picture so badly?

Her picture. Paid for. She remembered then that she hadn't locked the kitchen door and scuttled to do so. Only when she was sure he'd gone did she nip out to her car to get her shoulder bag and phone.

There was a WhatsApp message from Ash. Don't say he was still looking for her? She prepared herself for a row of question marks and a frantic *Where are you?* What she read instead brought the world to a momentary stop.

Offered contract, megabucks. Speak soon.

She messaged back, *What contract? Where?*

His answer arrived several minutes later and when she read it, she gaped like a cartoon cliché.

On way to airport. Will call 2 morrow.

Airport? Was he punishing her for abandoning him at the market? No – he'd been in the taxi before she'd got into her car. That's where he'd been going when they nearly collided. A sudden call back to work – really? Rupert James Ashton – always known to friends as 'Ash' – had worked in cyber security before they came to Lazurac. In their London life, crisis calls had been a regular thing. Ash's phone would buzz at inappropriate moments. He'd grab his stuff and go.

That's why they'd moved here, to the Gers, and started a hospitality business offering painting holidays. Eat-Sleep-Paint-Gascony. A simpler life, emphasis on eating, better sleep and, at some point, the inspiration to pick up a paintbrush.

If Ash's old company was summoning him back, he'd be on his way to London. She jabbed out a second message: *Call me before tomorrow! Couldn't you have swung by home to explain? Talk about leaving me holding the ticking hand grenade!*

He'd probably point out that grenades did not tick. They went from silence to detonation, pretty much what he'd done.

Hope went back upstairs to stare at the portrait of the

unknown woman until her panic over Ash receded. By every measure, it was a good picture. She'd picked up a bargain, even if you ignored the astonishing coincidence of the brooch. Hope had graduated in fine art, with every intention of becoming a professional painter, before swerving onto a completely different career path. As a student, she'd spent hours in galleries, visually deconstructing the great masters and many lesser ones. To her eye, this painting had quality, but if she looked into the soul of the painter, she'd say he'd got bored once the girl's face, hair and hands were completed. Only they – and the brooch – had real definition.

Taking the picture to the window, Hope tilted it to the light, looking for a signature. There it was, bottom left.

L.L. Shepherd.

Shepherd, as in sheep? Was the artist British, then, or American? Wouldn't it be a happy twist of fate if it turned out to be worth thousands! Though she'd feel obliged to share the profit with the woman from the market. Maybe its value explained why that dreadlocked typhoon had chased her home.

I need it, he'd said. Maybe he knew who L.L. Shepherd was, as well as the identity of the subject. Looking into the fathomless eyes, Hope murmured, 'Whoever you were, you knew trouble in your life.'

It niggled, how the man had shown up in Rue du Cathédrale within minutes of her arriving home. How exactly had he tracked her down? His accent had been tricky to place. Not mother-tongue English, nor Gascon dialect. Nor entirely French. Oh well. Slamming the door on him should have given him the message.

Hope drilled a small hole in the wall opposite her bed, twisting in a picture hook. She hung the portrait and stood back. Against the deep blue wallpaper, the girl's eyes shone jade. Her hair looked to be a natural, sandy blonde; it matched her eyebrows, unlike Hope's platinum highlights, which had come straight out of a salon. On her last visit to the hairdresser, she'd asked for a pixie cut and to go blonde and, after a tussle, the stylist had obliged. The woman in the picture had even shorter hair, almost punky, which struck a wrong note against her dress.

Maybe she wasn't French. Or ahead of her time. Or maybe the portrait was modern, the sitter wearing vintage. None of this answered why she had Hope's grandmother's brooch.

Hope went downstairs, conscious of the empty house, to her office which was a pine table in the corner of the kitchen. She powered up her laptop and typed 'L.L. Shepherd' into the browser.

It brought up any number of Will Shepherds. A second try brought pictures of German and Belgian shepherd dogs and puppies for sale. She tried, 'L Shepherd, painter' and turned up three contemporary artists, more dogs and the famous wildlife artist David Shepherd.

It was feeling unlikely she'd acquired a valuable piece but, having dived into the rabbit hole, she wasn't giving up. She found a discussion group specialising in 'Lost English Painters', joined and wrote a message, describing her purchase. *It's a portrait of a woman from the waist up, and to my eye dates from the 1940s. The artist is L.L. Shepherd but I'm drawing a blank online. I'll send a photo when I've taken one in daylight, but any insight would be appreciated.*

She then updated her social media pages, posting pictures she'd taken at the flea market, of *brocante* stalls piled with shabby-chic bygones. Her page had fifty new likes and twelve comments, mostly from regular followers. She replied to them before checking to see if there were any bookings.

None today.

Ash's departure in pursuit of what he'd described as 'megabucks' made sense in the context of their faltering business. Eat-Sleep-Paint-Gascony was a strong concept. They'd built it with passion and their location was great, deep in the heart of the Gers yet only an hour and a half from an international airport. So why was nobody booking? Ash must have felt he had no choice – but why go without a word? Because he feared she'd try to stop him? She still had faith in their business. All they needed was a decent summer season.

Leaning back in her chair, she stared through a skylight into purple dusk. She'd cleaned the glass not two days ago and saw now that she'd left a smear behind. A smiley emoji in window-shine.

She'd take it as a positive omen. There was plenty of summer left.

By eleven that night, Ash had still not replied. Anxiety sat in Hope's chest like a ball of screwed-up paper in a waste bin, un-crinkling itself in the cooling silence. Before getting into bed, she picked up the binbag she'd brought the picture home in and realised there was something at the bottom. Giving it a shake, a paperback book fell onto the floor. The front and back, and some of its pages, had been ripped away and the paper had that old-book smell. A key to the title was printed across the bottom of the exposed front page:

BARBED WIRE AND FALSE NAMES

If she'd been ready to sleep, she wasn't now. Propped up on her pillows, she began where the book began, mid-sentence, mid-thought.

...a million of us elbowing out of the city, frantic to escape.

4

Paris, 12 June 1940

The street where I live is a slow-moving tide of people, bicycles, handcarts and dogs on leads, all heading towards the southern gateways out of Paris. A man with a rolled mattress on his back has fallen and is floundering like a turtle. The stink of burned paper mingles with the screech of iron-rimmed wheels, the car engines of the rich, and the wailing of lost children in three languages. It's a sensory assault that edges me close to distraction. Are German tanks really on their way to bludgeon the life out of Paris?

I can't leave until my friend comes back. Her name is Pauline, and we have shared a room since the war made her homeless. At dawn this morning, I went out to buy bread and came back to find her bed empty and a note:

Popping out to see a friend, back in a twinkle.

She's been missing two hours, making it the longest 'twinkle' in human history. I'm standing in front of our lodgings, scanning every face in the crowd in case she sweeps by in the human current. I'll grab her, like the baby in the willow basket as the river races past. Pauline, Pauline, where are you?

We have an hour to get to the junction of Rue de Grenelle and Boulevard de La Tour-Maubourg where, God willing, a car will be waiting for us. The métro isn't running, so we must walk. On a normal day, it would take fifty minutes. Today, who knows? Even if the German army is two days' march to the north, as the creamy wireless voice assured us this morning, everyone knows what has befallen Holland and Belgium. And Poland, God help them. It's why the whole of Paris – so it seems – is on the move. Our bags are packed and sit by my feet. One piece of hand luggage each, and a shoulder bag, as per instructions. Our ride out comes courtesy of Monsieur and Madame Marshall, Pauline's wealthy former employers. They left months ago but didn't forget Pauline and have done what they can to ensure her safety. Everyone is very fond of Pauline, except me.

Me? I love her. Apart from my man who left yesterday, Pauline is the dearest thing in the world to me, though right now, I could strangle her.

Here she comes! I recognise her hat. It's from a 1938 collection, with a sloping brim and a chic veil. It was a parting gift from Madame Marshall. What on earth possessed Pauline to risk it in this crush? I shout her name and wave.

She fights her way towards me, flushed, out of breath. 'Sorry. Sorry. I had to say goodbye to someone.'

'So you wrote, but who?' We are on Rue Monge, a long and ancient street in the fifth arrondissement. Left Bank, the arty side of the city. It runs roughly parallel to the Seine, one end leading into the Latin Quarter, which is the direction Pauline has come from.

'Who did I meet?' she echoes, straining her voice above the noise of the crowd. 'Madame Marshall's seamstress, who used to do the family's mending. Did I never mention her?'

'Never.'

'Well, I wanted to call one last time because she was always kind to me.'

'Well, I'm glad you're here.' I brush white petals off Pauline's shoulders and wonder if her visit took her through the Jardin des Plantes. She's been walking under lime trees, at any rate. The gardens are where I and my darling Otto walked and talked almost daily – before life changed forever. Where we, *sh! don't repeat this*, made love in the twilight, before the gates were locked.

I hand Pauline her bags and shoulder mine. My free hand takes hers and she returns my grip. Our fingers fuse to the point of *rigor mortis* as we set off uphill against the flow.

We reach the big crossroads at the end of Rue de Grenelle after two exhausting hours and there it is, our saviour, our angel, a long-nosed Renault Nervastella, waiting exactly where Madame Marshall promised it would be. It shines like a ruby in a dirty wine glass because of the shreds of burned paper over its bonnet. The embassies and government offices have spent the last few days incinerating their documents to stop them falling into German hands. Ash disfigures every surface.

Standing next to the car, keeping people away from its paintwork, is a man in full chauffeur uniform. The Marshalls are in textiles and very rich. Monsieur Marshall is English, and they left for London a month after war was declared, but their son, who is a good friend of ours, remained to fight. I suspect it was he who alerted his mother to the fact that Pauline and I were still in Paris, and to please, help us get out. Using my body like a mortar chisel to cut through the crowd, I drag Pauline the last few metres. I hear her cry, 'My hat! Oh, wait – my hat!'

I don't wait. Hats don't matter. Not now.

A minute later, I'm sobbing my thanks to the chauffeur but he has no time for the courtesies. 'Get in.' He opens a rear door and desperate people surge up, begging for a lift. '*Get in!*' he shouts and shuts it the moment we're inside.

There's nowhere to put our feet because of all the paintings and other valuables filling the footwell. It's obvious from the chauffeur's attitude that he's salvaging the last of the family's treasures and considers us to be excess baggage.

Beggars can't be choosers. We hitch up our coats and perch, cross-legged, on the leather seat. Two exhausted but thankful gnomes. The chauffeur fires the engine. 'What kept you?' he growls over his shoulder.

I wait for Pauline to confess her ill-timed social call, but she is staring down at her hands, massaging fingers that almost got dislocated by me pulling her. I tell our driver it's mob rule out there. 'Worse in the fifth even than here. We did our best.'

He grunts. The crowd parts in front of us as the Nervastella starts moving. We edge down Boulevard de La Tour-Maubourg towards Montparnasse, heading south.

Heading, God and the Nazis willing, to safety.

5

HOPE

She woke early next morning, the memoir face down on her chest. 'God and the Nazis,' she mumbled to herself. 'And I think I have problems.'

Hope's second thought was – today is Friday the thirteenth. She wasn't superstitious, but the weight in her stomach fitted the date.

It was early still. She opened the window and the shutters and leaned out, letting in the dawn chorus. Leaving the shutters wide, she went down, airing every room as she went. Her neighbours, long-time residents of the Gers, had taught her how to activate natural air-conditioning. Stone-built houses like this one stayed cool in summer if you opened them up to the early-morning chill, then closed the shutters by eight to keep out the heat and the midges. In her kitchen, Hope lit the gas. The memoir had kept her awake longer than she'd intended. She put the coffee pot on the flame, then checked her phone. There was a message from Ash. He'd landed safely, he'd call soon.

'Elegantly brief,' she muttered. The thought of being alone for the foreseeable was dispiriting. She'd been so busy since coming to Lazurac, she'd had no time to make proper friends.

The soft-pawed approach of emotions she'd experienced when her mother died, which had returned after her father's death, was alarming. They were hard to label. Isolation? Abandonment? This must be how Robinson Crusoe had felt on his second day on the desert island.

As the coffee pot came to a murmuring boil, Hope opened her laptop and checked incoming emails. Nothing from the Lost English Painters community. On impulse, she fetched down the portrait, propped it on a chair under the kitchen skylight and took a couple of photos, which she attached to a new email, writing, *There's no date on the picture, but really interested to get your opinion.*

From her website, she answered a query from somebody in Florida, asking if there were direct flights to Gascony from Miami International Airport. She sent a suggested itinerary. That done, she took her first deep slug of coffee and weighed up the impact of Ash's departure. When guests began to book – and they must, there was no logical explanation for this void – she'd be cooking, cleaning, bed-making by herself. On the other hand, Ash's income would alleviate their financial stress.

She made toast from yesterday's bread, spreading it with white butter and apricot jam, and thought about the memoir's author rushing out in the Parisian dawn to buy bread, before joining the mass exodus. Were food supplies under pressure ten months into the war, or had the narrator wanted to be sure of bread before the journey? Hope opened a search engine and typed in, 'BARBED WIRE AND FALSE NAMES'. Pages of results appeared: wartime memories, research papers, black and white photographs of people with sad eyes and outdated hairstyles. On an online antiquarian bookshop, she got a hit.

BARBED WIRE AND FALSE NAMES: MEMOIR OF AN ENGLISH GIRL
IN OCCUPIED FRANCE

The book had been published in 1979 but there were no copies available, a fact explained in a footnote: 'Initial print-run of 750 in hardback withdrawn from sale following legal action. One or two salvaged copies in circulation, but generally considered a lost personal insight into a moment of history.'

An eBay search turned up the same information. It would be interesting to know what had triggered the legal action.

A knock at the front door stilled Hope's hands on the keyboard. Her first instinct was to ignore it and hide. Then, telling herself she couldn't afford to be intimidated, she went to the front and yanked the door open, prepared to shout if that man was back. There was a box on the step.

Ah. Five reams of printer paper, ordered two days ago. Feeling foolish, she put the paper away and returned to her coffee. Turning around on her chair, arms draped over the rail, she gazed at the portrait. Whoever the woman was, she wasn't what you'd call typically French with her light hair and a skin tone somewhere between English rose and freckly peach. Had the memoir hitched a ride home with the picture by accident, or were they connected?

Wait, though. If, as she thought, the portrait dated from the 1940s, almost four decades stood between it and the memoir's publication.

After a few minutes, the silence got to her. Had she missed Ash this badly in April when he'd flown back to the UK for a family party? Answer no – she'd got on with things. She started doing the washing-up but wherever she went in the kitchen, green, harrowed eyes watched her, whispering for attention.

In the end, it was too much. 'Whatever you went through, honestly? I can't live it with you.'

She came to a fast decision. The man with the sun-streaked dreadlocks could have the picture back – for the twenty euros she'd paid for it. She knew exactly where to go to find out his name.

6

Le Chat Célèbre, known generally as Le Chat, was the café where you found everyone in Lazurac. If not the actual person, you could prise out a telephone number or a home address. Lazurac often felt like a large village. Swollen with tourists in the summer, lured there by its medieval streets and stunning views, its permanent population had either lived here all their lives or had drifted in during the 70s and 80s when a crumbling townhouse could be bought for the same price as a Paris bedsit.

The portrait wedged under one arm, Hope cut through an alley into the main shopping street, crossing to the sunny side. Scents of warm stone, fresh bread and scooter exhaust lifted her mood. The lady from Florida had messaged again, asking if Hope offered a discount for a larger group. Hope had responded 'Yes!' and crossed her fingers. By the time she walked into Le Chat, she was remembering why she'd ditched a steady career in London to become this version of herself: feet in espadrilles, ten euros in her purse.

The café occupied a corner of a square by the cathedral gardens. Tables under green umbrellas made her think of lily pads, waiting for a splash of movement. The café's current 'famous cat' purred on an outside chair and Hope paused to stroke the smoky grey fur.

Inside, the proprietress was piling madeleines onto a tray with tongs. Hope greeted her. 'Jeanne, is Madame Royale in?'

Jeanne pointed towards the open rear doors. 'Outside, with her niece, in her favourite spot.' She glanced at the package under Hope's arm. 'Shall I bring your usual?'

'Please.' Hope walked out onto a vine-shaded terrace and at once saw Inès Royale: a thin woman who wore her age, her linen dress and abundant white hair lightly. The hair was caught up with a tooled leather clip, which looked as if it might give way any moment. Inès was a talented artist, born and bred in Lazurac and had agreed to be the tutor on Hope's painting courses. A real coup, people kept telling Hope. Inès was regarded as a very private person.

The woman with her, whose face was concealed by a bell-shaped woven hat, must be the niece. The pair sat in the shade of a trellis heavy with vine leaves. Each had a cup in front of her, which would contain mint tea in Inès's case. Hope and Ash had struck their deal with her here, at the same table.

'Ah, *salut*, Hope.' Inès looked up and smiled. 'Have you come with news of a booking? I'm so looking forward to teaching again, I was telling my niece. Have you met Manon?'

The bell-shaped hat turned. Kohl-lined eyes, regal brows, rainbow hair extensions tumbling from under the brim... Hope said, 'You're the lady from the market.'

'I'm Manon Taubier.' A heavily ringed hand was briefly offered, just as quickly withdrawn. 'I never did get your name.'

'Hope Granger.' Hope fetched a chair from another table and propped her picture against her leg, thinking, what appalling luck. She'll think I'm trying to sell it back to that man to make a quick buck. Her coffee arrived with a jug of hot milk and a plate of warm brioche.

'It's late for breakfast.' Manon Taubier had an offhand way

of speaking, as if using both sides of her mouth at once was too much bother. She glanced at Hope's parcel with more than curiosity.

Inès, oblivious to the atmosphere, asked where Ash was.

Hope explained the urgent summons to London. 'His old firm... all will be revealed when he has a moment to call.'

'*Ah, dommage.* I miss him.' Some mild, inter-generational flirting had been established between Ash and Inès. He said their neighbour was living proof that Frenchwomen never gave up being attractive. 'He won't stay in London long, will he?'

'I shouldn't think so,' Hope said vaguely. 'It'll be a contract, three months most likely.'

'But that is all summer! The best time in Lazurac.'

'Keep men on a short leash, is my motto,' Manon said.

'I don't have Ash on any kind of leash,' Hope laughed. Through rather gritted teeth.

'That is not wise.'

'Oh, what would you know, Manon,' Inès chided. 'The only man you ever stuck with left you twelve years ago.'

To fill the sudden freeze, Hope unwrapped the picture and balanced it on the table. Manon's eyes had been burning through the paper and there was little point putting off the reason for coming here. 'I bought this yesterday, on impulse,' she told Inès. 'I had no idea you and Manon were related, but one of you can perhaps solve a mystery. There was this man who must have had his eye on it because he followed me home.'

'Stalked you?' Inès sounded perturbed.

'Not really but I'd love to know how he found me. To be honest, it scares me a bit.'

'Describe him, Hope.' Inès always pronounced Hope's name as '*Ope*.

'Big and loud, could do with a shave and decent haircut.'

'Bad hair scares you?'

'No, honestly. It was his energy. It felt unpredictable. Thing is, if he wants the picture so badly, he can have it and I wondered if you knew him.'

'Manon knows a lot of men who need to shave.' Inès looked across at her niece, who had torn a vine leaf from the trellis and was shredding it. Having been so fascinated by the parcel a moment ago, now it was unwrapped, she was studiedly looking elsewhere.

Hope offered a fuller description of the man. 'Broad-shouldered, primitive. Dark blond hair in dreadlocks.'

'Ugh.' Inès pulled a face. 'I know who you mean. That aberration from the mill at Varsac. Yves Ducasse. You know him well, don't you, Manon?'

'I wouldn't say "well".' Manon threw down the mangled leaf and gave Hope an accusing look. 'He followed you home?'

'He found out where I live. So technically, no, he didn't, but he does want this picture and I'm inclined to let him have it. I need to know how to find him and I want to know something about the picture too. Like, who is it and who was the painter.'

'He lives at Varsac-les-Moulins,' Inès said, 'a little way out of the town, in the direction of Auch.' Auch was the regional capital. 'He came home recently from his travels, but honestly? You shouldn't concern yourself with him.'

'You don't like him?' Hope couldn't help noticing that Inès was sending meaningful looks Manon's way, while Manon's attention was now on a winged insect raiding the vine flowers. 'What is it about him, exactly?'

'He has tattoos.' Inès made a contemptuous motion of the lips. 'They make men look like vagabonds.'

Hope got the drift. Lazurac was a smart kind of place. Arty, but wealthy too. This man Ducasse did not fit. She lifted up the portrait so the other two could see it. 'This was what he wanted so badly.'

Manon's muttered, 'Don't!' came too late. Inès Royale's intake of breath told Hope that she'd made a gaffe.

Inès half-rose and stared at the painted face. 'No,' she said heavily.

'What is it?' Hope faltered. 'Who are you seeing?'

The answer was a single word. '*Her.*'

7

BARBED WIRE AND FALSE NAMES: MEMOIR OF AN
ENGLISH GIRL IN OCCUPIED FRANCE

We have covered one kilometre in the last two hours. Midday
sun hammers at the car windows, which we can't lower
because of the smoke in the air. A few days ago, before they
fled Paris, the government ordered the oil and petrol refineries
to be torched to stop the Nazis getting the fuel.

The odour of petrol permeates the car; our driver has
hidden a spare can under the front passenger seat. I'm getting
a headache and I'm sweating, though I've taken off my jacket.
Beside me, Pauline weeps quietly. When I ask why, she
answers, 'Because of what I've lost.'

'There will be more hats,' I soothe. 'When everything's
back to normal and we're in Paris again we can find you a new
one.'

She gives me her disarming, tear-filled stare. A friend –
male of course – once said that when Pauline gazes at you, it is
like being seduced by Rome's Trevi Fountain: you want to
throw in everything you have and know you will go back again

and again. 'Nothing will ever be the same,' Pauline says in husky despair.

Well, it was a Madame Paulette hat, and she saw it being crushed under the hobnail boot of boy who didn't even realise he'd done it. In a bid to cheer her up, I tell her it died a hero's death. 'Tell you what, we'll shop for a replacement in Marseilles.'

'You girls know I'm not driving you all the way to the sea? I haven't enough fuel for that.' Our driver shoots the comment over his shoulder. He must be melting like candle wax in his uniform. If he told us his name, I didn't catch it and nothing about him invites familiarity. He's about sixty years old, with a drooping moustache that, when he turns his head, appears a half-second before his nose. I know without asking that he fought in the last war. He has a look of disillusion, of despair that the world has fallen into a second catastrophe twenty-one years after the end of the last one.

'We understand,' I tell him. 'You are taking us as far as Poitiers and we can get the Marseilles train from there.'

'So long as you know.' His moustache quivers before he turns to concentrate on the road ahead. Out of nowhere we enjoy a burst of speed... a whole ten metres before the brakes are applied. Our driver beats his steering wheel. 'Why is the whole world and his mother leaving at once?'

From the frustrating to the surreal: we're surrounded by sheep. Farmers from northern France have joined those fleeing the Low Countries and of course they've brought their livestock with them. They are going nowhere, while we are lurching towards Gare Montparnasse where, the wireless announced last night, there are no trains. No trains because there is no fuel. No fuel because our government ordered it to be burned.

I start laughing, a hysterical response to the absolute, utter awfulness of the situation we're in. All these people, mothers, fathers, grandmas and babies heading towards a shuttered railway station. And what then? For days, the skies north of Paris have shaken with gunfire. A neighbour, who crossed the Seine and trekked up to the Butte de Montmartre, saw fuzzy, grey lines of tanks and guns on the far horizon. Planes were patrolling the line, like wasps in and out of their nest. The neighbour was relieved to hear that Pauline and I had secured a car ride out.

'Good. You're young and pretty. Don't wait to see how the Germans behave.'

I give up looking out of the window, exhausted by the fear in the eyes of those who will not make it. Every now and then, a gap opens and the Nervastella covers another five or ten metres. The driver's orders are to take the car to the Marshalls' château outside Poitiers and hide it there along with the valuables stashed in the footwells. Did I say already, the Marshalls took their younger children, pets and best pictures to London last September and urged Pauline – their au pair of two years – to go with them. The little girls were very attached to her and Madame Marshall felt a parental responsibility.

Pauline chose to stay. I had dug in too, for the simple reason that my man, Otto, was here and couldn't leave Paris until his visa for America came through. Just three days ago, the US consulate rubber-stamped the papers and he spent the following days bidding farewell to trusted friends, and queuing to withdraw money from his bank. He left yesterday to make his way to the Spanish border. He'll take the dangerous route across the Pyrenean mountains. I would have gone with him but knowing Pauline could never manage a journey like that, I'm travelling with her instead. In Marseilles, she and I will apply for permits from the British consulate – if it still exists, or from the American one if not – to get us on a ship to Lisbon. From Lisbon we can sail to Liverpool. One day, one way or another, Otto and I will be reunited.

Two hours pass in gridlock with Montparnasse just within sight. Fights break out between drivers. I get out to ease the cramp in my legs. Pauline joins me and hops around with pins and needles. Our driver winds down his window and snarls, 'Get back in! I'm only taking you because Madame Marshall asked. For two centimes, I'll leave you behind.' His mood is volatile because his precious Nervastella hates this stop-start going, and so does he. Pauline scrambles back in. Me – I dislike being ordered about and my attention has been caught by something in the sky. At first, I think it's a heron. But no, it's a fighter plane, writing a vapour trail in the blue. I watch, fascinated, thinking, 'The Germans aren't coming. They're already here.'

When I get back in and repeat this to Pauline, she whispers, 'Thank God he got away.'

'Julien?' That's her employers' son, with whom she is madly in love. Blessed with English good looks shot through with French charm, Julien Marshall was called up at the start of the war. Months of inactivity saw him back in Paris at every opportunity, but then things got serious. Since the debacle at Dunkirk, nothing has been heard of him. I'm not sure I understand Pauline's comment about him having 'got away'. When she adds, 'Will he have taken this road and headed west?' I realise she's talking about my darling O.

Actually, Otto's going by train, but as he's on the run and in danger of being recognised, I say nothing. Who knows if our driver is trustworthy? I squeeze Pauline's hand and thank her for caring.

The following day, we reach Chartres, its fragile spires like antique lace against the June sky. After Chartres it will be on to Tours, where the French government is hunkering. German and Italian planes track us, flying over then looping back for a second look. Pauline is silent. I pass the time sketching what I see out of the window, and when that palls, I draw the face of my beloved from memory. I kiss the sketches before tearing them into pieces to scatter like plum blossom onto the road. The news that the Germans have entered Paris catches up with us on June 15th, as the outskirts of Tours take shape under the setting sun. Yesterday, their army made a victory march through the Arc de Triomphe, we're told, and along the Champs-Élysées. It's happened. Paris is under occupation.

8

HOPE

Her.

Having spoken with all the venom she could muster, Inès left the café. Manon pushed back her chair while giving Hope a furious look. 'You should learn our history before you jump in with both feet.'

'Wait—' Hope followed Manon as she strode off in pursuit of her aunt. 'It wasn't intentional. Will you tell me what it's about?'

'Forget it,' Manon flung back at her.

'At least tell me how to find Yves Ducasse.'

'We told you already. Where the windmills are. His house is called La Cachette. He runs a café and a gallery, if you can call it that.'

'Why d'you think he wants the portrait so badly?' Hope needed to know, if only to ensure she never blundered again.

'Ask him, not me.' Manon put her bill on the counter, said something to the proprietress, Jeanne, and walked out. As the door clashed, Jeanne muttered, 'She is always trouble.'

Hope asked Jeanne if she knew Yves Ducasse.

'A little, by sight. He came in asking for you... was it Thursday, after the market?'

'You told him where I lived?' That explained how he came so quickly to Hope's door.

Jeanne apologised. 'I won't do it again.'

'It's OK. But is he as wild as Inès suggests?'

Jeanne made a face. 'I'd say more that he's a drifter who can't stick at anything. His mother was the same. I don't advise you getting close.'

'I'm not thinking of getting close,' Hope replied. 'I want to give a picture back so he doesn't call at my home again.'

Jeanne told her to drive out of town towards Auch. 'Pass the sign for Varsac-les-Moulins and you'll see a windmill on a hill. White sails. His place is after the bend. It's called La Cachette for a good reason and you'll probably go past. Leave the picture outside his gate, by the mailbox if you don't want to go onto his property.'

Hope was anxious about Inès's state of mind. 'You've known her longer than me, Jeanne. Should I phone and apologise? Only, I might have guests soon and she's our tutor.'

'Leave her for now.' Jeanne was printing out Hope's bill. 'She's most likely getting a migraine. It's what happens when she is stressed.'

Feeling even worse, Hope opened her purse. 'Hang on.' The reading on the card machine was way too high. 'I only had coffee and brioche.'

Jeanne looked embarrassed. 'Manon said you might want to show you're sorry and pay their bill too.'

'Oh... OK. I'll have to go home and fetch my debit card.' Anything to make amends.

It was late afternoon by the time Hope drove out of Lazurac towards Auch. The countryside on this edge of town always reminded her of her native Hampshire. When she was eleven, her family had moved to a village on the South Downs. It was the rolling hills and dips that felt familiar though the colour-canvas was very different. This area of the Gers was a mosaic, of sunflower fields and slopes striped with ripening vines, interspersed with the sudden shock of blue flax. With the sun now less intense, the colours glowed.

As Jeanne had warned, Hope saw the sign for Yves Ducasse's house too late to slow down. She continued on a short way, then reversed up a track that led to another of the ruined windmills for which Varsac was famous. Her left-hand-drive Renault Laguna was longer than the city car she'd driven in London, and she backed up cautiously. The day she'd driven this one home from the dealer's, she'd knocked down a row of dustbins. She returned the way she'd come and parked in the mouth of a long driveway. A sign nailed to a tree said 'La Cachette'. It meant 'The Hideaway' and a thick line of holly and chestnut trees kept the house secret as she trudged up the drive. Windmill sails above the treetops made a V-sign against the sky.

She started to question her decision to search out Yves Ducasse, clutching a picture capable of triggering a migraine. Unreliable drifters weren't her type. As she emerged into a rambling garden, the windmill seemed suddenly unnervingly close. It was a traditional redbrick pepper pot, three levels high. White wooden sails projected through a dormer in a pointed roof.

It wasn't its height or closeness that made her catch her breath, but the absolute certainty: *I've been here before.*

9

BARBED WIRE AND FALSE NAMES: MEMOIR OF AN
ENGLISH GIRL IN OCCUPIED FRANCE

It is June 15th and we have made it as far as Tours. We're
about to cross the Loire, beyond which the Germans will not
venture. Or so we believe. The river shines like bronze, the
city's cathedral towers are luminous against a pomegranate
sky. We made good progress yesterday from Chartres,
achieving twenty kilometres an hour on occasions. So many
vehicles have either broken down or run out of fuel, the road-
side is lined with woebegone travellers and their possessions.
People brought too much. Unlike us, a handbag and a holdall
each. Also, we've become part of a French miliary convoy and
each time a stranded vehicle blocks the way, soldiers jump
down and heave it into the ditch. I tell Pauline that once we're
across the Loire, we're safe.

I'm saying it to bolster my own nerve, as I've been hearing
planes all day. We don't see them as they're either too high or
behind the clouds. Pauline's reply is to mutter, 'D'you think

our driver would stop if I asked? I need to get out and take pictures.'

She has a camera that was her eighteenth birthday present from her parents. A Leica, precision-engineered in a leather case. When she proudly showed it to me on her return to Paris from her birthday trip home, it crossed my mind that her parents must have saved for a decade to afford it. I warn her against using it under these conditions. 'Somebody will steal it, Pauline. You've seen how people are behaving out there.' There's been violence on the road, unprotected women and families set upon. And worse. 'Honestly, if it were mine, it would stay in my bag.'

'But I promised I would record what I'm seeing.'

'Promised who?'

After a short silence, she whispers, 'Otto.'

Otto, my darling 'O'? 'When did you promise him?'

'I don't know. A few weeks ago, when we were all together. You know he wants to write about this time. He'll need photographs for the book.'

What book? Pauline tells me... the book he's planning to write, an eyewitness account of his escape from the Nazis. Which he never mentioned to me.

Pauline looks wretched. 'Don't be angry, darling, please. We were just chatting. It was in the Jardin des Plantes, you and Julien were striding ahead talking about art, as always. Otto and I fell into step and he said, "If the worst happens and the Germans invade, take pictures. It will be a moment in history." I should have captured everything as we left Paris, but I was too upset.'

'Fine.' I lean forward to speak with our driver. 'Next time we slow down, Monsieur, we'll jump out to answer a call of nature.' If I mention taking photographs, he'll rage at us and probably leave us behind. Pauline removes her camera from her bag, looping the strap of its case over her head, and I take out one of my travelling sketchbooks and a pencil. I shove our handbags on the back shelf, still feeling cross and hurt. Why does Otto want Pauline's photos when he can have my line drawings? I can almost hear the dry smile in his answer:

'Because the camera records and the artist creates. We cannot have two creators for one book. Don't be jealous.'

The car slows to a walking pace and Pauline gets out. She misjudges her footing and tumbles. Convinced she's fallen under the wheels of the troop lorry behind us, I shout 'Stop!' and our driver slams on the brakes. I find Pauline curled on the grass verge. The headscarf she's worn since losing her hat hangs in the rushes of a dry ditch and her thick, brown hair falls across her face. 'Pauline?' Please don't let her have broken her neck. 'Say something!'

She looks up at me, her eyes charcoal smudges in a pale face. 'I'm such an idiot.'

Suddenly, she's laughing, and I'm laughing. 'You are, absolutely a nutcase.' I hold out my hand to her. The truck passing us has an open back and its military occupants whistle and offer crude attentions as it steers around the Nervastella. I smooth down Pauline's skirt, which has ridden up. 'Get a picture of these military vehicles in a line, with the cathedral towers in the background.'

'Are you going to sketch it? Race you.'

I accept the challenge, my pencil raking out fast lines while Pauline struggles to get her camera from its case. I'm writing in the colour detail, in case I want to make a painting of this later, as she lines up the Leica. Film is so expensive; I feel her adding up the cost as she clicks the shutter release.

As I feared, our driver hasn't waited and I chivvy Pauline along until we're close enough to the car to see our bags on the rear shelf. Everything vital to our survival is in them – passports, money, stockings, my pencils bound with a rubber band. The blank sketchbooks I brought with me. But instead of exerting herself, Pauline stops, jolting my arm. She stares up into the sky. 'Listen.'

Shadows cross the sun. Our ears fill with a noise like flood-water cascading through metal pipes. The earth under our feet buckles and a monstrous pressure forces us down. We cradle our heads, our screams lost as the world explodes around us.

10

HOPE

Yves Ducasse's garden was lush, vines claiming every upright surface and containers spilling melons and courgettes. A silver estate car was parked alongside a stone cottage. The sight of it, normal and unthreatening, and the sound of children's voices gave Hope the confidence to walk forward.

Two diminutive figures in shorts and tee-shirts were playing swing ball on a patch of lawn. Each time their bats swacked at a candy-pink ball on a bungee cord, they shouted.

'*Vijftig!*'

'*Eenenvijftig!*'

They were counting, though not in French. A small white dog yapped and jumped, trying to join in. Jeanne at the café hadn't mentioned that Yves Ducasse had kids or a partner. The children were intent on their game but a call of 'Mitzi!' saw the dog tearing off across the lawn. A woman stepped over the low fence of a vegetable patch. She was holding a bunch of pink-stemmed chard. Late thirties, fair hair and a wide smile. This must be the children's mother. Seeing Hope, she came over.

'*Bonjour! Cherchez-vous quelqu'un?*'

'I'm looking for Monsieur Ducasse,' Hope answered in French. 'Are you Madame Ducasse?'

The woman laughed. *As if*, her amusement seemed to say.

'This is his place, though?'

'Yes. He is gone but for not long. You bring this for his gallery?' The woman indicated the picture under Hope's arm.

'Not exactly.' A pause set in and, on a hunch, Hope asked, 'Would you be happier speaking English?'

A grin split the woman's face. 'Yes! My French is coming on but I speak English much better. Or Dutch, of course.'

'I have no Dutch, sorry. Is it worth me waiting for Monsieur Ducasse?'

'For Yves? Well... the café is open. He dashed out on an errand but I'm not in his confidence. We're visiting, me and the children. On our vacation.'

Hope took in the woman's shorts and tanned legs. Three bicycles, one with a baby-buggy attached and a flag declaring 'Pup on Board' in three languages, as well as a car with foreign plates, completed the picture of a family unit on a summer break. The stone house might be a rented gîte. Did Yves Ducasse live in the windmill then? 'Is it worth me waiting?' she asked again.

'Probably. There's only him to serve in the café since his waitress left, so he won't be away long. Oh, have you come for the job?'

Hope shook her head. 'I already have one of those.'

'Shame. He's super-stressed. I'll make you a coffee if you like. Unless you'd like a cold drink? I'm Claudia van Beek.'

'Hope Granger, and some cold juice would be lovely.' There came a shout of '*Zestig!*' The children continued to punish the pink ball.

'Go, guys! They're trying to get to one thousand,' Claudia explained. 'But three hundred is their personal best. Why don't you go sit in the shade?'

Curiosity took Hope to the windmill. She climbed a path set into a slope, which somebody had made more foot-friendly with steps. Her sense that she'd been here before was fading. Nothing in the garden felt familiar and the presence of a static caravan behind a green privacy fence eroded the impression further; La Cachette felt like a work-in-progress. The windmill had a cedarwood extension on one side, where a painted sign advertised 'Gallery open'. Hope recalled Manon Taubier's disparaging comment: 'He runs a café and a gallery, if you can call it that.'

Inside, the rich coffee aroma suggested that Yves Ducasse knew his beans, at any rate and she liked the house plants in recycled oil cans decorating the artisan counter. The tables were old school desks, ink-stained and ingrained with graffiti. From a closed-down school, or the flea market? The effect was quirky. Better still, a glass cabinet contained a tray of walnut tarts and it flashed through Hope's mind that she could bring guests here. Though maybe not. Her brushes with the owner had been unnerving, and hadn't she just learned that his waitress had absconded?

Leaving the portrait on a chair, Hope walked through to the gallery, anticipating a presentation of local art. Sunflowers, more sunflowers and *moulins à vent*. Naturally, there would be windmills, sails angled against moody skies. What she encountered was indeed windmills and sunflower fields, but in monochrome photographs that sweated drama, as if the hand behind the camera wanted to punch a hole through every cliché. How did someone wring so much angst out of a summer sky? It wasn't until she'd made a full circuit that she discovered who their creator was.

There was something almost disturbed in Yves Ducasse's rendering of a landscape.

The sound of footsteps took her back into the café. Expecting Claudia, she blurted out, 'I've never been in a gallery where the owner seems hell-bent – oh.' Not Claudia. Hope recognised the unkempt tee-shirt skimming a honed torso. 'Monsieur Ducasse. Sorry. You, er, look a bit different.'

He didn't reply. Without sparing Hope a glance, he seized the portrait from the chair and held it at arm's length.

'You've had your hair cut,' she said. That was the difference. The dreadlocks were gone, and gold-brown hair, scraped back from his forehead, revealed a range of ear piercings and a tattoo on the side of his neck. She noticed that his fingernails were short, almost to the quick. Painful to look at. Tattoos on his hands too and down his arms. Frankly, he looked as though he'd had himself wallpapered. 'Am I talking to myself?'

Finally, he looked at her and she realised he had green eyes. A penny rolled, quivering and ready to drop. 'The woman in the painting...?'

'My grandmother.'

Knowing she was in danger of wildly over-explaining, Hope pointed to the picture, and the brooch on the woman's lapel. 'Did you ever see that in real life?' When he didn't answer, she spoke breathlessly. 'My father gave me the original. Told me it was the only thing he ever had of his mother's... the *only* thing.' Again, no response, so she blurted out the obvious. 'His mother's – my grandmother's.'

Even that didn't pull his gaze. Hope scrutinised Yves Ducasse, his profile, his physique, searching for anything that might indicate they were related. Before he went grey, her father's hair had been middling brown. His eyes had been blue-grey, as were hers. Like Yves, he'd been tall, but lean and as he'd aged, he'd gained a stoop. Nothing in Yves' profile, in the muscular neck or the biceps that pushed against the dog-eared sleeves of his tee-shirt, shouted, 'We share DNA!' Quite the opposite: studying him stirred ideas that were anything but familial.

She stepped back, disturbed that she found Yves Ducasse

attractive. Cue to exit, except that she could not turn her back on the breathtaking fluke of seeing *her* brooch on *that* painting. There was a story and she needed to know. He had to acknowledge it.

Claudia van Beek came in with a jug of juice, apologising for taking so long. 'Hi, Yves, I see you got to the barber.' She walked round him to judge both sides of his head. 'Very smart. What do you think, Hope, an improvement?'

'Definitely.' Likeable as Claudia was, Hope wished she'd go so she could pin Yves Ducasse down to an answer but in a frustrating twist, the little dog ran in, yapping at Yves for attention. He bent to stroke it.

'Hey, Mitzi, you thought I'd gone for ever?'

Next came the children, who stampeded towards the windmill steps. Yves called them back but they ignored him, forcing their mother to put down her jug and go off in pursuit. I give up, Hope thought. Time to go.

Yves stopped her with a touch to her arm.

'You're giving this picture back?'

'I am.'

He raked his hair as if bewildered by the change in texture he found there. 'This will take some getting used to. My dreads took years to grow. It's your fault.'

He didn't seem to be joking. 'OK, you've got me,' she replied. 'How is it my fault?'

He led her by the hand in a peculiarly intimate way to a bistro mirror on one of the walls and pointed at his reflection. 'After I came to your door yesterday and you looked so terrified—'

'Angry. I was angry.'

'And scared to hell. I came back and looked at myself and said, "Shit. Right. Now I see why they all run." So' – a quick smile altered his face – 'all down to you, and the poor girl who took the waitress job then couldn't get away fast enough.' There was a clear trace of a French accent in his English, and the other strand she'd heard before she now identified as Australian. It made her wonder where exactly he'd come back from, and how long he'd been away. 'Mind you,' he went on, 'you need to have a car to work out here. She only had a bike so—'

Hope interrupted him. 'I'll leave the picture but I need to go.'

'And I need to reimburse you. Was it two hundred euros you paid?'

She stared. 'You can knock a nought off that.'

'Twenty?' He looked incredulous, almost angry, when she assured him that was all she'd paid. He went to the counter, muttering, 'Twenty euros. She's such an effing liar. She said two hundred.'

Hope had an idea who he meant. 'Manon Taubier?'

'You know her too?'

'That would be overstating it. I got palmed off with the tab for her coffee this morning. More than coffee. I ended up covering the cost of a substantial brunch.'

Yves rolled his eyes. 'You've been done. You won't be again.' He lifted a cash box onto the counter.

'How well do you know her?'

'Pretty well. We go back a while.'

Hope didn't press. She suspected his personal relationships were tangled. 'How did you know I'd bought the picture? You turned up just as I'd paid for it.'

He explained that he'd got a tip-off. 'A secret call: "Get to the market at Lazurac, now." Only, I couldn't find my vehicle key. I arrived to see you walking away with a bag, and Manon laughed at me, so I knew I'd blown it. What made you want to buy a picture of my grandmother?'

He hadn't been listening, had he? Not wanting to open the familial Pandora's box again, she said, 'It's by L.L. Shepherd.'

He seemed pleased, surprised, that she knew. 'A prolific artist, a free spirit. Twenty euros is an insult.'

'I agree.'

Fishing a note from the cash box, he handed it to Hope.

She thanked him. 'And good luck.'

'Do I need luck?'

'In finding a waitress.' She took a last look at the portrait and asked impulsively, 'Did she write a memoir of her time in occupied France?'

The change in Yves Ducasse was startling. 'How d'you know that? She did, it got lost. No, wait – don't go.'

But Hope was out of the door. Not exactly running. She wasn't scared of him now but his reaction to her comment made her fear he'd want the book too. She was a few pages in and wasn't giving it up.

Yves Ducasse didn't follow. A new vehicle was parked between the windmill and the gîte: a Land Rover the colour of toasted orange peel, which looked as if it had been manhandled around a hot continent or two. Reaching the bottom of the drive, she found a card advertising Café du Moulin under the windscreen wiper of her own car. On the back was written, 'The potholes look worse than they are. Feel free to drive up next time, but watch out for children, dogs and existential *tristesse*.'

Existential sadness. Appropriate for Friday the thirteenth. Maybe the whole point of Yves' café was that nobody ever came to it, she reflected as she drove away. It was an uncomfortable echo of her own situation. No guests *chez moi* either. She was relieved to escape but couldn't shift the idea that she should have pressed that she-elephant of a question:

'Do you and I share a grandmother, Monsieur Ducasse?'

11

The moment she arrived home, Hope regretted giving back the picture. The house felt emptier without it. With the prospect of spending a Friday evening alone, she checked her emails. Finding nothing from Ash or the lady in Florida, she retreated to the sofa to eat pasta and watch television until self-loathing drove her out for a walk. It was a gorgeously warm night, the cathedral gardens alive with silvery moths and the scent of blossom. Inside the ancient building, somebody was practising on the organ and she crept in, found a seat at the back, and let the music clear her over-stimulated mind.

Heading early to bed, she found her place in the English girl's memoir, picking up the thread on the road outside Tours. Immediately, she got stomach cramp: she was identifying too closely with the narrator.

When, finally, the attack is over, Pauline and I discover we've rolled into the ditch. Probably, it saved us. Peering over its edge, I see a version of hell. Human carnage. Blackened, twisted vehicles, their blown bonnets grinning. Among them, the Renault Nervastella, no longer wine-red, but blistered and bronze. Inside, at the wheel, what remains of our poor driver. I hope it was quick for him.

These words triggered worse cramps and put paid to sleep. Echoing the writer's prayer that the driver had died quickly, Hope got up and located a map of France which had been left behind by the previous owners of the house. Opening it out on the bed, she traced the N10, the Route Nationale, from Paris to the Spanish border. The modern road might not follow the same route as in June 1940, when it would have passed through little villages, but she found Tours and ran her finger down the map to Marseilles in the south. It was a long way. Did they ever get there and board their ship? The narrator's loyalty to ditzy Pauline came through powerfully, but Hope couldn't help thinking the author would have done better on her own. Loyalty had stopped her crossing the mountains with her beloved 'O'. Did they ever reunite?

Read to the end, then you'll know.

Hope got back into bed, picked up the memoir and read on until sleep blundered back and claimed her.

She spent Saturday morning catching up with her accounts, and in the afternoon called on Inès Royale, but her knock went unanswered. The rest of the day passed rather slowly, with chores, some shopping and a film, which she watched on the wide screen TV she'd bought because Ash had liked the look of it in the store. On Sunday morning, woken by the cathedral bell, she was struck by the realisation that today was June 15th. Seventy-four years ago, German planes had opened fire on a convoy outside the city of Tours. Dozens had perished and two young women had narrowly missed the same fate. Hope lay under her duvet, allowing herself an extra half-hour in bed. Sleeping alone had its benefits. She could stretch out and grab a cool pillow. Usually, she ended up squinched on the edge of the mattress because Ash slept like a starfish, arms flung wide. She'd always considered the nocturnal battle for territory to be the price of partnership, though recently, he'd started to shift away when she curled herself around him. 'Personal space,' he'd mutter before hauling the duvet off her. As these thoughts tracked through her head, Hope reflected that their relationship had changed so subtly over the past months, it had taken a separation for her to see it.

'Poor me in my comfy bed,' she murmured. The memoir's author, locked in a version of hell on the road outside Tours, would have had little time for self-pity. It would have been fight or flight, stark choices made fast.

She found the memoir in a fold of her bedcovers and turned to the place where she'd fallen asleep. Within a few lines, the story brought the first life-or-death decision.

> By the grace of fortune, Pauline and I are alive but have lost everything, including our way out of France. The jaws of the trap have closed around us but we cannot submit to despair. Which route do we take now?

Going down to the kitchen, Hope checked for new emails and found three waiting for her. The community dedicated to Lost English Painters had messaged. So had the lady in Florida.

And Ash had made contact. She opened his first.

12

Ash normally preferred WhatsApp or texting, but his message explained this departure from habit.

> *Left my phone in the taxi from the airport, had to buy a new one. Course, it isn't charged.*

He'd inserted a meme of a man hitting himself over the head with a frying pan. It made Hope smile, more from relief than anything else. Losing a phone was so unlike Ash. The message was long, too, by his habitual standards.

> *Back with my old firm. Got taken out to dinner by head of Internal Security. Signed for a twelve. Also signed an NDA so can't tell you exactly what I'll be doing, except it's the usual.*

'The usual' being cyber security for large, financially sensitive organisations. Hope felt her chest tightening.

He'd signed off: *Hoping to get back to L for a weekend soon. XXX.*

Decoded, Ash was telling her that he'd signed a year's

contract with the firm he'd been working for when they met. They'd made him sign a non-disclosure agreement. Well, nothing strange in that. Hope had signed a few NDAs in her time. But... only 'hoping' to get back for a weekend? Not wanting to show how upset she was, she replied, asking him where he'd be living.

> *And what's the number of your replacement phone, so I can call?*

The second email was more uplifting. Goldie Solon, the lady from Florida, was asking if Eat-Sleep-Paint-Gascony had room for a party of three. *I got two of my girlfriends interested in coming over. So excited I can't sleep.* Hope glanced at the time. Wow. This lady must be emailing in her jimjams as dawn broke.

My friends don't paint much, Goldie had written, *but they eat and sleep. Two out of three ain't bad! Do we get that block discount?*

Hope created a discount code and emailed it, then opened the message from Lost English Painters, moving her laptop screen into shadow, the better to focus.

Her correspondent was a retired university professor and an enthusiast of inter-war English painters. He was writing from North East England and described L.L. Shepherd as 'a local lass'.

Lass? *Of course.* The creator of that portrait was a woman who understood instinctively what another woman's pain felt like.

I was already familiar with her by name as she was born not far from where I live, the professor wrote. *L.L. stands for Lavinia Linda but she was always known as Lally.* He provided a biography: *Born in 1913, in Jarrow.*

Jarrow... The hunger march, unemployment and hardship. Lally's father had worked in a shipyard on the banks of the

Tyne until injury laid him off. Her mother had been in domestic service and was of Irish descent. At the outbreak of the First World War, her father joined the navy as a stoker – presumably fit enough by then to shovel coal into a ship's boiler – and was killed at sea. Her mother and Lally's three siblings died at the war's end, possibly of the Spanish flu. Lally was raised by a grandmother in a two-room tenement shared with another family. They got by, collecting waste coal from the banks of the river and selling it door to door.

Wow. That a remarkable artistic talent had found expression amid such hardship made Hope want to know everything about Lally – L.L. – Shepherd. The professor gave a partial explanation:

> She was named for a well-to-do spinster who employed her mother as a gardener and handywoman during the 1914-18 war, when the men went away. After Lally's mother's death, this lady stayed in touch and gave Lally a leg up in life. I found a reference to Lally aged sixteen, as a pupil in a private art school in Durham. She was also employed as a life model there. See attached a picture taken in 1929, not great quality.

Hope clicked on it. It showed solemn men and one woman at their easels, drawing a posed figure. Lally, naked but for a draped sheet over her navel. She was gazing down, and all Hope could derive was that, at age sixteen, Lally Shepherd had been a flat-chested girl-woman with a short bob of blonde hair. She seemed tense. Perhaps it had been cold in the studio.

By 1932, Lally had graduated. She decamped to Paris a year later, shortly before her twentieth birthday.

She is listed in several galleries' exhibitions from 1935 onwards, Hope's correspondent continued, *and also as the subject of male painters' work, notably one Victor Ponsard. This is a pattern that's all too familiar with female artists of the time. Wants to paint, makes her money by sitting for others. WW2 breaks out and all goes quiet until circa 1972 when she is the subject of a retrospective exhibition at the Marshall Gallery on Boulevard de Courcelles, Paris. I can't find much about this, and Lally again disappears without a trace. She died in 1999 aged eighty-six. Shall I keep digging? Being retired, I have time.*

Yes please, Hope wrote back, attaching the photograph she'd taken of the portrait. From the sound of it, Lally could certainly have painted Yves Ducasse's grandmother early in the 1940s. The burning question – was it a portrait of Hope's grandmother too? She googled the Marshall Gallery, and learned it had closed in 2001, its collection now housed in the 'country residence of its retired owner, Julien Marshall'. That must be the Julien in the memoir, the son of the family that had employed Pauline. The one Pauline was in love with.

L.L. Shepherd, the Marshall Gallery, the memoir and its narrator... clear connections were forming. Hope still hadn't established if the memoir had been in the binbag by accident, or if it belonged with the portrait. 'Must talk to Manon again,' Hope muttered. Though she didn't relish another encounter, she didn't want to wait until the next Thursday's flea market either. A town called Saint-Sever, an hour's drive away, held a Sunday market where the same stallholders pitched up. It was worth a try. If Manon wasn't there with her vintage wares, it was a lovely drive anyway.

Within ten minutes, Hope was on her way, music playing from the dashboard. A particular song came on, and it hit her that the last time she'd done this journey, Ash had been sitting beside her, eyes closed, a low-level '*tsk tsk*' beat leaking from his earphones. What was lonelier, she asked herself: being alone, or being alone while with someone?

You're in danger of sinking into existential *tristesse*, she warned herself. Snap out of it. Just as the Marshalls had known they must leave France or be trapped, Ash had taken a well-paying job to safeguard their future. He would come back.

13

Saint-Sever was a *bastide*, meaning a fortified town. From its highest point, you could see to the Spanish border or look down on the ancient pilgrims' route that took travellers into northern Spain. Hope toiled up winding streets keeping the twelfth-century church in her eyeline, wishing she'd brought a bottle of water.

The market was crammed, every stall butted up against the next. She bought a can of artisan lemonade and went in search of Manon Taubier. She knew her gamble had paid off when she spotted a stall with a familiar, messy display. The crate stencilled 'Oranges d'Espagne' was still there, and this time, it wasn't packed with stuff. What was missing was Manon herself. Behind the stall was a sparrow-thin youth, his thumbs busily working a Game Boy. 'Pokémon Champ 2012' said the graphic on his tee-shirt. Chin fluff and a scattering of spots on his cheeks put him around fifteen or sixteen. She cleared her throat and he looked up.

'Is Manon here?'

He jabbed a thumb. 'She's getting a drink. You want to buy something?'

She asked him how much the planter was.

He didn't know. 'Mum does the prices.'

'Mum?'

'She's Manon.' He pointed towards a food and drink van. Hope went over but if Manon had been there, she was no longer. Sipping her lemonade, Hope circuited the market, keeping to the shade as the temperature was nudging eighty. She finally saw Manon Taubier by a children's puppet booth, talking to a man with a ponytail and mirror shades. Squawking puppetry and children's laughter meant that Hope was up close before realising she was interrupting an argument.

'Fifty euros, hand it over,' the man was saying.

'All I've sold today is a couple of lousy cushions.' Manon's shrug implied, *What d'you want me to do, wave a magic wand?*

'That's not my problem. You take a pitch, you pay the fee. It's not complicated.' There was a weariness in the man's reply, as if it wasn't the first time he'd had this conversation with Manon. 'Come on, or I'll stand in front of your stall. And don't offer me a dud cheque again.'

Again, Manon shrugged. *Still don't have a magic wand.*

Hope saw her chance. She tapped Manon's arm above a butterfly tattoo and said, 'I'd like to buy that wooden planter. Fifty euros?'

'Done.' It was the man who answered. 'Let's go to your stall, Manon.'

With a glance for Hope that was anything but grateful, Manon marched away. At the stall, Hope took out her card, offering another five euros if someone carried it to her car.

'Noah?' Manon tweaked her son's ear in a way that made him squirm. 'Help the lady.'

The transaction complete, the man with the mirror shades held out his hand and the argument began all over again.

Between them, Hope and Manon's son lugged her purchase to where she'd parked. She'd done all right, she reckoned. At any chichi London outdoor market, she'd have paid twice as much for the planter. They were on their way back when Noah, playing on his Game Boy as he walked, darted down a side street, shouting to get somebody's attention. Good. Hope still wanted her private conversation with his mother.

She found Manon completing the sale of an embroidered tablecloth, so casually that Hope suspected she'd done quite well today, despite what she'd said to the market manager. Going to the side of the stall, she said, 'May I ask you more about the portrait I bought off you?'

Manon's response was to pout lips painted so darkly red as to be almost black. 'I don't do money back. Everything here' – she drew an imaginary line over her stock – 'is bought as seen. Nobody in the market does returns.'

'I only want information about the book that came with it.'

'What book?'

'A wartime memoir, written by an Englishwoman. It was in the bag with the picture. There's no author name and it has no back or front cover, so I'm at a loss.'

Manon's expression seethed with suspicion. 'A loss about what?'

'Who wrote it. It was in the binbag with the portrait,' Hope repeated.

'But I didn't sell it to you?'

'Not exactly—'

'If I didn't sell it, you can't complain.'

'I'm not complaining. I want to know more about the book. And the picture. I know it's Yves Ducasse's grandmother—'

'So, what else do you want to know?'

'Where it was painted and when. Dates, a location.'

Manon waved her hands as if fending off hostile questions. 'I just sell stuff, and whatever Yves has told you, I looked after his grandmother at my own expense when she hadn't long to live. I never wanted thanks but I'm sick of it being shoved back in my face.'

She's such an effing liar, Yves Ducasse had said of this woman, words which armoured Hope against too much credulity. She asked crisply, 'Why did you tell Yves that I paid two hundred euros for the portrait?'

Manon Taubier slowly raised her chin. 'I warned you not to talk to him.'

'And I ignored your advice. I went to his place and sold the picture back to him. For twenty euros.'

This brought an unexpected effect. Manon threw back her head with a barking laugh. 'So, everyone is happy. I exaggerated the price because he would have a fit if I told him, only twenty euros for his precious *grandmère*.'

'Tell me her name.'

Manon pulled heavily drawn eyebrows together. 'She was Lally Ducasse in normal life. As a painter, she was Lally Shepherd.'

'Wait... so it's a self-portrait? The woman in the picture is – was – Lally Shepherd?'

'Yes and yes. *Oh la vache!*' Manon had seen something behind Hope's shoulder. 'Did you bring him?'

Hope turned and saw Noah jogging to keep pace with Yves Ducasse and, once again, Yves' face was set in an expression of intense emotion. He strode up to the stall, pushed aside a set of greengrocer's scales whose pan was full of empty, single-serve jam pots and bellowed, 'Where are they?'

Manon spread her arms in bewildered innocence. 'I don't know what you mean.'

'You do, Maman.' Noah had pocketed his Game Boy and with his eyes freed from the curtain of hair that fell forward whenever he was on his device, he looked younger. More fragile. 'They're behind the stall. I told Yves, so give them to him.'

Manon made a face of dry acknowledgement at being

caught out. It was obvious Yves didn't frighten her. '*Eh bien*, you can stop shouting. They're here, all right? Yves, why do you get so angry? You're like *her*, always on a trigger.'

'Leave Lally out of it.' Yves' voice had settled, but his emotion had not. He acknowledged Hope with a frown, as if her presence made no sense. He swung back to Manon. 'Pass them over.'

'Get them yourself.'

Yves squeezed past Hope, saying to her, 'She was going to sell them. It's what she does.'

'Sells things? Well, obviously. What do you mean by "them"?'

'The things she steals.' He sidled behind the stall, his hip knocking down a stack of old magazines, and said loudly, 'She doesn't even do it well.'

Manon yelled '*connard*', which loosely translated as 'arsehole'. Noah begged his mother to please, stop it.

'I can say what I want.' To prove it, Manon called Yves every obscene word Hope had absorbed since coming to the Gers, and a few she had to guess at. Yves meanwhile took a cardboard box from under the stall. As he lifted it to his chest, Manon hit him hard on the side of his face.

Hope couldn't believe what she was seeing.

'Could you take it?' His voice terse, because the strike had clearly hurt, Yves handed the box to Hope. It was full of old vinyl records, black edges poking out from creased sleeves. He fetched a second box, stepping back sharply as Manon aimed a punch at his midriff.

'Funny, she only hits me when my arms are full,' Yves said as he got out from behind the stall. He kept walking and Hope went after him, still carrying the box he'd given her. Noah came too and Hope had no idea where they were going. Behind them, Manon shrieked at her son to come back.

'I'll call the police. Noah? You're a minor – if you go with him, it's abduction!'

'You'd better go back,' Hope urged the boy. 'Your mother sounds angry enough to make the call, and then she'd be embarrassed afterwards.'

Noah turned on his heel without argument and Hope felt she could have handled that better. 'How far?' she called after Yves. The box was heavy.

He let her catch up. 'I'm parked down the hill.'

'Ugh. Then I need to change my grip.'

'I've got a better idea.' He plonked his box down on a café table and did the same with hers. 'Wait here, I'll get my car.'

'You won't find anywhere to park,' she said. 'The town's heaving.'

He made a face, agreeing with her. 'Plan B. D'you fancy lunch? D'you like Senegalese food?'

She'd never tried it.

'Wait here, and if Manon comes, ignore her.'

Easier said than done, Hope reflected, as Yves walked off in the direction of a food wagon. At some point, she'd put down her lemonade and went to buy two more. Yves had chosen a table in the shade of a plane tree and she sat down, pulled back the ring on her can and took a pleasurable gulp. A steel band nearby was bashing out a familiar tune. It took a moment to unravel the melody: Oasis, 'Wonderwall'. It made her laugh for some reason. Yves came back with cardboard cartons filled with rice and topped with chunks of salmon in a glistening sauce, a side of deep-fried pastries, and a bottle of sparkling water. He handed her a wooden fork and put bamboo cups on the table.

'I didn't check your tolerance for mustard,' he said.

'Or fish.'

'Or fish,' he acknowledged. 'Act first, think after. My fatal principle. Would you like something else?'

'Fish is fine. As for how hot I can take it, French mustard has nothing on English. That lemonade is for you.'

'Cheers.' He raised the can in a toast as she tried her food, drinking it down almost in one go.

The fish was fiery, but delicious. The rice had been cooked with chilli and spices which, like 'Wonderwall' played on steel drums, took Hope some moments to identify. The deep-fried pastries were packed with chicken and beans. Yves poured sparkling water and they knocked rims.

A red patch had blossomed beside his left eye. 'Smacking you like that was lousy,' she said.

'Manon knows when to aim her punches.'

She'd had enough of Manon and moved the conversation in a new direction. 'Do I detect some Aussie in your accent?'

'Probably. I worked in Thailand for nearly ten years, along-side loads of Aussies and Kiwis. As a child, I learned English from my grandmother and her accent was not like the ones you hear on the BBC.'

'She came from Jarrow.' Hope confessed to researching L.L. Shepherd. 'Escaped poverty, came to Paris. Painter, self-portraitist, model. Writer? And your gran, of course.'

'Mm. Now you know about as much of her past as I do. When you came to my place, you spoke of having her memoir, but how? They were all destroyed, bar one or two that were probably sent out to the press at the time of printing. I've tried for years to get hold of a copy.'

'It's at home.' Hope explained how she'd come by it.

'Manon again.' He said it wearily. When his interest was engaged, he had a way of looking right at you, Hope thought. Green eyes were often more brown or blue than anything else, but his were the same spinach-leaf shade as the portrait. His trip to the barber had revealed a face more Nordic than French. Viking ancestry? Could be, with ancestors from North East England. He had good cheekbones, scattered with daytime beard, the hairs of which, when they caught the sunlight, were flecks of golden shrapnel. The sides of his neck were reddened.

'You ought to wear a hat,' she said. 'Like mine.' Hers was straw with a brim.

'I might invest in a Stetson,' he said. 'It would feel more manly.'

'Fine but wear one. Under your tan, you're fair-skinned. Melanoma knows no borders.'

'What a cheery person you are. Where were you born, Hope?'

'South East England. Fareham in Hampshire for the first few years then a village outside Petersfield.'

The names meant nothing to him, as his vague nod bore out. 'What is your second name, you are Hope...?'

'Granger.'

'Were you a long time coming for your parents?'

She got her finger stuck in one of the fretwork holes in the metal table, wiggling it out irritably. Over the years, she'd heard every play-on-words levelled at her name. Hope-less, Hope-full. In Hope we trust. Hope-on-a-Rope. 'I like to think I was longed-for, but actually, my mum just liked the name. They had their honeymoon in Hope Cove, Devon.'

'It's a sweet name. I was called Yves after Yves Duteil.' At Hope's blank look, he said, 'You have to be French, maybe. He's a singer.'

'A good one?'

'He sings in a tone of warm molasses and plays his guitar like a harp made of silk, or so it says on one of his fan-sites. Handsome, too, when young.'

'Your mother liked him, I take it?'

'No, Maman would have called me something bizarre like Gandalf. My grandmother was the Yves Duteil fan. Listening to him took her back to Paris, she said, before the war, when men knew how to sing and make love. Yves Duteil isn't from that generation, but he channelled my grandma's youth.' Yves tapped one of the boxes from Manon's stall. 'There are some of his records in here. I don't mind lending them to you, if you promise to give them back.'

'I always give things back, as you'll have noticed.' She'd sneaked a look in both boxes. The LPs were a mixed bag. Bach, Beethoven, Wagner. 'Big' German composers, alongside French male vocalists with razored moustaches, and *chanteuses* with soft waves and passionate lips. 'I don't have a record player,' she said. 'I download stuff onto an iPod.'

'Then come to the windmill and I'll play them to you, on my grandmother's ancient gramophone.'

Was he hitting on her, inviting her back to his place? The moment passed, and he asked about her parents. Were they still living in Hampshire? Did they mind her relocating?

She reloaded her fork with sweet-chilli rice. 'They've both passed. Mum in 2005, Dad in 2011.'

'I am sorry to hear that, one orphan to another. Didn't you want to stay where you'd grown up?'

'Did you?' Yves had told her, hadn't he, that he'd worked for years in Thailand. 'There was nothing to root me in Hampshire or in London either. That's where I was working when my dad died. He'd remarried by then, and she took over rather.'

Yves gave her a quizzical look. '*She...* Wicked stepmother?'

'Not wicked. Just... thorough.'

'Interesting choice of word.'

'Stephanie made Dad happy after we lost Mum. Just, there's no connection there. She has grown-up children and grandkids who always come first.'

'You feel shoved out.'

'It's more that I feel she pulled off a hostile takeover. She replaced my mum and replaced me with her own tribe. After Dad's funeral I went back to London, to my little, private cave. I thought I'd never leave. "My friends are the family I choose."

You know the feeling?' Something moved in Yves' eyes: a bleak flash of recognition. 'Anyway, I met my partner, Ash, and found my own path.' Ash had made her feel cherished again and being suddenly reminded that they were on the brink of a year's separation made her body temperature plunge. She said to Yves, 'I want to know more about your grandmother. You didn't say she was also L.L. Shepherd.'

He regarded her from under thick, straight brows. 'She wasn't L.L. anything to me. She was Lally Ducasse and I only speak of her to those I trust or who ask for the right reasons. You understand?'

Hope opened the photo app on her phone, and enlarged the close-up she'd taken of the portrait, pushing it towards Yves. 'See that?'

His vague reply reminded Hope of a dog's warning growl. He minded that she'd taken a photograph? Tough. The picture had been legally hers at the time. He hadn't commented yet on the Grey Eyed Dove, which she had fastened to her shirt this morning. She unpinned the brooch and put it on the table where he couldn't avoid seeing it. 'What do you think?'

He inspected it, then passed it back to her. 'It's like the one in the painting. What am I meant to say?'

She flared up, certain he was being deliberately obtuse. 'It's not "like", it's totally the same.'

'If you say so.'

'Not because I say so! Look again.' She held the brooch out; he didn't take it. 'Don't play games with me. Not over the only damn thing I got from my dad.' She sat back, steadying her breath. Actually, not the only thing. Another little memento had come to her on the day of her father's funeral.

Stephanie been tidying up, Hope assisting. It had been a good turnout. As Stephanie kept remarking, 'A good tea always brings them in, doesn't it? While I'm remembering, Hope, your dad wanted you to have this.'

Taking a rusty tin from the dresser, Stephanie watched as Hope prised up the lid. Hope was anticipating her dad's wedding ring or his watch. Inside was a dry-as-dust sprig of vegetation. Lavender? If so, it hadn't been attached to a bush in a long time. She'd put it to her nose, and without thinking, had said, 'It's French.'

Stephanie had agreed. 'Your father told me once, his mother was French, though he couldn't ever name her. Isn't that odd? I was all for tracking her down, but he wouldn't have it.'

'He wouldn't let Mum do it either,' Hope had said.

'I'll be honest' – Stephanie had wrinkled her nose at the lavender-sprig – 'I chucked that out three times at least, but he tipped up the dustbin every time. So, there you are, Hope. Never say I haven't carried out his wishes.'

Hope took back her phone and said now in a hard voice to Yves Ducasse, 'This brooch is called the Grey Eyed Dove. You're sure the woman in the portrait is L.L. Shepherd, your grandmother?'

'Course I'm sure. You must have noticed the resemblance between her and me.'

She had because it was indisputable. The eyes, alight with passion, the complexion. The mouth, straight and long, hinting at a steely character. Yes, she saw the resemblance of Yves to Lally Ducasse-Shepherd as clearly as she saw its absence when *she* looked in the mirror.

He asked, 'Why do you care so much?'

'This brooch was my dad's and he got it from his French mother.'

His narrowed gaze told her he had finally started to listen. 'You think Lally is your grandmother too? Not possible.'

'Yes – possible,' Hope countered. 'Else, why would she be wearing this brooch? There can't be two in the world. Look at it properly and you'll see I'm right.'

Reluctantly, he picked up the Grey Eyed Dove again. 'It's nice workmanship. Silver inlaid with enamel but it needs a clean.'

It was her turn to growl in frustration. 'Forget that. I've compared it with the painting and every detail is identical. Why won't you concede? Is it that you don't want to know?'

He leaned towards her. 'A stranger, claiming my grand-mother as her own? You want it to be, because you have nobody else. Your mind is creating it, like seeing faces of angels in the clouds.'

'You're coming close to calling me nuts.'

He gestured that away. 'You've found a vague similarity in a brooch that needs cleaning to a picture that needs restoration. Lally painted a brooch on her dress in a few quick strokes. There's no detail.'

'That's not true.' The brooch in the portrait had been care-fully executed.

'It's there to balance the picture's composition. It's a coinci-dence, Hope.'

'It's the same brooch. My father, Joseph Granger, had a French mother. He didn't invent her. They got separated during the war.'

'How, where?'

Hope admitted she didn't know. As her conversation with Stephanie at the funeral had illustrated, Joseph had been hyper-private about the circumstances of his birth and could never be cajoled into doing research. When Hope's mother was alive there had been talk of visiting France, to pick up the trail. Hope had an insubstantial memory of standing at the rail of a cross-Channel ferry, her mother with her, but wasn't entirely sure she hadn't created the image to fit with a conversation she'd overheard.

'Your dad was raised by his grandparents and something about his birth cast a great, black cloud,' Hope's mother had confided once.

What kind of dark cloud, illegitimacy?

Her mother had shrugged helplessly. 'Your dad's gran was still alive when we married, but would she talk about his mother, her daughter? Not a squeak, unless she was angry with him for something, when it got thrown in his face. She and his grandfather rescued him from France and your dad's terrified what he'll find if he looks too deeply.'

A trauma in childhood so great, Joseph Granger could never speak of it, except once, when he gave Hope the Grey Eyed Dove. 'It's all I have of my mother. They took me from her because of what she was, and who my father was.' And that was it.

At the end of one of her university terms, with time on her hands, Hope had joined an ancestry site. Mapping her family tree had been a guilty secret she kept from her father. Her mother's side had been easy to trace whereas the Granger side yielded virtually nothing. Only child upon only child, two world wars obscuring the records. She'd concluded that she had everything that remained of her father's French origins, a brooch and a faded sprig of lavender, until she'd lifted the portrait of Lally Shepherd from a wooden box at a flea market.

'Thousands of people got separated during wartime.' Yves jammed his elbows on the table, making it creak. 'Lally had one child, my mother. My mother had one child, me. Sorry, but we are not related, Hope.'

'It's not you I want to be related to! What if Lally had a child, during the war, that nobody knew about?' An illegitimate child would have been a massive source of shame at the time.

'She didn't,' Yves said.

'Or she didn't tell you?' Hope planted her elbows too. She wasn't going to let a man dominate the table. 'This is what I know. My dad was born in France when it was an occupied country. From something my mum said, I believe he was fetched away by my great-grandparents – his mother's parents – who brought him up.'

'Near Peter-somewhere, you said?'

'Petersfield was where we moved to but they lived in Fareham, on the edge of Portsmouth Harbour.'

'The south coast?'

She nodded.

'We've already agreed,' Yves said, 'my grandmother came from the other end of the country and was called Shepherd, not Granger.'

All true. Hope felt deflated.

'I'm not denying you have a French grandmother, Hope. Ignore what I said a minute ago about you seeing faces in the clouds. I was being an arse. I'm just saying, your grandmother wasn't Lally.'

'Fine. We'll see.'

'Come back to my place.' His voice had lost its edge, as though he'd decided to coax instead of blasting at her. By sitting down to lunch with him, had she given the impression of wanting to grow the friendship?

'I'm in a relationship,' she said coolly.

'Good for you. I was saying, come to my place, to look at Lally's portrait again. You can't tell anything from a photograph.'

'That portrait spent an entire night on my bedroom wall.'

He explained patiently, 'View it in a good light and tell me honestly if you see a resemblance to your family. Do you have a picture of your father?'

She did, in her wallet.

'OK, let's go then. We'll show the brooch to Claudia.'

Claudia...? For a moment, Hope was at a loss.

'My holiday guest,' he reminded her. 'With the ball-obsessed children? She's a silversmith, from an Amsterdam diamond dynasty.'

'Wow. Why's she slumming it at yours?'

He made a face, taking the hit. Her remark had been spiteful, instantly regretted. 'The fortune took a side-step some time ago. Claudia makes her own jewellery, but she learned from her grandfather so she might tell you something about your green eyed dove.'

'Grey eyed. Fine.'

As they left, Hope noticed someone watching them go. She touched Yves' elbow. 'Manon's boy wants to talk to you.'

Almost as if he could lip-read, Noah Taubier came running up, his expression naked and eager. He asked if he could go home with Yves.

'Sorry.' Yves ignored the boy's crestfallen look. 'I don't want to be arrested for kidnapping. Come to La Cachette when your mother's stopped hating me. You're sixteen soon, aren't you?'

'August,' the lad said.

'So, after your birthday, I'll give you a Saturday job.'

'What job?'

'Caffeine delivery operative.'

Hope could almost see the words ticking through the boy's brain. 'You mean a waiter?'

Yves grinned. 'Till then, keep your head down and be nice to your mum.'

A teenage sneer cut across Noah's lips. '*Ma mère est une vraie catastrophe.*'

'Hey – that's not cool. You only ever have one mother, right?'

'Right.' Noah sounded as if he wished otherwise.

Sitting in her car, waiting for sight of Yves' Land Rover in her rearview mirror, Hope considered Noah's comment about his mum. *Catastrophe.* Car crash. Noah exuded such raw feeling when he watched Yves, there had to be something complicated going on. When the dented bumper and caged headlights of Yves' vehicle appeared, she thought about Manon Taubier lashing out at him, literally punching low. Manon thrived on hostility. Consider the petty way she'd got even with Hope for upsetting her aunt. That café brunch had cost twenty-five euros, and Hope hadn't enjoyed more than three bites of her own brioche.

Good relations with Inès Royale were essential, but the niece? 'Avoid, avoid,' Hope muttered. Should she extend that to Yves too, now she suspected he was embroiled with Manon in some way? Yes.

Definitely yes.

Yet, when he honked his horn and gave her space to pull out ahead of him, she knew she was on her way to La Cachette. The portrait had captured her, and now she could put a name to it. Lally. Proving it was the face of her grandmother was more important than avoiding Manon Taubier. More important than getting home in case Ash called and asked where she was. And that was saying something.

14

When Yves had promised they'd view Lally's portrait 'in a good light' Hope hadn't expected to be taken to the top of the windmill. Removing the 'No Entry' sign as he went up, he informed Hope that she was honoured.

'Really?' The stairs were steep, the air hot and still.

'My grandmother let only trusted friends up here and you are the first person I've brought since I came home.'

'Apart from Claudia and her kids,' she pointed out. There had been no sign of Claudia, the dog or the children when she and Yves had arrived. Yves had speculated they'd gone for a cycle ride along the pilgrims' path.

'Apart from them,' he acknowledged, 'but they come up here without permission.'

Aware he was relaxing boundaries, she cut the teasing note from her voice. 'Have you done all the renovation yourself?' The mill's stairs and walls had the patina of recent sandblasting.

In answer, he displayed his beaten-up hands. 'My grandmother hardly touched the place in all the years she lived here and I was away, on and off, for thirteen years. When I got back I had either to sell up or stage a rescue.'

'Will you stick at it?' The 'drifter' tag given by Jeanne at the café was seeming less accurate by the minute.

'I am stuck, like the fly in the web.'

As she stepped onto wooden boards at the top of the mill, Hope was surprised at the light and the freshness. Looking up was like seeing the inside of a conical hat. Knotty beams held up roof tiles through which daylight poked. Other than that, the space seemed restored, including the black-painted arm and brackets that supported the sails. 'Where's the turning gear?' she asked. Apart from a big, old cupboard, a chair and a single easel, the room was empty.

'There's been no corn ground here since the war,' Yves told her. 'There weren't enough able-bodied men to work the mill. The grinding wheels and all the iron would have been melted down as scrap. This was Lally's studio from 1944 until she died. That was the year the liberation of France began, and it happens to be when she painted the portrait.'

'Oh?' She'd dated the portrait to the beginning of that decade. Ah, but perhaps the dress had been a few years old. People did not shop for fashion in wartime. 'Was the date accidental or significant?'

He didn't know. 'But it has to be. The year, the month, the day of liberation is cataclysmic if you live through it.'

It was a perfect studio, in Hope's estimation. An unsealed opening led onto an iron balcony with a view to the horizon. The balcony would be a place from which to watch the sunset – if you were OK with heights. Next to the opening, on a rush-bottomed chair, sat Lally's portrait.

She took out the photo of her dad to compare features. Yves watched, saying nothing. Nor did she speak, because there was no chime of recognition as she looked from one to the other, no similarity between man and painting. Disappointed and self-conscious, Hope let the view claim her attention, asking, 'How far can we see?'

'Step out. It's quite safe.'

'Only quite safe?'

'I'm still alive, aren't I?'

She edged out, disliking the way the pierced metal panels rang beneath her feet. Yves followed, leaning his hands on the rail. 'You can see to Auch when it's clear. Too much heat haze today. That snaking line is the River Gers, flowing towards the Garonne. See, where it gets very dark green? Those are the foothills of the Pyrenees. You can't make out the mountains exactly, but you can see the snow on their tops.'

She could indeed. White peaks against an intensely blue sky. 'This is a fabulous studio.'

He agreed. 'In Paris, you will always want northern light to paint by, as it's the purest. Here, we angle towards the mountains and colours show true. It's why Lally made this her nest.'

'I'm not sure I'd get much work done if I was standing here all day.'

He agreed. 'I'd often see her framed in this doorway, staring out. She didn't like stepping out onto the balcony, said it made her sad.'

'She moved here while the war was still going on, I think you said?'

'Yes.' He sounded vague. 'She came from over there.' He was indicating a house partially screened by poplar trees. A double line of them ran towards the road, suggesting a long driveway.

'What's that place called?'

'Lally referred to it as Madame Taubier's place.'

'Taubier, as in—'

'Manon. *Oui*. But don't be surprised. Anyone whose grandparents were born in Lazurac is related. The proper name of that house is Le Sanctuaire.' The Sanctuary. Pressing his stomach against the rail, Yves pointed to a scrubby treeline that meandered behind both properties. 'That's the pilgrims' path,' he said. 'The Via Podiensis. It follows a stream for some distance then crosses the site of a Roman villa.'

She'd love to see that. 'How far does your land go?'

'Not far enough,' he said, his voice snapping back to its gravelly register. He went back inside. Hope drank in the view a little longer, daring to step up to the rail. It felt lovely, the breeze playing into the roots of her hair, fluttering her shirt collar. This mill made a perfect summer studio but what about winter? 'Did your grandma work here all year round?' she asked over her shoulder.

'Every day, every season. I remember coming in and finding snow on the floor, and her wrapped up in shawls and hats, still painting. She lived in what's now the gîte but up here, she entered her real life, that of the artist.'

'Why do I get the impression she was sad much of the time?'

'Because she was. She drank, and more so after my mother died, which made everything worse, though she laughed too. She wasn't a misery guts. I'm one of those so I know the difference.'

Was he? There were moments his face lit up, but it didn't take much to knock him back into growling fury. As Hope went back inside, she noticed an iron hook above the doorway. Links of rusty chain dangled from it and she wondered if it had once supported a lantern, perhaps to warn low-flying aircraft of the mill's height. She made the chain swing as she passed beneath.

Yves had moved the chair, placing the portrait in the pure light he'd spoken of. In Hope's bedroom, Lally's brushstrokes had seemed messy, the colours indistinct. She now saw that every stroke had meaning and the colours sang. Hope imagined Lally at her easel, wearing that same summer dress, a long mirror reflecting her image back to her. 'Was it painted up here?'

'Probably. Or while Lally was lodging with old Madame

Taubier next door. I remember the dress hanging in our wardrobe, though. Grandma told me some nuns gave it to her, and that it was sewn in the 1930s.'

'D'you still have it?' Hope had studied vintage textiles during one of her terms at art college. Imagining Lally here in all weathers, driven by passion for her art, aggravated Hope's growing dissatisfaction with herself. She had stepped away from the artist's life... to study accountancy. It had made sense at the time, less so now.

'Do I have the dress? No. It walked.'

'Walked? Oh, you mean—'

'Manon adores old things. Come on, let's do what we've come to do.' When Hope stared back, not catching his drift, he said, 'The brooch?'

'Oh, yes.' She fumbled at it.

'Let me.'

She stood, inches from him, seeing where the sun had caught his skin, and the stubble on his chin and throat that had grown since lunch. His fingers were ill-designed for releasing a delicate catch and it was a mistake to look up. They both felt it, the flicker, the instant where desire punched through the film of polite reserve.

She stepped back, thinking of Ash, even though she still had no clear idea where he was. 'Will it work to compare a three-dimensional object with a two-dimensional one? That's what we're going to do, I suppose?' She was blathering, covering the moment of chemistry.

'It's all we've got.' Yves held the dove brooch next to its painted double. For fully two minutes, neither of them spoke.

Hope broke the silence. 'They're the same.'

Yves did not answer.

'Look at the beak,' she persisted, 'how it's broken off at the end? It's the same angle of break on the picture.'

'Maybe... you can't tell. If any part of your brooch was going to snap off, it would be the beak.'

'What are you saying – that there's a flock of grey eyed doves, all with broken beaks?'

He smiled. 'Why should yours be unique? Look at the eye.'

She knew what he was going to say. In the picture, the eye was rimmed with gold but missing on her brooch. 'The gold fell out,' she said.

'When?'

'I don't know. It's how it was when my dad gave it to me, but obviously it was there because you can see the groove.'

'You don't know it was gold. It could have been enamel, or silver.'

'You've made up your mind.' She took the dove from him and stalked to the stairs but didn't go down as her sense of justice won out. Of course he was reluctant to consider that his beloved grandmother might have given birth to a secret child. Her claims, coming out of the blue, must seem wildly eccentric.

Yves hung up the portrait, standing back to look at it, and answered the question she hadn't voiced. 'I don't think you're my cousin, Hope, and I don't believe you're Lally's grand-daughter but why does that matter?'

'It matters.'

Why? He came to her, the question in his eyes.

She hesitated. She could leave and her quest would fizzle out. She'd be no worse off than before her visit to Lazurac's Thursday market. But the flame had been lit. 'I have no family,' she said. 'Mum had a sister, who died without having had children. Dad had nobody but his grandparents, and they died before I was born.'

'You want a flock of your own. That's understandable. Make your own dynasty, Hope, with your boyfriend.'

A few days ago, that suggestion might have had meaning.

Now it only stoked her sense of isolation. 'I need to know where I come from.'

'Sure? It's not always a happy ending.'

'It doesn't have to be happy.'

'The way I see it' – Yves put his hand on her shoulder – 'you're somebody's granddaughter. So start with a question, not the answer.' He began to make his way down. 'Want a coffee?'

'In the least busy café in France?'

He smiled casually up at her, the comment bouncing off him. 'There's a painting on your website, people sitting outside a café in the sunshine. Your work?'

'Um, yes.' She flushed. 'I made the sketch at Le Chat, during that warm spell at Easter. I was on my own, time on my hands. I'm not really a painter. I gave up.' He hadn't said he liked her work, just that he'd noticed it. She turned her embarrassment back on him. 'You've looked me up on social media, then?'

'Isn't that what people do? Your website is good. Clever and aspirational. I need one like it.'

'Then build one.'

He raised a hand. 'We're all good at something... And my coffee is excellent.'

While Yves ground the beans, she studied the artefacts on his walls. They must be odds and ends he'd found here or excavated. 'Why do you have a café?' she asked when the grinder stopped.

'For an income.'

'But nobody comes.' She counted eight tables, every chair pushed neatly in.

'They did before,' he said, lifting a carton of milk. 'Ugh. Gone off. Black OK?'

'Fine.' She touched an iron lamp with lattice-mesh sides. 'What stopped them coming?'

'My neighbours. Would you like some tart? Fresh this morning.'

'Go on then.' She dragged out a chair and Yves brought their coffee and plates piled with walnut tarts, the nuts glistening under thick daubs of caramel. She reached for one. 'By "neighbours", you mean the people at the house next door?'

'At Le Sanctuaire, yes. It still belongs to the Taubiers. When I opened this place, I planted a sign on the pilgrims' path. "Best coffee this way". People started coming and I could hardly keep up. Varsac is about fifty minutes' trudge from Lazurac and people would see the sign and think—'

'Time for a break, with cake.'

'Exactly. Just as money was coming in, the Taubiers got arsy about people crossing their land.'

'Their land?' Yves would be the type to overlook that detail.

'The land isn't registered to anyone, but the Taubiers have the money to go legal if I argue. The old man's a bastard and one of his sons is a lawyer, the other's an estate agent.' He made a sound of disgust. 'They put up a barbed-wire fence and I lost my business overnight.'

'And your waitress left.'

'Not because of the fence. Because of that.' Yves gestured to his gallery. 'The pictures spooked her.'

'Your windmills? I think they're stunning. You're an accomplished photographer.' She might have guessed that overt admiration wouldn't please him.

'Whatever. Maybe she heard gossip in town. The end result was the same, no customers, so she left. Here I am' – he flung an angry gesture at nothing in particular – 'my income the gîte, and only three more bookings this year.'

That's three more than I've got, Hope thought. 'May I ask a question?'

'You ask nothing but questions.'

Then one more wouldn't hurt. Remembering how the

colour had fallen out of Inès Royale's cheeks at the sight of Lally Shepherd's portrait, she asked, 'What was the grudge between Lally and Madame Royale?'

'Manon's Aunt Inès?' He made a non-committal sound. 'People in Lazurac don't like the name Ducasse.'

'Are you going to tell me why?'

'Because they don't know their own history. They tell themselves they do, but they only see what they want to see.'

Hope remembered Inès clenching her teeth together. *Her*. Hope hadn't shown the memoir to Manon – there had been no chance for that conversation to develop – but Yves deserved sight of it. She was about to go to her car to fetch it when the van Beek children raced in, Mitzi the dog scampering behind. Claudia followed more sedately.

'Can we go up the windmill?' the children begged Yves.

'How many times must I say? If you fall off the balcony, my insurance won't pay out.'

The children laughed, suggesting they knew Yves wasn't serious. 'We won't go on the balcony, we promise,' one said. 'We need to talk to our dad and our phones work better up there.'

'So, you've been up, despite the sign telling you not to?'

'You know I took them up.' Claudia came up to the table. 'I trust them, Yves. I can say to you, they'll climb the stairs slowly, and not step onto the balcony.'

Hope had the idea Claudia wanted to speak without the children present. Yves conceded. The kids could climb the mill, but on no account to kill themselves. 'Mitzi stays here though. Dogs and windmills aren't a good fit.'

As the children began their slow climb to the next level and Yves got up to make more coffee, Claudia sat down and unrolled a scroll of paper: a laminated notice with a drawing pin at each corner. 'The Café du Moulin is closed permanently'.

'It was on the path, nailed to a tree trunk,' Claudia said.

Yves shrugged. 'More of the same.'

'Can they do that?' Hope asked. 'Isn't it, I don't know, restriction of trade or something?'

'Probably.' Yves brought their coffee over and sat down, hands behind his head and his weight perilously balanced on the chair's back legs. 'I could sue them, but losing court cases is a family tradition.'

The memoir, she thought. Withdrawn from sale owing to legal action. Assuming it was Lally's autobiography of course. She still lacked proof. She'd read a bit more of it, she decided, before showing it to Yves.

'Maybe you should sell up and go, Yves.'

At Claudia's comment, the chair dropped forward and Yves replied sharply, 'They tried to bully my grandmother out. My mother had so much crap to put up with, brought up without a father... They won't get another Ducasse scalp.' He saw Hope's frown. 'What do you want to say?'

She was thinking – was having children out of wedlock another Ducasse family tradition? Instead, she asked where the surname had come from.

'It's the name Lally assumed and called herself until her death. During the war, having a French surname became a matter of survival.'

'She signed herself "Shepherd" on her paintings.'

'Once the war was over, yes.'

Hang on... 'You said the portrait was painted in 1944. The war was still going on, yet it's signed L.L. Shepherd.'

That silenced him. He frowned. Nodded. 'I can't explain that. "Ducasse" was the name she took on. Stole, really.'

Barbed wire and false names. With that one revelation, Hope had no doubt it was Lally's memoir she was reading.

Yves said to Claudia, 'Hope has something she'd like you to look at.'

'Oh?' Claudia was stroking Mitzi, who had jumped onto her knee and was panting in the heat. Claudia had caught the sun and her hair shone all the blonder for it. An attractive woman. Wholesome, likeable. Hope wondered about the children's father, and whether he was intending to join his family. She showed Claudia the brooch, explaining how she'd come to own it. 'It's of little value, probably, but Yves thought you might be able to tell me something.'

Yves fetched more of the tarts, saying he'd save some for the children. 'They ought to be eaten today. I buy them frozen, so they can't go back in the freezer.'

He watched Claudia turning the brooch in her fingers, saying, 'To me, it looks from the 1930s, when enamel was fashionable.'

Claudia didn't answer at once but held it in front of her eyes for at least a minute before shaking her head. 'I need to put it under a loupe for a proper inspection. A watchmaker's magnifier,' she explained. 'When you're looking at tiny joints, the naked eye misses a lot.' Turning it around, squinting at the pin, Claudia's focus sharpened. 'Have you read the inscription?'

Hope hadn't known there was one. 'What does it say?' An inscription might include a name.

'Without a loupe I can't really see.'

'Don't you have a magnification app on your phone?'

'Course I do. Duh! My children are always getting at me for not using my tech.' Claudia powered up her phone, only to frustrate Hope again by saying, 'No, it's too shadowy in here.' They followed her outside into better light.

'Is it a name?' Hope asked anxiously. Claudia was taking too long.

'Erm... it's not, no.'

'So what does it say?' Yves sounded just as exasperated, undoubtedly because he wanted proof that the brooch had nothing to do with his family.

'It says... "*Mit Liebe*".' Claudia looked at them both. 'That's

German for "With love".' She smiled at Yves, appearing oblivious to the denial that shook his body.

'That can't be right,' he said.

'Sorry.' Claudia was realising she'd put her foot in it. 'It's what it says.' She held out her palm, displaying the dove's dull underside. '"*Mit Liebe*". Whoever first had this little brooch had a German boyfriend.'

15

BARBED WIRE AND FALSE NAMES: MEMOIR OF AN ENGLISH GIRL IN OCCUPIED FRANCE

Crawling out from our ditch as the smoke clears, we run across a meadow into some trees and hunker there all night, hungry, thirsty, our nerves shattered. At dawn, I emerge to watch the sun rise through low-lying mist. What now, with nothing to our names but the clothes we stand up in?

Pauline comes silently to stand beside me. She tells me she's hungry.

'Me too. We can't stay here.'

'Where shall we go? We could try and catch up with Otto. Is Spain a long way?'

'Yes.' The Spanish border is several hundred kilometres away and outright dangerous as Spain's government is sympathetic to the Nazis. We don't have passports either. We have no documents at all. I voice a thought; we could strike north to St Malo and try to get home from the Brittany coast. 'But it would be a gamble, as we don't know if the Germans are there or not.' My best suggestion is to stick to our plan and go south to Marseilles, to the British consul. Seven hundred kilometres but if we rejoin the exodus, we might pick up a lift.

Pauline droops. 'Nobody is giving lifts. We didn't, did we? I can't walk seven hundred kilometres, Lally. I'm not sure you could, either.'

'All right. Spain it is, in the footsteps of Otto.' But when we reach the main road that is scarred and littered from yesterday, smell the stench of burning and see the smoke rising from the heart of Tours, we realise at the same moment that we have only one option. Though we went through so much to leave...

We must go back to Paris.

We trudge into the ravaged morning, falling in with other survivors, all in that bedazed state that follows horror and noise. It's gridlock yet again because columns of refugees are still flowing towards us. These newcomers have heard rumours of the bombing, and ask what things are like further along. 'Can we cross the river at Tours, can we get through?'

I shake my head. Meaning, *Don't try*.

'Why are you going the wrong way?' a man asks us and when I tell him our plan, he looks at us as if we're mad. 'Paris is German now. You won't even get there, there's a bloody war going on, pitched battles between Blois and Orléans. You'll be killed. Or raped.'

We keep going. There is death for mile after mile. I try to ignore those I see picking through the corpses, like ravens on a battlefield. A man in his shirtsleeves levers a tooth from a dead woman's mouth. A flash as it disappears into his pocket tells me he's a gold prospector who has found a miraculous new seam. I feel I'm witnessing the disintegration of humanity.

Hours later, hearing bells, Pauline raises her chin and says in wonder, 'It's Sunday.'

So it is. The 16th of June 1940. This day last year, we

borrowed bicycles and took a two-day trip to Fontainebleau. There were five of us: me, Pauline, Julien, an artist friend of mine called Victor Ponsard and Otto. Pauline took a photograph or two and I sketched. Victor drank from a hipflask, critiquing my work over my shoulder. Otto and Julien talked politics and literature. Just one year ago.

In a silent village, we gulp water from a fountain. Pauline gags, because she can feel it travelling from her mouth all the way down to her stomach, a cold and comfortless stream.

I tell her to fill up on it. 'Better a bellyful of water than air.'

'When will we get something to eat?'

'As soon as we find a kindly soul.' This village and all the others along the road have closed their doors to refugees. Charity dies when hunger mobilises. Homes are shuttered, suggesting their owners have fled. This is grain country, a landscape of fields and river valleys. There are no mountains to hide out in.

The sole is coming off one of Pauline's shoes. My feet are rubbed raw where my shoe leather has split. We sleep in a barn that night.

The following day is so hot, the road coughs up dust until our throats are raw. In another deserted village, we creep into somebody's kitchen garden and gorge on their strawberries. We drink water from their pump, then crawl into an empty stable and sleep. I am woken by Pauline giving a series of sharp screams and realise there's somebody in the stable with us. A man, from the blunt silhouette and the sound of his breath. I can make out the outline of a rough beard, a hat or beret pulled low. He seems to be crouching over Pauline, who is shrieking and he is trying to silence her.

I reach into a corner where I left a wooden bucket that I'd filled from the pump and hurl it, water and all, at his head. He emits a sharp 'Ahh!' of pain and pitches sideways, swearing furiously.

In German.

I retrieve the bucket, prepared to club him to death with it. Just as I'm raising it to bring it down on his head, he shouts, 'Lally, it's me. Put it down.'

'Otto?' I let the bucket fall, torn between joy and dismay. He struggles upright and I hurl myself into his arms. We both collapse into the straw. 'Otto, my darling, I didn't recognise you. Did I hurt you? How are you here?'

'I walked, of course.' The words are squeezed through gritted teeth. I really have hurt him and because he's in shock, he's temporarily forgotten to speak in French. 'I saw you pass through a village a short way back and followed. I waited till dark to come, just in case.'

Pauline, who is wet from the water in the bucket, says incredulously, 'You're meant to be at the Spanish border by now.'

'How fast do you think I walk?' Otto replies. He shoots out a hand to help Pauline up from the straw. 'This is as far as I got. I was injured.'

I and Pauline echo, 'Injured?'

'Got knocked over on the road two days out of Paris.' He caught a train at Versailles, he tells us, the day he left Paris but got off at Chartres because of the enemy planes swooping over the railway line. 'I decided walking was safer, until some madman on a motorcycle clipped me as he went past. I thought I'd broken my elbow. I holed up in a churchyard, watching the people go by. I couldn't believe when I saw you walking in the other direction. Something went wrong with the car?'

I explain about the attack, in as few words as possible because I cannot bear to describe, or visualise, the death of our reluctant chauffeur. 'We're going back to Paris, because we haven't a franc or a change of stockings between us,' I tell him.

Otto is horrified. Go back to Paris? He has heard the refugees flowing past him describing the city they escaped. 'It is no longer in French hands,' he says and because he witnessed the military build-up in Germany, he has a better idea than us what occupation actually means. 'We must keep to our original plans. We'll go together as far as Bordeaux or Toulouse, yes? I've just about enough money to feed us.'

The dread I've been carrying since we turned back melts a little. But Pauline, who is holding Otto's arm the way a child clutches a cot blanket, repeats what she said before. She can't walk south. She can't walk that stretch of road where our car was burned either, with our driver inside. 'I'm not tough like Lally. If you both want to go, I'll understand. Leave me here.'

'What, to die?' I say, angry with her because my chance of escaping with Otto is again being snatched from me. 'As if we'd do that.'

She sinks down, smothering a sob. Otto exhales and says, 'Fine, we'll go back to Paris and lie down till we can get a train out.' He means 'lie low'. He is remembering to speak French again, but his command of the language is not perfect. 'We'll need more money if we're any time in Paris, though. And you'll need French papers.'

In a macabre way, the flames have done us a favour by consuming our British passports.

Morning comes and we get on our way. Two have become three, heading into the sunrise beyond which lies the most dangerous city in France.

16

HOPE

Hope lifted the planter she'd bought from Manon out of her car. On her return from Yves Ducasse's house, she'd gone straight inside and picked up the memoir. She had finally discovered the author's name: *I'm not tough like Lally*, Pauline had said and Hope wondered if, in recounting this darkest of moments, the author had forgotten her desire to stay anonymous.

The memoir was not easy reading, and once again, Hope had put it down after a few pages. It felt good to be out in the sunshine. Balancing the planter on a sack-barrow, she wheeled it to the terrace and into the shade of a mimosa tree. It would look good filled with hostas and hellebores, she decided.

She swept the terrace but the exercise didn't shift Lally's story from her head. Imagine, nearly dying, then heading back to occupied Paris. How extraordinary, that meeting with her German lover. Otto must be German, if he switched into the language when he was flustered.

Was it Otto who had given Lally the Grey Eyed Dove and engraved it '*Mit Liebe*'? If so, he became a person of interest to Hope. She felt her father near, blocking her. Telling her, 'Don't ask. Don't look. Don't see.' Joseph Granger had been spoon-fed shame by his grandparents. Had they erased his parentage because his mother had loved a German? The truth couldn't be any worse than the trauma Otto, Lally and Pauline had experienced. Most people went a lifetime without seeing a dead body. Lally and Pauline had seen dozens on that road outside Tours. How had it left them, psychologically? These days, it was understood that trauma could lead to a dissociative state. To self-harm and depression. 'She drank,' Yves had said of his grandmother.

Hope leaned on her broom and recalled her father saying once, when they were walking a coastal path and the crash of waves had ensured complete privacy: 'All I knew of my mother, apart from the fact that she stayed in France, was that she wasn't fit. Not a fit person.'

Not a fit person? The Lally of the memoir sounded, frankly, pretty darn heroic.

Hope was emptying fallen mimosa petals onto a compost heap when the phone in her pocket chirped. She'd got an email. Oh! From Goldie Solon in Florida. She opened it, preparing herself for a disappointment.

Paid deposit, confirm receipt. Please send travel advice and a what-to-bring and what-not-to-bring list. We're whooping with excitement. Oh, should have said. We're four, not three. My friend Paloma's brother wasn't going to be left out.

'I have guests!' Hope spun around in pleasure and immediately messaged Inès Royale. *Guests arriving Friday 28th, tutoring begins Monday July 1st. You must join our welcome dinner on the Saturday night.*

She remembered to ask Inès if she was feeling better: *Your migraine resolved?* Afterwards, she called Ash, using the number in her frequent-caller list. After a few rings, it went to message.

'Hi, Ash, you found your phone? Just letting you know, we're in business. Four guests from Florida, USA. Call me, yes?'

Ash hadn't replied by the time the sun went down. Hope pulled the cork on a bottle of wine and told herself that he was busy settling into his new job, but as the buzz of anxiety amplified, she did something she never did.

She looked at his personal Facebook page. What she found struck a cold, hard note.

17

When they'd first come to Lazurac, Hope had scaled down her personal social media, instead promoting Eat-Sleep-Paint-Gascony. Ash, by contrast, had splattered his Facebook and Twitter accounts with daily updates of their new life. He took pictures of every meal, every country walk, the morning bakery run. A constant stream of 'Isn't this amazing?'

Around eight weeks ago, the pictures had stopped. Nothing posted since Easter when Ash had flown back to the UK to spend the holidays with his family. He was one of four children, and his eldest brother had come home after a year on the road. There'd been a family reunion. It wasn't that Hope hadn't been invited... it was just assumed she'd want to stay here, in case they got a booking.

Scrolling back through months of Facebook posts, Hope couldn't avoid the obvious. Ash's enthusiasm for their life here had switched off while he was with his family. He'd posted pictures of an Easter Saturday barbeque, his mum and dad raising glasses, clearly delighted to have their adult children home. Ash's sister was there in a striped apron behind a smoking griddle. His younger brother appeared to be explaining to her how to spear a sausage. Ash sat at a table with his elder brother, Nick, happy grins on their faces. Hope wondered who had taken the photograph. She and Nick hadn't hit it off. He'd called her boring. No, correction. He'd said that accountants were boring. Same thing, really. He'd also slammed their decision to move to France.

'Buy a holiday home, for God's sake. Do you know how slowly house prices rise in rural France? You'll be priced out of the UK. You'll never get back.'

Ash had laughed at the time, insisting they knew what they were doing.

In another of the photos, a girl Hope didn't recognise had her arms looped round his shoulders. Younger than Hope, she was bending to get into shot, her chin grazing Ash's shoulder. His almost-black hair and the girl's glossy auburn layers made a striking contrast.

Course, she might be Nick's latest girlfriend. Nick liked to joke that he had a revolving door fitted in his flat.

Hope messaged Ash again. *You still haven't told me where you're living. What if I need to get hold of you? It would be fab to have you here when our guests arrive. Any chance you could get back that weekend?*

Questions, questions. Even to herself, she sounded scratchy and needy. After her second glass of wine, she called Ash and he picked up.

He seemed unsettled, hearing her voice, but quickly righted himself, saying he'd been about to phone her.

'Ash, what's going on?'

'Hey? Nothing. I'm working. You know that.'

'Working so hard you can't return a call? I'm glad you got your phone back.'

'Hey?'

'The one you left in a taxi.'

'Right, yeah, that was a pain.'

'How did you get it back?'

'How did I get it back?'

She left a silence. One he had to fill.

'They, er, biked it over.'

'Over to where?'

'My office. What's this about, Hope?'

'That was good of them. Beyond usual customer service.'

'Not really. I had to pay.'

Another silence.

'Ash, we need to talk.'

He agreed. They did. He'd come to Lazurac as soon as he could. She asked again where he was staying, but before she completed the question, he'd disconnected. A few minutes later, he texted.

With a friend, near Old Street. I'll grab a break soon and come but I'm pretty run off my feet. Great news about the paying guests. XXX

Old Street was central London. Central-*ish*, a smart area for young professionals, and not all that convenient for the Docklands, where Ash was working. All in all, there was a lot to unpack.

Over the next seven days, Hope perfected every detail of her guest accommodation. With the party arriving at the tail end of the month, she had time to repaint a bathroom she'd previously decorated in a hurry, to fill shelves with soaps and shampoos and clean the windows until they shone. Three days before they were due, Hope went to call on Inès Royale. She'd waited for as long as she dared for a reply to her prompt about teaching and to the Saturday dinner invitation. She was hoping her message had simply got lost. Walking the short distance to Inès's home, she rang the doorbell, crossing fingers that it wouldn't be Manon who answered.

It was Inès but, seeing Hope, she said in a quick, agitated way, 'My niece is not in. She is visiting a sale, buying stock. I'll send her round when she's back.'

'I didn't know Manon lived with you.'

'She has her own place, but it's very small.' Inès seemed to run out of words and stared anxiously at Hope.

Hope said, 'It's about the tuition, Inès. Didn't you get my message? We need to talk about hours and start-times, and I invited you—' She didn't get as far as saying 'to dinner' because suddenly, Inès's eyes fixed on the brooch on Hope's shirt front.

'Why do you wear that?' It was an accusation.

'Because I like it. Clearly, you do not.'

'Lally Ducasse flaunted it. I wish they'd made her swallow it.'

Hope gaped at this outburst from her elderly, and previously amiable, neighbour. 'They?'

Inès shook her head. 'I don't want to speak about that time. Where did you get the brooch?'

'My father gave it to me.' Hope steeled herself. 'It was his mother's.'

Inès's pupils flickered as she worked out the implications. 'Then his mother was a German's whore,' she said, before shutting the door in Hope's face.

Hope was home, cleaning the legs of the outside dining table, when the click of the side gate told her she had a visitor. Inès, coming to apologise? That would be a miracle, but welcome as otherwise, she was going to have to do some emergency re-planning.

Dropping her abrasive cloth as the visitor came around the corner of the house, Hope adjusted her expectations. '*Salut*, Manon. I suppose Inès told you I called? Take a seat, why don't you?' In her experience, people were less combative when sitting down. 'Can I get you a glass of something chilled?'

Manon stayed on her feet and ignored the offer of refreshment. 'I've come to tell you that owing to ill-health and other commitments, my aunt won't be giving tuition to your visitors. She asks me to say she's sure you'll understand, age catches up with us all in the end. Her words.'

Despite this being much as she expected, Hope felt a stab of panic. 'My guests arrive on Friday and they're paying for painting lessons. They're coming on a painting holiday, for heaven's sake. Your aunt gave me her word.'

Manon's trademark shrug was expressed in the lift of an eyebrow. 'As I said, my aunt is feeling her age.'

'She wasn't feeling it four months ago when we agreed terms. Sorry. That was out of order. I know it's about the portrait.' Hope had taken off her brooch while she cleaned the table legs. 'Only, what the hell am I going to do?'

Manon picked up the brooch, saying, 'Memories last a long time here. Inès was very young at the time, but she has never forgotten. You were cruel, shoving it in her face again.'

'I didn't shove it. I was wearing it, and what exactly is it Inès hasn't forgotten?'

'What Lally Shepherd-Ducasse did. The misery she inflicted.'

'Am I tarred with the same brush?' Hope asked tersely.

'Why should you be? She's Yves' grandmother not yours.'

'There's a chance she's also mine. I'm researching it.'

'*Mon Dieu*, that will be a shock for the Golden Boy, discovering a rival grandchild.' Manon turned the brooch over, though Hope doubted that in the terrace's dappled shade she'd notice the inscription. Manon bounced the brooch in her palm. 'It's worth its silver-weight, maybe ten, fifteen euros.'

Hope commented that she hadn't asked for a valuation.

The quick, cool smile came and went. 'You look nothing like Lally, except for your hair, and that isn't your natural colour. That blonde is too extreme for you.'

That was rich, coming from someone with eight shades of hair extension. Ash had said pretty much the same thing when Hope had come back from the salon. Rather than compliment her on her powerful new look, he'd muttered, 'Most women are happy with a few highlights.' The following day, he'd announced he'd be spending Easter with his family. Coincidence? Hope wasn't looking forward to telling him that she'd lost their painting tutor. Perhaps her distress showed because Manon suggested, 'Why not teach your guests yourself?'

'I'm not a professional painter. I wouldn't have the nerve to teach.'

'You studied fine art, Tante Inès told me. You have a degree, no?'

'Yes… but I jacked in painting for accountancy.'

'That's what she said.' The black-cherry lips pursed in contempt. 'Who gives up art for money?'

'That's rather a leap, Manon. You don't know my motives.'

'Why else? I can't stand people who have the world in front of them, then pretend they're too blocked, or too scared and choose the safe route.'

'Well, that's me.'

Manon regarded her speculatively. 'Why not ask Yves to be your teacher?'

'Yves's a photographer. I need a painter.'

'Oh, he paints when he thinks nobody's looking. Like you, he has space and time, but it tortures him to lift a paintbrush. Dare you to ask him.'

Hope doubted enthusiastic amateurs were Yves Ducasse's cup of tea. 'But thanks for the suggestion.'

Manon put the brooch on the table. 'You shouldn't wear this, not here.'

Hope's expression asked the inevitable, *Why not?*

'Because Lally Shepherd sold sex in return for favours from a German who was our bitterest enemy.'

'How the hell could you know that seventy years on?'

'One of Inès's uncles was in the Resistance. To her, it is lived experience. Lally sold them out. She must have hoped the Germans would be here forever, but when her protector fled, she had to pay.'

'Pay how?'

'That's for you to find out, if you're so curious. Or ask Yves – if you're brave enough.'

As a provocation, it did its job. As soon as Manon had gone,

Hope texted him. *Can we talk?* That done, she went for a stroll in the cathedral gardens. Returning home, the sight of the ginger-orange Land Rover outside her house came as a shock. She hadn't been inviting him to drop everything.

He was sitting at her terrace table, legs stretched out. Seeing her, he got up and indicated the Oranges d'Espagne container, which was now filled with greenery. 'I admire your taste,' he said. 'My grandmother had pretty good taste when she bought it from a salvage yard near Auch.'

Hope pulled out a seat for herself. 'How come Manon Taubier is selling yours and your grandmother's property on her market stall?'

'Good question.' She felt he was deciding how much to reveal. 'I let Manon use La Cachette when I was away.' He explained, 'I was running a beach bar in Koh Samui but came back to France in 2010 for a few months. I bumped into Manon and she asked if she could store her stuff on my property because she'd been kicked out of her shop. For not paying rent. This is Manon, right? I said yes, but only for a few weeks. I went back to Thailand then returned home for a quick visit in the summer of 2012. She was still there, and wasn't just storing stuff, she was using La Cachette for her business.'

'What kind of business?'

'Furniture upcycling. Nothing bad. But her friends were also using it as a kind of drop-in. I found some idiot, totally out of it, in his pants on my grandmother's sofa. I told Manon to get out, and she said she would. I had to go back to Koh Samui to tie things up financially—'

'At the beach bar?'

'Giving it away, basically.' He shrugged. 'I'd decided by then that I was coming home for good and told Manon to be out of my house by November first. When I returned, expecting a vacant house, same situation.'

'She hadn't moved out?'

'Same dude on the sofa, who told me to back off, show some respect. I flipped.'

Hope could picture it. 'Then what?'

'Manon called the police and I was escorted off my own property. She accused me of assaulting her.'

'Which you didn't?'

Yves' glance said, *What do you think?*

'And the police?'

'They took Manon's side. Everybody did. I'm a Ducasse. I was barred from my own home.' In the end, he told her, Noah had broken the impasse, refusing to live with his mother until she cleared out of La Cachette. 'He was fourteen, basically squatting in the static caravan next to the mill, which meant his mother could be charged with child neglect. He threatened to call Social Services and she's never forgiven me.'

Hence the low punch, Hope thought. 'Noah sounds rather amazing.'

'He's great. Not to look at, though that'll change in a year or two. He kind of looks on me as his mentor, God help him. Manon accuses me of driving a rift between them.'

'That's not true, though? You wouldn't let him call his mother a car crash.'

'If you challenge Manon's ego, watch out. Inès should look out, because Manon has a nose for vulnerability, and no scruples.'

'They don't seem to match as aunt and niece.'

'No,' he agreed. 'Inès's brother was Manon's father, and he married a woman with a hell of a temper and a shady past. There was always scandal around them, though nothing that could be proved. Inès puts up with Manon because she feels sorry for Noah. You know, having no father around.'

Hope reached out, touched the fading bruise on his temple. 'Is Noah... Actually, you don't have to tell me.'

'Is he my son?' Laughter burst from him. 'I was young when Manon picked me up in her talons, but not that young. His dad lives in Toulouse, smokes weed and thinks the government is spying on him. Noah sees him now and then, but they don't connect much.'

'You and Manon go back a bit, clearly.'

'I was seventeen and she was thirty-four. Sounds like the start of a rock and roll anthem.'

'Was it love?'

He rolled the question around. 'When you're seventeen, getting sex for the first time, anything is love. I mean, she was this passionate older woman, amazing-looking, lighting up joints for me.'

'Passion and weed... potent. Only, now she thumps you and steals from you.'

'My grandmother broke us up. Lally turned up one night when I was with Manon in a nightclub. Lally made the DJ stop and grabbed the microphone. "That woman is screwing my underage grandson. Take a look at her, everyone."'

Hope covered up a gasping laugh. 'To be called "underage" at seventeen... I bet you wanted to die.'

'I'd been drinking shots but I remember the silence that dropped. Only time I've heard silence like it. Sure, I was morti-fied, but I was also going down the tube and thank God Lally staged an intervention. She sent me to England for the summer. I must have been my host family's worst nightmare, a sulking, French school dropout doing cold turkey from hot sex. But after a while, I threw off the mood and they grew to like me.'

'It sounds more like a coming-of-age novel than a rock and roll anthem.' Hope tried to peel the years from him but it wasn't easy, his features and physique carved by sunshine, salt and surf, and more latterly, from sandblasting brick. Hard to imagine the vulnerable youth a grandmother had saved. 'How was England for you?'

'Wet, to start with, then humid. I fell in love with a girl in a park. I learned to speak slangy English, came back home and restarted school. When I bumped into Manon, I was embarrassed. Here was this beautiful woman who told me she'd been looking out for my grandmother while I was away and all I could do was mutter and go red. It took me a long time to work out what Manon had really been doing.'

'Stealing?'

'By another name. She'd invited herself into Lally's studio and found hundreds of unframed pictures. Lally worked every day for half a century. Manon told her, "These are wasted, let's make some money." Lally fell for it. I hadn't realised she was surviving only on a state pension. You don't see, when you're young, how the machinery turns.'

'Manon told me she looked after Lally for you, at her own expense.'

'Ha,' Yves snorted. 'It would be at everyone's expense but hers. She organised an exhibition for Lally. Her grand gesture. It was in a gallery in Auch, where they take forty percent commission on sales. You can bet Manon got a finder's fee. The exhibition made Lally a few hundred euros and she was grateful. She credited Manon with giving her one last moment of validation. It's why, when I went abroad after her death, I let Manon use La Cachette. Only, Manon kept on selling my grandmother's work, without permission, and when I came home for good—'

'You found her squatting, got arrested—'

'I counted up what was left.' His expression changed, from sorrow to anger in one sweep. 'Manon took everything. Even her record collection. Her sketches, her private papers. I don't even have her paintbrushes or paints. The easel in the windmill got left because it's got a broken leg. I see my grandmother's work at fairs and markets and in antique shops and I buy it whenever I can. Everyone can describe the woman who sold them.'

Hope believed it. 'And I beat you to the self-portrait, at the Thursday market. No wonder you were furious.'

'Noah tipped me off.'

'I wish you'd explained, and not shouted.'

Yves smacked a mosquito away from his forearm. It was that time of the day, when the air began to bite. 'What I can't get from Manon is, where did Lally's sketchbooks go, her letters and her writing? You mentioned a memoir the other day.'

She fetched it. Her bookmark was a quarter of the way in. Wordlessly putting it down in front of him, she left him to it, going to the kitchen where she took a bottle of white Burgundy from the fridge, grabbed glasses and a jar of olives. She returned to find Yves holding the torn memoir as if he couldn't quite believe it. Seeing her, he said, 'Is this what I think it is?'

'*Barbed Wire and False Names: Memoir of an English Girl in Occupied France.* The front and back cover has gone, and a dozen or so pages.' She described finding it. 'I started reading and got hooked, but it took ages to discover the author's actual name. Lally had a friend, Pauline, and a lover, Otto. Did she ever mention them to you?'

He screwed up his face, clearly struggling to remember. 'No. Yes. Maybe. Lally felt betrayed by all those she loved, well, almost all.' He read the first few lines. 'This is definitely Lally because she described leaving Paris with a million others. She told me when I was studying the war at school that the Germans had every intention of bombing the city to pieces. Did you know, it was one telephone call from the US ambassador to Adolf Hitler that stopped that happening?'

Hope had never heard that.

'I knew she'd written her life story, but she'd never say why the book got sabotaged. It was one last insult in a life of insults.

There's a couple of copies out in the wild, so to speak, and her own personal copy which disappeared while I was away.'

'Now it's found.'

They sat, not speaking, as the sky deepened, citronella candles keeping a midge-free space around them, until Yves stroked the book and asked, with a tilted smile, 'Are you giving this to me?'

'Of course.' He really was dangerously attractive when he was in this mood. 'But, erm, I'd like to finish it first and since it's my bookmark keeping the place...?'

'I'll let you finish it.'

She poured wine with a mildly unsteady hand and offered the olives. Her phone screen lit up, alerting her to an incoming message. She ignored it, focussed on Yves and the very big favour she hadn't yet asked. The moment couldn't be put off.

He must have thought the same because he said, 'Did you text me for a reason?' He speared an olive, knocking the brine off on the side of the jar. 'I was driving through town and wasn't sure whether to stop or not.'

Now or never. 'Inès has backed out of being the art tutor for the holidays I'm running.'

'Well, she's entitled to her retirement.'

'It's not that.' Hope described Inès's reaction to the brooch, though not the gross accusation levelled at Yves' grandmother. Maybe he guessed because he pulled a face.

'Where do I come in?'

'Um, Manon suggested you. She said you paint and you were good. *Are* good.'

'She'll have a hidden agenda. Manon won't have suggested it for my benefit or yours.'

'But you're good?' She'd already discovered that flattery wasn't the way to his heart. 'I haven't time to call a dozen people, see if they're available only to discover they're not.'

'Of course I will.'

She refilled their glasses, unsure whether he'd capitulated or was playing her. 'You'll teach oil painting technique to some lovely American guests, starting Monday?'

'Only if they are lovely. Maybe you could do me a favour in return.'

'Try me,' she said.

'You're a chartered accountant, right? It says on your website. "Hope Granger left a high-pressure role as a chartered accountant to live life at a slower pace, along with her partner, Ash…"' Yves glanced around, provocatively. 'Where is he, by the way?'

'In a flat in Old Street, London.' Apparently.

Yves made a teasing noise. 'So, here's the deal. In return for me changing my plans last minute, would you look at my accounts? I should have filed them six months ago.'

Instantly, she reverted to the London version of herself. 'They'll fine you.'

'No, they won't, because I didn't earn anything, so I have no tax to pay. But still, I have to file accounts.'

'What state are they in?'

'On life-support. I've entered some figures but I get bored. Twitchy. Don't worry, I keep my receipts and things. They're all in one place.'

'That being a cardboard box?' She groaned when he nodded. 'You do know that chartered accountants' fees are astronomical?'

'Are you aware that internationally celebrated photographers' fees are off the scale? Maybe we can cancel each other out.'

'Barter our services?' she suggested, then wished she'd found a different way of saying it.

'Something like that,' he said. 'So long as your Americans come to my place and buy coffee.'

'Get some herbal teas in, in case they're caffeine sensitive.'

'I will. I'm starting to believe we have a lot in common, Hope.'

'Including a grandmother?'

'Oh, shut up about that.' He leaned forward.

She was convinced he was going to kiss her but when she opened her eyes, he had leaned forward to spear another olive.

'It would not be a good idea,' he said, stepping straight into the current of her thoughts.

She felt her cheeks scorch. 'I don't know what you think you saw.'

'OK. Whatever.'

'There was nothing to see!'

'I won't contradict you.' They held eyes for long seconds, the summer's evening wrapping them in shadows, a breeze stirring the trees, and then Yves said something that shocked her.

'He won't come back.'

It took her a second or two to absorb the comment. 'Ash? I don't recall asking your opinion.'

'I've seen this many times. An English couple buy a big place, they bring their furniture, dogs and horses and when the money gets tight one of them, usually him, goes back to Britain to take a quick job. Only it isn't so quick because he gets used to the nine-to-five and not having to argue with impossible Gascon tradespeople. Then he meets somebody else—'

'Amazing. My life as a book-blurb. Do I meet someone else?'

'You have the sense to fall for a good-looking Frenchman.'

'Not my style.' Hope got up, riled but also pierced by the fact that she, for a moment at least, had wanted Yves to kiss her. Saved by the absence of any attraction on his part, a kick up the rear for her ego. She retreated into the house and took a second bottle from the fridge and a pizza out of the freezer, which she stuck in the oven. She sliced up the remainder of the baguette she'd bought that morning and tumbled the pieces into a basket. Actually, she thought, I ought to be asking him to leave.

Wanting to kiss a man who I think is my cousin does not make sense. Now he'd agreed to be her painting tutor, they'd be seeing each other several times a week. Something had to give.

She opened her laptop, found an ancestry site and ordered two DNA kits. The whole process took less than five minutes.

She took the bread out to the terrace.

'I'm not Gascon,' Yves said as she returned, continuing their conversation from an odd angle. It was a habit of his, she was discovering. 'My grandmother was English, my grandfather came from Paris. His name was Victor Ponsard and he was an artist too. My father was from the Loire valley. He came here searching for open skies and windmills.'

'Like Don Quixote?' She put down the basket. 'Have some bread, soak up the wine.'

'My papa turned up at La Cachette one day, asking if he could camp on the lawn so he could watch the sails turning in the wind. By that point, they'd stopped turning but that didn't stop him. He stayed long enough to get my mother pregnant, then *pht*, was off again.'

'You never knew him?'

'No. Not at all.'

'Then no wonder you're screwed up, Yves.' She had intended to mention the DNA kits, but suddenly felt how inappropriate it was, ordering one for him without his consent.

He reached for some bread. 'I'm not screwed up. I am damaged, but that's not the same. How are you coping with your partner away?'

Ash had been gone just over two weeks, as she pointed out. 'A relationship can sustain a little separation.'

'Ash and Hope. Doesn't that tell you something?'

'Ha ha ha,' she hit back. 'We're good, he and I.'

'Then why are you so downcast, and on your own?'

'I'm not alone. I'm with you, a new friend. A work partner. That's what life should be about. And what you said about

British couples moving here, then one of them losing their nerve – there are expats who've been happy here for twenty or more years.'

'Sure. I was exaggerating.' He was looking not at her, but at her brooch, and it felt as if they'd walked to the edge of a cliff and he was going to suggest they jump.

She broke the tension, asking him if he had someone in his life. 'Or does living in a windmill render you celibate?'

'I don't actually live in the windmill and I'm between relationships.'

'What about Claudia?'

'She's a mother of two, going through a bad breakup. Her husband left her.'

'Oh, I didn't know. That's horrible.'

'I don't sleep with my holiday makers.' He sniffed the air. 'Is something cooking?'

'Oh, crumbs.' She'd forgotten the pizza and went to check on it. It was ready. While it cooled a little, she stole a glance at her phone. The message that had arrived earlier was from Ash, following on from one he'd sent over an hour ago, which she hadn't seen. The timing was unsettling, messages coming in as she drank wine in the semi-dark with a man Ash had never been introduced to. Her desire to kiss Yves, or be kissed, had passed. It had been a momentary aberration, an emotional misfire because she was going through stress.

Outside in the street, a car hooted and Hope wondered if Yves' Land Rover was blocking somebody's way. He came into the kitchen and she was about to suggest he go out and check when he took her hands. She felt the brush of calluses under his thumbs.

He said, 'It's the same brooch.'

Her heart gave a bump. 'Are you saying that to be nice?'

'Honestly, I'm never nice. I'm saying it's the same brooch.'

'Why the change of mind?'

'Because Claudia told me after you left my place that two such brooches could not exist.'

'How can she be so sure?'

'She knows her stuff. Just *knows*. I could explain but our pizza will go cold. Shall I take it outside?'

'Please, and could you grab that big candle from the kitchen table?' It was too dark to eat outside without additional light. Hope took a dish of tomato salad from the fridge, located the pizza cutter and collected two sets of knives and forks. When she went out, the candle was lit, throwing gold over Yves and her heart skipped a beat. God, he was handsome in profile. She walked forward, impelled by feelings she wasn't in control of, tripped and almost threw the pizza onto the table.

'Whoops.' She laughed, then stopped as Yves' hands went around her waist. 'Hey—'

'Hey what?'

She'd drunk too much wine. She heard the side gate close, quick footsteps coming around the house, which activated an outdoor light. Into its glow strode a figure in sweatpants and a hoodie. It took Hope only a second to realise who it was.

'Ash – hell.' She pulled away from Yves. 'When did you get back?'

Ash's stance, the balled fists, robbed Hope of further speech. Yves asked quietly if he should go.

'Yes.' Hope watched him walk with the confidence of a man who knows the other fellow won't throw a punch, or if he does, it will bounce off. Ash, to Hope's surprise, accepted Yves' handshake, remaining silent until the click of the gate told them that they were now alone.

'I texted you from the airport,' Ash said.

'Come and have a glass of wine. You just met Yves Ducasse, our new art tutor. It's a long story, but Madame Royale—'

'I texted to ask if you'd collect me.'

'I'm sorry.'

'I had to get a taxi. Obviously.'

'Again, I'm sorry. I didn't see the messages. Come and eat.' Why wasn't he moving?

'I flew in to see you because you wanted to talk. I didn't expect you'd have company.'

'Nothing was happening, Ash. Yves and I had a few glasses of wine. I tripped.'

'The way you do.'

'Oh, come on!' The unfairness of the remark diluted her guilt. She was sorry. Mortified, in fact, but how many times was she supposed to say it? Clearly, several more. 'I'm really, really sorry.'

'I'm out, Hope.'

She stared, understanding the phrase, but not its intention. Out of laughs? Out of a job?

'Out of all this.' He gestured up at the house, taking in the terrace, the garden that fell away in the darkness towards the town's ancient ramparts.

'I don't understand.'

'You've changed.'

'How?'

'Everything. Your attitude, your hair.'

'It's a bleach job and it'll grow out. You're a fine one to talk, taking off without a word then blanking me.' She went to him, gripped his arms, tried to make him look at her but he wouldn't meet her gaze and it was too dark, even with the outside light shining, to know what he was feeling. Or concealing. He freed himself. 'Take care, Hope, be safe.' And then he left.

She followed him to the street, sacrificing dignity as she begged him to wait. Anything was better than a cold walk-out.

His taxi was coming back; it would pass the house and she watched in dismay as he flagged it down. Grasping at straws, she demanded, 'Who's that girl, the one at your family barbie? Tell me about DeeCee, who called you so late the other day.'

'Now you're embarrassing yourself.' Flashing her a contemptuous look, he climbed in. Hope watched her partner of two years leave in a glow of taillights, the red discs blurring with her tears as the taxi reached the end of the street, turned and disappeared.

She sat out on the terrace until the air chilled. The untouched pizza and the undrunk wine collected a little scum of midges as the citronella candles sputtered: forensic leavings of a moment of emotional violence.

She'd blown it, and now she was alone, with the weight of this house bearing down on her. She had only Lally. Yves had left the memoir on the table, and she took it to bed with her.

BARBED WIRE AND FALSE NAMES: MEMOIR OF AN ENGLISH GIRL IN OCCUPIED FRANCE

We edge back towards Paris, living off the land. Scavenging from deserted orchards and kitchen gardens becomes our day job. Otto is also good at trapping rabbits. He and I grew up beside rivers and learned how to set weirs of hazel sticks to catch fish. We follow the Loire whenever we can, keeping to fields and woodland, occasionally straying onto back roads or trekking along the railway line.

Is it wrong of me to say that, despite the danger, the privations and our nightmare memories of Tours, this is a happy time? We are evaders, heroes of our own story, reliant on each other. We're existing in no-man's land, hemmed in by land and air battles, but somehow untouched. Like the deer we see running for cover, the foxes slinking along the field edges, we have shape shifted. More creature than human. I have learned that I can trust Otto in a crisis, and he me.

Watching him lighting a campfire, his sleeves rolled, neck and forearms tanned and his hair gleaming like oiled ash wood, I am tugged by longing and pride. Otto has a good physique and the most beautiful grey eyes. In Bremen, in north-west Germany, he was a mathematician and teacher. He was also the man who wrote 'The Grey Eyed Dove', a poem about the River Weser that runs through his city. It praises the river but, reading between the lines, it's a protest against German remilitarisation. He refused to join the Nazi party and spoke out against the war, which is why he had to flee his homeland. Why he's now on the run in France. Returning to Paris is to walk back into the lion's mouth. Am I wrong to resent Pauline for forcing this choice on him, on us? Without her, Otto and I would be on our way to the Spanish border. I try to keep these thoughts inside. I include Pauline in our conversations. Otto and I avoid speaking German together because that would exclude her. Did I say already, I am pretty fluent in German, thanks to Otto's skill as a teacher? Only when Pauline is sleeping – and she sleeps rather a lot – do he and I find a sheltered niche and whisper that language as we make frantic love.

The cathedral towers of Orléans come into sight on the first day of July. From conversations with people met on our journey, France has now surrendered completely making Pauline and me, officially, enemy aliens. Otto is a German hunted by other Germans. Our adventure is over and reality floods back.

Reaching the city's edge, we stare across the Loire through the white breath of dawn. The priority is to get identity docu-ments for me and Pauline, so we can pass through checkpoints as we enter Paris. They're everywhere, we've been warned.

Otto knows someone here and we are given beds in an attic near Orléans' centre. Utter bliss, to bathe and sleep on a mattress again. Our host points us towards someone who can provide *cartes d'identité*.

This individual operates from within a maze of medieval

streets, in a secret back room. He used to run a left-wing printing press churning out anti-Fascist newsletters until a desire to remain alive persuaded him to stop. He now does arguably more dangerous work, creating false papers for unfortunates like Pauline and me. In the event, we're not so unfortunate; our forger has two artfully aged cards in stock, made for sisters who lost theirs when the train they were on came under fire. As they haven't collected them, our new friend assigns them to us. He's already written in birth dates, birthplaces and a surname:

Ducasse.

All that remains is to add our physical descriptions and decide what our first names are to be. 'Pauline' is a perfectly usual French given name, so that's easy. Mine's more of a problem. I've been Lally as long as I can remember, but it won't do on a formal document. My baptismal names, Lavinia Linda, won't do either. The last thing you want at a check-point, our forger says, is to be asked by a twitchy guard with a machine gun why you have an English-sounding name. 'What if I call you Marie-Laure, then Lally can be your pet name, if someone forgets and calls you that.'

It's a good solution. We have our photographs taken at a nearby studio and, a couple of days later, I leave the forger's premises as Marie-Laure Ducasse aged twenty-eight, a year more than my actual age. Pauline is reborn as my sister, aged seventeen. In reality, she's nineteen but can pass for younger. I'm worried about Pauline. While I have caught the sun, she's stayed pale and her eyes look huge, smudgy and sad. I'm always catching her gazing at Otto and me as if she would cut off a limb to have what we have.

Nine days after entering Orléans, we leave. Carrying food and wine provided by our host, we make our way to the railway station. Trains are running again, to an erratic timetable. Otto tells us to go on ahead. 'I'll sit in a different carriage. If anybody stops me, if anything happens, stare right ahead. Don't get involved.'

'And vice versa,' I tell him, wrapping him in a trembling embrace. 'See you at Rue Monge.' My room's paid up until the end of July and that's where we will meet, to plan our next move.

20

9 July 1940

Our train is bulging with returning Parisians. Now France has surrendered, the great exodus is going into reverse. The Germans have split the country into two. The roughly northern half is under their direct occupation while the southern portion remains under the control of a French government-of-collaboration, now based at Vichy. Thousands have found themselves on the wrong side of the line.

As we travel through ground-up countryside strewn with the carcasses of tanks and military vehicles, I feel a sense of shame. It emanates from everyone I see. Nobody, *nobody*, saw this coming. Just as nobody knows what we're returning to. A woman in our compartment tells me there are more swastikas in Paris now than in Berlin. I'm not sure how she knows as she's been absent since the beginning of June.

'Don't go out in the evening,' she warns. 'Those German troops are sex-starved and our police are rounding up women for them, dirty collaborators. Even you won't be safe.'

Even us. She glances at my threadbare cuffs and ragged

nails. Pauline's best jacket, which she unwisely wore with her lovely hat the day we left, and has not taken off in almost a month, looks fit for a scarecrow.

In third class, even with the blinds down and the windows open, our carriage is soon stifling. All the men smoke. After eight gruelling hours, we pull into Gare d'Austerlitz. Pauline and I clutch hands. German soldiers are checking identities at the barrier. As we shuffle forward, I lean close and say, 'If they comment on our ID cards, say only what we practised.'

I fight the urge to look around for Otto and when it's our turn, I flip my identity card open to show my unsmiling likeness. The little booklet is taken from me by one of a pair of guards. I see a grey-green cuff and a man's wrist-knuckle covered with fine, brown hairs.

I'm asked something in German and, looking up, I encounter a squarish face under a helmet like an iron pot. He must be boiling. His tunic has dark stains under the arms, and I smell a sharp, animal scent. He inspects my face, then the photograph. He has a handgun tucked into a leather holster, leather straps across his chest. A silver crescent hangs around his neck, like a dog-tag for a mastiff, the word *Feldgendarmerie* emblazoned on it. He's about forty.

He repeats his question. I gape at him stupidly, my ill-nourished brain unable to muster a word of the educated German Otto taught me. He tries in guttural French: 'Date of birth?'

'*Pardon.*' I rattle off Marie-Laure Ducasse's birthday.

'Where born?'

I tell him, Pau, in Gascony. 'We were hoping to get home but it became impossible, so we are returning here to find work.' He grunts and pushes the identity card back at me in a way that suggests he finds me indescribably tedious. I imagine I would feel the same, were I manning a barrier in Berlin as frightened foreigners inched past. Now it's Pauline's turn.

Our German peers at her open card, then back at Pauline. I quietly slip my hand into hers.

He demands her birth date. She answers without hesitation. 'The eighth of—' I kick the side of her foot, and she gasps and starts again. 'Twelfth of February 1924.'

'How many years you have?'

She shakes her head, not understanding.

I hiss, 'He's asking your age, Pauline.'

'Oh, um, seventeen.'

Our German asks his colleague something like, 'How old do you think this girl looks?' A chill descends to my legs. The other military policeman dissects Pauline with his eyes before answering, '*Dreissig?*'

'Oh, come off it!' I retort. There isn't an inch of Pauline that looks thirty. Even so, my response is risky. Humour can work, or it can open a trapdoor under your feet.

For seven heartbeats, the older German teeters on the edge of something. Violence, rage, or the cold execution of power... it's like waiting for a gunshot. And then he shoves the document at Pauline and jerks his chin. *Get lost.*

'Had we better wait for Otto?' Pauline whispers as we leave the station.

'Sh! Don't even say his name, it's not safe.'

'What if he's stopped, Lally?'

'You heard what he said. We keep going.'

'But—'

'Helping him would be suicidal. It might make things worse.'

Outside the station with the summer dusk upon us, I choose our route and make her keep up with me. Passing the railings of the Jardin des Plantes, we see our first swastika. It's mounted on the bonnet of a black car that sweeps past. In the back are military figures in grey, high-fronted caps. I get the impression of stony profiles, replete with the confidence of men who own the territory. I tell Pauline to stop looking over her shoulder. As we turn onto Rue Monge, we're stopped by a French gendarme who asks us roughly what we're doing out at this time of night.

I tell him we've just got in by train and what does he mean, 'This time of night?' My watch says it's a few minutes to eight.

'Don't you know there's a curfew? If you're caught out after nine, you can be arrested. Where's home?'

'About five minutes away,' I tell him, 'and we'll be there way before nine o'clock.'

He makes a sound of exasperation. 'You don't know? Paris time has been reset to Berlin time, making it two minutes to nine. So run!'

Now I'm worried for Otto, who must be behind us and will be caught out by the curfew. Despite everything I've said, I'm consumed by the urge to find him and I'm suggesting to Pauline that she goes on ahead to the flat, when I hear footsteps coming up behind. It's that gendarme again.

'Keep walking, you two,' he says as he passes us, 'or I'll arrest you for soliciting.'

We reach the door of my lodgings as the tower of nearby Saint-Médard clangs nine times. Ha, so even the saint is collaborating. Knocking at the door, thinking that the twenty-seven days since I was last here feels like twenty-seven months, I pray someone will answer. It takes a terrifyingly long time. The door is opened by the last person I expect. 'You – how on earth?'

Otto hasn't time to respond as Pauline throws herself through the doorway, crying, 'I thought you'd been caught.' She sobs against his chest, and Otto looks at me over her head like a man shown his reflection in a mirror, loathing what he sees.

21

When the street door is shut behind us and we're standing in the vestibule, Otto reveals how he beat us home. And why.

'I was recognised.' Not by the ticket barrier guards but outside the station. 'Some German high-ups in a car. One of them looked my way and I saw his face change, and a moment later, the car stopped. I ran like hell.' A section of railing alongside the Jardin des Plantes has been removed and he scrambled through, sprinting across the park. He is safe for now.

He has seen our landlords, Monsieur and Madame Arnaud, and told them why we're back. The good news is, they haven't relet my room. The bad news is, they are visibly alarmed by our return. The Arnauds know Otto as my companion, and they know he's a fugitive from Nazism and, of course, everything changed overnight on June fourteenth. 'I told them we wouldn't stay long,' Otto says.

He leads the way, up to the attic where, for the past three years, I have occupied one room, alternately sweating and freezing under the sloping zinc roof. He talks as we climb, detailing the mattress and the bedding the Arnauds are pulling out for him, so he can sleep on the landing. 'You won't mind?'

I get the impression he's talking to cover up fear. Or embarrassment. Pauline throwing herself at him was awkward. It's how she is, her emotions unleashing themselves like shaken champagne. Me, I'm more the aged variety, the fizz matured out. Otto is passionate when appropriate and the rest of the time, reserved. I've never seen him this edgy, and it stokes my anxiety. Looking back at the narrow stairs, I can't help but think how we could get trapped up here. He is on a Gestapo death-list, and even now, the word will be out. The search will have started.

My bedsit smells of warm dust. There are dead flies in front of the dormer. My bed is still made up, as is the couch Pauline used since she moved in with me last year. She pulls off her cardigan, flushed already from the heat. I open the window and sweep up the flies, throwing them out over the balcony. Seeing the familiar rooftops, the hospital dome glossed with ruby light, I feel a wrench. I wish we could stay and not have to move on again.

Otto watches Pauline as she tenderly places her camera on the bed. 'Take any good pictures?' he asks.

She twitches, as if the question is a personal one. 'I'll only know when I've had them developed. I've had this film in the camera for ages.'

He persists. 'Did you capture the road after the planes came over?'

'When they bombed us?' She shakes her head. 'No. I couldn't. I just couldn't.'

'It happened too fast, Otto,' I tell him. 'We leapt for our lives.'

'*Na gut.*' Fair enough. He means it, but Pauline seems to feel she's done wrong. She touches his arm, making him look at her. 'I took some shots in one of the villages we stopped in.

There were people playing accordions in the churchyard, women and old men dancing. And I took one out of the car window. Of a poor grandmother with a handcart, piled high with pots and pans, and a myna bird in a cage balanced on top. You'll like that one, for your book.'

'When I write it. If I write it.' He moves from her grasp. He looks at me. 'We need to discuss our next move.'

I unfold the table I've eaten at a thousand times and turn the two flimsy dining chairs to face it, then put what's left of our food onto a plate. 'Cheese and tomatoes. Come on.' One of us will have to sit on the bed. 'Chop-chop, I'm starving. Oh—'

Otto has taken Pauline into his arms, and she's pressed up against him, eyes closed. He shoots me an apologetic look. She is human ivy, and he the nearest solid surface, I suppose. I wish she'd stop doing it. I wish she'd find another room, so Otto and I can be alone. I want to kiss him, before getting down to talk. Talk we must because we need money for three train fares. I'm not sure how we'll acquire it as I don't have a supply of rich friends in Paris. Otto has contacts, but now he's been seen, he can't risk going out and about.

I'm struck by a sudden good idea. 'I'll visit Dorienne Ponsard.'

Otto blinks. 'Victor's sister? What about her?'

'To ask her to lend me some money.'

His response is instant and sharp. 'No. I don't like her.'

'You mean, you don't like the house she keeps.' Dorienne herself is an angel.

'I still say no.'

I'm not used to being ordered about. I left all that behind years ago. I say in a curt voice, 'Alert me when you have a better idea.'

Footsteps on the stairs shut the conversation down. I fling

open the door and see Monsieur Arnaud on the landing, pressing a hand to his ribs. The stairway is very steep.

'My wife invites you to dine, Mademoiselle Lally. And your friends, of course. A simple meal, but you are welcome.'

'That's so kind.' The prospect of a good dinner gets us moving. We wash in the tiny bathroom, one after the other, in cold water. Opening my wardrobe, I stroke the clothes I had to leave behind and thought I'd never see again. Mine hang on the left, Pauline's on the right. Lifting out a blouse, I pick up a hint of perfume in its folds. Lanvin's Arpège, the first gift Otto ever gave me and I've been eking it out. Pauline tugs out a favourite dress of apple-green check. The colour goes wonderfully with her dark hair.

Dinner is fish stew, more potatoes and turnip than fish, but delicious. There's an excellent white Burgundy to go with it. The Arnauds do most of the talking, itemising the changes that have struck Paris since we left. Silent streets, empty parks. 'They've shut the schools.' So many new orders have been issued, delivered through megaphones, posted on the sides of buildings, the Arnauds hardly dare leave the house in case they violate one unwittingly. 'Nothing much in the shops,' sighs Madame, 'butter has almost doubled in price... oh, and of course, there is the demarcation line.'

This is how we learn that the line separating France into Occupied and Unoccupied Zones is more than a theoretical squiggle on a map. It is a tightly controlled border, over a thousand kilometres long, with barriers and guards. You cannot cross it without a pass, an '*Ausweis*' stamped by the German authorities. While Bordeaux and a section of the Spanish border are in the Occupied Zone, mine and Pauline's destination of Marseilles is the other side, in what the Arnauds refer to as the 'Free Zone'. It's a new shock to fret over.

It doesn't make us any less hungry and, when we've mopped our plates clean with bread, Pauline takes out her camera. She has one last exposure left. 'Everybody scrunch up,' she says, gesturing us to make a huddle.

'For God's sake, Pauline,' I bark, 'Otto's face will be in every police station by tomorrow. At every German guard post. All it would take is someone to see your prints...'

I break off as our hosts glance uncomfortably at each other. I think this is the moment they truly grasp how much of a wanted man Otto is. Pauline says warmly, 'I'm not stupid. Otto will stay out of camera shot, as he always does.'

'Not always,' I remind her. 'Remember that snap you took of us all at La Closerie des Lilas?' That's a café in Montparnasse, a favourite of our little gang. A mixed bag of Parisians by birth and Parisians by inclination, we'd been confident that Otto was safe in this freedom-loving city. He was less convinced, but he hadn't got out of shot and Pauline had taken the picture. I suppose it's on the camera still.

Otto steps aside and the rest of us pose. The Leica gives its beautifully engineered click. Pauline winds the film on and takes out the canister, putting it on the table. 'Would you like it?' she asks me. 'Am I too dizzy to be trusted with it?'

'I didn't say that.'

'Well, I can't get it processed now, probably not for ages. I'll keep it safe. It has some irreplaceable moments on it.'

I know what she means. She took photos of me, Julien and Victor the last time we were all together in the park. Otto was there too but, as Pauline rightly says, he kept out of camera range. We eat the cheese I brought down with me and finish the wine. Pauline drinks water. She never got to like wine, whereas I took to it rather too enthusiastically. I'm longing for my bed and am about to suggest we help with the washing-up, when, from outside, comes the gunning roar of a vehicle. Tyres screech, doors slam, a man shouts, 'That house there!'

French, not German, but nevertheless it's the voice of authority.

The five of us turn to stone, our expressions pure, distilled dread. We hear more shouting and then a woman screaming.

Monsieur Arnaud goes to see and comes back to say that a police unit are arresting a couple two doors down. 'For breaking curfew.'

'What will happen to them?' Pauline whispers.

'A visit to the cells, probably. Nobody's been shot for it yet. The Germans are ruthless about curfew violations, and our police are catching the same disease.'

I say firmly, 'We'll go tomorrow, Monsieur. It's not safe for you or Madame Arnaud while we're here.'

Neither he nor his wife argue. I ask them if they will reimburse me the rent I paid to the end of the month. They nod. 'Of course.'

It won't be enough for our needs, so I ask what time curfew ends. They tell me, five in the morning. 'Then I'll walk to my friend Dorienne's and borrow the rest.' As I speak, I look straight into Otto's eyes.

He takes off his watch and lays it on the table. 'It's Swiss, though it got a bit dented when I was knocked over by a motorbike. Could you sell it, Monsieur?'

Monsieur Arnaud works for the city authorities, in the street-cleaning department, but he repairs watches on the side. He inspects Otto's Rotary, listens to its tick, and hands it back. 'I couldn't offer enough to make it worth your while. And you'll need it on your journey.'

'Then what about this?' Otto is wearing a waistcoat, and he delves into its lining and removes something colourful, which he lays on the cloth. 'Is this worth anything?'

I say, 'Oh, Otto, not that!'

It's a brooch, finely made from silver wire, infilled with enamel. It's the dove of peace, its gold-rimmed grey eye conveying a gentle sense of hope. Otto's sister had it made for him, a parting gift before he fled Germany. I know how precious it is to him and, as Monsieur Arnaud turns it over in experienced fingers, I make a desperate audit of my own stuff, thinking which of my possessions I can put on the table. I don't come up with anything, frankly.

'It's pretty,' our host says of the Grey Eyed Dove. 'The silver is worth a bit, if melted.' He makes a low offer.

'Don't do it,' I say to Otto, who replies that if we're to leave Paris by train and not on foot or broken-down bicycles, we can't be sentimental.

'Let me ask Dorienne Ponsard for a loan,' I persist. 'I don't know what you've got against her. If Victor was around, he'd tell us to go to his sister.' It's unbearable, the thought of Otto relinquishing the one keepsake from a family who are lost to him. Me, I had lost everyone but my grandmother by the time I was six, and she died when I was fifteen. She never saw me escape the poverty I was born to. It's why I feel ridiculously protective of Otto's family, though I've never met them. I hope one day to. 'I could sell my winter coat.' Or my half-used bottle of Arpège. What about my oil paints, which are in a blanket chest upstairs? Hm. I've rolled up the ends of the tubes almost to the neck to eke out the last squeeze of pigment, but still...

Pauline's soft voice cuts into my thoughts. 'If you would like to buy this, Monsieur Arnaud, we can negotiate but I will need the money by morning.' She puts her camera on the dining table.

After a moment's astonishment, Monsieur Arnaud seeks his wife's eyes, silently gaining her consent. He has money in his safe, the deal is done. By five a.m. the following morning, we are on our travels again.

22

HOPE

Hope woke to cool air through her open window. The gentle thud as the memoir slid to the floor summoned back the previous night. Ash had come home, caught her having terrace drinks with Yves Ducasse and, in disgust, had turned on his heel.

He would come back. He had to come back. Their life was here. And she'd done nothing to deserve abandonment. Even as she thought it, Yves' cynical observation bounced in. 'When the money gets tight one of them, usually him, goes back to Britain to take a quick job. Only it isn't so quick because he gets used to the nine-to-five—'

Ash didn't do nine-to-five. More seven a.m. to nine p.m. He would have just woken up in the flat in Old Street. Had he told her if the friend he was staying with was male or female?

She stumped downstairs and emptied the dregs of yesterday's coffee onto the garden. The sight of two glasses on the terrace table drew a groan. Blame it on the night and the wine.

She made fresh coffee and repeated her new mantra: Ash would come back. He'd wanted this life as much as she had. More, even. She'd been prepared to spend another few years at her accountancy firm, building financial security. It was Ash who'd been burned out, craving change. Seeing her with Yves had shattered his trust. Course it had. She'd have reacted the same if she'd found him with a strange woman on the terrace. Give it time.

Going back into the kitchen, nursing her coffee, she knew she had to talk to someone. Someone non-judgemental who would let her vent. Her finger hovered over Yves' number. Was he unjudgemental? Not wholly and, chances were, he'd be fast asleep, and find a missed call from her and be too embarrassed to respond.

For some reason, she pressed 'call' anyway. The number rang six times before she heard, 'Hope, that you?'

'Yves, hi, sorry.'

'What for?'

'Last night.'

'What happened last night?'

That floored her, until it occurred to her that he'd driven away before Ash had made his speech and left. He wouldn't know how things ended. 'My partner walked out on me,' she said.

'Not surprised,' was Yves' response.

'Is that all you can say? "Not surprised." We've been together two years and he broke it off, just like that. I did nothing wrong!'

'Didn't say you did. Just, I saw it coming.'

She heard the *zhoosh* of automatic doors and the hum of traffic and realised that, far from being dragged out of sleep, Yves had already started his day. 'Where are you?'

'That's a wife's question.'

'I'm curious, that's all.'

'I'm at this moment leaving a builders' merchants outside Auch where I have bought three sizes of rawl plug and beige-coloured grout—'

'OK, enough, enough. You can't pass judgement on Ash, or on our relationship, based on one millisecond of a meeting.'

'Yes I can.'

'How?'

'He's flaky,' Yves said. 'Is that the word?'

'It's *a* word. Flaky people are unreliable, they turn up late, or not at all.' Her voice faded. Maybe Ash was flaky. 'What makes you think you know?'

'Thirteen years working in and around bars. In your first year, you meet every kind of person. After ten years, you realise that there are three or four basic kinds of people, and they're just circulating. *Un moment—*' Someone was saying something to him. She heard him reply, 'Sure. I can cut them in half for you, if you like. Give me two minutes.' Then he was back with her. 'A lady is trying to get three-metre planks into a small Citroën. I've offered to—'

'Saw them up for her. You're quite the gallant knight, Yves Ducasse.'

'No, I'm the man with a hacksaw in his Land Rover. All I said was, with Ash, I saw it coming.'

Now Hope felt she was fighting for Ash's good name and briefly described his arrival and departure, the bare ten minutes of it. She could hear Yves rootling about in his vehicle. Was he listening?

He asked, 'Did he bring a suitcase?'

'Ash? Er, no, but he'd only flown in from London. He wouldn't need a suitcase.'

'Travel bag? One of those little wheely things men seem to need these days?'

'He had a bag, a sort of in-flight satchel.' Its strap had been across Ash's chest.

'Proves he wasn't intending to stay then, doesn't it? Think about it, Hope. No luggage, no phone call to tell you he was on his way—'

She butted in. 'He texted me from the airport.' If only she'd opened his first message, instead of focussing on Yves. 'His schedule is hectic. He'll have got a last-minute flight.'

A sceptical sound reached her ears. 'Who calls for a lift when they've already landed? How did he get back to the airport?'

'Taxi. The one that brought him was passing the house as he walked out.'

'Convenient, that. Is your home in joint names?'

A cold feeling slid in, because she knew what he was saying. 'No. Just mine.'

'That's good, though when you think about it, isn't that a danger flag?'

'What – a red flag? I don't think so. Ash put seed capital into our business.'

'Then he'll want his investment back. Hope?' Yves must have read something in her silence, because his voice shifted. 'Hard times always have a beginning and an end. You'll get through.'

She thought, I don't want to 'get through'. I want to be loved, cherished, partnered. What she actually said was, 'I don't know how.'

'Get busy. You have guests any minute. And you know what, I'm going to get you painting... and I don't mean windows and doors.'

'Dream on.'

'And there's your search for your grandmother. Isn't that something to interest and excite you?'

'I don't know where to start.'

'You start with a name. You look online.'

Could she? A few years back, she'd confessed to her father about doing the online ancestry search and he'd been so distressed, she'd promised faithfully she'd never do it again. Even agreeing with Yves, yes, all right, felt like a betrayal.

Though what would you call sending off for DNA tests? 'My dad never had a birth certificate,' she said. 'It's why he wouldn't travel. He was scared to apply for a passport.'

'How did he get through life?'

She could hear him walking across the car park and thought, he probably wants me to get off the phone so he can help out the lady with the planks. Keeping people talking was what you did when you were lonely. I'm not lonely, she told herself. 'With an adoption certificate. His grandparents officially adopted him.'

'From an orphanage?'

'No, from France... It's what he said. His mother was deemed unfit.'

Yves said warningly, 'This isn't your moment to mention Lally.'

'I wasn't going to.'

'Wouldn't that adoption certificate be the place to start?'

'Mm. I'd have to ask the second Mrs Granger,' she said. 'She has all Dad's stuff, unless she's chucked it out.'

'Call her. Hope, I have to go now, but does this change anything?'

She wasn't sure what he was driving at. 'I still want you to come and teach my guests, if that's what you mean.'

'Good.' He sounded businesslike. 'And I still want you to do my accounts, so we are fine. On the same page.'

'Cousins. Colleagues.'

'Colleagues yes, cousins no. I don't want you as my cousin.'

She seized the moment, asked him if he'd consider taking a DNA test.

'What?' He sounded outraged. 'I hate those things. They put you on a database that anyone can look at, ex-wives, insurance companies, police, God knows. I would rather have my feet skewered.'

'I'll take that as a no, then,' she said, making a horribly

embarrassed face in the privacy of her kitchen. 'Colleagues but not cousins.'

She'd just wasted two hundred euros with an online DNA company, Hope reflected as she ended the call. It crossed her mind that they might refund her, if she sent them back unopened.

It was mid-morning by the time Hope found the resolution to call her father's second wife. Hope never referred to Stephanie Granger as 'stepmother'. Neither of them had wanted that. Her first call went to answer message, but as Stephanie lived in fear of fraudsters and screened everything, Hope identified herself, adding, 'I'll ring back in two minutes.'

This time, Stephanie picked up. 'Hello, Hope. Are you in England?'

Hope explained that she was still in France.

'I see, then this call is costing a lot?'

'It's costing me, not you. I'll be quick, though.' Hope asked about any Granger family documents that might be hanging around. 'Particularly Dad's adoption papers, please, for posterity.'

Her timing was provident. Stephanie had just that week taken a suitcase full of stuff from the loft. She'd been wondering what to do with it.

What's to wonder, Hope thought fractiously. She restrained herself, saying pleasantly, 'Could you send them to France?'

An edge came into Stephanie's voice. 'It would be a big parcel.'

'If you could get everything into a box, I'll have a courier pick it up. I will pay,' Hope assured her. The conversation took an odd turn as Hope spelled out her address.

'Oh, *that* Lazurac? Isn't that where your dad wanted some of his ashes to go?'

What?

'I'm sure that's what he wrote down. In the end, it wasn't possible. Yes, I'm sure it was Lazurac. Does it have windmills?'

'Outside the town, yes. Let me get this straight – Dad asked for his ashes to come here after I moved?'

'No, he talked about it when you were still living in London, before you even met that chap of yours,' Stephanie said. 'It never made much sense to me.'

Nor to Hope. For a moment, she was back at La Cachette, coming up the drive and seeing the windmill, knowing she'd had a similar moment at some other time in her life. Thanking Stephanie and hanging up, Hope called an international courier and arranged collection of her family papers. She touched the Grey Eyed Dove. From reading the memoir, she now knew it was German, the gift of a sister to a beloved brother. '*Mit Liebe*'. With love. But how had it ended up with her father?

'You are my link to Lally and it proves nothing.' Hope's surname was Granger, not Shepherd, not Ducasse. Her dad had been adopted by his own grandparents because his mother had been... well, the probability was, she'd been unmarried, which at the time was all it took to be 'unfit'.

Due to set off in four hours to pick up her guests, she took Yves' advice and got on with her life, working up a sweat, hoovering the already-spotless bedroom carpets, adding an extra gleam to the bathroom taps. That done, she started prepping that night's meal. It was to be chicken chasseur. A series of emails between Hope and Goldie Solon had established that this French classic, with garlic, onions and wine, was a safe choice. She would serve it with salad and crusty bread. The casserole called for slow cooking and, as she put it into a low oven, Yves called again.

His opening words were, 'I have a feeling I need to apologise.'

'Go ahead, though I'm not sure why.'

'My reaction when you mentioned DNA. I sounded off like a crazy conspiracy-theorist.'

'Oh, that. I did wonder how many ex-wives you have, spying on your every move.'

'Just the one,' he said. 'She's in Thailand and has remarried. I didn't mean to go off on a rant, that's all.'

'I could have been more tactful. Given you a glass of wine, then asked you.'

He laughed. 'You're learning, Hope. What are the arrangements for our labour exchange?'

So that's why he'd called. 'I'm thinking we could pile over to your windmill middle of Monday morning. While you're teaching, I could familiarise myself with your financial position. Actually, why don't you join us tonight at dinner?' As far as Ash was concerned, she had crossed a line and there was no going back. Why not make it six for dinner instead of five? She then pictured Yves' tattooed limbs and unshaven chin. 'I hope you don't mind me saying, while it's not exactly a black-tie affair, it mightn't be a good idea to arrive in shorts.'

A full-on pause before he asked coldly: 'What do you consider suitable?'

Great. She'd alienated him again. She wanted suddenly to cry. 'I don't know what my guests' cultural assumptions are. You understand? I don't know anything.'

'You see, there's a danger my knees would send them wild.' His voice down the line grazed her ear.

'I walked right into that one, didn't I?'

'Totally. I'll be smart, and I'll bring wine. I'll even shave. À ce soir.'

She set off early for Toulouse-Blagnac airport, arriving well ahead of her guests' arrival time. She bought a coffee and found a seat in the terminal, taking Lally's memoir out of her shoulder bag. The women and Otto were on the move again, making another try at getting out. They must have been jumping at every shadow, Otto having been recognised by a car full of German military elite.

Otto is on a Gestapo death-list. Lally's brusque narrative style said everything necessary. Yes, they would have been scared half to death.

23

Hope lifted a sign reading 'Eat-Sleep-Paint-Gascony' as passengers surged out of arrivals. Eye contact was established.

'Honey, we made it!' Goldie Solon, Elkie Warberg, Paloma Findlay and her brother TJ came through the barrier, so excited, so pleased, to be on French soil.

Counting the hardshell suitcases they had between them, Hope knew at once her car would never accommodate so many. She went to find a taxi willing to take two passengers and four suitcases to Lazurac. This was something to chalk up to experience. Check how much luggage your guests are bringing.

Goldie and Elkie fell asleep on the journey and were glad to be shown immediately to their rooms on arrival. The Findlays, brother and sister, wanted a tour of the house. Hope took them out to the terrace, and down steps to an open-fronted stone barn. 'This is painting HQ, but I plan to take you to other places too, to work on location.'

That was when TJ mentioned that he'd never picked up a paintbrush in his life.

'Well – great. Let Lazurac inspire you,' Hope answered, wondering how Yves would react. He might not actually enjoy teaching beginners. When he arrived for dinner, she'd gauge his reaction.

By eight p.m., her guests were sipping drinks on the terrace, dipping bread into olive oil. Hope was whipping up a raspberry coulis to go with a lemon tart. She realised Yves had arrived only when she heard a change of pitch in the chatter outside. Putting down her sieve, she wiped her hands, meeting Yves in the kitchen doorway. He had two bottles of wine.

'From the vineyard the other side of Varsac. I thought, keep it local.'

The white was nicely chilled. 'Did you introduce yourself?'

'Of course. Will I pass?'

She gave him a tilted look. He was wearing beige trousers and a new-looking black tee-shirt, a leather belt and sandals. When she went outside with him, to formally introduce him, she saw a cotton sweater over the back of a chair. Smart casual, just the right note, except for the tattoos his tee-shirt did little to hide. Yves asked the guests about their flight, sounding very French tonight. It seemed to go down well, so she left him to it. When she brought out smoked prawn pâté and toast, Goldie was holding his arm, having pushed his shirtsleeve up to the shoulder.

'Young man, I've seen less paint on a Manhattan subway. What's this one, a plant of some kind?'

Yves turned his arm so Goldie could see better. 'It's the Gold Leaf Bauhinia, a native plant of Thailand.'

'It looks like a heart, honey. I was thinking you were romantic.'

Yves glanced at Hope, who was trying to decide if she minded that he had become star of the show, that eyes were not on her, nor her food. 'I am not romantic,' Yves said, 'I am passionate.'

'My kinda guy,' laughed TJ, whose skin was weathered to

teak-brown from his two hobbies, playing golf and sailing the Florida coast.

'Would you open the wine?' Hope asked Yves. A note in her voice hinted, *Dial it down.*

Dinner was a success. They were perfect guests, having good appetites and a clear intention to enjoy themselves. Only as darkness crept across the garden, and Hope lit tall candles and citronella tealights, did their energy fade. Jetlag had kicked in.

She escorted them to their rooms, bade them goodnight and urged them to sleep as late as they needed. 'Breakfast is a flexible meal. I'll see you when you're ready.'

On the terrace, she found Yves uncorking the red. 'You didn't drink much,' he said.

'A hostess should always stay sober.'

'You're not a hostess now.'

'You're still here.'

'I don't count.'

'I doubt the ladies would say that. They couldn't stop feeling your biceps.'

'Sure.' He shrugged. 'Sandblasting a windmill, inside and out, builds muscle. Have you heard from your boyfriend?'

'Partner. And no, I haven't.'

'So it is over?'

'Let's not, ha?' All afternoon and evening, Hope had kept her thoughts neutral and busy. 'Tell me some more about yourself. Did you leave Thailand and come home because of the ex-wife you mentioned?'

'Sort of, but it was time anyway. After Lally died, I didn't know what to do. I'd dropped out of college, I'd pissed off my friends. Travelling halfway across the world, living among people who didn't know my past, gave me time to work out that life was worth living. For the first couple of years, I was a nomad, then settled in Thailand. I worked in beach bars, and at my photography and grew up. Eventually, I bought my own bar.'

'In Koh Samui.'

'Uh-huh. I met a woman, we got married.'

'And divorced.'

'*Ouais*. She kept the bar and one day I woke up on a beach being bitten to death by sandflies, and realised nobody needed me. Literally, I could walk away and nobody would care. I'd been thinking of coming home for a while and, one night, I dreamed the windmill had fallen down and that I had been declared dead.' He gave a dry laugh. 'I wasn't far wrong. I flew home a couple of times to test the water. To see if I could reacclimatise to living in Europe and found Manon... well, I told you all that. I told her to move her stuff out—'

'And it turned unpleasant.'

'Sure. I arrived back in Varsac on the first of November 2012, and was granted the right to occupy my near-derelict home in the middle of February 2013.'

'That's bleak.' Gascon winters sometimes dropped down to minus ten.

'What hurts most,' he said, 'is that Lally told me to take care of her stuff, and now it's gone.' He met her eye. 'I should never have left for so long. I get it. Have you finished the memoir yet?'

'Not yet. They're back in Paris, hoping to take a train out. Did Lally ever tell you what brought her here? Why Lazurac? Because they were intending to get to Marseilles.'

'She'd drop the odd anecdote, when she'd had a drink,' he said. 'She got out of Paris ahead of the invasion, but the Germans attacked the refugee column at a village called Parçay-Meslay, outside Tours. She described it or tried to. She couldn't find the words, which is why she wrote them. That made it easier, somehow.'

'These days, she'd be diagnosed with PTSD,' Hope said. 'Back then, people just had to get on with it.'

They sat without speaking, wrapped in the warm dark, listening to the owl that used Hope's studio roof as a perch. Yves asked, 'Will you sell up and go back to England?'

'I hadn't really considered it.' In fact, her thoughts were tending the opposite way: how to keep this house if Ash really had detached himself.

'You want him back?'

'Yes. Very much.'

'Then why are you still here?'

Was he kidding? 'The four people you were flirting with not half an hour ago are staying two weeks.'

'I don't mean packing right now. I mean making plans to put this place on the market so you can rejoin your man. Summer is the time to sell property in the Gers.'

The casual comment triggered a sharp response. 'I don't reach for my passport the minute things get tough. I've made my life here.'

'Mm, but he hasn't.'

'It's not your business, Yves Ducasse.'

He reached across the table, picking up two corks stained red from the bottles they'd been pulled from and stood them in front of Hope. Pointing to one, he said, 'Home.' Then to the other, 'Your relationship. Choose.'

'I'm not playing games.'

'I'm not playing. If your Ash is everything to you, go to him. Tell him I pushed my way in and kept topping up your wine so you weren't in control. Tell him you want nothing but to be with him, whatever it takes.' When she stared blankly at the corks, he dropped his challenging style. 'Listen, those few people who cared for my grandmother would ask her why she stayed here, where people abused her. Why didn't she go back to England or to Paris, or anywhere she could turn a page and start again. She told me that La Cachette was as much a prison as a refuge. She'd invested her life here and couldn't leave because she was waiting for someone to return.'

Hope pushed aside her irritation. 'Otto. You know she was in love with a German fugitive?'

'Do I know… sort of. Lally would reel off old friends, as if I knew all the people she'd met in her life but if I asked about them, she'd turn vague, or say they'd betrayed her, or died. Conversations like that aren't easy for a teenage boy with limited emotional insight. If I had her archive, I might piece it together. Maybe the memoir will say more. All I know is, she was trapped. You don't have to be. You can decide if your life is here, in the place you have created, or with Ash, who I suppose you'll say you love—'

'I do love him.'

'Then your choice is clear because you love one more than the other.' He flipped a cork onto its side with a chewed fingernail. 'Once you choose, you will have no more confusion or sleepless nights. Won't that feel good?'

The candles were guttering but Hope wasn't ready to end the evening. Yves' presence brought conflict but kept her from delving too deeply into her own confusion. 'Coffee?' she invited.

'No, too late.' She felt disappointment, until he added, 'Do you have green tea?'

She did. 'Let's go in,' she said. A persistent insect was landing on her arm. 'Find the lounge while I make it.'

While the kettle boiled, she checked her phone. Nothing from Ash. If 'radio silence' was to be his style from now on, then Yves had nailed the truth. She was facing a life-altering choice. Leaving the tea to brew, she ran upstairs and fetched the memoir from her bedside table.

She found Yves lying on a couch she'd bought from the Thursday market. Squishy brown corduroy with a chrome frame, it shouted '1972'. He'd switched on side lamps and had his phone to his ear. Hope experienced a flash of mistrust. Was he calling a girlfriend?

'You don't mind having me for another couple of hours?' he asked, cutting the call.

'That would make it midnight,' she answered coldly. 'Anyone I know?' she asked, aware that she sounded clipped and judgemental.

'Taxi Rapide. They've only got one driver on tonight, and there are three customers ahead of me, so *rapide* they aren't. Is it OK? I don't mind if you go to bed.'

'You came by taxi?' She'd assumed his Land Rover was outside.

'Yes, because I knew I would drink. What have I said? You're smiling at me.'

'I'm not. I mean, good for you. Thinking ahead.'

'Running bars all those years, I lost count of the number of times I had to take people's car keys off them. But if you want to kick me out – it's not beyond me to walk home.'

'You don't have to walk. In fact, I wondered if you'd like me to read you a story.'

'A bedtime story?' A slow smile crossed his face, and Hope had to look away.

She held up the memoir. 'There are things you'll understand better than me.' Names, places. It would be like having page notes, or Lally herself offering insights. 'Shall I?'

'Sure, yes.'

Hope switched on a reading light. Getting comfortable against her sofa cushions, she found where she'd left off earlier. Yves linked his hands behind his head, looking just a little too at ease. God, if Ash walked in now... though, actually, what would he see that he hadn't spotted yesterday? Yves and herself standing with their hipbones touching, something in her body language that had instantly turned Ash's love cold. If she'd been a gambler, that moment would have been the one where she lost the lot.

She recapped where she'd got to in Lally's story. It was dawn, July 10th 1940. Curfew had just lifted. Lally, Pauline and Otto were walking to the railway station, the women carrying carpet bags stuffed with clothes and other personal items they'd salvaged. Monsieur Arnaud had given Otto an old suitcase, and some spare clothing including a street sweeper's beret, which Otto had pulled hard down to hide his light hair. They had taken back-streets, this time making for the Gare Montparnasse, the station for trains to Bordeaux. From there, Otto would journey on to the Spanish border. Lally and Pauline would take their more complicated route to Marseilles.

Yves frowned. 'There were bound to be checks at the Spanish border. How was he going to pass through with a German name, and his face on "Wanted" posters?'

'Good question.' Hope flipped back a few pages. 'Lally explains it. Otto travels on a forged Swedish passport. He has the right colouring to pass for Swedish and he speaks the language too.'

'Good, so long as I know. Go on then, get to the drama. I like your voice.'

She began to read.

BARBED WIRE AND FALSE NAMES: MEMOIR OF AN ENGLISH GIRL IN OCCUPIED FRANCE

The last time I saw Gare Montparnasse, it was surrounded by homeless nomads. The streets are now clear, the early morning air sweet with lilac blossom.

As it's too early to catch a train, we stop at a café for some breakfast, and oh, is it a relief to sit down and ease off our shoes! The short walk has torn open our blisters. Speaking low, we discuss our plans which have slightly changed. Pauline and I will head to Marseilles, as we always intended and get on a ship for Portugal. Otto will go across the mountains but this time, we've agreed we'll meet in Lisbon, Portugal's capital. The idea of separating to different continents is unthinkable, fate having brought us back together.

The first leg is Bordeaux, however—

'We can't travel together.' Otto is firm about it. He glances at Pauline, who is drinking milky coffee from a bowl, as is common still in France. Otto and I have cups of strong, black coffee in front of us. 'We'll say our goodbyes now as there's no telling when I'll reach Lisbon. I could be weeks crossing the mountains. In fact, you might beat me to it.'

I find that unlikely, as Pauline and I will have to apply to cross the demarcation line, which could also take weeks. Otto says he will give us the address of a safe house in the Free Zone in case we need to find refuge.

I ask what he means by 'safe house'.

'Owned by a sympathiser who will give you shelter, should you need it.'

'Who is this sympathiser, can we trust him?'

'Her,' Otto says with a half-smile, catching my flare of jealousy. 'She's well over fifty. She wrote to me when "The Grey Eyed Dove" appeared in a poetry magazine she subscribes to. We got into correspondence and she said if I ever needed sanctuary, to come to her. She will welcome you as my friends.'

'What's her name?'

He tears a scrap of paper from a notebook and writes. Folding the note in half when he's done, he says, 'Hide this inside your shoe, under the lining. No, don't look. In case you're arrested and interrogated.'

I drag off my shoe, assuring him that I wouldn't talk.

'You think?' He glances at Pauline, who is listening to us as if through a drugged veil. Her eyes look dreamy, and I know what's passing through his mind. Pauline will betray his literary admirer on the spot if a Gestapo officer so much as looks at her. To be fair, I might too, if tortured, so it's best I don't acquaint myself with the directions until I need to, and hopefully, I never will. Having eked out our breakfast of bread and rancid butter we pay and leave.

Outside, Otto tells us to wait five minutes. 'Follow, but don't approach me inside the station. I will get the first Bordeaux train out. You take the next. When you arrive, make for the cathedral and I'll find you.' Once there, he promises, we will enjoy a last few days together before striking out on our separate journeys.

The same rules apply as before. If anything happens to him, we're to look straight ahead and get out of Paris. He kisses me, then Pauline, then me again, then Pauline, tears in his eyes. 'Be safe, goodbye for now, my sweet loves.'

My *loves*. The plural pricks my ready jealousy, spurring me to do something I will feel ashamed of for years to come. While he is accepting a portion of the money Pauline got for her camera, I slip my hand into his jacket pocket.

I take the brooch his sister had made for him. I plunder the Grey Eyed Dove.

25

Inside Gare Montparnasse, I witness a most un-Parisian sight. People standing meekly in line at the ticket windows. The city suffered such a profound shock from its invasion, its character has altered. Those queueing remind me of the survivors I saw walking back along the road from Tours, eyewitnesses to the unthinkable, their expressions locked in the moment between heartbeats.

A train pulls out, the one Otto will be on, and as steam fills the vaulted space, I remind myself that we'll be together again by the end of the day. Someone walks past carrying new-baked bread and Pauline flinches at the smell. She must still be hungry. I tell her we'd best not buy more food in Paris. The Germans have mucked up the exchange rate. One of their Reichsmarks now equals twenty French francs, meaning everything in Paris is cheap as dust for them and unaffordable for us. Pauline's camera-money will buy our train tickets out, and food and lodgings until we get our boat – *if* we are frugal. I consult a timetable. 'There's another Bordeaux train in just over an hour.'

We join a slow-moving queue, reaching the ticket window

twenty minutes before our train is due. I ask for two third-class tickets and Pauline pays. I take one, hand her the other. As I'm doing it, a scuffle breaks out in the line next to us. I quickly see why: the ticket seller has pulled down his blind, and people who are desperate to get on that Bordeaux train are pushing forward. The ones who already have their tickets are battling to get away. A man hammers on the glass, letting out a tirade of fury, and a woman and her children are trapped in the crush. Someone starts screaming.

I spoke of Paris being on the edge... the panic is infectious. Travellers behind Pauline and me start to push forward and when the frustrated queue alongside us stampedes towards our window, everything disintegrates into a shoving, shouting melee. I lose sight of Pauline as I'm pinned up against the counter, my bag wedged against my ribs and my forehead against the glass. All I can see is the employee on the other side mouthing and rapping with his fist. I'm losing consciousness when gunshots ring out. All at once, the crowd disperses. I fall to the ground, gasping and retching, still clutching my travel bag.

A policeman helps me up, asks if I'm all right. I can't find my ticket, and I ask if he's seen my friend.

He suggests I stay where I am and let her find me. The place is chaos. She could be anywhere. Except, she is not. Our train for Bordeaux comes in and goes out. I call her name, I scan every face, hunt in every corner for almost two hours.

Pauline has disappeared.

26

HOPE

Hope put the book down. 'Poor, poor Lally. I cannot believe how unlucky she is.'

Yves agreed. Only someone psychologically robust could have dealt with that new disaster. 'Lost her friend, lost her ticket. Hardly any money and prices in Paris have tripled. Her great stroke of luck was to be outside the car when it was hit on the road to Tours, but apart from that, life dealt her a crappy hand.'

'I wonder if Otto waited at Bordeaux for them,' Hope said.

'Maybe Pauline got on the train,' Yves suggested, 'leaving Lally stranded.'

Hope wasn't having that. 'She's a drip, and flaky as they come, but she wouldn't have abandoned the friend who had her back all those weeks.'

'No? People never leave others in the lurch, because it suits them?'

Hope knew perfectly well that he was thinking of Ash.

'Do we have a surname for Otto?' Yves asked. 'We could google him, see what became of him.'

'Not yet.' Hope read on a little way, then gave up. 'It gets worse. Lally traipses back to Rue Monge, her feet bleeding, in case Pauline is there. Monsieur Arnaud opens the door, says no, she's not, then shuts it on her. Their neighbours being arrested the night before has spooked him.'

Yves asked, 'Do they ever find each other? I don't mind a spoiler.'

Hope had no idea how the story ended. 'But Lally had the Grey Eyed Dove in 1944, when she did her self-portrait, which implies she never gave it back to Otto. Or he let her keep it.'

They mulled on that until Yves said, 'I'm not so sure about him.'

'In what way?'

'His intentions. His integrity.'

'Oh, come on! He escorted them back to Paris, when he should have kept going towards the Spanish border.'

'Mm. But did he love Lally?'

'She loved him, for sure.'

Yves said wryly, 'That wasn't my question.'

She closed the book. 'I can't answer for him. But whatever misery she went through, Lally stood a better chance of survival without Pauline clinging to her.'

Yves' phone buzzed. 'My taxi's outside. What are your plans for tomorrow night?'

Astonishing, but for a moment, she'd forgotten her guests. 'Dinner out. Want to join us?' She immediately feared she was being pushy. It didn't help that Yves' expression clouded.

'Have you booked somewhere in Lazurac?' he asked.

'No, Le Sentier, not far from your house. You don't have to.'

'Oh, they're all right. They're young, not burdened by history. They won't spit in my wine. Yes, I'll join you. Can I bring Claudia?'

'Sure.' Conscious of sounding less than gracious, she amended her reply. 'Course. And the children.'

'They're girls, by the way,' Yves said. 'I put my foot in it when I first met them, saying, "Hi, guys." They're going to Bordeaux tomorrow, to their dad's.' He read her unspoken response. 'I know, life imitating art. Claudia's husband moved there to live with another woman, but he and Claudia are still married.'

'I see. Complicated. And yet, strangely predictable.'

Yves gave a half-smile. 'What time tomorrow?'

'Seven o'clock?' She couldn't shake the guilty feeling that somehow, Ash could hear her making a date with another man. It wasn't a date, of course, but still, she felt like a thief caught red-handed who goes out and steals again.

Yves kissed her cheek. 'Seven o'clock, Berlin time.'

'French time, obviously.'

'Same thing,' he said, telling her to stay put, he'd find his way to the front door. 'The Germans imposed their time on France when they took over, and we never changed it back.'

Hope headed for bed. She ran the shower and the water was tepid. Another thing for the list – make sure, with five people in the house, you put the immersion heater on. Now thoroughly awake, she punched up her pillows, put on the bedside light and picked up the memoir, which she'd brought upstairs. This was cheating, but Yves didn't have to know...

There was a riddle at the heart of this little book. *Barbed Wire and False Names*. She understood the false names. Lally had morphed into Marie-Laure Ducasse, and Pauline was masquerading as her sister, but where did the barbed wire come in? A running theme, as barbed wire had scuppered Yves' café. Had Lally been forced to climb over some, or under it?

It would be in these pages.

BARBED WIRE AND FALSE NAMES: MEMOIR OF AN ENGLISH GIRL IN OCCUPIED FRANCE

I've walked and walked, taking a route through the Jardin des Plantes in case Pauline had the idea of waiting for me there. I've spent the entire day checking all the places we liked to go. No sign of her anywhere, so I've returned to Gare Montparnasse. The German Feldgendarmerie with their dog tags scare me, and one of them addresses me in German. Something about us 'going for a little walk'.

I pretend not to understand. It's curfew in under an hour and I pray Pauline has found a refuge somewhere. At least she's got the bulk of the money from selling her camera. I urgently need to find shelter for myself and have one prospect. Thankfully, it isn't far.

From the station, I limp the ten minutes to the Rue du Maine.

It's the kind of street you find near railway stations, full of cheap hotels and lodging houses. Halfway down, I give a coded three-rap knock on a black door and wait for what feels like a century. Probably it's only a minute. It is opened by a woman in a well-cut dress, a cigarette between her painted lips. One glance at me, she says wearily, 'We're not hiring, dear. Try up on the Butte.'

I rasp, 'Dorienne, it's me, Lally. Victor's friend.'

Victor Ponsard's sister peers at me before gasping something akin to, 'Good God, what the hell happened?' She pulls me into the lobby. As she closes the door, a man tramps down the staircase, his peaked cap pulled low. He passes us without a word.

Dorienne gives a 'Tsh!' as he leaves. 'A month ago, I wouldn't have let the likes of him over the threshold, but trade's fallen off a cliff. This bloody curfew. All we get now is policemen, being the only ones who can stay out late, though getting them to pay the going rate is a bloody battle.' She regards me thoughtfully. 'Where's your little shadow?'

'You mean Pauline?' I explain what's happened, though I don't mention Otto.

'You know what? Let her go,' Dorienne advises. 'Last time I saw her, she came with my brother's handsome friend. They wanted a room. I was a bit shocked, which is quite something for me.'

'A room – when?' The handsome friend would be Julien Marshall.

Dorienne thinks it was two months ago. 'In May.'

So, before Julien was deployed to northern France. I can't help being a little shocked myself. It's bad form, him bringing his sisters' au pair here. Pauline was under his family's care. When I meet him again, I'll tear him off a strip. Before I hug him. As for Pauline, the fool, it's the oldest misstep in the book.

Fatigue closes in on me. 'Can I stay a little while?' Dorienne takes me in her arms.

'There, there, course you can. Victor would want me to take care of his dearest Lally.'

For now, I am safe but my fears for Otto and Pauline gnaw at me. I sleep cradling the Grey Eyed Dove in my palm.

28

HOPE

Next morning, after a trip to the baker's, Hope took a tray loaded with baguette, croissants and jam through to the dining room.

'I thought this morning you might like to explore,' she said to her guests who were drinking their coffee.

'We were just talking about that,' said Paloma. 'Will they let us walk around the cathedral?'

'Absolutely. And the Saturday food market is on this morning. They block off all the roads through the middle of town, so we can stroll at leisure. Get your cameras and sketchbooks ready because it's a blaze of colour.'

She sat down to her own breakfast as they chattered away. Unexpectedly, Goldie reached over to touch her hand. 'You OK, honey, are we too much? Only you're toying with that croissant. I guess, if you can get them this good every day, the novelty wears off.'

Hope glanced down and saw a croissant shredded. 'My mind's running ahead to dinner tonight. Remember, we're going out? But we'll want lunch. I'm suggesting a buffet with lots of salad, yes?'

'Sounds good.'

Hope helped herself to raspberry jam, demonstrating that all was well in her world. The effect was dented when Elkie Warberg asked when they might meet 'your lovely man'.

'Yves? He's joining us tonight for dinner.'

A silence told her she'd walked into a trap that only she could have dug.

'I meant your partner, Hope. The one on your website, that you're married to... Ash, is that his name?'

'We're not married.' She felt herself blush.

'Uh-oh.' Elkie raised a finger. 'Shoulda put a ring on it.'

'He's gone back to London, on a temporary basis.' That sounded lame. 'We always knew our first two or three years here would be a transitional time. He takes contracts now and again.' Put like that, it sounded totally reasonable.

TJ asked what line Ash was in.

'Cyber security in the banking sector.'

'Gee, money, money,' Goldie laughed. 'You get to play house, he gets to earn the bucks.'

Hope laughed unconvincingly. Their financial arrangement was rather the reverse. Reaching for the coffee pot, she offered everyone a last refill and escaped to the kitchen. Grabbing her phone, she messaged Ash.

Stop ghosting me and come home.

Later that morning, while her guests changed into walking shoes, Hope sneaked back to her laptop and opened an ancestry site she'd subscribed to. Yves had suggested she start with a question, not an answer. Fine. She typed in 'Joseph Granger', giving her father's year of birth as 1941, and the location as Fareham, where he'd lived as a child.

'Sorry, Dad,' she muttered as she waited for results. 'I know you were afraid of what I might find, but it can't be that bad...'

The result wasn't bad, or good either. Other than a reference to her father's death in September 2011, his record was blank. She set up another search, this time for the grandparents who had adopted Joseph after the war, taking him from his mother.

With no details other than their names – George Granger and his wife, Mary – she guessed a probable birth-decade and location. Her search brought up a dizzyingly long list of Georges and Marys. Frustrated, Hope closed out of the site and typed a new line into her search engine. 'Poem, The Grey Eyed Dove'.

Up came dove-inspired verse of all kinds, but none attributed to a German poet. Wasn't the internet supposed to contain every fact known to humanity? She typed in, 'Otto and The Grey Eyed Dove'.

Those weren't the magic words either.

'Ready when you are,' Elkie called from the hall. 'We've decided we'd like to visit the cathedral first.'

'Coming.' Hope closed her laptop and grabbed a shopping bag.

29

Usually, Hope loved being inside the cathedral, listening to the organ or just tuning in to muted conversations and soft footsteps. Today, the reverential atmosphere fuelled her exasperation. Her guests were entranced, however, so she invented an excuse to leave. She'd better hit the market before the best stuff went. 'How about we meet in Le Chat in two hours, for a coffee or beer?' She gave them directions.

In the sunshine, Hope checked her phone, finding a couple of spammy messages and a notification from her bank. From Ash, zero. Jaw clenched, she threaded through the market-day shoppers, heading for Place de la Libération where, in her view, the best food stalls were to be found. A narrow street off the square was named Rue d'Août – August Street. Only now did Hope wonder if it was in honour of August 1944 when four years of Nazi occupation had come to an end. Something had inspired the name and she stared at the street sign until a pedestrian behind her coughed politely because she was blocking the pavement.

She shopped for lunch. Her guests had paid handsomely for their holiday and into her bag went charcuterie, local cheeses, huge tomatoes which would be bursting with flavour, ripe peaches and melon. She bought rustic loaves, pâté and butter. Heading home, weighed down, her phone pinged, alerting her to a message. Ash?

She put down her bag and fished out her phone. It was her dentist, advising that she was due a check-up. Life was still giving her lemons. Reaching home, she saw that the garden gate was off the latch, which was odd. She'd come out last, shutting it behind her. Maybe a parcel had been delivered... those ill-advised DNA kits, perhaps?

There was no parcel at the front door, nor on the mat as she let herself in. Taking her shopping through to the kitchen, she looked out over the terrace and gave a gasp. A man wearing a dark top was descending the steps towards the lower part of the garden, the sun glinting off his near-black hair. Tomatoes spilled over the counter as Hope dashed out yelling, 'Ash, Ash, I'm here!'

Alerted by her voice, the visitor stared up at her. It wasn't Ash. It was a man with expensive-looking sunglasses, wearing a black linen jacket over a smart-casual tee-shirt and trousers. He came back up the steps. '*Bonjour, Madame Granger?*'

'Ye-es. Who are you?'

He held out his hand. 'Jonny Taubier. We were to meet twenty minutes ago?' He said it as a question.

Hope shook her head. 'I'm confused.'

He took out a phone and scrolled through. Checking his diary, no doubt. 'This morning, at eleven.'

'Meeting about what?'

His reply was to give her a business card. *Taubier et Fils, Agence Immobilière.* Taubier and son, estate agents. Yet another Taubier? This must be 'and son'. Now thoroughly churned up, she said, 'I'm not buying and I'm not selling. Who arranged this?'

'Monsieur Rupert Ashton.'

Hope reeled slightly, hearing Ash's legal name. She'd never called him Rupert, except maybe once, to tease him.

Jonny Taubier gave a brisk, apologetic smile. 'Clearly there's been a mix-up. I thought he would have informed you.'

'He didn't.' He'd said not a damn thing. 'I'm afraid you've had a wasted trip. My home is not for sale.'

Hope emphasised 'my', and tried to return the business card, but her visitor said, 'Please, keep it.'

'I'll call Ash – Monsieur Ashton – and get to the bottom of this,' she said. 'Apologies if your time's been wasted.'

He said it was no problem, sorry to have disturbed her, but when he took off his shades and gave the house, its creeping vine and pastel-blue shutters, a speculative once-over, Hope felt he was contemplating giving her a price there and then.

She knew it when he said, 'I could always look round, in case you change your mind.'

'I can't change my mind,' she said crisply, 'because my mind has not been consulted.'

'Monsieur Ashton was quite—'

'I don't care,' she butted in, her composure shattering. 'My name is on the purchase deeds of this house, mine alone. No man alive can say when, if and how I sell. How much more clearly can I put it? Now, please, just go.'

'Hope, is all well?'

She hadn't heard Yves come through the gate. 'I don't know,' she said. 'Something's going on, but this gentleman is leaving.'

It was obvious the two had met before. Seeing them giving each other the once-over, Hope was reminded of a wildlife programme, tusked boars encountering each other on a wood-land path. Yves stepped aside. Jonny Taubier walked past, giving the faintest of nods.

After the garden gate clashed, Yves took a moment to study the view from the top of the steps. 'It's a desirable location,' he said, smiling dryly. 'Impressive vista.'

'To die for.' All the houses this side of town were built along ancient ramparts, and from her terrace, she could see over a railway line to fields of sunflowers and the forested hills beyond. On the highest of those hills was the *bastide* of Saint-Sever. She gave a ragged account of coming home, finding Jonny Taubier, 'Scoping out the size of the plot. I suppose I should be grateful he didn't try to get in the house.'

'The Taubiers are an entitled bunch despite their chequered history.'

She looked at the business card, which in her agitation she'd folded in two. 'How is Jonny Taubier related to Manon?'

'Second cousin. Third cousin. Their family tree spreads wide.'

'Can I get you anything? I have peach juice in the fridge.'

'Perfect.'

When she came out again, he'd made himself comfortable at the outside table. She joined him and asked, 'So, "chequered history"?'

He looked at his watch. 'Have you got an hour spare?'

'Twenty minutes max.' It wouldn't take long to put a buffet lunch together. Everything was being served cold.

'Then come with me.' Yves had already drunk his juice.

'Where to?'

Only to the cathedral, it transpired, though not inside. He led her under a stone arch into a courtyard enclosed on three sides by ivy-clad walls. The fourth wall was the cathedral's flank. A fountain leaked water into a trough that, from its colour, could not have been cleaned out in years.

'I didn't know this little enclave existed,' Hope said.

'It's Lazurac's closest-kept secret. I only know it's here because, years ago, Manon showed me.' Yves pulled at a vine of ivy, revealing a stone of a lighter colour than the wall with words carved into it. Hope had brought her phone in case her guests called, and she shone its torch onto the surface, reading,

'"On this spot, August 5th, 1944, twelve men of Lazurac were shot by the German SS. *Vive la Résistance*." My God. An hour ago I stared down August Street and wondered what happened back then.'

Names were listed, five surnames between the twelve men, suggesting members of the same few families had perished. Some were familiar to Hope from businesses and shops still operating in Lazurac.

'A Resistance cell was active here,' Yves told her. 'Early in August 1944, they were sabotaging the railway line to stop the Nazis moving south to fight the Allies on the Midi coast. They were betrayed.'

He was showing her this... why? Hope was almost afraid to ask. 'Who betrayed them?'

'Nobody knows. They didn't know at the time either, but distraught people will blame someone. Whose name is not on the plaque?' he asked, his voice soft and savage.

Any number.

'Taubier,' he said.

'As in Jonny and Manon. And the family next door to you.'

'Uh-huh. Three Taubier boys were members of Lazurac's Resistance, yet none were caught.'

'You're saying one of them tipped off the Germans?'

'I'm not saying it, but yes, I *am* saying it. Lally said it too, but nobody was listening.'

Hope's phone buzzed. Yves urged her to answer it. 'Your guests might have got lost.'

She took the call. It was not Goldie or any of the others. It was Ash.

30

Hope's tentative greeting, 'Glad you've called' was met with a tirade of fury. She stood, shocked, as Ash raged at her across seven hundred miles of ether for having 'that effing creep Ducasse' in the house.

'He called by, that's all. And you have some explaining—'

Ash wasn't hearing her. What was she up to, sending the estate agent away when he'd gone to so much trouble to organise it, and didn't she get it?

'Get what?'

'We can't afford this life, Hope. It's over. Done. It was nice pretend-time but while I was prepared to work my butt off to dig us out, you sat around, swigging wine, entertaining your boyfriend—'

Woah. 'Back up, Ash. Firstly, Yves was not in the house. He called round.' Why had he, actually? She hadn't asked. 'Secondly, who says our life here is over?'

'Anybody with a brain would say it.'

'But you're saying it. When did you get to decide my life?'

'I get to decide mine, Hope, and I'm out. Get that house on the market, now. Today.'

Hope's heart measured each hard second as she concentrated on breathing. She managed to say, 'We have guests. It's starting to work.'

'Four guests after all these months? Grow up.'

'Don't patronise me! I do the books. Things are tight, but this has got us through and if you would only put in your share—'

'Throw good money down a pit? I might have, except you had to go and sleep around, didn't you?'

She was now as angry as he was. 'You read too many lads' mags in your bedroom when you were growing up, Ash. It's stunted your development.'

'Jonny Taubier told me who that bloke is. If you don't want a reputation, Hope, don't hang out with deadbeats.'

'Who the hell is Jonny Taubier? An estate agent whose number you found online, I suppose. You had a nice, cosy chat about me and a man you've never met. Ash, I don't know what you've become... or what's brought this on.'

'Reality. I want my money out.'

'What money? We had an agreement. I bought the house; you got us up and running.'

'But it's not my house, and there's no business either. I want my forty thousand back.'

Forty? He had to be kidding. 'I couldn't raise half that.'

'Course you can't. Hence the estate agent.'

She flinched at the sarcastic edge. A stranger had hacked Ash's phone. Except it was Ash, the man who had told her she was 'the one': the woman he wanted to marry. 'You said you'd lost your phone,' she rasped, as the details of their separation galloped past her eyes. 'Your excuse for not contacting me, true?'

'Stop changing the subject, and who cares? Get Jonny Taubier back, get a valuation.'

'Just piss off.' She cut the call and sank down on the edge of the fountain. Yves came and sat beside her.

'That sounded volcanic. He really has left you, I guess?'

She nodded, a tear hitting the knee of her trousers, making a dark spot. 'He wants me to sell.'

'He can't make you, and even if you decide to, there are other estate agents in Lazurac. You need at least two valuations.'

'It's my home and business. I can't sell.'

He put his arm round her. 'Let it flow. You can't solve this while you're distressed and in shock.'

'You sound like a wise agony aunt.'

'As your agony aunt, you need a lawyer.'

'Can't afford one.'

'You need legal advice. Ash can't force you from your home, and he can't demand money with menaces. He lived there for a year?'

'Over a year.'

'Which makes him responsible for some of the expenses. You're an accountant, you can work out what you reasonably owe him and vice versa.'

She let out a breath. 'It still isn't do-able. Forty thousand is surreal!'

'Let's go back to yours. You need to get lunch ready, yes?'

'Yes.' She glanced towards the plaque on the wall. 'I'm crying over first-world problems.'

He extended his hand and pulled her to her feet, bent his head and kissed the bridge of her nose. Stepping clear, she said, 'What made you call on me? We're not at the restaurant till this evening.'

'I wanted to talk to you because I've been thinking.'

'Dangerous,' she joked awkwardly. 'What about?'

'Having my feet skewered.'

'You've lost me... oh, you mean—'

'Taking a DNA test. If it means that much to you, I'll do it.'

So moved, her eyes brimmed over. Yves made a tutting sound and dragged a cloth from his pocket. It had engine oil on it. '*Non*,' he said, shoving it back.

She wiped her eyes with the hem of her shirt. 'If we turn out to be cousins?'

'Then I can never kiss you, except like this.' He pressed his lips to her cheeks, one then the other.

'Fine with me,' she replied, and in the midst of pain, it felt like a really good deal. A friend, who kissed her on the cheek and overcame a deep distrust of something, because she asked it.

They walked home and got on with making lunch. Yves was dicing the tomatoes for a salsa when Hope gave a gasp. 'I'm meant to be at the café!'

'Le Chat?'

'I said I'd meet them in...' She checked the time. 'In two minutes.'

'Then you'll be ten minutes late. Get the table laid.'

'OK.' Being ordered about wasn't her favourite thing, but right now, having someone put the head back on the headless chicken was comforting. When the table was set, she rejoined Yves and he pointed at bowls of salad he'd prepped. 'Those go in the fridge. And the pâté. Put a cloth over the cheese, leave that on the side. Bread, butter and peaches too. Just lay cloths over, in case of flies, and we're good to go.'

She watched him finish the salsa, the flash of his knife. 'This is something else you're secretly darn good at.'

'Did I make a secret of being able to cook, *hein*?'

'The pastries in your café come from the cash and carry.'

'Because this is France, and they're as good there as in the Paris Ritz. Why mess around with pastry when there's no need?' Before setting up his own business in Thailand, he'd mooched from bar to bar, restaurant to restaurant, learning from amazing people. 'They don't let you cut so much as a radish until you've learned knife skills.' If he had more time, he said, he'd cut turnip lotus flowers for the table.

'D'you miss it?' she asked. 'That life?'

'I'm trying to get it back. My café...' He stripped basil leaves from their stems. 'Starting from zero for the second time in your life is tough. Doing it for the third time is horrible.' He frowned. 'Sorry. Didn't mean to crash the mood.'

'I'm going to dig in and fight,' she said.

'An invisible foe?' Yves added the shredded basil to his salsa.

'Ash has to come back at some point. I'm not being dumped by text, or in a one-way phone rant.'

Yves added olive oil, chilli, salt and black pepper to the bowl, gave it a stir and put a plate on top. 'Done, let's go.'

Jeanne at Le Chat greeted Hope and looked askance at Yves. All she said, however, was, 'Your friends are outside, at the back.' The café was crowded, with tables pulled away from the wall. Three people were busy mounting photographs.

Two of them, a man and woman, were strangers to Hope, but the other woman was not. She went up and said, '*Salut*, Inès.'

Inès Royale cast a wary glance at Yves and returned Hope's greeting uncomfortably. 'You look well, Hope. I met your Americans, in such good spirits. They love our cathedral.'

'We're about to join them. You know Yves Ducasse, of course.' Hope was giving Inès no excuse to ignore him. Inès managed it, however, turning away to fix up another photograph.

Hope's eye travelled along the display. The photos were black and white, and shouted 'wartime': they were of men sitting on the tailgates of trucks, wearing short leather jackets, caps and loose trousers. Almost all of them balanced cigarettes between their lips as they stared into the lens with savvy intensity. Straps across their torsos supported skeletal machine guns.

'Seventy years ago,' said the woman Hope didn't recognise,

leaning past her shoulder, 'in June 1944, these men were practising warcraft in secret. They were meeting in cellars. Some had only two months left to live.'

'And some had less,' Inès Royale added harshly. 'Lazurac's Resistance was betrayed. Wasn't it, Ducasse?'

To Hope's surprise, Yves answered quite steadily. 'True, Madame Royale. And the guilty ones paid, would you say?'

'Not all.'

'No. Some scuttled into the woodwork, like cockroaches when the lights go on. Isn't it always the case? The well-connected get away with it, the vulnerable take the punishment.' Yves spared a moment for the picture Inès was hanging. 'Powerful images. Maybe you inspire me to do something of my own, at Varsac-les-Moulins.'

'At the café that is closed?' Inès smiled thinly.

'My door is always open. Just as in Lally's day. Open door, open mind. They tend to go together. *Au revoir.*'

They found Goldie and the others sitting beside a trellis that was almost overwhelmed with scented jasmine. They were enchanted with the café and the exhibition. 'Seventy years since Liberation,' said Goldie. 'Those ladies were saying that Lazurac was quite a centre of Resistance.'

'It was,' Yves agreed. 'It was also a nest of collaborators.' The Milice – the French paramilitary police – were firmly onside with the Germans, with the Gestapo, and had informants betraying anyone suspected of being a Résistant.

'Way it goes,' Paloma said. 'Societies under occupation always split.'

'My pops flew a Liberator bomber,' TJ said, adding that he was famished and could they order food? Hope reminded him that lunch awaited at the house. 'Come on,' she said. 'Let's walk home by the ramparts. It's part of the pilgrims' route. Ancient footsteps.'

'The Resistance used the pilgrims' path,' Yves said, his

words covered by the scraping of their chairs, and only Hope heard him.

As they walked back through the café, the door opened to let in Manon Taubier and her son Noah. At the same moment, Inès stepped back to judge the hang of a photograph she'd just put up. It was a street scene, a crowd of townsfolk surrounding a woman who was held by the arms. The woman's stiff, back-leaning posture was that of a victim being dragged to execution. Either she'd known a camera shutter was about to click, or she had looked into the lens the second before it did. Her hair was short as a convict's, sheared off at the roots. Her eyes were huge, a syringe-full of terror in each one.

It was Lally.

Manon came up, interpreted Hope's expression and said, 'So now you know Lazurac's second-best-kept secret. *Voilà, la collaboratrice.*'

The best-kept secret being the plaque in the cathedral courtyard. Twelve dead souls. Hope stopped Manon from walking past. 'If you are repeating unsubstantiated rumour—'

She felt Yves' hand on her arm. 'Join your friends, Hope. Let me deal with this.'

BARBED WIRE AND FALSE NAMES: MEMOIR OF AN ENGLISH GIRL IN OCCUPIED FRANCE

I first met Dorienne Ponsard when Victor brought me to her house. I was Victor's friend, and his model too. Not his muse as I'm not muse material. He was fond of his sister, but also embarrassed by her business. To avoid awkwardness, he only ever brought me on a Sunday, a day of rest even for the proprietress of a bordello.

A top-floor room here catches the purest light in Paris, and over a succession of Sundays, Victor painted me. Dorienne would bring wine, and we'd chat as he worked. I grew to like her very much, and I thought Otto did too, which is why his refusal to let me come to her for a loan both surprised and nettled me. Not even the man I adore tells me who I can be friends with. As the stifling July of 1940 rolls by and Paris blooms with swastikas, I settle into the routines of Dorienne's house, lucky to have found a safe haven. I never expect anything for free, of course.

In return for the room under the eaves, I mop the hotel top

to bottom twice daily. I change beds, carry laundry up and down. In the kitchen, I chop and slice vegetables for the broth that is our main source of nourishment. Every afternoon around four, I flop onto my mattress, sleeping three hours straight. Dinner is at eight, Madame Dorienne and her girls sitting together around a large table. By nine, the knocks begin upon the door, which is when I retire to the little snug where the girls gather between clients.

I brought as many of my art materials from Rue Monge as I could ram into my bag, and I sketch whoever comes my way. Not the clients, for obvious reasons, but the girls like having their portraits done and they bring me scrap paper, whatever they find, to make sketchbooks. I cut the pieces into squares small enough to fit into my pocket and stitch them together with a darning needle. Somehow it's got out that I'm English and, oddly, the only person in the house who doesn't like me is another Englishwoman. Norma-Rose Foster is her name. Perhaps she realises that just as she can spot my fakery, I see through her carefully constructed veneer. Norma-Rose's false fable is that she is in no way a prostitute. No indeed, she is simply obliging Dorienne's gentlemen-callers from the goodness of her heart. She smirks when we pass each other, as if she's guarding a secret I'd die to know. She complains that I don't mop properly under her bed.

Really? She goes down on her knees to check for dust? Under normal circumstances, I'd enjoy pulling Norma-Rose down a peg or three, but I feel vulnerable. Along with others in the house, I'm involved in serious crime. That of listening to the BBC.

London calling, London calling, the French speaking to the French. I, Dorienne and other girls huddle round the wireless set after dark, a sofa against the door to stop anyone bursting in on us. We hear Général de Gaulle denouncing the cowardly, collaborationist French government. We hear how London is being bombed and other British cities too, which is harrowing though it gives the lie to the propaganda that London has surrendered, and Winston Churchill is in prison. Churchill's resolute voice on the BBC Home Service, or de Gaulle's smooth tones over the airwaves, teaches us the meaning of hope. Even so, we jump at every creak and footfall. The majority of Dorienne's customers are still the policemen whose wives and families left Paris in the great exodus and haven't come back. Some root for Churchill and de Gaulle, but many have snuggled up to the Germans. Learning which is which is impossible, so it's easier to mistrust them all. In this way, caught between boredom and anxiety, August arrives and I am still ragged with worry for Otto and Pauline. For a while, I was sure Pauline would track me here, because she knows Dorienne is the only friend I have left in Paris. Not a whisper. As for Otto, I can only imagine he waited for us in Bordeaux until shortage of money pushed him onward. Whenever I can, I walk in the Jardin des Plantes, and sometimes I think I see him, or Pauline, in the distance. I run, calling their names, but it is never them.

Towards the middle of August, Madame Dorienne calls me into her office and my tenuous security comes to an end. She says, 'Have you heard, it's compulsory now for all enemy aliens to register.'

I ask what she means.

'To declare your British identity, have it recorded in the Kommandantur on Place de l'Opéra.'

The Kommandantur is the hub of German rule in Paris. It's where you get those precious permits to travel, or to remain. Or not. Making sure nobody is listening, I hiss, 'Nobody's supposed to know I'm British. How can I show a forged identity card?' My genuine one, belonging to Lavinia Shepherd, was incinerated along with the Marshalls' poor chauffeur. I daren't present myself at the Kommandantur as Marie-Laure Ducasse.

Dorienne tells me I'll have to do what Norma-Rose has done. Go to the American embassy on Avenue Gabriel and ask for the 'British Interests' desk. There, an Englishman, who must wish he were elsewhere, provides new papers. Norma-Rose also receives a few hundred francs a month through his good offices. 'And that would be nice, wouldn't it?'

I'm not convinced. 'Couldn't I just stay here, and not go out?'

Dorienne is firm. She has to consider the welfare of everyone. 'If we get an official police visit, or someone blabs...' She looks tense and I know she has a lot on her plate. The Germans keep bringing out rules to control brothels, and just the other day, a letter arrived calling up her brother for forced labour in Germany. Victor left Paris weeks ago and is on the run, and Dorienne fears he might be registered as a deserter in his absence. Since I'm in a similar state over Otto, I sympathise. When I mention Otto's plight, Dorienne comes out with something odd.

'Don't love any man too much, will you, Lally? I'd hate to see you made a fool of.'

I sigh, and say, 'Too late for that. But I trust my man.'

'Ha,' she answers. 'I trust men to cheat. It's easier that way.'

Her trade has made her cynical. 'I'll go to the US embassy in the morning,' I promise.

And I do, crossing the river at Pont de la Concorde, sticking my tongue out at the swastika flapping morosely from the top of the Eiffel Tower. From the Right Bank, I walk to Avenue Gabriel. The métro is running again, but I always stay in the open when I can. At the US embassy, I'm escorted to the British Desk where a man with a well-bred accent listens to my confession. He tut-tuts at my identity card, tells me I'm very silly to pretend to be a Frenchwoman when I'm not, but he will help me. 'There are rather a lot of you we still have to mop up,' he says, meaning, I think, that I'm not the only Brit lying low in Paris.

'What are your plans?' he asks.

When I tell him I want to get out of the country via Marseilles, he tells me that the British consul there, along with his counterpart at Nice, evacuated weeks ago. There's nobody left on the southern coast who can get me on a ship. No point going to Brittany either, as the port of St Malo has been bombed, and that coastline is heavily restricted. I wonder why he bothered asking me my plans, as it seems my only option is to stay put.

He asks, 'Anyone at home I can write to, let them know you're tickety-boo?'

Nobody, I answer.

'Right-o,' he says and adjusts his spectacles. 'I say this to all of you. Don't *even think* about writing a letter home, d'you hear? No parcels or telegrams. The Germans tolerate us stranded ex-pats if we keep a low profile. Do anything silly, you'll get arrested on a spying charge for which the penalty is—'

'Six nights in the Ritz with the man of my dreams.'

He doesn't appreciate my quip and removes his spectacles to stare piercingly at me. 'This is serious, Miss Shepherd. The Germans pounce. They don't drop in for a chat.' As if I haven't realised. I feel like describing to him the road outside Tours after the Germans 'dropped in for a chat'.

Within five days, I have new papers. Lavinia Linda Shepherd is risen again, Alleluia! Born in Jarrow, County Durham, on the Ides of March in 1913. I am reunited with my former self.

August 1940 ends with a volley of thunderstorms and lashing rain, which hammers on the roof above my head and makes me dream of biblical floods.

September dawns, the first anniversary of war comes and goes. Leaves blow along the embankments and in the hour before curfew, when I slip out for a brisk walk through the Jardin des Plantes, or along the river, I feel a chill. True to my word, I go each day to the Kommandantur and by now, I've notched up so many trips, I've stopped being nervous. You queue. You receive a glacial glance from a German clerk. Sign, stamp, out.

I go to the British Desk at the US embassy every week for my three hundred francs, and very grateful I am for it. Until, one day in mid-September, I arrive and find the desk closed.

My helpful Englishman has been sent with a cohort of other British men to an internment camp. The news travels like iced water through my veins but I assure myself that they won't take women.

I balance on the razor's edge through the rest of autumn and into the winter. On December 5th, 1940, the first wisps of snow graze the windowsills on Rue du Maine. I am clearing away the breakfast crockery when I hear a rap at the door. It's the wrong time of day for a client. Dorienne comes in. She's white-cheeked.

'Lally? Stop what you're doing. There are some policemen here to talk to you.'

32

HOPE

Le Sentier was an ancient, fortified manor house on the Lazurac to Varsac road. Hope, Goldie, Elkie, Paloma and TJ were snacking on bread and olives. Yves and Claudia were late.

The chef-patronne had handed out booklets detailing the manor's history, and Elkie wanted to know what was meant by 'dating from the time of English occupation'.

'Do they mean the war, Hope?'

'Not the last one.' Hope pulled her eyes from the door. 'It goes back to Eleanor of Aquitaine, who married King Henry II and brought territories to the English crown, of which Gascony was part.' Explaining the long influence of the English in this region kept the conversation flowing. Reading another tranche of Lally's memoir after leaving Yves at Le Chat had done little to steady her emotions. Breaking off at the point in Lally's story when the police arrived was like an injection of adrenalin after a near-miss on the motorway.

Hope was desperate to know what Yves had said and done after she left the café. She'd taken her friends home for lunch, expecting him to join them, only he hadn't. She'd called him and got no answer. She didn't think Yves was the kind to ignore calls without good reason, but what did she really know about him? And if Lally was her grandmother too, she should have stood alongside him, demanding that horrible picture be taken down.

At least now she knew how the Grey Eyed Dove had come to be in the portrait. Lally had swiped it from her sweetheart's pocket. Love did strange things to people.

The interior temperature of Le Sentier was a medieval sixteen degrees centigrade, and she'd advised everyone to bring a jersey. She was wearing a short jacket with an inner pocket, which was why she felt the vibration of her phone against her ribs. Yves? Making her excuses, she went to the ladies' loo to check.

It was another message from Ash. *Have you called Jonny Taubier yet?*

Was he demonstrating that he could reach into her world any time he liked? An irrational part of her mind clung to the idea that this was all a bad dream. Ash would come back, opening his arms and telling her he'd been a fool. Overworked and overwrought. Deleting the message, Hope ran cold water over her hands, then stared at herself in the mirror. You have blue-grey eyes, she told herself, but isn't there a speck of green in there too?

Her phone vibrated with a fresh message. It was from Claudia. *On our way but Yves says, please order for us.*

They arrived five minutes after Hope returned to her seat. Seeing them come in together, Claudia helping Yves off with his jacket, made her flinch. Her jealousy shocked her. Was this what they called 'rebound'? Only when Claudia pulled a chair out for Yves did Hope realise that his right hand was heavily bandaged. 'What happened?'

'I got on the wrong end of a piece of glass. Blood, ambulance, a lot of fuss.'

'At Le Chat?'

'Uh-huh.'

'He needed stitches,' Claudia cut in. 'He phoned me to pick him up. Course, he can't drive now.'

'We came by taxi,' Yves said. 'Silver lining, means I can drink wine.'

'Except you're on antibiotics, so you can't.'

'Ha. Watch me.'

They sound like a married couple, Hope reflected with a panicky flutter. 'You won't be driving for a while, by the looks of it,' she said.

'No. I'm grounded. I can't paint, either.'

Her heart plunged. Oh, no. 'You can still be our teacher?'

His eyes held reproach and a dose of teasing. 'I can teach, just can't do anything with my right hand. *Tant pis*, that includes driving into Lazurac.'

'OK. I can pick you up every morning.'

Yves glanced around at his audience. 'Or you can bring everyone to La Cachette and I'll teach them at the top of the windmill.' This was greeted with whoops of enthusiasm.

'D'you have a stairlift, for TJ?' Paloma asked.

'She's so funny,' her brother hit back. 'I can climb a windmill so long as I take it a stage at a time. Did we order yet? Do we get to eat, ever?'

Hope had ordered duck confit for them all, with side salads and *roste*, grilled bread rubbed with garlic and duck pan-juices. Yves chose the wine, and bottles of Côtes de Gascogne arrived, white and red, and Diet Coke for TJ, who resisted the catcalls of his compatriots.

He hit back. 'I am what I am. Wine gives me heartburn.'

Hope found a moment to snag Yves' attention. Despite Claudia's tutting, he'd poured himself a generous glass of Merlot. 'What actually happened?' she asked.

He said, 'There is a gap in Inès and friends' "Memories of

Resistance" exhibition. And a nasty bloodstain on one of Jeanne's tablecloths. That is all I am saying.'

'You can't button up on me. I want to know.'

'I'll tell you when we're alone.'

'When's that likely to be?'

He lifted his glass and narrowed his eyes at her over the rim, but he didn't offer an answer.

33

The day after their meal, Hope drove her guests to Saint-Sever for lunch in the market square. Goldie and Paloma went off to hunt out vintage jewellery, TJ chose to sit under an umbrella and catch up on his emails, and Paloma stayed in the shade with a novel she was engrossed in. Hope welcomed the chance to wander, in company with her own thoughts.

She wasn't intending to seek out Manon's stall, but there it was, laden with bygones. Manon was perched on a high stool, flicking through her phone. She glanced up and saw Hope. The way she got off her stool and moved a vintage patchwork suggested that among the pre-loved treasures lurked something she would rather Hope did not see.

Hope waited until a customer came up. With Manon's attention on a possible sale, she moved casually to the stall. Many of the artefacts were familiar. That heavy-bottomed kettle would struggle to find an owner. The old smoothing irons would make excellent doorstops, but were overpriced, in Hope's opinion. What was new was a cardboard box with twenty, maybe thirty, little fat books inside. Manon was spreading out a threadbare quilt, giving the patter to the would-be buyer –

'Such patient work... fabrics cut from old dresses and skirts. You won't find another...'

Hope pulled the box towards her. The spines of the books were stitched with twine, bringing to mind a young woman sitting on her bed under a sloping roof, surrounded by squares of paper, plying a darning needle. Hope picked one out and opened it at random. What she saw took her breath.

'They aren't for sale.'

Manon was at her side. Hope held the book up. 'This is Lally Shepherd's. These are her working drawings.' The subject matter – an all-too-recognisable windmill – left Hope in no doubt.

Manon gave a dismissive shrug. 'They're not signed. You can't prove whose they are.'

Hope didn't need proof. A quick way with line, a deftness in the execution. It was the work of someone who drew every day, for years. On another page was a view of a distant mountain range which Hope herself had seen from Lally's studio. 'Does he know you have them?' Yves, she meant.

'Just go.' Manon snatched the sketchbook from her, replacing it in the box.

Hope went and bought an espresso from a coffee shack and sat down in the shade. Taking out her phone, she called Yves. He didn't answer, so she left a voice message. 'I'm at Saint-Sever and you need to get yourself here.'

Nothing to do but drink her espresso and see if he picked up her message.

Hope used the time to read a new email from her contact at Lost English Painters. In the subject line was written, *Heading down the rabbit hole.* Hope's interest in L.L. Shepherd had prompted the professor to delve into the archives of the auction house he occasionally consulted for.

Some years back, he'd helped value a probate sale, when the auction house was selling a lady's lifetime collection. *She was an*

avid collector of art and everything art-related. I don't think she ever
threw anything away. See attachment.

It was a flyer advertising an exhibition at... 'Oh, wow.' At the Julien Marshall Gallery, on Boulevard de Courcelles, Paris 8. Her helpful friend had mentioned an exhibition in his first email to her. The date on the flyer was June 1972, when Lally would have been in her late fifties. Hope was typing a reply when a voice interrupted her.

'*Salut, Madame.*'

She turned in her seat. Noah Taubier was thrusting a plastic supermarket bag towards her.

Scenting some kind of Manon-inspired trickery, she asked, 'What's in it and does your mother know?'

'What you looked at before, the little drawing books. I heard you and my mum arguing just now.'

Hope took the bag. By the weight of it, it was the whole boxful. 'I can't accept them,' she said, 'unless you've paid for them. Or I should pay.'

'They're for Yves.' Noah dropped his gaze. 'Mum stole them. She took loads from Yves' house when he was away...' He gave an awkward jerk. 'I hid stuff under my bed, but she found it.'

Hope made a fast decision. 'OK, but if she realises this box has gone, make sure Yves doesn't get blamed.'

Noah nodded. 'Is his hand all right now?'

'You know about that?' But of course, Noah had come into the café with his mother. 'Sit down.' Hope pointed a bossy finger at the second chair. 'Tell me everything.'

Noah began at the point where Hope had left the café with her American guests. He had heard Yves ask politely for the picture of his grandmother to be taken down. 'My great-aunt said no.'

'Great-aunt,' Hope interrupted, 'being Inès?'

'*Ouais*. She said to Yves, "Together, these pictures tell the story of Lazurac's Resistance. You cannot whitewash truth."'

Yves wasn't having that. 'What's truthful about a defence-less woman being dragged by a mob?' It was perpetuating a gross abuse. Giving legitimacy to violent injustice. 'Without context this picture is nothing but pornography for every *misérable* in town.'

'*Misérable* – every outcast?' Hope queried the word, but Noah nodded, apparently certain. Yves had once left her a note talking about *existential tristesse*. So, maybe.

Noah continued: 'Then Great-Aunt Inès says, "It was 1944. Our boys were murdered. You expect people to forgive and forget?" And Yves shouted back, "What about the men who sided with the Germans?" He was losing his cool. "I don't see their pictures up here. Or the Milice who enforced the rules, saving the Nazis the trouble. Why aren't you displaying them or the respectable folk who loaned their homes to German officers?"'

Noah's reedy voice was no substitute for Yves in a fury, but Hope could easily imagine the café falling silent, his accusations finding every eardrum. He had pointed to the photograph of his grandmother, singling out two stocky figures looming over her. 'What about Alain and Étienne Taubier, who sold flour to the Germans while their neighbours went hungry? My grandmoth-er's punishment was a put-up job. After the war the Taubiers carried on a vendetta against Lally. They're still doing it only now they have me as a target.'

One of Inès's companions had intervened at that point, implying that Yves was seeing conspiracies where there were none. It only fuelled Yves' rage.

'He roared, "You come to my place and see for yourself the barbed-wire fence that's been put up, but this isn't about me. My grandmother was tormented in front of her neighbours – *by* those neighbours – and it went on for years. She was assaulted, abused, and some pig took a picture of it. And you want to put it up on the wall?" He ordered my great-aunt to take the photograph down.'

'I take it, she refused?'

'I think she would have done,' Noah said, 'only my mother had to butt in, telling Yves that people needed to know what happened in the past. Maman told him, "That picture is a feminist statement."'

'Oof.' Hope made a painful face. She expected to hear that Yves had cracked the picture over somebody's head, or over the back of the chair, but according to Noah after an astonished pause, he'd burst out laughing.

'He said, "Fuck's sake, Manon, one for the sisterhood?" That's when he called them all "*misérables*". Jeanne, the café owner, said if we didn't shut up, she'd ban us. Then she called an ambulance.'

'The word is "*mysogyne*",' came from behind Hope's shoulder. 'Not "*misérable*".'

Hope hadn't seen Manon's approach.

'Noah, go mind the stall,' Manon directed her son with a jerk of her thumb. As Noah shambled away, Manon took his seat. 'Yves called that photograph misogynist, and in a way he is right. The punishment given out to women who fraternised with Germans was far more brutal than that given out to men. Inès doesn't see it, but I do because I *am* a feminist.' Manon lifted her chin, as if she expected pushback from Hope.

Hope's response was to think back to Yves' bandaged hand, and what must have been a bloody trip in an ambulance, and ask, 'Did you stab him?'

'You think I'd pull a knife on him?'

'I wouldn't be entirely surprised.'

Manon Taubier leaned closer. 'If you think a punch to a muscular belly is the same as a stabbing, you are stupid or grew up wrapped in cotton wool.'

'Neither,' Hope said lightly. The carrier bag full of sketch-pads was pressing against her ankle. So far, Manon hadn't seen it. 'You didn't stick up for him, did you? Or for Lally, whom you claim to have cared so deeply for.'

'I didn't stab him,' Manon said stubbornly. 'The glass on the photograph broke. Noah bandaged Yves' hand with a tablecloth and Jeanne is furious. So now I'm banned from Le Chat too. Yves Ducasse is trouble. I warned you.'

'And the photograph?' Hope asked, as Manon got up to leave. 'Not still on the café wall, surely?'

'Aunt Inès took it home.' Manon tossed her braids and the beads woven into their ends clicked. 'Yves is in denial about his grandmother. She wasn't simply a German's whore, she sent Lazurac men to their deaths. Maybe you can help him see it.'

'Don't you ever wonder if there might be more to the story?'

'There's plenty more and it is even worse. Lally Ducasse was a more-than-decent artist. Whether she was an equally good human being is quite another question.'

'It is a question I'm going to answer, and I look forward to sharing the results with you,' Hope flung as Manon walked away. She could chalk up a small victory; Manon hadn't noticed the sketchpads. She finished her coffee, gathered everything together and went to find her guests. It was obvious Yves hadn't got her message and it wasn't until ten that evening and she was brewing herself a last cup of peppermint tea that he finally got back to her.

He began by apologising. He'd slept virtually all day. 'Did you know you shouldn't drink wine and take antibiotics?'

34

'Idiot,' Hope replied, ridiculously glad to hear his voice. 'Claudia said it first, but you weren't listening. Is she around?' She tried to sound casual.

'No, and she's a bit depressed. Taking her kids to her ex and the ex's new woman being there.'

'I can empathise.'

'What time are you all arriving tomorrow for the first tutorial?' he asked.

'Mid-morning... but I've just thought. You don't have enough easels for everybody, do you?'

'I don't have five, no. You can use Lally's. I mended it. But you'll need to bring the rest.'

Hope knew she wouldn't get four easels and as many passengers into her car in one trip. Her solution was to say she'd whizz them over separately, first thing. 'If that's all right?'

'Sure. I'll give you coffee. Why did you want me to come to Saint-Sever, by the way?'

'I've got a present for you.' Hope couldn't wait to see Yves' face when she put the bag in his arms. She ended the call, before she ruined the surprise. In life as in art, seeing was better than hearing second-hand.

Next morning, she drove towards Varsac-les-Moulins through a pearl-and-chiffon sunrise. As windmill sails appeared above the trees, she said out loud, 'I saw those once, long ago. Just as now.' The impression was there and gone, like a moth flitting past the windscreen.

Yves was waiting for her outside. He hardly glanced at the bulging bag, saying, 'I hope you don't mind company.'

'Oh. OK.' She hadn't wanted to share this moment with anyone but him. Mitzi ran out barking. Hope saw no sign of the dog's owner. Inside the windmill, she put the bag down, and her laptop, which she'd brought along. 'Is Mitzi "the company"?'

'Uh-huh. Claudia went off on her bike at four thirty this morning.' Yves put cups under the espresso nozzles.

'I like having my own personal barista,' Hope said.

He held up his bandaged hand. 'Took me ages to get the lid off the coffee beans. Is my present in that bag?'

'All in good time.' She powered up her laptop while he made their coffee left-handed. 'Where is Claudia off to so early?'

'Beauville. It was beautiful this morning and she decided to go before the heat set in.'

'You, erm... waved her off?' Hope despised possessiveness, but she had to ask.

He brought over their coffee, and a plate piled with his customary sticky pastries. 'I did,' he said. 'I slept badly last night. What happened in Le Chat churned me up and my cut is hurting. So, when I heard the dog barking, I got up and there was Claudia, pumping up her tyres.'

'Outside your caravan?'

'Sorry, did I miss out stage directions?' He sat down, giving her a measuring look. 'I got up, put on some clothes, walked out. Yes?' His eyes glinted. He sensed her jealousy.

'Yes, all right.'

'She was going to leave me a message to let the dog out, but I said, "Claudia, my friend and guest, allow me to look after Mitzi for the morning. It will be a pleasure to have some company."'

'Understood.' She bit into a pastry. 'I must go to the cash and carry,' she said, inviting a change of direction.

'I'll take you. Or you can drive me. Come on, what's in that bag? I'm assuming it is linked to Saint-Sever and somehow to Manon?'

'You're psychic, obviously.'

'No, yesterday was one of Manon's days to be at the market there. I also got a garbled text from Noah. Cut to the chase, Hope.'

'Something else first.' She opened yesterday's email, from Lost English Painters, turning the laptop so Yves could see the attachment.

'Some background,' she said. 'I've linked up with a professor who does consultancy for a London auction house and he knows of Lally and admires her work. Some years back, he prepared a collection for sale. Its owner had passed away, and they got everything she'd ever acquired, including this...'

Julien Marshall Gallery
Boulevard de Courcelles, Paris 8
23rd to 30th June 1972
Work by L.L. Shepherd
Private view 6 p.m.
Friday 23rd June by invitation only

'I knew there had been an exhibition way back,' Yves said. 'It was going to be her relaunch, only something went wrong.'

He sat back. 'Julien Marshall... *that* Julien, who comes into her book, I guess.'

'Has to be. His family lived in Paris and Pauline worked for them.'

'And the eighth arrondissement is *plus chic*,' Yves agreed. 'Lots of money there.'

'This flyer proves that Julien got through the war, and he and Lally stayed in touch.' When Yves continued frowning at the laptop screen, Hope added, 'What went wrong? Wasn't the exhibition a success?'

'I only ever heard Lally speak of it once.' Yves rubbed his chin. He hadn't yet shaved. 'A throwaway remark, followed by a shudder. What I can say is, inviting my grandmother to Paris for a big fuss would be like throwing a ball for a donkey and expecting it to fetch. She always had a morbid fear of Paris. She never went back after the war.'

'Because...?'

'Of what happened. Before you ask, I don't really know what that was either. I don't know what led her here to the Gers, to Lazurac. She took refuge next door, at La Sanctuaire, but how she found it, I don't know.'

Hope could offer an answer to that. 'Otto gave Lally the address of a safe house and the woman you call "Old Madame Taubier" could have been the admirer Lally mentions in the memoir. Otto wanted Lally and Pauline to have a bolthole if things went wrong for them.'

'So that's how she came,' Yves said thoughtfully.

'If staying here in Varsac-les-Moulins, hated and victimised, was preferable to going back to Paris, then what happened there must have been unspeakable.' Hope closed her laptop. 'I googled the Marshall Gallery, and it closed down a decade or so ago. Julien might be alive.'

'It would be worth trying a search for him online. Now show me my present.'

Hope untied the bag's handles and spread it wide. 'Noah smuggled these from under his mother's nose. Manon doesn't yet know.' Feeling he should be left to make the discovery in private, she pushed back her chair. 'I'll get those easels out of my car.'

Hope brought them in one at a time. Yves, engrossed in one of his grandmother's homemade sketchbooks, offered to help but she declined. 'I need the exercise and we don't want to split your stitches.' The book balanced in his bandaged hand looked absurdly small.

After four trips up and down stairs, she was ready to sit down to finish her cooling coffee. 'Well?' The sketchbooks were now in three neat piles.

'They're from early in the war to 1965,' Yves said. 'Some scenes I can interpret because they're of La Cachette. There are drawings of my mother as a little child.' He sounded almost drunk, and Hope guessed that pleasure and sorrow had created a strong cocktail. 'Others... I don't know. I don't know where they were done.'

'And there must be more,' Hope said. 'You told me that Lally worked solidly for half a century.'

That brought a slight smile. 'It would be too much to expect everything to survive.' His hand covered hers. 'Thank you, Hope.'

'Thank Noah. I dread what his mum will do when she works out they've gone.'

'Oh, she will go nuclear. But not with Noah.' He gave a resigned shrug. 'The worst she can do is kill me.'

Hope noticed how he cradled his injured hand. She offered to help him change his dressing; perhaps she sounded too anxious because he said, 'I'll let Claudia do it. You need to go home and get your people ready for their first art bootcamp.'

'Bootcamp?' That wasn't encouraging.

He laughed. 'Joking. I'll be gentle.'

Two hours later, she was back with her guests and a crate of art materials. It might not be bootcamp, but it felt like a moment of truth. The first hands-on moment of Eat-Sleep-Paint-Gascony. When she'd discover if Yves had talent as a teacher, or the patience.

And it was her moment to draw again. To find out if the artist-self that she'd put into mothballs ten years ago wanted to come out and play. It was why she'd come to France, after all. It was also why Lally had come to France.

As she stood in front of Lally's battered A-frame easel, her pulse began to drum.

Yves was at her shoulder. 'Well?'

'I've got artist's block.'

'There is no such thing.'

'I'm terrified.'

'Then feel the fear. Who are you trying to impress, me? Them?' He meant the others.

She stared at the white art paper in front of her. 'A smaller sheet would have been less intimidating,' she muttered.

'Tear it up, then.' He sounded brusque. Bossy. It was like the first week of art college again. *Stop being precious, you're not here to make pretty pictures.* 'If Lally could draw every day when her life fell into a sinkhole, you can now.' When still she hesitated, he made a noise of irritation. 'Go down to the gallery. There's something that might inspire you.'

Glad to escape, she did as he suggested. In the gallery, she stepped into a cone of light. Yves had cleared space on the wall and set up a projector. One of Lally's sketches was cast onto the white wall, showing every pencil mark, scuff and line.

The scene was some kind of courtyard, women standing in line. Some wore coats and hats in styles of the late 1930s. Others had scarves tied around their heads. Their posture was cowed, or was it that they were cold? You could tell that they were standing in snow. Some had no boots, but what looked like strips of blanket tied around their shoes.

At each end of the sketch were armed guards, clutching guns. The caption read, 'Winter 1940'.

That last page of Lally's memoir had been dated early December 1940. Lally had been washing up in the kitchen, on Rue du Maine. A knock had come at the door. Was this what happened next?

Yves joined her. Without turning, she said, 'This isn't in Paris.'

'I don't think so.'

'I'm guessing she never did get a safe train out.'

BARBED WIRE AND FALSE NAMES: MEMOIR OF AN ENGLISH GIRL IN OCCUPIED FRANCE

'Lally? There are policemen here to talk to you. They're in the entrance lobby.'

With these words from Dorienne, the world as I know it stops dead. In the lobby I find Norma-Rose Foster and, for once, she has nothing to say to me. Two policemen in snow-flecked capes stand between her and the door. Seeing me, one of the policemen checks a notebook. 'Lavinia Shepherd?'

Oh, good grief, he's the policeman who stopped Pauline and me the day we returned to Paris. He ticked us off for not knowing about the curfew. Did we present fake identity cards on that occasion? I can't remember.

Avoiding his eye, I acknowledge that I am Lavinia Shepherd. He notes this down. He then tells us we are to accompany him to the *commissariat de police*. It's the other side of the river. We have five minutes to pack a bag.

Norma-Rose finds her voice. 'For what purpose?'

To sign a register, we're told.

'But we sign a register every day, at the Kommandantur.'

'A different register.'

'Why must we pack a bag?'

A shrug. 'Maybe you're going elsewhere. *Uh?*'

'What kind of "elsewhere"?'

'No more questions,' raps the officer. They don't have to tell us anything.

Sensing the mood turning, we go silently upstairs. Norma-Rose peels away to her room, and I take the narrow flight up to the top. There, I try to make wise decisions about which clothes to take. How long will I be away, a few hours, overnight? Remembering how much I'd wanted my coat when sleeping outdoors in June, I take it off its hanger. I pack my warmest jersey and change my indoor shoes for sturdy brown ankle boots. I pack stockings, changes of underwear. Pencils and my home-made sketchbooks go into the bag. Anything official these days involves hours of waiting.

I always wear the Grey Eyed Dove next to my skin. Even so, I pat the place on my blouse to make sure.

I hesitate over taking the *carte d'identité* in Marie-Laure Ducasse's name. I should have burned it by now, but I could never bring myself to do that. It's so imbued with my last days with Otto. Tangled in decisions, I don't hear the door opening until it is shut harshly. It's the policeman who asked me my name. The one who accosted me and Pauline on the bridge.

He's taking off his cape. He's undoing his flies. 'Get on the bed,' he says. I stare, my mind refusing to comprehend. He whips the identity card out of my hand, his free hand still working at his trousers.

'Whose is this?'

'A... a friend's.'

'Don't lie. It's fake, isn't it? I could report you as a spy. D'you know what they'll do? Put lit cigarettes under your tongue and pull your fingernails out, till you confess to anything. Get on the bed.'

A flash of defiance holds off the moment. 'I wouldn't confess.'

'Course you would. You'd tell them the names of everyone you know who listens to BBC propaganda, the names of all your friends who are hiding in cellars and attics. That girl who was with you that time – you'd hand over her name and address.'

'I don't know her address.' But I do know the penalty for listening in to the BBC. I have no choice. I get on the bed and close my eyes. It's rough but it's quick, I'll give him that.

Afterwards, he watches me adjusting my dress. I tell him to go. I must wash. 'Give me five minutes.'

He repeats, 'Five minutes,' and leaves.

I'm shaking so badly. The last man who touched me was Otto. That policeman has scoured a precious memory, and I must scrub his scent off me.

There's no bathroom up here, just my jug by the washstand. I pour a disinfectant called eau de Javel into the water, and douche again and again. I straighten my clothes and put on an extra cardigan. My movements are jerky and the five minutes are up before I'm ready. What else will I need? Money. My correct identity papers, of course. The Arpège goes into the bag and finally, obsessively, I check that the Grey Eyed Dove is still anchored inside my blouse, behind the pocket. I'd cut my hand off rather than lose it. I ram on a woollen beret and find my gloves. In a final act of defiance – insanity? – I cut a slit in the lining of my travel bag and slide Marie-Laure Ducasse's identity card inside.

I go downstairs, and they shove Norma-Rose and me out into the icy cold.

At the commissariat, we join a throng of women, mostly middle-aged or older, and the cacophony of English tells me all I need to know. This is no mere registration exercise, it's a round-up. The first comers have all the seats, so I sit on my bag. I'm hurting between the legs and sitting makes it worse, a pain like acid burn, cramp in my abdomen. I'd give anything for a hot bath.

I distract myself by discreetly scanning the faces of my fellows. In a corner sit a group of nuns in starched wimples. They've dragged nursing sisters from the bedsides of the sick. A governessy-type in grey serge knits methodically in another corner, tears sliding down her cheeks. A group of street-walkers trade profanities.

For hours, we wait, hungry, thirsty, bursting for the toilet, the holy and the respectable, the outcasts and the sinners. The Germans shout at us in garbled French. 'Stand over there! Stand over here!' 'Make groups of six!' 'Mothers with children this way!' 'All of you with dogs, send the dogs out. You cannot take them!'

Take them where?

My name is recorded by a German military official at around two in the afternoon. At last, I am given permission to go to the toilet.

Seven hours after we arrived, I and Norma-Rose along with six other women are chivvied into the back of a police van. There's a crow-black flock of them. We're driven away at speed without concern for our comfort. I try to keep track of the streets through the tiny square of back-door window, giving up when my forehead makes sharp contact with metal.

Twenty or twenty-five minutes later, we're prodded out into the freeze. I thought I was scared before, but my blood shunts in my veins as I recognise the fan-shaped glass frontage of the Gare de l'Est. This railway station serves the east of

France, Switzerland and Germany. Not Germany, please, God.

'Lally?'

I turn, and my heart stops. A fragile-looking woman is being helped out of the latest van to arrive. Her voice flies towards me. 'Lally! Lally! It's me. It's Pauline.'

I stare at her, open-mouthed. A sympathetic policeman is attending to her but Pauline looks scared half to death. I can understand why: she is at least six months pregnant.

36

HOPE

She was back at her easel. At Lally's easel, still to make the first mark on her paper.

Yves had set up a table of items for them to sketch and paint. Wine bottles, a knocked-about aluminium coffee pot, tin mugs and saucepans. He'd provided a vase of majestic hydrangeas from the garden.

'Take something from the table. Take a pencil, or charcoal, or paintbrush and paint. Whatever medium you like best. Draw without overthinking. Just start.'

Everyone looked dubious. *Be like Lally*, a voice whispered in Hope's head. Lally sketched through the darkest moments of her life. That line of women in the courtyard, some smart as couture house models, others resembling bag ladies, suggested that the German net had scooped up rich and poor alike. That drawing was of a prison, and Lally had survived.

Yves walked from one person to the next, moving and shifting their easels with his good hand. 'Now you can't see each other's work. Find yourself something to draw, take it to your table. Let's do some fast work. You have ten minutes.'

He paused beside Hope. 'You're staring into space.' The

Grey Eyed Dove was in its usual position, on the front of her shirt, and he nudged it with his knuckle. 'To be a serious artist, you must draw every day. No excuses.'

'Slave driver.' She fetched the hydrangeas, liking their bold shape. Placing the vase a couple of feet away, she trained her eye on the contours of the air around them. *Don't draw what you think you see, draw what is filling the space.* She made the first marks, writing the name 'Lally', which she then rubbed out with her elbow. Then 'Pauline'. She rubbed that away too. It messed up the paper nicely.

After ten minutes was up, Yves told them to turn their paper around and start again. 'This time, we'll draw until you all want to stop. I shall draw too. *Au boulot.*' To work!

This time, starting felt easier, Hope's brain sinking into a mindful lull. So much so, she jumped when Yves came up to her shoulder and said, 'Lunch.'

Stepping back, she felt the urge to rip the paper away from the board. It was all wrong.

'Don't you dare,' he said. 'I can see exactly the moment you loosened up. You must keep every sheet and see yourself evolve. And you will.'

'Evolution is slow. Can we grab a moment after lunch?'

'Sure.'

Goldie claimed his attention. She wasn't happy with what she'd done either. Hope left them to it.

Everything for lunch was in Yves' fridge. He came down while she was unwrapping cheeses.

'That seemed to go well,' he said.

'You're a natural teacher. Precisely the right balance of bossy to inspiring.'

'Thank you,' he said. 'After you went yesterday, I was here for hours, looking through those sketchbooks and you know one thing that struck me? There is not one drawing of Pauline.'

'They met up again, at a moment of crisis.' Hope explained

that she'd read ahead in the memoir. 'I stole a march on you, but I'll let you catch up.'

'Not one drawing of her,' he repeated. 'Lally loved to sketch people, friends and strangers.'

It did seem odd. The women had shared so much. Perhaps Pauline hadn't wanted to be drawn. 'Do you know where that prison lineup was?' Hope asked, the one he had projected onto the wall.

'I looked up British women under the occupation and I think she was interned at Besançon. That's eastern France, about two hours' drive from the Swiss border. Two hours on modern roads, in a modern car. The way it was reported in the British press at the time, you'd think they'd been shipped off to a health farm.'

'A health farm with guns and guards?'

He nodded. 'Even there, she kept a sketchbook in her pocket, the way a chain-smoker always has a packet of cigarettes. She was still doing that in her seventies and eighties and because she never had much money, she'd cut the edges off letters from the bank, or the backs off envelopes, and use the paper. Her pencils were sharpened until they were shorter than her thumbnail.' He put a piece of spiced sausage in his mouth. 'After the war, Lally could never eat dark bread or anything served with a ladle. And she never slept on her back. Never.'

'Why not?'

'The war screwed with her head and her digestion.'

They heard TJ yelling from the floor above, 'The Yanks are coming.'

Yves kissed her cheek. 'Can you get away tonight, and come back here?'

Exactly her thought. 'I'll bring the memoir and read to you again.'

'Yes. I don't mind you being late. Or staying, if you want.'

. . .

After dinner that night, worn out from an emotionally draining day, Hope opened her laptop and, once again, researched the name 'Julien Marshall'. This time, she found a mention of him on a museum's website.

> *In the summer of 2002, having graciously opened his historic château near Poitiers to share his private art collection, Julien Marshall spoke at length about the period after the Second World War, before the dawn of 1950s modernism. A vigorous ninety-year-old, Monsieur Marshall held his audience spellbound with his evocation of an era when he might drink coffee with Picasso in the morning, take lunch with René Magritte and meet Marc Chagall for a stroll in the Jardin des Plantes in the afternoon.*

A few more clicks and up popped an obituary. Julien Marshall, long-time owner of the Marshall Gallery and patron of many artists, had died in April 2004 at his château on the banks of the River Clain. That clinched it for Hope. It was the same man. The Renault Nervastella had been heading for the Marshall family château in the same area.

'At least you survived,' she said, addressing the distinguished-looking face pictured alongside the editorial. 'You saw out the war, and the long years beyond. Did you get married and have children?'

Actually, no. The obituary stated that Julien Marshall had remained unmarried, and his estate had passed to the descendants of his two sisters. Ah – the sisters would be the little girls Pauline had been au pair to.

It was fully dark when Hope picked up her car keys and the memoir. Yves had sounded sincere when he said he didn't mind how late she arrived. At the front door, she noticed a white package, opened it and what fell out jolted two words from her.

'Oh, crap.'

The DNA kits had arrived and a match would prove they were cousins. 'No match' would open the door to feelings she was trying very hard to ignore. Was now the moment to remind Yves that he'd changed his mind about the test?

'If not now, when?' she muttered, and took the kits with her.

BARBED WIRE AND FALSE NAMES: MEMOIR OF AN ENGLISH GIRL IN OCCUPIED FRANCE

I am reunited with Pauline and we are on a train, leaving the city. Just not in the way we'd hoped.

We sit on slatted wooden seats in a compartment with twelve or more others. Norma-Rose has seized a space between a nun and a wealthy-looking woman, forming a predictable new allegiance. As if it matters, as we're all equals in misery. If one of us needs to stand, everyone must stand. I thought of jumping out as we left the station, literally throwing myself onto the track. However, Pauline was clutching my hand and anyway, as I discovered, the train doors are sealed with festive wreaths of barbed wire. They cannot be opened. Nor the windows. My need for the lavatory becomes an obsession. There are no facilities.

There is so much I need to ask Pauline and in the consternation that breaks out as a woman on the bench opposite suffers an asthma attack, I throw the first question. 'Who is the baby's father?'

Pauline looks at me as if I have asked her to quote Einstein.

I have done the maths. If, as I think, she's six months pregnant then she conceived early in June. 'Is it Julien's?' She was so in love with him. The last time I saw him was at Easter when he was expecting to be mobilised and was in uniform. He assured me that he'd visit Paris whenever he could get leave. 'If only for a bath.' I remember him giving a smile that was both boyish and absurdly confident. So... if he came back in June, there was time for him to have impregnated Pauline in the room at Dorienne's. 'Is it his?'

Pauline gives an abrupt acknowledgement. 'I – I didn't realise I had caught...' She swallows. 'Caught for a baby until I fainted one morning. Someone fetched a nurse, and the only thing she asked was if I was married.' She looks up, suddenly defiant. 'I said yes, my husband is a victim of this war.'

'Does he know?'

'Julien? No. What could he do anyway?'

I feel sad for her and him too. Yes, Julien was one of those impossibly spoiled French eldest sons for whom the world is a gilded playground. But there was a kindness to him, a talent for seeing the best in people. The asthmatic woman on the bench opposite is gasping into a brown paper bag, aided by a pair of nursing nuns, and we fall silent, our heads nodding with the bucking of the train. Questions continue to crawl over me like ants and I can't bear it after a while. 'Pauline, where did you get to that day? What happened?'

'At Gare Montparnasse? What happened to you, Lally?'

I tell her I narrowly escaped being crushed at the ticket counter, then hunted for her high and low. 'I walked the whole day, hours and hours, and only stopped because I'd have got caught out after curfew. Where the hell did you go?'

'To Bordeaux,' she says.

For a moment, I'm dumb. When I speak, it is in a voice I hardly recognise. 'Without me?'

She nods, biting her lip, which, I note, has a ragged sore in the corner. Because we've had no fat in our diets for six months, we all have flaky, dry skin and brittle nails. 'I saw you getting onto a train,' she says. 'I thought you'd left me!'

I didn't get onto a train, what's she talking about?

'I got mangled in the crush too,' she explains, 'I had to crawl out through people's legs. By the time I was safe, you'd gone. I ran up and down, and out onto the street to see if you were there. I ran all the way around the station, nearly fainting with the heat. I went back inside and I saw a woman with yellow hair, with a bag just like yours, heading for the Bordeaux train we were supposed to catch. I saw you climb on.'

'It wasn't me.'

'She looked just like you. She even walked like you. I jumped aboard a second before it pulled away. Then I couldn't find you there either.'

'Because I wasn't there.'

'I thought you'd left me. I was so frightened.'

'What happened at Bordeaux?' I refuse to be moved by her tears. Until now, I'd not realised how angry I am with her. 'Did you find Otto?'

She nods. 'At the cathedral, that night.'

And? My face, the way my breath dips in and out of my throat, makes a nun opposite glance at me anxiously.

'Otto made me come back to Paris. He said you'd be at Dorienne Ponsard's.'

'He was right. And yet you didn't come.'

'Because… I couldn't.'

That fuels my anger. 'Sure, it's a brothel, so what?' That gets the nuns staring. Norma-Rose sends me a furtive, threatening look. 'You could have knocked on the door or shoved a note inside.'

'I didn't feel well enough to walk so far.'

'Posted a note, then. Nothing stopped us posting letters within Paris. I've been worried day and night.'

'I'm sorry, Lally.' She breaks down so violently, I think she's going to either collapse or be sick.

'It's all right,' I tell a nun who is about to come over, and I take Pauline in my arms. 'You're making yourself unwell. There, there. I would never intentionally abandon you, you know that.' I ask where she's been living. Not under a bridge, I hope.

Between sobs, she tells me, 'At the YWCA, on the Champs-Élysées.'

'Why haven't I seen you at the Kommandantur? I've been registering there every day since September.'

'Oh... medical exemption.' She clasps protective hands to her stomach. 'I had to be certified by a doctor every month but it meant I didn't have to go in person.'

That explains why we haven't bumped into each other. She was living on the Right Bank, me on the Left. It's almost funny, Pauline ending up at the Young Women's Christian Association and me at Dorienne's. Almost funny, but not quite. 'I'm surprised the YWCA let you stay, unmarried and expecting.'

In reply, Pauline peels the glove from her left hand, displaying a gold ring.

'Ah. Clever.' That's when I notice Norma-Rose Foster staring at Pauline's swollen belly, and at the ring. 'Put your glove back on,' I whisper. The last thing we need is that woman unleashing her spite.

I've been holding back from asking about Otto but it bubbles out. How was he, what were his plans when they met, how long did he stay in Bordeaux?

'His plans were the same,' Pauline says, speaking like me, behind her hand. 'To cross into Spain, make for Portugal and then England.'

'Wasn't he worried about me?' I need to hear that he was out of his mind with anxiety.

She nods. Yes, he was worried. 'And someone stole his Grey Eyed Dove, which he felt was a bad omen for his trip. He was firm with me, I had to go back to Paris and find you. He wants us to go to that safe house he told you about.'

A bit bloody late for that. Why, why, did Pauline not make contact in the summer, when we might have had a chance? 'He told you about it too?' I ask.

'I overheard you and him talking about it in the café, on our way to Gare Montparnasse. You still have the address?'

I do. I'm wearing it, face down beneath the insole of my boot.

'Left or right boot?' she asks.

'*La gauche.*' Left. I've always been a Left Bank type.

'Did you look at it, Lally?'

'The address?' I hesitate because the Grey Eyed Dove burns like hot iron against my conscience. I wish I had never taken it and am frightened that by doing so, I've undermined Otto's resolve. Guilt and self-loathing won't make me incautious, however, and I fudge my answer. 'Otto trusted me not to peek.' Inside my shoes, my toes curl.

Our barbed-wire train tears through the winter evening as we head east. By dawn, white-capped mountains fill our view and we see our own breath when we speak. We've reached the département of the Jura, closer now to Switzerland than to Paris. We arrive in a town called Besançon long after dark and are off-loaded into a snowstorm.

We stumble onto the platform. All those hours on wooden slats have taken the feeling out of our legs. We are prodded into line, shouted at in French and German, and the older women are marshalled into waiting trucks. Some of the shouting men wear French military uniforms but are under German command. There's no transport for us younger ones. We are herded through a town whose residents gaze down from their balconies and top-floor windows, their faces washed with lamplight.

Something hits me hard on the cheek. Above my head a woman shrieks, 'Bitches! Spies!'

They hate us, but what have we done? We plod uphill towards a massive edifice perched on the summit. I thought Paris a trap, but this place, which I hear being referred as the Citadelle Vauban, looks exactly like a prison. It is absolutely unprepared to receive hundreds of women in one go.

After an hour kept standing outside, shuddering with cold, we are split into groups of about forty and chivvied up stone steps to an upper level. Our clumping feet and the breathing of the less-fit are the only sounds we make. We're too wretched to express anything. I hear one of the French guards, 'trustees' as I will learn they are called, saying this was an army barracks in Napoleon's time. I don't think it's been touched since.

Our dormitory is a long room with a cement floor and a beamed ceiling infilled with mouldy, cracked plaster. There's a coal-burning stove in the middle and, of course, there's a rush towards it. It's not lit. Metal beds, in pieces, are stacked at one end of the room and it dawns on us that we are expected to put them together. Nobody has the strength. For our comfort on our first night, thin straw mattresses are laid out. I get myself and Pauline adjoining berths halfway between the stove and the door. Norma-Rose and the 'respectable' woman she sat next to on the train, who wears a fur hat and coat, battle for the mattress nearest the fire.

We are ordered back outside to queue for our meal. If we want a fire, we will have to fill buckets with fuel. 'You need to organise teams,' a trustee tells us, with a glint of malice. 'Or we can do it, but you have to pay us.'

Nobody steps forward. He shrugs. 'Then freeze, bitches.'

What I am starting to understand is that France, traumatised by its violent defeat and the collapse of the army it hero-worshipped, has to blame somebody. That somebody is us British. They believe our troops abandoned theirs at Dunkirk, opening the way for the Germans.

Mine and Pauline's neighbours on the mattresses are robust girls in their twenties, wearing breeches which smell of stables. They come from Longchamps, the racecourse. Like Pauline and me, they stayed too long – though in their case, it wasn't the men they loved who pinned them, it was the horses. Love is dangerous to women.

At some point after a miserable supper, I drift into a kind of sleep, until I sit up, making sounds of disgust. So is everyone else. I hear screams.

Somebody lights a candle and we discover our pillows and blankets – and hair – are crawling with red-brown mites that have tumbled from the cracked plaster above. They're all over the floor, our blankets, and the walls.

Nobody sleeps after that.

Next morning, we pool money to bribe our jailers for fuel and get the stove going before we head out into the courtyard to queue for breakfast. I'm worried about Pauline. She should never have walked last night, but she chose to, rather than risk being split from me. She's stopped shivering, which is never a good sign. I send her back to bed, telling her I'll bring her food to her. Stamping my feet on the frozen slush in the courtyard line, I look up at the forbidding walls, the barred windows. If she's got her timings right, her baby will arrive early in March. She can't give birth here. We must get out. I cannot envisage Pauline surviving winter, or a newborn baby surviving a week in Frontstalag 142, which is what the Germans call Citadelle Vauban.

When I get to the end of the queue, I'm asked where my pan is. And my bowl. Apparently, we were meant to collect cooking and eating utensils from a store, but I was helping build the fire and didn't hear the order. Norma-Rose passes me on her way back, walking carefully so as not to spill the contents of her pan. I look at her helplessly. She looks away.

I grab two hunks of mouldy rye bread and return to find Pauline curled up under her thin, grey blanket. When I lower myself onto my mattress, I smell a familiar smell. I grew up where the river lapped the back wall of our yard. I know the stink of rat when it's nearby.

From now on, every sound will feel like a threat.

Again, that night, the bugs patter onto our faces, stinging as they hit our skin. I hear Pauline slapping at herself, making an appalled burbling noise. All evening, she's been cradling her stomach, in pain from eating unfit bread. Last the winter? She won't survive a month. Stupid idiot girl, getting herself pregnant. There's only one person in the world who can help her and her unborn baby survive.

That person had better learn how this place works and make a plan.

38

Before first light, I'm up, creeping between the rows of mattresses to where Norma-Rose snores. I steal her saucepan and snap off its handle so she won't recognise it. I hide the handle under my mattress. At least now I can get some proper food. My bag sits like a faithful dog beside my pillow, and I reach inside for an extra pair of socks. I wish I'd packed more woollens.

Needing occupation, I take out a sketch pad and draw the sleeping forms around me until my fingers seize up from cold.

A bell clangs. Rumpled figures stir, blankets are unwillingly pushed aside. Nobody gets undressed for bed or even takes off their coat. I read the same dawning despair on every cold-mottled face. This isn't a nightmare; it hasn't gone away.

I get Pauline up and to her feet. She mustn't give in.

'Where's the toilet?' she asks.

Ah, the great existential question of our time. So far, we've used buckets but this morning, we discover the sanitation block.

Our latrines are long trenches with wooden boards flung across. Forget privacy. Imagine, housewives, mothers, lady-teachers and nuns being faced with that. It's a feat of acro-batics to get on and off without slipping into the trench, and as it fills – I won't go on. Suffice to say, some slipped and some did not get out.

Pauline can only use this ersatz lavatory with help. Fortunately, the Longchamps girls are good sports, and unlike most of us, not that bothered about outdoor ablutions. Being with horses all day long must blunt the sensibilities. But those poor nuns. They go in threes so two can hold a blanket as a privacy screen for the third. The trustees come to gawp. They find it hilarious, snooty British women being humiliated.

One man in particular makes my skin crawl. He has a name, no doubt, but Pauline and I christen him Raton, 'young rat', because of his narrow face and protruding front teeth. He has other rat-like qualities, such as lurking near the dormito-ries at night, and moving around close to the walls. I see him looking at me. I don't know what he wants. Yet.

After our introduction to the latrines, it is time to queue for breakfast. Norma-Rose is vociferous about the disappear-ance of her pan. She knows someone took it. Her eye finds me. Nonchalantly, I turn the pan in my hand to display the bracket that held the handle.

I like to think of myself as a good person. I grew up in a community where we looked out for each other. Norma-Rose has proved herself willing to watch me go hungry, so I'll keep her pan and she'll have to ask for another and clean it, and perhaps pay precious money for it. It's called survival.

Our breakfast is soup made from last night's leftover bread and what I think is potato water and boiled-up cows' feet. I don't think the feet were washed before they went into the cauldron. It is beyond revolting.

After that, our first task of the day is to assemble our beds. They're bunks, and I will sleep on top because, obviously, Pauline can't climb. 'You'll get the benefit of the rising heat,' she says sheepishly, handing me a cross-piece to screw in.

'There isn't any heat to rise.' I'm worried about our coal supplies. We burned all today's ration last night when it dropped below zero outside. 'Being on top means I get all the bugs.'

'I'm sorry.' She really means it, and I suspect she's referring to more than just the sleeping arrangements. If she had been willing to press on after the air strike, we might now be home in England. But then, I wouldn't have seen Otto again. I ask Pauline what he said to her before he left for Spain. 'Anything about him and me meeting up again in London, when all this is over?'

She shakes her head. 'He saw me to the station, put me on the train back to Paris, and then went. He's one of those men who don't chatter when their minds are heavy.'

That's true but I don't like that Pauline has discerned it. It's my prerogative to know my man's odd quirks, and to forgive them. I heave Pauline's mattress onto the lower bunk, then roll mine so I can lift it onto the top. As I reach up, a griping pain gets me in the abdomen. Mouldy bread is doing horrible things to my insides and from being assaulted, I've developed a bladder infection.

After a rest, I get my mattress in place, but I forgot the pan handle. It's on the floor and Norma-Rose notices as she's passing. She picks it up, stares at me.

'Filthy thief,' she shrieks. 'You did steal my pan! You dirty little whore!'

'I'm none of those things,' I say in a voice that reaches to both ends of our dormitory. 'I've had lovers, but never been paid. Unlike some…'

She throws the handle, towards me but not *at* me, and I know I've found her Achilles heel. In the midst of all this filth,

Norma-Rose Foster has been reborn as a virtuous woman. Fine. So long as she leaves me alone.

Why did I imagine she would? That night, as we head towards our beds, she comes up behind me and whispers, 'I knew I recognised your pregnant friend.'

'Pauline? How?'

'From Rue du Maine. She and a man hired that top room of yours, several times.'

'One time,' I correct her. 'Dorienne told me anyway.'

'No. Five or six times. They couldn't keep their hands off each other, panting their way up the stairs.'

What Norma-Rose is saying is not just crude, it is impossible. Pauline comes from primly genteel stock, white gloves and church flowers. She'd no more make a public display of lust than she'd step into an abattoir. I tell Norma-Rose to stop being disgusting.

'I'll tell you what's disgusting,' the woman leers. 'Going upstairs with a German. Called himself a poet though there was nothing poetic in the way they worked those bedsprings. Thought you'd like to know, Lally.'

It's all I can do not to tear Norma-Rose's brassy curls from her head, dark roots and all. I'm stopped by the urgent need to relieve myself, which I control by clutching the side of the bunk.

'Lally, what did she say?' It's Pauline, already in bed, her blankets wound so tightly around her she resembles a wooden clothes peg.

'She said you came to Dorienne Ponsard's place, with a man.'

'That's rubbish. What man?'

'Oh, let me see. Yes, Otto, I think.'

Pauline's silence lasts perhaps a second longer than it should. It's followed by a furious denial. 'You don't believe her, do you? She is so spiteful.'

Oh Pauline, why did you need to think about your answer?

At the same time, I cannot allow this monstrous suspicion to enter my mind. If I do, I will begin to hate Pauline and everything I believe in, and yearn for, will fall apart. It comes down to survival for me, for her and her baby. So I say, 'Yes, she's the most vindictive person I've ever met.' I feel my heart freezing over and to distance myself from the sensation, and from the stinging pain in my bladder, I dab my neck and wrists with perfume, putting on too much. Norma-Rose, who is watching me, wafts at the air in an exaggerated way.

'One smell to cover another,' she says loudly.

I get through the days after that by drinking litres of water and drawing like a demon. My art links me to the woman I was a week ago. I take off the Grey Eyed Dove, hiding it in my bag, under my clothes. I can't bear to feel it on me. When I go to the toilet, it's like passing razor blades.

At this point, I believe nothing can get worse. I'm wrong.

Fifteen days into our imprisonment, rodent-toothed Raton makes his move.

39

It is a few days before Christmas and I am in the corridor outside our dormitory, shivering in the darkness. I've discovered that if I lean into a stone window embrasure, I can see the lights of the trains arriving and departing in the lower part of town.

By staying awake night after night, I've learned the timetable and formed the basics of a plan. A train leaves Besançon bang on five every morning but Sunday. It heads south, probably for Lyon.

If we could get on it, me and Pauline, we'd be free of this hellhole.

On this particular night, I am envisaging the two of us slithering and stumbling down the long hill to the station... by some miracle we've passed through the locked barriers that stand between us and the road... we have our bags and just enough money.

Deep in my fantasy, it takes me a few seconds to attune to a scuffling sound. I go still, every inch of me listening. A torch dazzles me, and before I can get away, I'm hauled from the embrasure, my shoulder smacking violently against its edge.

'Caught you! What are you doing, what are you watching?'

'The moon and stars,' I gasp. It's Raton. I know his wheedling voice, even in the dark. The pain in my shoulder is excruciating.

'It's against rules to be out of your dormitory at night. I can have you put in solitary for this.' Raton pushes me up against the ice-cold wall, one hand to my throat, the other trying to get my skirt up. 'You want me to do that, or are you going to be nice?'

The threat, the groping touch, and I'm back in my room at Dorienne's, being told to get on the bed. Something snaps inside me. It was going to, sooner or later. I keep Norma-Rose's pan handle in my pocket, mostly to scrape ice off the window glass, the better to see the trains. In a single movement, I jab the ragged metal into Raton's thigh. He howls, clutching the top of his leg. I tear back to my bunk.

Pauline wakes. 'Lally?'

'Shush. Play dead.' I cannot break the habit of protecting Pauline. And now I am protecting a baby who may not be Julien Marshall's at all, but the seed of someone far dearer.

I'm hopeful, when morning comes, that Raton will decide that discretion is the better part of valour and leave me alone. And indeed, over the following days, he keeps out of my way. Christmas arrives. Our dormitory sings carols, hunched around our stove. On New Year, we link hands and belt out 'Auld Lang Syne'. Dysentery sets in and a hundred women succumb before 1941 is a week old. Bronchitis and pneumonia have been culling our numbers since we arrived, but nothing sweeps faster than dysentery. It is so cold in our quarters, the water you bring in freezes overnight unless you are right by the stove.

As a consequence of the outbreak, a new infirmary is opened. It's run by German Red Cross nurses and though it's a long way from adequate for the number of patients, I scent an opportunity. It isn't guarded, you see. Pauline gives birth in two months. The clock is ticking.

Fleshing out my plan keeps me preoccupied and I forget about Raton.

January shuffles out, February comes with arctic snow which piles up on the window ledges until we can hardly see out. Escape in this? Not a hope.

Around the 21st or 22nd of the month, I'm queuing for our food, carrying a metal jug in the hope of cadging some hot water for Pauline. It's too bitter for her to come outside and she's desperate to wash. The wind razors off the top layer of snow and hurls it in our faces. Even the guards in their great-coats and mufflers look miserable as they pace and stamp across the courtyard.

Norma-Rose, directly in front of me, wears stolen pelts. The woman she fought for a place by the stove died a few days ago, before a doctor could be fetched. Norma-Rose wasted no time stripping her of her furs. The coat's collar has frozen into peaks, like silvery pen-nibs. I cannot resist; I strip off my gloves and draw her, my fingers too numb for subtlety and it's more a cartoon than a sketch. Norma-Rose resembles a mountain gorilla, her feet splayed for balance. A German guard comes alongside, glances at my page, and gives a faint snicker. His reaction germinates an idea.

I have discovered two important things since we got here. Firstly, that the trustees will get you anything within reason if you can pay. That includes what passes for coffee, decent wine and tins of anchovy fillets, which Pauline has developed a craving for. The second is that just as the girls at Dorienne's loved my sketches, so do the women here. They buy them, paying in money or cigarettes. As I don't smoke, cigarettes are tradeable currency.

With this in mind, I start to sketch the German guards. I begin with the one who laughed at my picture of Norma-Rose, giving him as heroic a profile as I can. We don't get elite troops here but the rejects, the ageing, the drinkers, the ones unfit for campaign duty. They're still Nazis of course, but they're potential customers. I let him see my picture, and hey presto, he says, 'You give?'

I say, '*Zehn Zigaretten.*' Ten cigarettes.

We agree five. Next day I repeat the process with one of his chums. Again, five cigarettes. And so it goes. A few days later, I'm finishing off a picture of a newly arrived German guard, adding some inches to his shoulders and taking a few off his waistline under his greatcoat, when I notice Raton looking at me.

I immediately put the pencil and sketchbook away and look straight ahead. When I sneak a glance, Raton is talking to the man I was drawing. They look at me. A moment later, that guard is striding towards me, roaring, '*Was zum Teufel machst Du da?*'

What the devil am I up to! He demands to see the sketch.

I'm shaking so badly, I drop it as I take it out of my pocket. He picks it up, looks at it and snarls, 'This is of me?'

Raton picks his way over and tells him I have made a record of every guard, and that I spend my nights logging the arrival and departure of the trains. 'She's a spy,' he says in terrible German.

I'm dragged across the yard, my arm all but wrenched from its socket. Inside the guard room, the reasons for my detention are given to the officer in charge, in German that is too fast, too enraged, for me to follow. My sketchbook is presented. I'm realising that a new detachment of Germans has arrived, and that this place is a punishment posting. These new men hate us. I try to explain; nobody listens. I'm thrust along a stinking passage down steps and into a cell with a barred peephole in the door.

Unthinkingly, I grasp the bars and scream. They're frozen. Ripping my palms away leaves skin behind. The door is locked on me.

I shout and plead, knowing I won't survive if they leave me here overnight.

40

HOPE

It was midnight when Hope drove up to La Cachette. Her headlights briefly illuminated Yves' Land Rover and Claudia's car. The gîte was in darkness. Good. Though why should she feel the need for secrecy? She was a single woman and not in her most desperate moments did she believe her relationship with Ash was retrievable. He'd accused her of infidelity and sent her a bill for their time together. That was about as 'over' as it got. So why was she cutting her engine with a sneaky look towards the gîte's upstairs windows, fearful in case a light went on?

'Hard-wired social conditioning,' she muttered, dropping her car key next to the gear stick. She picked up her bag containing the memoir. Her permit to pass.

She made her way to the static caravan, knocked, then tried the handle. The door was open. 'Hello?' The interior smelled of something woody and resinous, which she associated with the burning of joss sticks. Which in turn, she associated with a desire to cover up the smoking of a little light weed. Though why Yves should care about hiding it, living out here... 'Hiya?'

'Hope?'

'Who else? Unless you have an ant-trail of women coming to see you at midnight.'

'I'm in here.'

'Here' was his bedroom. He was lounging against woven cushions, wearing tracksuit bottoms and a tee-shirt with the silhouette of an elephant on the front. She told him he looked like the rajah of La Cachette.

'You can be what you like when you live on your own.'

'As I'm discovering.'

He held out his hand. 'Come and be my queen for the night. There's a bottle of red and two glasses in the lounge. I could get them, but you're on your feet and my hand still hurts.' He held it up. He'd changed the bandage at some point. Or Claudia had.

'I'm not going to help you sink a bottle,' she said. 'I have to drive home.'

'The glasses are tiny.'

They weren't, but she poured small measures. Yves made space for her beside him, and she wriggled into a comfortable position, her back against cushions smelling of sandalwood. Placing the memoir on the bedcover, she shared her most recent finding. 'We're a decade too late for Julien Marshall.'

Yves made a sound of regret. 'Pity I didn't know before. I could have found him, maybe visited him.'

'D'you think he ever came here?'

'He could have.' Yves seemed to be dredging for memories, like fishing for old tyres at the bottom of a lake. 'I came home from school, one time. I'd have been about thirteen, and I went into the house, where Claudia is staying, and nobody was there so I walked up to the studio.'

'In the windmill.'

He nodded. 'There was my grandmother with an elderly man, both of them sitting beside the wooden crate that acted as her tea table. It wasn't tea on the table, it was a carafe of red and a very full ashtray.'

'Lally didn't smoke. It says in her memoir. At Besançon, getting paid for her sketches in cigarettes gave her a side income.'

Yves sniffed. 'She started at some point, and once she started, couldn't stop. When I gutted the windmill, the plaster that came off the walls was yellow with nicotine. She developed neurotic habits. Smoking, drinking, stitching the spines of countless sketchbooks. Her way of coping.'

'With the loss of your mother?'

'In part. Maman died and, suddenly, Lally was parent to a tiny baby. I might as well tell you, since somebody will, my mother took an overdose. She got really down after I was born but wouldn't seek help. I think – believe – the overdose was accidental.'

Hope breathed out her sadness at hearing this. 'How grief-stricken Lally must have been.'

'Yes, it was tough. One after the other, she lost everyone she cared about.'

'What makes you think the visitor that day was Julien Marshall?'

'Hmm. Maybe because she beckoned me in and said, "Yves, here is one of my dearest friends from when I was young, and the most forgiving man in the world." Something like that. That makes me think it was him.'

'In what way was he forgiving, d'you suppose?'

'If the Paris exhibition he went out on a limb to stage misfired, costing him a bomb.'

That fitted. 'What did he say?'

'Nothing much to me. He was friendly, but I was too young to think that conversing with old men was interesting. I left them to it. Afterwards, Lally cried for days. If it was Julien, they would have talked about Victor, Pauline, Otto. Other friends.

Lally was part of a Bohemian crowd. Who knows what scars it opened up for her.'

'Victor and she made contact again, didn't they?'

Yves gave a dry laugh. 'Totally. Between them, they created my mother. Otto... as I said to you before, if Lally mentioned his name more than once I don't remember. As for Pauline' – he took a swallow of his wine – 'we must keep reading the memoir. Lally said once, "I was lucky not to be sent to Ravensbrück." That was a concentration camp many women ended up in, the SOE agents and others the Germans caught out in clandestine activities. She said, "Pauline saved me on two occasions and, all the time, I thought I was saviour-in-chief."'

That was a turn-up. 'Pauline was the reason Lally got interned in the first place,' Hope pointed out.

Yves screwed up his face. 'I looked again through those sketches and there's still none of Pauline. Quite a few done at Besançon. The women, views from the windows. One or two guards. It's a unique archive but not a few pages have been ripped out.'

'I might know why Pauline was deleted. Someone dropped a bombshell on Lally.' Hope gave a potted version of the chapters she'd read that day. 'Lally's arch-nemesis had caught Pauline and Otto sneaking up the stairs of the house on Rue du Maine. Or so she claimed.'

'You mean, as lovers?'

'Definitely not as painters and decorators.'

'My God.' Yves whistled. 'So Pauline's baby...'

'Don't know yet. Lally obviously made that connection. She's heartbroken, trying to cope with betrayal while also forming a plan to spring them from prison. Right now, on the page I'm on, she's in the cooler.'

'In jail?'

'In some kind of coalhole below ground level, and if she doesn't get out, she will quite literally freeze.'

'She must have, or I would not be here.'

'Have you got a reading lamp?' Yves' bedroom lighting was heavily on the side of sleep or seduction, certainly not designed for reading a faded memoir. 'Before I start, can I, er...' She found herself ridiculously tongue-tied and, in the end, shook the DNA kits out of her bag onto the bed.

Yves picked up one of the packets. 'Right. OK.'

'You don't have to but, you know...'

'Maybe tomorrow?'

Clearly, he'd changed his mind. 'Fine. Or we just forget about it.'

'I mean, we've both drunk wine. Won't that affect the results?'

'Good point. Tomorrow it is.'

'How long for the results to come?'

'Ten days-ish.'

'That's enough time to finish the memoir, and maybe by then, the results will be redundant.' He suggested she lend him her phone. Shining its torch as she opened the memoir, he invited her to start reading at the point where Lally was incarcerated, and fearing she'd never get out.

BARBED WIRE AND FALSE NAMES: MEMOIR OF AN ENGLISH GIRL IN OCCUPIED FRANCE

Listening for any sound, terrified I've been forgotten, takes me to the edge of despair. I'm reaching the point of 'move or die' so I march on the spot. Later, I discover that guards were sent into our dormitory to confiscate my sketchbooks and search out proof of espionage. That's how Pauline learned what had happened and followed them to where the camp administrators are housed. Shy, self-effacing Pauline demanded an audience with the prison Kommandant himself, only to be told he wasn't present that day. She could have left me to my fate. Instead, she does something that only a naive, heavily pregnant Englishwoman could do. Gets down on the floor with her legs out straight and refuses to move until she has seen somebody in authority.

They bark at her to get up and attempt manual force. At which point, she delivers, in English, a tirade on civilised behaviour, or the lack of it. She then goes into labour. I should say, she feigns it, but with such gusto, it convinces those military gatekeepers who immediately send for the prison's second-in-command.

I, meanwhile, remain in ice-bound solitary, marching like a wind-up tin soldier. I overdo it, and my abdomen ties itself into an agonising knot. I thought I'd got over my bladder infection but fear has brought it back. The pain is so crippling, I go down on my hands and knees and pant. In this state I'm discovered by the guards who have come to take me to be interrogated by the deputy Kommandant. They have to half-carry me.

I am taken into an office adorned with swastika banners each side of a portrait of Adolf Hitler. A man in officer's uniform sits behind a desk, hands placed either side of a pile of items I realise are my sketchbooks. Not just the one I took out with me this morning, *all* of them. They've raided my travel bag, upturned the mattress of my bunk. This man will know, then, that I have been sketching his soldiers at their duties for quite some time.

A magnificent fire crackles in the grate, its heat almost overwhelming me. Another twist in my abdomen leaves me breathless and I hardly answer when the officer demands my name.

'She is Lavinia Shepherd,' my escort tells him. 'She was seized this morning on suspicion of spying and creating images liable to create dissent and aid enemies of the Third Reich.'

The man behind the desk has a double braid on his tunic collar. The tunic has wide, padded shoulders. It is a uniform to create an air of authority and strike fear. He tells the guards to wait outside. I am now alone with him and he introduces himself as Oberleutnant von Salzach, second-in-command of Frontstalag 142. 'The Kommandant is absent, and so you have me, Fräulein Shepherd. That makes you very lucky.'

Gritting my teeth, I tell him that I'm not a spy. Even if I

was, what information could I send out? 'That it's wretchedly cold, and that your soldiers have red noses, either through drink or frostbite?'

'That in itself is incendiary information.'

We are speaking German. I had begun unthinkingly and I'm less rusty than I would have supposed. He has a pleasant voice, this von Salzach. A different accent to Otto's and it is many years later that I discover him to be Austrian, though that's not why I'm lucky.

I point at the tower of my sketchbooks. 'How is it you have those? I hid them under my mattress.'

'One of your dormitory companions revealed their whereabouts.'

Pauline? Please, no. Because at that moment, I know nothing of her role in getting me out. 'A pregnant woman brought them?'

'Ah, no. Though a very pregnant woman made a scene outside. You are lucky to have so good a friend. You might have frozen to death.'

I nod. One half of me is still ice-cold. The other half, nearest the fire, is cooking like a crumpet on a grill. 'Who betrayed me?' I'm determined to know, though I'm halfway to guessing.

'A lady in a fine fur coat.'

Norma-Rose Foster. 'She's hoping I'll be punished and either it will put her in good odour with you, or she can steal my boots.'

'What she has done instead is bring your talent to my attention.'

'I'm not a spy.'

'Well, you may be but you are also an artist, Fräulein Shepherd. Your work impresses me. I spent some time in Paris before the war, observing and studying. At home, I am also a painter. Where did you train?'

I tell him about the private art school in Durham, where I was helped to get a place by the middle-class spinster my mother worked for prior to her death, and who retained a kind interest in me. I mention that I sat as a model at art school to help pay my fees but not that the life-drawing tutor took a shine to me, and asked to draw me in private, and then more. Instead, I jump to Paris, where I arrived in 1933, enrolling in evening classes at a painting academy. 'I modelled there, too, to earn my way. I learned as much from watching other painters work as from doing it myself. I always drew. Even here, in this vile place, I draw. It's like breathing. If I stop—' A fresh surge of pain gives my words authenticity. Von Salzach fetches me a chair.

'You are ill?'

'Probably. Undoubtedly.'

'Can I get you something, water?'

Water, no. I won't be able to keep it down. From being half-frozen, I now feel feverish and flop on the seat. 'What are you going to do to me?'

'Nothing. Unless there is something you would like me to do?' I must look scared, or disbelieving, because he says, 'I am not a monster, Fräulein Shepherd. I am loyal to my Führer' – he acknowledges the portrait behind the desk – 'but I do not agree that it involves crushing the human spirit. I have enjoyed looking through your pictures and will like to see more. Tell me what you need most.'

42

HOPE

'Here's my theory. Lally falls for von Salzach,' she said, lowering the book. Yves looked sceptical. Hope persisted. 'What if von Salzach fathered a child with her and that's why everyone called her a collaborator, a traitor. Because she had a child with the enemy.'

'My grandmother was in love with Otto. She wouldn't tumble into an affair because a man in uniform was nice to her. Have you given up believing that Lally is your grandmother?'

'I'm keeping an open mind and putting my faith in DNA.'

'In which case, consider the fact that Pauline is pregnant, and will give birth in a matter of weeks. See where I'm leading?'

'Perfectly, except what are the chances of the poor little child surviving in that place?' Hope touched his face. 'Do you take after your grandfather Victor Ponsard?'

'A bit, from pictures I've seen, though it's hard to know because he grew a bushy beard at some point. I look like Lally.'

'You have her irises. Green as jade.'

His eyes, which until now had been lazy with wine and lack of sleep, flared open. 'You know what they say about jade. It's not always green.' Their gazes locked. 'Hope?' It was a seeking of permission.

Permission denied. She took their empty glasses and set them on the floor. 'It's not going to happen, Yves.'

'No? I've wanted you since I first saw you,' he murmured.

'Not true. You wanted Lally's portrait.'

He agreed. 'OK. But I wasn't seeing you then. Next day, when I came to your door, and you slammed it on me, it was a punch in the gut. I wanted the picture, sure, but even more to get to know you, this blonde hurricane. I knew I'd screwed up. When you gave the picture back, I was devastated. I thought – now I don't get to see her again.'

'The Grey Eyed Dove links us, and Lally and Pauline. However the story ends – and we don't know, do we?' He said something in reply, which Hope didn't hear, her attention snagged by sounds outside. 'Is that a car pulling up?'

Yves turned to the window beside the bed and raised the blind. 'Claudia must have been out and come back,' he said. 'I didn't hear her go.'

Claudia's car had been in its usual place when Hope arrived and she was saying this when they heard glass breaking.

Yves was off the bed in a second, Hope following.

The area in front of the windmill was awash with head-lights. Yves tore past her, returning the way he'd come. Hope gasped as she saw flames in front of the windmill. Had they heard the gallery window shattering? Passing a small, grey van with its engine running, she grabbed the fire extinguisher from her car and was on her way back with it when Yves reappeared with one of his own. Together, they jetted the flames until only wisps of smoke rose from a pile of debris.

Boots crunched on the gravel behind them. 'You can put on a turn of speed, the two of you. I'll give you that.'

'Manon?' Yves gasped. 'You did this?'

'Stay away from my son.' Manon Taubier strode up to Yves

and pushed him in the chest with the heel of her hand. She turned on Hope. 'You too. I don't want to see you sniffing round my stall, ever.'

Yves got between them. 'Don't you dare threaten Hope. You're insane, Manon. You could have burned down my windmill.'

'I was burning rubbish.'

They were interrupted by Claudia coming out of the gîte, Mitzi barking in her arms. She was wearing a thick jersey over her pyjamas. 'I've called the police and the fire brigade,' she said.

Manon spat contemptuously. 'I'll have gone by the time they find this dump.'

'I photographed your number plate,' Claudia told her and when Manon flung an insult back, said calmly, 'I may be all that and more, but at least my vehicle MOT is up to date.'

The effect of this was astonishing. Manon ran to her van, flung herself into the driver's seat, wheel-spinning in a chaotic five-point turn before driving off in the wrong gear.

They all let out a breath. Claudia released Mitzi as Manon's headlights disappeared in the direction of Lazurac.

'How did you know her vehicle isn't legal?' Hope asked.

'I have the nose.' Claudia tapped hers. 'I didn't call the police, but Yves, I'm happy to be a witness.'

'Me too,' said Hope.

'Let her be,' Yves said. 'For Noah's sake.' He fetched a shovel and began to spread out the smouldering heap.

Hope joined him, only to shout, 'Stop!' What Manon had described as rubbish was several black binbags which had melted to reveal a hoard of small, stitched pads and dozens of black and white photographs. Hope picked out a photograph and shone her phone torch on it. 'Paris,' she said. 'Friends lounging outside a café. Oh my goodness...'

Yves came to peer over her shoulder. 'There's Lally and

that's my grandfather, Victor.' He pointed. 'Before he grew a beard.'

'You have the same look sometimes,' Hope agreed. 'The fellow sitting between Lally and Victor is Julien Marshall, I'm pretty sure.' The bone structure of the smiling young man was that of the distinguished gentleman from the obituary. 'And this man at the side, leaning in...?' Her pulse upped a gear. He appeared a little older than the others, his sensitive face marked with worry lines. His eyes were light-coloured under a mop of sandy hair. 'It's my dad,' Hope said in awe and disbelief. 'My dad, Joseph Granger, but younger than I ever knew him.'

'Then it isn't your dad, is it?' Yves said. 'I think we have found your grandfather.'

Claudia invited them in for hot chocolate. Hope drank hers quickly, then left, knowing if she didn't, she'd be too tired to drive. Confused or what... A fairground carousel was spinning inside her head. The night had involved smouldering chemistry between herself and Yves, quickly doused. Then a genuine bonfire and Manon's threats, ending with a photo of a man who was the spitting image of her father. Only the picture had been taken in the wrong lifetime.

At home, too twitchy for sleep, she made rosehip tea and checked her phone. There were five messages from Ash, the first four being curt demands that she message back immediately, the final one informing her that he was taking advice on 'the monies owed to me. Kindly advise on your intended payment date'.

Unequal to composing a reasonable reply, she opened a different message. It was from a friend of her London days, whom she hadn't spoken to since coming to France. She wondered what had inspired Katie McDougal to contact her now, out of the blue. It quickly became clear.

Hi Hunny, bit of a curveball, but I bumped into Ash in
Brighton, at a café with a woman he introduced as his business start-up partner. Bit freaked out bcs I thought you were
his business partner. WGO?

WGO meant 'What's Going On?'

Good question. Ash had told her he was staying in London
'with a friend'. Katie's message suggested the friend was female.
Sure, he was entitled to get on a train to Brighton and sit in a
café but not with a new business partner. Not when he had an
existing one: Hope. And a home, here.

Fuelled by herb tea and a simmering rage, Hope spent the
rest of the night creating a spreadsheet in which she itemised
every expenditure that had come out of her purse since they
moved to Lazurac, for which Ash was fifty percent liable. It
included a reasonable rental for the roof over his head. She sent
it to him, and sat back, surprised to discover that the skylight
above her head was milky pale. She went outside and watched
dawn seep through the shrubby borders.

Could Katie have got the wrong end of the stick? No,
because it was a stick with two right ends. Katie hadn't
mentioned if the 'start-up partner' had been young and attractive but Hope recalled the woman with great hair at Ash's
family barbecue, her arms looped around Ash's shoulders.
They'd both been smiling.

It made her think of that little gang at an outdoor Parisian
café table, the men in shirts, cravats and waistcoats, Lally in a
square-shouldered blouse, her smile vivid with lipstick. Pauline
was likely to have taken the picture. In fact, it was possible that
the photograph had been on the film she'd taken from her
camera before she sold it to the landlord. Lally must have
acquired it and kept it. It still felt extraordinary that Lally,
Pauline and Otto's story should end up here, hundreds of miles
away from Paris.

Stephanie's casual comment came back to her. 'Oh, *that* Lazurac? Isn't that where your dad wanted some of his ashes to go?' Why would Dad want any part of him to come here? Yet his second wife must have heard him say it. It was mind-bending. The more Hope discovered, the less she knew.

All right... start at the beginning, as Yves had advised, with a question and not an answer. What had made *her* choose Lazurac?

She and Ash had agreed, over a memorable Indian meal, that their favourite destination for relocating was south-west France. They'd both visited the region, and loved the scenery, the food. She vividly recalled the drive from Toulouse airport in a hire car. Ash had been at the wheel, and they'd been on their way to look at a property they'd found online. She remembered them rounding a corner, and seeing—

A windmill against a turbulent sky. The conical top and white sails catching sunlight flooding through thunder clouds. Something had clicked. She had seen it before. Not déjà vu, but factual reality. She'd seen Lally's windmill at some earlier point in her life. She just couldn't pinpoint when.

Not with her father, because he had never travelled outside England. Hope placed her fingers on the Grey Eyed Dove. For all his shame, his crippling fear, he'd kept this brooch. It was the link between him and his parents. He had given it to her, so a part of him must have wanted her to do what he never dared to do: search. Keep searching.

A courier rang the doorbell as Hope's guests finished breakfast. He had a box for her to sign for and she recognised Stephanie's hand in the heavily inked address. This was synchronicity in action. You think of the person...

Stephanie had wrapped enough brown tape around the box to bind an Egyptian mummy, and though Hope itched to cut into it, there wasn't time. Yves had texted, asking if she and her guests could delay their arrival at La Cachette until mid-morning.

Still painting out the scorch marks in front of the windmill.

It was now ten to eleven. She had done her DNA test and posted it. She wondered if he had done his or if Manon's shenanigans had wiped his promise from his mind. She'd remind him and offer to post it on her way home tonight.

'Ready in ten minutes?' she asked Goldie and TJ, who were the last at the breakfast table.

'No way. I need half an hour to put on my socks,' Goldie said.

As they trailed off to their rooms, Hope cleared the table and stacked the dishwasher. She havered between opening the box or reading another few pages of Lally's memoir.

The memoir won.

BARBED WIRE AND FALSE NAMES: MEMOIR OF AN ENGLISH GIRL IN OCCUPIED FRANCE

We need blankets, I tell Oberleutnant von Salzach. 'You know, don't you, that children and elderly women freeze to death overnight? And more coal. Better food, medicines, proper mattresses. And for those horrible bugs to be dealt with, the ones that drop out of the ceiling. They stink.'

'I understand.'

'And we need human conditions in the latrines. They stink too. And baths, please.'

With a flat palm, the deputy Kommandant pushes back this tide of impossibilities. 'I will find more blankets for your dormitory.'

'For all of us!'

'And I will ensure you have paper and pencils for your art, but do not sketch my soldiers.' He goes through my sketch-pads, ripping out everything depicting a German and feeds the pages into the blazing fireplace. Later, I will find out he missed a few. Deliberately? While his back is turned, I notice some cards on his desk. The word '*Arbeitsausweis*' jumps out. It means 'Work permit' and the top one bears an official stamp. There is a dotted line for a name to be filled in.

Two of those might get Pauline and me over the demarcation line. No waiting around for official passes to be issued or refused. I reach out. Von Salzach is still staring into the flames. He says, 'To destroy art is as bad as burning books.' Two are all we need – *do it, Lally*. Von Salzach turns back to me and I've lost my moment. To cover my horror at almost being caught, I ask for something else. 'My friend Pauline shouldn't be here, in prison.'

That brings a smile. 'Isn't that the opinion of you all, that you should not be here?'

True. 'But Pauline needs to be somewhere she can have her baby in safety.'

'Ah... the one who cries, with the smoky eyes? You have drawn her many times.' He finds a sketch I made recently. Pauline, curled on her bunk. 'May I keep this one?'

Oh, not him as well. I watched Julien fall under Pauline's spell, and Victor too. I didn't see it with Otto. I tell von Salzach he can have the picture. 'But will you get her out of here? She's frail.' I suggest he sends Pauline to the infirmary, with me as her attendant.

He will see what can be done. Before I'm escorted back to my dormitory, my somewhat thinner sketchbooks are returned to me, and I overhear him saying something to one of the guards. I hear the word '*Bad*'.

Bath.

In the dormitory, I can't climb onto my bunk as I'm racked with pain in my lower back. While I was with von Salzach, I could take my mind off it. Now, I gasp. Pauline, still rolled in her blankets, asks woozily what's going on. Norma-Rose comes up, her eyes darting as if she expects guards to come in any minute, either to take me away or her.

'What's wrong with you, then?' she asks.

I press my hand to my groin. 'Nothing. I and the Kommandant's deputy are the best of friends. Now stay out of my sight.'

Somebody gives me aspirin, which takes the edge off things for a while.

It grows dark, we've had our slop and potato supper, when a grim-faced German Red Cross nurse calls my name. I start to cry. I can't go back into that cell.

But far from being locked up, I'm being given a special privilege. How everybody's ears prick up! I can't resist glancing at Norma-Rose, who now looks terrified. She must imagine that I've seduced the second-highest-ranking German in the prison. Let her think it.

I must bring my sponge bag, I'm told. I'm escorted to the German nurses' section, shown into a bathroom, handed a small piece of white soap.

'You have half an hour,' the nurse says. 'You will find a towel there.' She points to a wicker laundry basket.

The bath is vast and when I turn on the taps, it sounds like a culvert disgorging floodwater. I could drown in there. Yes, there are towels in the basket. Damp and used, mingled with nurses' crumpled uniforms, no doubt on their way for washing. To my abused eye, they look pristine white. Peeling off my clothes, I cannot do justice to the sensation of hot water on my dry, goosepimpled skin. On my aching back, over my red-mottled knees. It is heaven.

I wash myself and my hair, I refill with hot water. I almost hear the minutes ticking away. Would it be so bad if I drowned?

Yes, for Pauline because I don't trust Norma-Rose Foster not to fall on her like a hyena and strip her of her few possessions if I'm not around to protect her. Has my request for Pauline to be transferred to the infirmary found fertile ground? If I'm allowed to go with her, I might be able to negotiate a transfer to lodgings in the town. We could stay until Pauline gives birth, which would be an easier route to escape. My ordeal has weakened me. I feel unequal to heroic action. The bathwater has dulled the pain in my back, but suddenly it returns. It's like a wooden wedge being hammered into my lower spine. I cry out, swallowing water before managing to grip the sides. At the peak of this agony, I let out a hideous scream. Someone rushes in and I'm hauled out, coughing and spluttering. The bathwater is violently red.

I come to in the infirmary. I've been granted my wish, in circumstances that are utterly bewildering until the German nurse who fetched me from my dormitory tells me, without inflection, that I have had a miscarriage.

'How long were you with child?' she asks in halting French.

I have no idea. It cannot be Otto's because the last time we made love was in woodland outside Orléans. The would be the beginning of July, and if I'd become pregnant then, I'd be the size Pauline is now. The only possible explanation is that the gutless policeman who coerced me in Dorienne's attic put a child inside me. 'Ten or eleven weeks,' I mutter. Near enough as makes no difference.

I let the blood flow, wanting only to be purged. I can't rid myself of the notion that I did something that made that policeman think I was giving him a come-on. Should I have looked more frightened? Or less? Why didn't I lock the damn door while I was packing my bag? Otto, I'm so sorry, so sorry. I am still locking out the truth of him with Pauline, taking the blame on myself.

I'm given a medicine that probably contains laudanum. I don't know how long I'm in that bed, dawn and dusk circling the infirmary and time unhinged. It's probably five days.

Pauline comes and sits beside me, or maybe I hallucinate her, until one day, I wake from deep slumber and there she is.

'Hello, you.' She's brought me the Frontstalag 142 version of a basket of grapes. A tiny, wizened apple. She has news. Thanks to my intervention, she got an appointment with the French doctor here. He's a prisoner of war, but lives in the town under some system of parole and is known to be sympathetic. He has confirmed she's unlikely to survive childbirth in this place, and that release is a priority for her. 'He sent me to the German doctor in charge here, and honestly, it was like being inspected by a Boy Scout. I suppose all the proper doctors are at the Front or looking after the officer class. Anyway, he agreed with Monsieur Huguet, the French doctor, and it's all down to you, Lally. Whatever magic you wrought with the Oberleutnant, it's got me a ticket out.'

'Where are they sending you?'

'I have a permit to cross into the Zone Libre.'

'Into the Free Zone?' I'm so relieved for her but envious too. A few days' coddling in the infirmary, warm and clean, with wholesome soup brought to my bedside, makes the prospect of going back to our bug-infested dormitory unsupportable. 'How did that happen?'

'You, my friend.' She lowers her voice. 'You made a conquest of Herr von Salzach. One artist to another.'

'Where in the Free Zone?'

'I'm not supposed to say.'

That's not good enough. 'I'll need to find you one day, so tell me, Pauline.'

Again, she equivocates. 'Of course we'll meet again. In Paris,' she says lightly. 'Spring, in the Jardin des Plantes. You'll bring a picnic and I shall be pushing a perambulator.'

I can't imagine a day when we're free to stroll through Paris again. 'Where are they sending you, Pauline? I want the town, the street, the house number.'

She presses my hand. 'Well, I told them I have a relation living in a village near Vichy who will take care of me.'

Vichy is the capital of the Zone Libre. 'What village?'

She puts a hand to her mouth. 'Grandeville. I know, terrible name. I made it up. But I have a permit to travel, so it doesn't matter.'

'In your condition, you shouldn't be travelling at all. How will you get there?'

'Train, obviously.'

'Pauline, you must insist I come with you. I can't stay here.'

She shakes her head. 'Some Red Cross workers are accompanying me,' she says. 'I can't suddenly produce a travelling companion.' She leans as far forward as her swollen belly allows. 'Of course you must get out, and now.'

Easy for her to say. 'I need a pass to get over the demarcation line and I can't just conjure one up.'

She suggests I try getting over the border to Switzerland instead.

I roll my eyes. Does she imagine I haven't run through every possible escape plan? The Swiss border is two hundred and fifty kilometres away and is heavily guarded. I'd be trekking through wintry foothills for days. 'You shouldn't be travelling as far as Vichy, Pauline. You're too far gone. I'll petition the deputy Kommandant to let you go to a house in the town and ask if I can join you.'

She shakes her head and it is Gare Montparnasse all over again. She's moving out of my reach. 'I'm not losing this chance, Lally,' she says earnestly. 'I owe it to my baby. I've brought you something.' Her coat is lying across her knee and she smuggles something out of the pocket. An identity card, mine – the fake one belonging to Marie-Laure Ducasse.

'*Dieu,* Pauline, put it away!' Two German Red Cross nurses are conferring over their notes on the other side of the room. Since first encountering them on the train from Paris, I've learned that these nurses are fully paid-up Nazis. Enemies in white aprons. 'Hide it, for goodness' sake.'

Pauline pushes the ID card into a travel bag she's brought in with her. *My* bag, I realise. It seems she's absolutely serious about me escaping now. Tonight. She tells me that while I was having my bath, Norma-Rose came to our bunk and asked to borrow my perfume. 'I told her, absolutely not! So she upended your bag, and the ID card fell out. Now she's got something on you, Lally. She demanded your bottle of Arpège to stay quiet.'

'She's not having it. Let her report me.'

'You don't mean that. She's trouble. Everything you need is right here, by your bed.' Pauline whispers that my coat is hanging up in a cupboard in the corridor. I don't need to go back to the dormitory for anything. She adds something chilling. 'Norma-Rose is telling the trustees that while you were living in Rue du Maine you listened to the BBC in your room.'

'Not in my room. And we all listened.'

'She's saying you would slip out at night and meet with communist spies. She's requested a meeting with the Kommandant. He's back.'

All because I stole the woman's saucepan! Unlike Herr von Salzach, the actual Kommandant is unlikely to take a sympathetic view of my sketching. Or of my supposed allegiance to communist infiltrators. I'll be back in that frozen cell. Or it will be deportation. They might interrogate me, and if Otto is not yet in a place of safety, I might say something that leads them to him. Pauline is right. I have to escape. I just don't know how because things are moving too quickly.

Pauline gives me her purse. 'There's four hundred francs in it. Enough for your train out.'

I ask how she got the money. On arrival here, she was pretty much broke.

'I sold my blankets.'

'Pauline!'

'Your sketchbooks and pens are in the bag. Like I said, everything you require. Don't forget your coat.' She pushes herself up with some effort. 'It's time I went.'

'Wait! Pauline, wait!' In the past, it's always been me pushing Pauline on, holding her up. Making the decisions. I can't believe I'm on my back, drained and weak, needing her. 'Tell me the truth.'

'What... about what?' Late pregnancy has put a little colour back in her cheeks.

'Your baby. Is it really Julien's?'

'Oh, not now, Lally.'

'Yes, now, or I'll scream. I'll scream that we're both communist spies.'

She plonks herself down again. 'It's his. He came home on leave. It would be early in June, I think. And we... you know.'

'In my room on Rue Monge?' I was often out, sketching by the river or in one or other of the parks. 'Or at Dorienne's?'

'No. Heavens, no. Neither. You know he has a flat in the eighth? I didn't say because I'm ashamed. I had such a silly schoolgirl crush on him.'

'Does he know he left you with a bun in the oven?'

She shakes her head.

'And you wouldn't lie to me?'

'If you're thinking about what Norma-Rose said, you told me yourself, she's venomous.'

'She recognised you. She was so specific.' 'German poet' was how she described Pauline's companion, creeping up the stairs at Dorienne's. 'How would she know that?'

'Because Otto was Victor's friend,' Pauline reminds me. 'Victor will have taken Otto to see his sister, won't he?'

I want to believe that my native mistrust has warped my thinking. But didn't Dorienne also mention Pauline visiting her house accompanied by a man she described as 'my brother's handsome friend'.

'They wanted a room. I was a bit shocked, which is quite something for me.'

I assumed she meant Pauline and Julien. But Otto also merits the description 'my brother's handsome friend'.

'Swear to me, Pauline.'

'It's Julien's child. I swear it, Lally.'

A nurse claps her hands. Visiting time is over. Pauline puts on her coat, belting it under her breasts as she hasn't a waistline any longer. What is it they say about babies in the womb? If it's a high bump all at the front, you're having a boy.

I flop back on my pillows and watch her go. I'm not sure if Pauline has saved my life or stuck a dagger into my heart.

When the lamps are dimmed and the nurses are dozing at their station, I push back my covers. My bleeding has all but stopped and Pauline is right, this has to be the night because once I'm deemed fit, I'll be sent back to my dormitory and be watched round the clock. Soundlessly swinging my feet to the floor, I reach for my moth-eaten bag. From its bulk, Pauline has rammed in everything I own. I grope around inside it, searching for the Grey Eyed Dove. I have never felt such need to hold it, to run my fingertip along the almost-invisible inscription. *Mit Liebe*, with love.

It should be at the bottom. But it's not there.

I can't risk a return to the dormitory. I have to leave but, without it, I feel robbed and naked. Like Otto when he discovered it gone, I fear it's an ill-omen for whatever lies ahead.

44

HOPE

Though Goldie and TJ had gone to their rooms for last-minute adjustments to their outfits, they didn't emerge until half eleven. And then Goldie couldn't find her sunglasses and Paloma had mislaid her shoulder bag. Hope texted Yves to warn him they were running late. They finally got going at midday.

Hope put the box from Stephanie in the car, saying to Yves when he came out to greet them, 'I'm relying on you to have a Stanley knife or similar.'

'I have everything,' he said. 'What's inside?'

'My father's documents, and other stuff, judging by the weight.'

They got to their lesson, only to break after an hour for lunch. Afterwards, Yves told everyone to wander around the garden and find something that inspired them. 'You will not be drawing it yourself, you will give it to one of the others. So be kind, and creative.'

Hope found a massive, rusty horseshoe leaning against a wall. It must have come off a drayhorse long ago. She caught Yves' eye. 'Got mine. Can we open the box now?'

'Sure.' He fetched a knife from his caravan and met her in the café.

Hope slit through the tape and opened the cardboard leaves. 'Oh.' She'd expected a stack of papers to sort through. What she took out could have fitted into a large padded envelope. The box's weight was explained when she realised that Stephanie had sent a wedding photo in a silver frame. Seeing her dad with shoulder-length hair, wearing an obviously hired suit and a kipper tie, brought a tear to Hope's eye. Her mum in empire-line satin, false eyelashes and kiss-curls looked incredibly young. And beautiful. The idea that Stephanie might have even considered throwing the picture out made Hope grit her teeth.

'I can see you in both of them,' Yves said. 'But you have your father's eyes.'

'Blue-grey. Oh, and here's his adoption certificate.' She would look at it later. 'Did you do your DNA test?'

'I did. I even drove out to the post office, so we'd get the results at the same time. Shocked?'

'Pleasantly surprised. In ten days, we'll know.'

'We'll know something. We won't know—' He was interrupted by Elkie Warberg coming up the café steps lugging an old pig-trough filled with a flowering succulent. 'Can I take this?'

'If you can carry it up the steps, you can, Elkie.' The others came in after her, bringing an array of found objects, and then it was back to work. Hope invited Yves to dinner at hers later. 'We can go through these papers afterwards, if you'd like.'

'Sounds good,' he said. He had something to show her too, something he'd retrieved from Manon's bonfire. It just needed a little restoration work first.

.   .   .

Yves helped her cook dinner and clear up afterwards. By eleven, they were alone, sitting each side of Hope's sofa. She angled a light on the adoption certificate. 'It's the one that was kept in a file at home. I sneaked a look once or twice, when I was little. It names him as Joseph Paul Granger. See what you think.'

Yves' eyes tracked across the columns and when he'd finished, he said, 'It says his date of birth is sixth of March 1941. It doesn't name his mother.'

'No,' Hope said. 'But I'm thinking she has to be Pauline. I know,' she said, catching Yves' expression. 'What a U-turn. But do the maths. Pauline arrived at Besançon in the first week of December 1940, six months pregnant. Three months later, we're in March 1941. It's bang on.'

Yves reread the adoption certificate and frowned. 'According to this, your dad wasn't adopted by George and Mary Granger until September 1946. That makes him five years old when they took him on.'

Hope had already puzzled over the discrepancy, until the answer became obvious. 'The war had to be over before the grandparents could find him and take him back. They couldn't have travelled to France any earlier than June 1945, and perhaps not even then.'

'Do you think your father came to England with his mother, or without her?'

Hope gave a shrug. 'I did a quick ancestry search for my grandparents and got forty-nine possibles. I haven't had time to study them.'

'But was Pauline's name there?'

'I wasn't looking for her at the time, but nothing jumped out.' The truth was, her promise to her father, to refrain from digging, still had power and she was beginning to realise how unpalatable reality could be. 'Pauline is an enigma.' And not an entirely likeable one. Pauline had sworn that her baby's father was Julien Marshall, but Lally had clearly had doubts, and Hope shared them.

'You can search birth records in France, too, you know,' Yves pointed out. 'If Pauline remained here, there might be records. Or if we knew Otto's surname, we could try that. It might lead somewhere.'

'You're convinced Otto and Pauline are my grandparents, then?'

'Aren't you?' He seemed surprised by her ambivalence. 'It was pretty clear from that photo that he's your grandfather.'

'The photo we rescued from Manon's bonfire? Assuming the unsmiling man was Otto.'

'You were pretty sure it was. Hope?' He was homing in on her hesitation, scenting avoidance.

'Yes. I am sure.' She sighed. 'I'm trying not to believe something because I want it to be true. Or not true. I've made that mistake enough times.'

'Otto is the most likely claimant to be your father's father. That's not a problem, is it?'

'It is, because it means Pauline lied to Lally.'

'Or she was being evasive.'

'No,' Hope said fiercely, 'she lied. I'll dig deeper for Otto's records… though a baby born to an unmarried woman would most likely be given the mother's name.'

'So, search for Pauline Granger. In Britain and in France. She can't have vanished from the face of the earth.'

'You reckon?' Hope folded up the adoption certificate. 'Thing is, my great-grandparents erased the tracks and because of their attitude, Dad was afraid to ask questions. All he had was the Grey Eyed Dove, and this…' She showed Yves the sprig of lavender Stephanie had given her after her dad's funeral. She was going to tuck it into the frame of the wedding photo. 'A brooch and a twig – Yves?' He was tapping on his phone. 'Am I boring you?'

'No, but my eyes are drooping. It's the antibiotics. I'm ordering a taxi.'

On impulse, she offered him her spare room. 'I'm too tired to drive you.'

'Offer accepted.' He closed down his phone and gave her a hug. 'Would you think me rude if I go upstairs now?'

In the morning, as Hope set the breakfast table, she reimagined that hug. It had been no more than a friendly clasp, but had it gone further, she wasn't sure she'd have pushed him away. The probability that her grandparents were Pauline and Otto brought desolation and a need for comfort. Two treacherous people. It was the worst result and made Hope feel complicit, as though by knowing what Lally had discovered the hard way, she was compounding the betrayal. One heart-rending line had lodged in Hope's head: *I feel robbed and naked.* Lally had survived, but at what cost? It was Lally whom Hope identified with. Not weak, dishonest Pauline.

In the kitchen, on her way to pick flowers for the table, Hope checked her emails.

Heck. She had another booking, for the first and second weeks of August, three generations of a family, mum, mum's sister, gran and teenage daughter. And there was a message from her friend Katie, sent early that morning. Hope opened it nervously, not sure if she wanted another update on Ash.

Katie had copied a Facebook link. Hope clicked on it and just stared.

'Heya.' Yves came in, looking showered and less shadowy around the eyes than he had last night. 'Sorry for crashing out yesterday.' He came to stand by her, looking at her laptop screen and the Facebook page. 'Who is Rupert Ashton?'

'Ash. My ex.'

'Didn't realise Ash was short for Ashton. He looks happy.'

Didn't he just? Relaxed in a shirt the colour of butternut squash, enjoying a drink at an outside venue. The caption read, *My new favourite place and my new favourite people*. It had been posted four days ago. Hope scrolled down, discovering a montage of sun, sea and a stony beach. Brighton, she concluded, from the skeletal outline of the pier. 'I've never seen this page before,' she said. 'He's living a life I knew nothing about.'

'What happened to that job in cyber security?' Yves asked.

'My friend who sent the link said he mentioned a start-up business. I've no idea what happened to the job he supposedly left to do. Even if it exists. Is there a way of finding out when he created this Facebook account?'

Yves told her to keep scrolling down. 'See when he put up the first post.'

It didn't take long. During the last week of April, Ash had posted a picture of the frothy surface of a coffee cup. *Always need caffeine after a flight.*

Someone called DeeCee1988 had commented: *Double strength, I hope? Whoops, delete Hope* followed by a row of 'I've screwed up' emojis.

Ash had replied, *Give me a chance! Getting the courage up. Love you.*

Love you back. Heart, heart, kiss, kiss.

Hope slammed her laptop shut. DeeCee was the name that had come up on Ash's phone. A late-night call a few days before he'd left, which he'd been suspiciously quick to conceal. Hope hadn't smacked into a wall; a wall had smacked into her. 'It was all planned out. He created this page during a trip home to his parents at Easter.' *Delete Hope. Getting the courage up.* She said in a voice she hardly recognised, 'He must have met this DeeCee, whoever she is, then. Or maybe they knew each other and hooked up again. Ash didn't leave me for a job, he left for a new life and a new woman.'

'Are you sure about the woman?'

'No. But it figures. The last pictures he put on his old Facebook page were of a family get-together and there was a girl there. Big lips. Glossy hair. It's obvious. He's stepped out of one life into another.'

'D'you want me to make cooing noises and say you're overthinking?'

She didn't want that.

'Then I agree with you. He has left, and he has somebody else. A new life, a new interest.'

'After he found us together, he had me grovelling to him, begging him to stay. God, he judged me! I wish I'd given him something to judge.'

'That's not healthy thinking, Hope.'

'Sod healthy thinking.' She remembered the conversation she'd had with Yves the following day. 'You asked me if Ash had a suitcase with him when he flew back. Course he didn't. He wasn't intending to stay. His taxi happened to be going past when he walked out—'

'Because the driver had been told to turn at the top of the street and return slowly.'

'He was coming home to break off with me, wasn't he? He'd told that DeeCee person he was getting the courage up. Why didn't I realise?'

'Why would you?'

'D'you think this job in Docklands is a lie?'

'You do, that's the point. He's not in London, is he?' There'd been a picture of a seagull on Ash's page, perched on a rail, the sea in the background. The caption had read: *This guy tried to eat my chips again today*. 'I don't know London,' Yves went on, 'but I don't think it's by the sea.'

'No. Brighton's the home of chip-stealing seagulls. He's got a start-up business, and he's moved on. That's why he needs

money so badly.' It all suddenly felt so obvious. Katie had done
her a solid good turn. 'He took off while I was buying Lally's
picture at the market. *Pht*, gone. Next thing, he was on a plane,
then claimed he'd left his phone in the taxi, which was why he
couldn't call to explain.'

'It happens. I've left my phone in a taxi many times.'

'Ash doesn't. Know what makes me want to spit?' She was
digging her fingers into Yves' shoulders. He didn't flinch. 'The
way he made me ashamed when he caught us. The scarlet
woman. Oh, the curl of his lip, when really, I'd saved him the
trouble of explaining he was bailing out on our life together. It's
what you said, isn't it?'

'What did I say?'

'That couples come over to France for the life, and the
dream always goes sour for one of them, and the other gets left
behind. What am I going to do?'

Yves looked at her steadily. 'I know what you shouldn't do.'

She waited. 'Well?'

'Anything fuelled by hurt or anger.'

'Like this?' Putting her hands to Yves' face, she drew his
head down until their lips met. Finding no resistance, she kissed
him passionately. After a moment, he gently pushed her away.

'I'm not going to be your revenge, Hope. I'm worth more
than that.'

He was right and she felt mortified. 'I'm sorry. I shouldn't.'

'You can. Just not to get even, OK?'

Week two of Goldie, Paloma, Elkie and TJ's holiday was
interrupted by days of heavy rain when the heat broke. With
the road between Lazurac and Varsac-les-Moulins awash, they
stayed home and spent the time watching films, playing cards
and reading. It gave Hope free hours to run through her
finances and conclude that she needed full bookings right

through to next Easter to allow her to pay Ash what she believed she owed him. They still had to agree a figure, but whatever it was, she hadn't got it.

Her mind lingered on the kiss she had sprung on Yves. Afterwards, it had been business as usual. Over to La Cachette for another tutorial and a long lunch in the garden. At the end of the day, as the others packed up their art materials, she'd followed Yves down to the café, wanting a private moment with him. 'I need to know,' she'd said, 'you don't think I was only kissing you to even the score with Ash?'

Before he could respond, her guests trooped down the windmill steps, ready to go home for their evening meal and drinks. That same night, the rain had begun, postponing the chance of a conversation.

Studying her financial figures again, Hope felt a gnawing dissatisfaction. She'd gone into this business with rose-tinted specs firmly on. She should have bought a smaller place, and not in the centre of Lazurac, where, because of its special historic status, living costs were high. 'Benefit of hindsight,' she muttered.

She redid the figures, only to arrive at the same bottom line. Taking a break, she went out onto the terrace and saw a rainbow spanning the sunflower fields, its ends buried in glowering rain cloud. This wouldn't be her view much longer. That was the hard truth.

Jonny Taubier's business card was still on her kitchen table. She went back inside, picked up her phone, dialled the number then cancelled the call, turning the card on its face. She needed time to prepare for a sudden, new change of direction. Perhaps it was walking past her parents' wedding photo every time she went into the lounge, but a harrowing conversation, one that had thrown her sideways, had come back to life in her head. It had taken place ten years ago. Hope had just staged her art college graduation show and was considering her future. Her mother had come up to London on a surprise visit and they'd met in the café at Tate Modern.

Tina Granger had come straight to the point. 'I'm not well, Hope. I've had tests. It's serious and, well, there's a chance I won't get through.'

Hope felt it again as she returned to her accounts, staring through blurred eyes at her spreadsheet. The pop of shock in the stomach instantly followed by denial. Her mum had looked fine. 'You were on top form at my graduation show,' she'd said. 'Things don't happen this fast. Are you sure they've done the right tests?'

She'd been told to, please, listen. 'I need to speak, and you not to interrupt.' Tina's next words had imprinted themselves deeply.

'I'm not one for false good news, as you know. Course I'll have all the treatments going, but I'm realistic. I'm here because I'm worried about you. Your father has had no practice at being alone, and he's going to be very needy.'

'I would be there for him,' Hope had said, putting it into the conditional tense. *Would be*, not *will be*. She still couldn't accept her mother's shocking disclosure. Tina had shaken her head.

'I'm not having you taking my place to prop him up. You have your own life to live.'

'Mum, you've never spoken like this before.'

'I've never had cancer before. Me and your dad love each other, but marriage isn't a poem, Hope. It's paying the bills, finding woodworm in the attic, and dealing with the fact that they snore.'

'Dad doesn't—'

'I do. I snore. Marriage is watching your child leave home, and realising you have to find another way to be just the two of you. Love changes. When I'm gone, get on with your life. Your dad will find somebody else, take my word on it.'

The very idea had made the tea in Hope's cup taste suddenly foul.

'Don't cry.' Tina had been matter-of-fact, though she too was welling up. 'We need to talk about you. Every woman should be able to support herself. How much will you make in your first year as an artist?' When Hope had vaguely shaken her head, Tina had swiped a napkin off a neighbouring table and dealt with her tears. 'You need a proper qualification then, something that'll pay the bills and let you save for a pension. Do that a few years, then you can paint to your heart's content.'

'Maybe I'm like Dad, taking every day as it comes.'

Tina Granger's face had expressed her opinion of that. 'Trouble is, days do come. I never thought I'd get lung cancer, but the day came last Thursday, when my consultant asked me to sit down. You know they say, there's none so blind as they who won't see? If you want to do something for your dad, take him to find his windmill.'

'Windmill? As in "dreams"?'

'No, an actual creaky windmill and the old lady who lives in it. If she's still around. Don't you remember?'

Hope really wanted to talk about her mum's illness, and when treatment would start. Tina Granger had her own agenda.

'He's always looking for his mother, but never plucks up the courage to go to the one place she might be.'

'Where?'

'France,' her mother had answered. 'How many times have I said, "Get a passport, Joseph, and we'll go to that place you mutter about when you're half asleep." He always says the same thing. "If I send off a form, I'll get a load of questions I can't answer." Honestly, I could wring his grandparents' necks and if I meet them in the better place, I will.'

Hope turned Jonny Taubier's card back the right way up as her mother's voice faded. *The old lady in the windmill.* Had her mother meant Lally? That lunch had been life-changing for Hope in so many ways. Nobody had understood why she'd ditched a career in fine art and started an accountancy degree. In that café by the Thames, Tina had spoken and, like a photographer giving a twist to a camera lens, had adjusted Hope's focus. She had to earn a proper living. There was no time for soft-edged artist's dreams because her dad would need her. Hope had rejected the prediction that Joseph would remarry within months of becoming a widower.

Huh. Enter Stephanie.

The rain began again, and thunder rolled in. Hope called Yves to confirm that they weren't coming over. 'Fine,' he said. He could do with catching up on a few things himself. Was she imagining a sliver of relief in his voice? Had her kiss made him step back?

An hour later, she called again. No answer. He must have turned his phone off, or maybe the storm was affecting signal. Not liking the fact that she was grasping at straws, Hope resolved to let him respond in his own time. Meanwhile, she could prove herself capable of listening.

She spent the next hour on the ancestry site. Her original search for her grandparents had, in fact, turned up over fifty couples named George and Mary Granger. She began looking at them, one after the other. Where they'd lived, their births and deaths and the children they'd had.

On her eleventh try, in the National Register of 1939, a married couple with the right names showed up in Fareham. Going back to the 1921 census, she found the same couple and there was a child too, aged four months. A daughter, name of—

Her phone lit up. It was Yves. They both spoke at the same time. Both said the same thing.

'I've found her. I've found Pauline.'

. . .

Hope sped to La Cachette and found Yves sitting outside his caravan, a fire pit glowing on the gravel. The storm had passed, leaving a spicy freshness in the air. He fetched her a chair from the café and made coffee for them in large mugs.

'You go first,' he invited. 'What I have to show you is up in the studio.'

She told him what she'd found in the records. 'George and Mary Granger of Palmerston Road, Fareham, had a daughter, Pauline, who was four months old when the census was taken in 1921. It fits with what Lally says about Pauline being nineteen in 1940. The clincher is, Pauline doesn't appear on the National Register of 1939. That was carried out so identity cards could be issued—'

'And Pauline was in France.' Yves nodded. 'You are convinced now? Lally's friend is your grandmother?'

'Sure as I can be.'

'We didn't need to have done those DNA tests, then. We aren't cousins.'

She gave a dry laugh. 'Another of my brilliant ideas.'

'Oh, well. They're bound to show something interesting.' Yves asked what else she'd uncovered for Pauline Granger.

'Nothing,' Hope said. 'She's in the 1931 census as a school student, then she disappears.'

'Because she went to Paris as an au pair and never returned.'

Hope drank her coffee. 'You said how your gran never trusted anyone after the war. Everyone she loved hurt her. I think it's inevitable that Pauline did that and I'm reading the memoir, waiting for the moment Lally crashes into the incontrovertible truth.'

'We don't know how the story ends.'

'No. We don't, and we can search for Pauline in France, as Pauline Granger.'

'Or as Pauline Ducasse,' Yves said. 'For a time, she lived under a false identity, remember.'

Hope gave a sigh. 'Don't I have to know which département she settled in, and died in? Assuming she *is* dead.' Pauline could still be alive, in her nineties. What a thought.

Yves got to his feet. 'Time to show you what I found.' He reached for her hand.

BARBED WIRE AND FALSE NAMES: MEMOIR OF AN ENGLISH GIRL IN OCCUPIED FRANCE

I've grown soft from a week in a hospital bed and my lungs catch as I walk through the infirmary door and into the bitter outdoors. Yes, it is that simple. As the nurses dozed at their station, I hoisted up my bag, collected my coat, stole a change of clothes and left. Leaving the infirmary is the easy part. As I approach the main gate of the compound, I must summon the courage to call out to the guards. In German.

With as much authority as I can muster, I ask to be let out. I add that it's an emergency.

A light goes on in a cabin next to the gate and a man in uniform comes out, a barking Alsatian straining on a leash. His flashlight bounces off the white cotton cap I'm wearing, and I point to the Red Cross insignia on the front. I've left a gap between the lapels of my coat to show a white collar and a section of blue-striped tunic. His torch drops to my travel bag, which I'm holding in a rigid grip.

'Who are you?' He narrows his eyes. 'I thought I knew all the nurses.'

Including the one who owns this uniform, I have no doubt. I took it from the laundry basket in the nurses' bathroom, leaving my old rags in exchange. I pray he won't shine his flashlight at my lower legs because my stockings are the wrong colour and my shoes are the boots I put on in Paris, the day I was arrested. Ankle-high brown leather, not the usual black.

'I'm filling in for a few nights,' I explain. 'They've sent me to get Dr Huguet from town. A prisoner has gone into labour, and it's...' I would like to say 'a breech delivery' but Otto never taught me medical terms, and all I can manage is that the baby is positioned the wrong way. 'You won't imagine how much blood the mother's losing.'

Does breech delivery involve blood loss? Probably not. At least, not until afterwards. I planned what to say in a hurry, and I'm banking on the guard having even less experience of childbirth than I. I dread him telling me that Dr Huguet is in the infirmary tonight and sending me back to search for him there. He shines his light on my bag again. His dog is finding it interesting, the black nose snuffling at the buckles.

'What's in there?'

I open the bag to reveal a tangle of blood-soaked linen, also from the laundry basket. At least I prepared for this eventuality – though not the presence of the dog, to be fair. The guard lurches back from the sight, yanking his animal away. 'I know,' I say. 'Not very nice, but the doctor needs to look at it. You know how it is with medical men. They always know best.'

It's worked. A door within the great gate is opened for me. Just as I'm going through,

my arm is caught. 'What's your name?' the guard asks.

'Sister Klara Müller.'

'How long will you be, Klara?'

'If I'm not back in half an hour,' I say, with a poor attempt at humour, 'you'd better pray for that poor mother.'

He grunts and wishes me a safe walk.

The station is essentially on a straight line from the prison. Just once, I look back up to the glacial hill and vow never to return. I'd rather die out here on the hard-packed snow.

The station is dark but my obsessive train watching should pay dividends. God willing, at five, a train will come from the north-east and after stopping for forty minutes, will continue south. Direction of Lyon. I'm no more than an hour behind Pauline, but she is probably already travelling the first leg to Vichy. I pray she has a safe delivery and that, one day, I get to know if she had a girl or boy.

The station, which is called Besançon-Viotte, has shallow window bays between stone columns. I push my bag into a corner of one of the bays and sit on it, huddling in my coat and with a cardigan tied over my nurse's cap like an ersatz Russian hat. I soon lose feeling in my feet. It's midnight, so I have five hours to wait. Five hours for my escape to be discovered and guards sent to find me.

I smooth out the knots in my stomach by inventing elaborate dinner menus for myself.

Lobster thermidor followed by roast beef and confit potatoes, then brandy soufflé, ripe Camembert, coffee and mint chocolates. Though to be frank, I'd be glad right now for a pickled mackerel eaten from a jar.

Somehow, I sleep only to wake and hear men speaking German close by. Soldiers, by their shape in the darkness. Padded service coats with belted waists, machine guns slung crosswise. Alsatians on leashes, with sloping haunches. They crunch past me and one of the dogs growls. His handler quiets him.

It's not the same dog that sniffed my bag. I'm not being

hunted. So far. From what they're saying, these troops are on their way 'to hold the line'.

What line?

They'll also be taking the first train out. I just want to get as far away from here as I can, to a place nobody knows me from where I'll take a series of onward trains to Otto's safe house.

More people arrive. Some on foot, others on bicycles. Workers, by their garb. I peel from my hiding place and follow them. The German soldiers are occupying the foyer seats. Everyone gives them a wide berth.

I ask for a ticket to the city of Lyon. In French, of course, mumbling to disguise my accent, which is a hybrid of English and Parisian, and which will give me away faster than anything. The ticket clerk says, 'Where, again?'

I repeat, 'Lyon.'

Not a chance. I can go as far as Lons-le-Saunier, where the demarcation line runs, and... here we go... I'll need a permit to get further. Why, *why* didn't I have the guts to steal one of those forms from von Salzach's desk? Apparently, Lons-le-Wherever is an hour and a half's journey. I'd hoped to get much further before negotiating my way across the line.

The clerk is looking hard at me. 'You're the second one tonight who thought she could glide all the way to Lyon.' He asks, with rising impatience, if I want a ticket or not.

'Yes, please, the place you said.'

'Lons-le-Saunier.'

I pass over some of the money Pauline gave me and ask casually if any Red Cross personnel arrived last night.

'Yes, a posse of them, and there was a kerfuffle.'

I can't ask more as people are tutting behind me. My stomach rumbles. I didn't smuggle so much as a lump of bread out with me. First, I need to get out of this nursing uniform. In the ladies' cloakroom, I remove the dirty sheets from my bag and dump them in the cistern. In the neighbouring cubicle, I do the same with the nursing uniform and change into my warmest things. From the lining of my shoe, I take the safe house address. It's too dim in the cubicle to read it but I memorised it months ago anyway. The house of Madame Taubier, Varsac-les-Moulins near Lazurac. It goes down the toilet. The final thing I destroy is the *carte d'identité* bearing the name Lavinia Shepherd. Once again, and for all eternity now, I'm travelling as Marie-Laure Ducasse.

At the mirror, I wash my face, horrified how pale I look. I dab Arpège behind my ears. Conjuring up Otto's face when he presented me with this gorgeous bottle pumps confusion into my veins. Otto and Pauline, together upstairs at Rue du Maine... truth or lie?

I have concluded that Norma-Rose stole the Grey Eyed Dove and the thought of it gracing her smug breast gives me back my faith in Pauline. Norma-Rose couldn't tell the truth if it left a thousand-franc note on the dresser. Searching for a handkerchief, I find the wizened apple Pauline brought to my hospital bed. 'Oh, my sweet friend.'

Sometimes, truth is as simple as that.

The train arrives and I climb aboard, still expecting at any moment to be dragged off. I find an empty compartment but don't keep it to myself very long. Men enter, light cigarettes and eye me up.

At six forty-eight, steam hisses from the train's skirts and pistons groan. Metal on metal, we pull away. I am leaving Besançon after eighty-five days. I realise it's the 1st of March. Pinch and a punch for the first of the month.

At Lons-le-Saunier, I see at once that there's going to be an identity check at the turnstile. The familiar sensation starts up, an electric needle poking the lining of my stomach. At the barrier, I present my false card.

The French official on duty looks at me, at the card. The

usual comparing glance, because the photo was taken in Orléans before I lost over a stone in weight.

'Where are you from?' he asks.

I spout the information that came along with the ID card. 'Originally from Pau, but I'm heading to Lyon, to join relations.'

He hands it back and says what I already know. 'You'll need a permit to get across to the Zone Libre.'

I nod, but as I pick up my bag, he catches the belt of my coat. 'Try the Café Suisse on Rue du Ronde. Ask for Le Vieux.' The Old Man.

'Is it safe?'

'He's your best hope.' The inspector is whispering now, because the German guards who embarked at Besançon are coming towards us, the dog sniffing the ground. 'Same as I told your sister.'

46

My sister...

I find the Café Suisse and learn that the Old Man isn't expected until later. A waitress confirms that another woman has been in, asking for him. 'Yes, very pregnant,' she says in answer to my question. 'I sent her to the Auberge de la Paix. The patronne there is sympathetic.'

That's where I head and ask at the desk if there's a Pauline Ducasse staying, and if so, could I please join her?

The hotel's patronne looks relieved. 'I'm so glad she has someone. I was really worried about her, being so far gone. You don't look very alike, if you don't mind me saying.'

'Different mothers,' I answer glibly. 'I'm the elder.'

The woman hands me a key and points me towards the stairs. 'Room four.'

Pauline is curled up, asleep, but wakes as I sit on the bed. 'Lally?' Her eyes are pools of astonishment.

'Did you think I was going to stay put after your warning?'

'I didn't expect you to get out so quickly.' *Or to find me*, her expression says clearly.

'When a door is left open, you walk through it, don't you? I thought you were heading for Vichy.'

'Oh, that changed.'

'I see. And the Red Cross folk?'

She sits up. Pauline's pale complexion is an easy canvas for embarrassment and, on this occasion, her blush is deep. 'I – they, well, they left me.'

'Left you? They're nurses, they're meant to take care of people, not abandon them.' I'm remembering what the ticket clerk at Besançon told me. Last night, on the station, a kerfuffle. My newly restored trust in Pauline drains away.

'We got separated,' she says nervously, 'and I climbed on the wrong train.'

'What wrong train?' She attempts an answer but I know the timetable. I tell her to stop blustering. 'You came here alone, didn't you?'

She sighs. 'Yes. I gave the nurses the slip. I did genuinely get on the train with them but as the whistle went, I said I was desperate for the toilet and got off. They were bashing on the window and one of them opened a door and screamed at the guard to stop the train. He wouldn't, and I hid in the lavatories. When the next train came in, I jumped on board. I thought it would get me to Lyon.'

'Not realising it would stop here, and you'd have to cross the demarcation line.'

She nods. 'You know about the Old Man?'

'Mm. He's due back later tonight. Where are you heading, Pauline? What's your plan?' I need to know if Pauline and I are heading to the same place.

'I am going where Otto said we should go,' she tells me, sibilant and defiant.

'So you know about the safe house?'

She nods. 'My baby must be born in Free France.'

Free? The Zone Libre is a contradiction in terms. It has a

collaborating government and a police force which does the Germans' dirty work for them but I'm too tired and hungry to discuss it and suggest we go to the Café Suisse for some food.

While Pauline makes a trip to the bathroom, I search inside her travel bag and find a map. A broken line begins at Besançon, then tracks diagonally south-west to a place heavily ringed in red. In the margin, she has written, 'Lazurac. Madame Taubier. Windmill.'

Did Otto decide at some point to tell her about the safe house or did she sneak a look in my shoe? If the latter, it would have had to have been while we were in the prison, but she'd have had plenty of opportunity in the dead of night, my shoes left upside down beside the bunk bed.

I tear the map into tiny pieces and push them behind the wardrobe.

47

The Old Man is precisely that, a veteran of the last conflict with a white moustache and a merry eye, which becomes less merry when he sees Pauline.

'*Mon Dieu*, Madame, this will be a great risk for you and your unborn infant. To get across the line, you will have to run across rough ground having climbed through a wire fence. If you falter or fall, you will be caught. If you are caught, there will be no mercy shown either to you or those with you. I beg you to change your mind.'

Pauline adopts the face I have learned to recognise. Blank as the back cover of a prayer book. I realise belatedly that it is the face that drove us back to Paris when we should have pressed on south.

'I will do it, Monsieur,' she says. 'I got myself off a train at Besançon, onto another without falling over or giving myself away.'

'The territory either side of the line is patrolled with men and dogs.'

'I will do it.'

The Old Man looks at me. 'Madame?'

I shrug. I'm still trying to comprehend that Pauline was on her way to the sanctuary entrusted to me by Otto, without me. I can't help it; I feel breathless and betrayed. But... we have the decision of our lives to make, so I look into the old gentleman's anxious eyes and say, 'I will make sure my sister gets safe across. How much will it cost us?'

About as much as a skilled man earns in two months. Each. After all this risk, I haven't got enough. Success so often comes down to money, or the lack of.

Pauline calmly opens her coat and produces a wad of thousand-franc notes. 'This will cover us both.'

'Pauline?'

'A friend gave it to me...'

'Who? Julien or Otto?'

'Neither. I'll tell you later.'

The old gent asks to see our identity cards.

He glances at them and hands them back. 'They're good.'

'Because they're genuine,' I reply.

That drags a chuckle from him. 'Sure, and I'm Général de Gaulle. Ducasse is a good name,' he adds. 'If you're heading south-west, Ducasse is a name of that region. Where are you staying?'

I name our hotel and he nods. '*Oui, c'est parfait.* Keep your heads down. I'll let you know when the *passeur* is ready.'

'*Passeur*' means a smuggler. I don't need to ask if getting fugitives over the demarcation line is a dangerous job.

48

HOPE

Time to show you what I found.

With these words, Yves led Hope to the top of the windmill. The easels were where they'd left them after their last teaching session, each with its work-in-progress. With luck, this spate of storms was over now and her guests would get a sunny finale to their holiday.

Yves switched the light on. Lally's self-portrait gazed down on them from the hook where he'd hung it. The cropped hair looked more jagged than ever and Hope ran her fingers through her own. She said, 'Show me what you found.'

Yves beckoned her to her own easel. Her drawing had been replaced by a large square of card, on which a montage of black and white photographs had been stuck with Blu Tack. Some were badly burned, others faded but otherwise perfect.

'Rescued from Manon's attempt at arson?'

Yves confirmed it. 'But don't you see what they are? I've put them in the order they might have been taken.'

There were twenty-four pictures, the first twenty clearly taken in Paris. Hope recognised, if not the actual locations, certainly the Haussmann buildings in the background, the awnings of cafés, the kiosks lining the quays of the River Seine. She also recognised some of the people. 'These are from Pauline's last roll of film.'

'Exactly. See the final one—' Yves pointed to a picture of Lally and an older couple at a dinner table. There was a carafe of wine and the edge of a serving dish. 'Taken at Rue Monge, and the old people must be Madame and Monsieur Arnaud. Otto was standing out of shot. Shame, really.'

'The Arnauds look so nervous. Feeding those guests could have got them sent to a firing squad.' Hope tracked all twenty-four of Pauline's pictures through a chestnut-blossom spring, a summer of café tables and riverside walks, until she found the one taken through the window of the Renault Nervastella. What a contrast. Still – 'That's an amazing picture,' she said.

It was of a very old woman, bandaged fingers gripping the handles of a pushcart, pots and pans lashed to it and a bird in a cage balanced on the top. The bird's beak gaped wide. Its owner's traumatised eye was a stark match to the creature's distress. 'Victims of war,' Hope said. 'I wonder if she made it.' Another photograph, taken on the journey, was rather underexposed. You could make out figures dancing in the glow of camp-fires. 'These pictures document history,' she said.

Yves didn't disagree. 'Let me show you the thing I brought you here to see. It survived Manon's fire because it was sandwiched between sheets of cardboard.'

Yves turned the photo montage around. On the reverse was pinned an unfinished sketch, done in charcoal, partly coloured with pastel crayon. It was of a young woman lying on a bed, her eyes closed. Her hair was gathered up in some kind of cord, and she was wearing a loose, buff-coloured blouse, the top buttons open. Pinned to the camisole that showed in the open V of the blouse-front was the Grey Eyed Dove.

'It's Pauline. And Hope, if you let your hair go back to its normal colour and grow it out, this face could be yours.'

She'd seen the resemblance at once. It reinforced every conclusion she'd arrived at over the last few days. Only... 'I don't want to be Pauline's granddaughter. She's a cheat.'

'We don't know for sure.'

'The jury's out as to who fathered her baby but it's indisputable that she was heading for the safe house, leaving Lally behind.'

'Having tipped Lally off, brought her bag and given her money. Pauline had a baby to think of.'

A baby, and one chance herself to get out. All right, but would I do that? Hope asked. Would I set out to reach safety, not knowing if my best friend was stranded behind locked gates?

'It proves one thing,' she said. 'Lally sketched her friend, at least once.'

'Once, for sure.' Yves gave her a squeeze. 'There's no doubt now, is there? Here is your grandmother.'

'Yes.' Pauline was beautiful. A cute nose and immense, long-lashed eyes. A tumble of mid-brown hair held off her forehead by the length of cord. Had pregnancy lent her that bloom, or had Lally added it with her chalk-pastels? Hope saw her father in the brow and the shape of the mouth.

'Ask it.'

Without a pause, Hope asked the question for both of them. 'When did she die? I've been thinking about it, and I'm convinced she died, or my father wouldn't have been adopted with only a piece of jewellery to remember her by. Lally writes about the Grey Eyed Dove as her most prized possession. She stole it from Otto, then lost it at the prison. How does Pauline get to pass it on? Unless *she* took it from Lally's bag and lied about Norma-Rose tipping everything out. Yes. That fits.'

They stood in silence until Yves said, 'We're agreeing, we're not cousins.'

'Agreed. Our grandmothers were partners in a wartime epic but you and I share no common bloodline.'

He lowered his lips to hers, his hand cupping the back of her head. Hope turned to put her arms around his waist. She felt him come alive, his breathing quicken. The lines attaching her to Ash and their shared dream frayed a little more, and she knew it wouldn't take much for them to snap completely.

But tonight was not the night. She didn't like leaving her guests alone in her house. They'd be going home in a few days, and then she and Yves could do what they liked. 'I'll finish reading the memoir and then you can have it for keeps.'

He stepped back reluctantly. 'Go home, Hope, read it, but don't stay awake all night. The forecast is good tomorrow so let's go out on the pilgrims' path, find a place to draw and have a lunch *sur l'herbe*. There's a spot from where we can see this windmill and the Taubiers' place.'

'La Sanctuaire. That was where Pauline and Lally were intending to go.'

'Uh-huh.'

'I'm tempted to jump to the ending,' she said.

'You can't,' he said, giving her a final regretful kiss. 'The last pages have been ripped out, remember?'

BARBED WIRE AND FALSE NAMES: MEMOIR OF AN ENGLISH GIRL IN OCCUPIED FRANCE

4 March 1941

We're still waiting for news of the *passeur* who will get us over the demarcation line. I'm desperate to be moving and Pauline's condition is worrying me. She's sleeping constantly and her ankles have swollen. By her calculation, her baby is due in the next couple of days.

It's madness to think of taking her on a journey, but she is determined. Unable to stay cooped up any longer, I call at the Café Suisse, where I receive awful news. Just hours after we sat talking to the Old Man, our *passeur* was arrested. Everything is off.

A day and night limps by as we wait for word. We haven't enough money for a long stay in this town, and there is always the danger of someone guessing we're English. Though we've had nothing but kindness, my time at Frontstalag 142 has scarred me. Betrayal sits in every shadow, in every footfall.

Who tipped off the authorities about the *passeur*, and who will dare take his place?

I grow so anxious about funds, I ask the patronne if I may exchange my hotel bill for work. She steers me towards a Mont Blanc of bedsheets that need laundering. 'Are you sure?' she says, rather embarrassed.

Scrubbing linen with grated soap, the only detergent available, my hands redden but I'd rather be working than pacing a small room. I left Pauline asleep, supported on pillows because her back hurts so badly. I'm really alarmed by her ankles. Pregnancy is very badly designed, I've decided.

She is still asleep when I take a break from the laundry. Even in this state, her mouth slightly open, Pauline has a particular way of capturing the attention. It's the delicacy of her features, so full of unexpressed emotion, even our friend Victor Ponsard, who peppers his speech with profanities, treated her with veneration. Pauline is no Mata Hari, nor a vamp. It's her innocence that mesmerises. It worked on Herr von Salzach. It mesmerised me and Victor, and Julien. And Otto?

I go back down to the laundry. Five hours later, I return to our room taking a cup of camomile tea to her. She must have woken because there's a glass of water by the bed and she's fastened the hair off her face with a strand of curtain cord. She is wearing a pale brown blouse made of brushed cotton. The top three buttons have come undone, revealing a silk camisole beneath. Something shiny catches my eye.

She's wearing the Grey Eyed Dove. For an instant, I'm tempted to rip it off, but what I do is reach for my sketchbook. I drew her so often in the past, and then, when I lost my trust in her, tore all those drawings out and fed them into our dormitory stove.

I draw her in charcoal, adding colour here and there. It's

like note-taking, to be turned into something more permanent later.

Her eyes open and she blinks at me. 'Lally. Oh.'

'Don't move, I need to finish your hands, how they're resting on your bump.'

She sinks back down. 'I must have drifted off. I only lay down for a quick rest.'

'Stay as you are.' I shade in the folds of her blouse and because I look closely to draw the Grey Eyed Dove, she gasps and tries to cover it, then, knowing the cat is out of the bag, blurts out, 'You know that I fought Norma-Rose for this? But you must have taken it from Otto in the first place.'

'Guilty as charged. I wish I hadn't.'

'He was so distressed.'

'Don't, please. Pauline, can you promise me one thing?'

She waits, in fear of what I will ask her. I can't bring myself to and say instead, 'You will speak up if crossing the demarcation line is too much?'

'I'm fine, Lally. Anyway, what choice do we have?'

'Still planning on going to your friend's house? Where was it... Grandeville, near Vichy?'

'I told you I made that name up.'

'Oh, yes. Well, I'll save you the trouble of inventing anything else. I know where you're heading.' I mention the map with the crimson line tracking all the way to Lazurac.

She blushes and says, 'Otto told me the address in Bordeaux and he made me memorise it. But I know you kept that bit of paper in your shoe, Lally, which wasn't sensible. Why did you, when you're better than me at remembering things?'

So she had looked. 'I kept it because it was the last thing I had from Otto.' I sound stupid even to myself, so change the subject. 'Even when we get across the line, Lazurac is an awfully long way. Several changes of train, I should think.'

'That's all right. I have enough money.'

Ah yes, the money. She confessed last night that she'd taken it from the fellow prisoner who died, the one whose fur coat and hat Norma-Rose appropriated. Apparently, the poor woman had hidden thousands of francs in her sponge bag. It gave me a new insight into my friend. In a way, I admire Pauline. Like a gracious swan, a joy to behold, she can break your arm with a strike of her beak.

I go back down to the scullery and finish the washing. Glancing out of the window, I see it's snowing heavily, and it's cold enough for it to settle.

The patronne knocks at the bedroom door the following day as darkness falls. 'It's tonight, at midnight,' she whispers. 'They have a new *passeur*. Go to the rear of the Café Suisse, and you'll be given directions. Don't delay. They won't wait for you.'

As is always the case when life is pivoting on a pin head, we have five minutes to pack. Pauline is once again so deeply asleep, I have to shake her. 'Hey, get up. We're on the move.'

I gather up all the clothes she's left lying around, her washing things, cramming everything into her bag. That's when I discover it has a false bottom. I run my finger beneath and pull out papers.

'Oh, leave those.' Pauline sits up, bunching the bedspread.

I ignore her. 'Pauline, my God. You've kept letters from your parents!'

'Why shouldn't I?'

'English stamps, and postmarks.' They are addressed to 'Miss Pauline Granger, care of the Marshall residence, Paris 8'. 'You put yourself in serious danger, and Julien too.'

'Why Julien?'

I make allowances as she's just woken up. 'Because it's his address.' These letters, in the wrong hands, would demonstrate that our friend sheltered an enemy of the Reich.

'Julien's a prisoner of war,' she says, slowly putting her feet to the floor. 'He's in an Oflag in Germany, protected under the Geneva Convention. He was captured in northern France, near Dunkirk.'

'When?'

'Oh, not long after the Germans crossed into France. The tenth or the eleventh of May, I think. Darling Julien, I hope he's surviving.'

'Wait, hang on.' I stop her. 'How do you know this?'

She explains. The day we left Paris the first time, in June, she met with an acquaintance. 'D'you remember?'

Do I remember waiting on the pavement of Rue Monge, chewing my lips to a rag, wondering if Pauline had forgotten that we had one chance of a car ride out of the city? *Back in a twinkle.* That twinkle lasted two hours, then suddenly, there she was, wading through the crush in her best suit, wearing the Madame Paulette hat. Lime-flower blossom on her shoulders, implying a walk through a park. So yes, I do remember. 'The friend you went to see had worked for Madame Marshall.'

'As a seamstress,' Pauline confirms. 'She remained in Paris, and when I was staying at the YWCA, I called on her. She had news of Julien through a friend at the American embassy. You can pull strings if you know the right people. That's how I found out what happened to him.'

The hotel patronne taps urgently on our door. 'Hurry up. They won't wait.'

Wordlessly, I pick up my bag and Pauline's. Walking down the hotel stairs, I'm breathing like an asthmatic. Pauline hasn't yet realised what she has revealed.

If Julien Marshall was captured during the second week

of May 1940, there is no possibility he can be her baby's
father.

The *passeur* is surprisingly youthful. Sixteen, maybe? A farmer's son, scared but eager. As well as Pauline and me to be taken across the line, there are two young brothers from Paris. Jewish, I think. There is a French matron who got stuck the wrong side of the divide after she went to look after her mother. There's an older man with his daughter and her baby. I gather that he has got his whole extended family across the line two at a time. This is his last trip. The baby grizzles and our *passeur* begs the mother to quieten it.

'There will be times when we're a hundred paces from the German checkpoints.'

I think of the soldiers who caught the same train as me, their dog on a leash. I might be passing them in a short while. I catch the company taking stock of Pauline, and it's obvious what they're thinking. She tells them she's not quite seven months pregnant, which is not the biggest lie she's ever told, but possibly the most dangerous.

'I've got weeks to go yet.' To prove her point, she insists on carrying her own bag.

We set off, taking a back road out of town. It is fiercely

cold, but though it's stopped snowing, our feet leave prints, clear and treacherous. At some point, we leave the road and, after a hard trudge across fields, reach lightly wooded country. Now, the going gets harder because snow-covered brushwood and frozen leaves cover all kinds of pitfalls. Pauline duly tumbles. I help her up.

'I'm all right,' she insists, but doesn't object when one of the young boys picks up her bag. I take her arm with my free hand. The wood goes on and on. We walk for about four hours, stopping occasionally for a gulp of water, a nip of red wine from a canvas flask our guide offers round. The infant has stopped crying, lulled in a sling behind its mother's back. I worry for it, in this chill.

Dawn the colour of cheese rind rises as we come out of the trees into meadows dotted with farming hamlets. The pasture is marshy. Our guide calls us to come close. In a whisper, he tells us that the demarcation line follows a road that we can't yet see. To reach it, we have to get past a barbed-wire fence.

'The Germans patrol it on bicycles, or on foot with dogs,' he says. 'They move between guard huts, and there's an interval of about eight minutes when this stretch of road is empty. We will go in two groups and you will have about five minutes, no more, to get under the wire, across the road and over the meadows beyond. The woods on the far side are your goal. Five minutes. If anyone is seen, they will unleash the dogs. So do not fall or stumble or make a noise. If you believe you can't do it, now is the time to turn back.'

None of us will. Six hours back through those woods, to be stuck in Lons-le-Saunier for the duration? I look across what I privately name 'God's forsaken land' and think – those woods look an awfully long way off.

After a few minutes' wait, the first glimmers of daylight pick out the metal of helmets and bicycles of an advancing patrol. The baby has woken and its mother puts it to the breast. 'Shh. Shh.'

It's decided she and her father must go in the first group, along with the French matron. I, Pauline and the brothers from Paris will go in the second. It means waiting for the patrol to go, to come back and then go again. Twenty ice-cold minutes.

Pauline needs to relieve herself and asks me to help. We go a little way off. I ask how she's doing.

'My back's murder,' she says.

'Like a pickaxe to your vertebrae?' I ask.

'How— Oh, darling, Lally, I'm so sorry. Your miscarriage.'

'You don't have to be sorry,' I whisper, astonished at how calm I am. 'We're all human. Our mistake is to think those we love are ever any more than that. Human.'

Pauline is adjusting her skirt, belting her coat above her bump. 'What are you saying?'

'That I will do everything in my power to help Otto's child,' is how I answer.

I hear her intake of breath. 'How—'

'I should have realised before. You are his Grey Eyed Dove, not me.'

She looks down. 'Oh, Lally.'

'I always thought it was inspired by a poem about a river.'

'It was. Everyone thinks it's a poem about peace, and it is. But Otto wrote it originally about the River Weser, in Bremen.'

'Well, it fits you perfectly. My eyes are the wrong colour. Where is he, Pauline?'

'I don't know. Truly, I don't. It's why I have to reach the safe house. That is where he will find me. Find us.'

Us. The correction was an afterthought. Norma-Rose told me the truth, it transpires, in her spiteful fashion. 'How long was this going on for? How long were you, Otto and me a triangle?'

'Lally, I don't know. A year, or less. We wanted to tell you—'

'*Hst, Mesdames!*'

We're being summoned. It's our turn to go. I pick up her bag and Pauline, out of habit, lets me take the lead. The truth, I will discover, is like the piece of wedding cake you put in your handbag and forget. For weeks, you're picking bits of it out of the lining.

51

When we reach the barbed-wire fence, Pauline's breath sounds like sandpaper on brick. Our *passeur* uses wooden batons to push down the lowest strand of wire while raising the strand above. This gap is wide enough for a normal person to wriggle through.

He looks nervously at me. 'Madame, you first.'

Chucking my bag ahead of me, I step through the gap, feeling barbs snatch at my coat. They are released by unseen hands. 'Keep going, Madame.' A step to the right, and I'm there, both feet on free ground. The two boys follow, and now it's Pauline's turn. She cannot bend double, with her pregnant stomach. Our *passeur*, out of breath from sprinting both directions in under five minutes, urges her to go flat on her belly.

'You will have to go underneath.'

She does her best, but she can't lie flat either.

'Roll onto your side, Madame. Quickly, please.'

She rolls then can't move at all, stuck, like a mare in a snowdrift.

I hunker in front of the wire. 'Try going on your back.'

With a groan of pain, she rolls again. The *passeur* and the boys lift the bottom strand as high as it will go and I place my hands under her shoulders. 'Push with your feet, Pauline.'

Her belly is so big, it catches on the wire. 'Wriggle and push, Pauline.'

'I can't.'

'You have to or we're all dead.' My anguish, my rage at her, finds a target. She will not cause my destruction, nor that of our fellow travellers. She's not going to dodge accountability for her lies by dying. 'Bring your knees together. Boys, get that wire up higher.' With them keeping those vicious teeth a hair's breadth above Pauline's bump, I flatten my hands deep under her shoulder blades and haul her like a roll of carpet. She whimpers and the snowy grass makes sucking sounds. But she's through.

We get her onto her feet. 'Now run.'

Pauline manages a few steps before buckling in pain. 'No. No. I can't.'

'You have to!' I've forgotten the need for silence. 'Move. Move or we'll leave you.'

'No, Lally, don't, please don't.' Her pleas come from a primal place, from the terror of abandonment. 'I'm sorry, so sorry. Otto hated what we did. He hated me sometimes, it broke his heart.'

The *passeur* is scouring the distance. The German patrol will be heading back by now. Right. I tell the two brothers to take mine and Pauline's bags and to run. They stumble away, slowed by the extra luggage but thankful to be free of us.

I support Pauline under one arm, the *passeur* takes her other side. We get her moving. Every now and again, she manages a few strides but essentially, we lug this nine-months pregnant woman over the ground, knowing we could be shot, or brought down by dogs, at any moment.

By some stroke of fortune, on this one night, the German patrol takes an extra minute to return to its position. We reach the woods to the breathless cheers of our companions. I have bitten through my lip out of stress, and all I want is to sink down and weep. But we've made it.

Pauline crouches against a tree, gasping and shuddering. 'It's coming, Lally.' Her eyes are wide and scared. 'The baby's coming.'

Please. Not here, not now.

'My waters have broken.'

The matronly French lady comes over and asks Pauline if she's felt a contraction. Pauline's answer is to screw up her face as pain engulfs her. The young woman with the baby says, 'She can't give birth out here.'

Pauline grips my hand. 'It's Otto's child.'

I already know. We had that conversation, remember?

She doesn't remember. She has only one thought in her mind. 'Don't leave me, Lally.'

52

We carry Pauline between us to a farmhouse and the boys in our party are dispatched for a midwife, who arrives within the hour. She's a nun from a convent on the edge of the village and she brings a novice with her who carries a basket filled with useful things. Pauline's silence since she was laid on a bed is more alarming than her screams. She's haemorrhaging and her brow is clammy to the touch.

'Lally?' Her eyes cannot locate me, though I'm holding her hand, which, in contrast to her forehead, is cold. 'You will take care of my baby?'

'You're going to be fine, Pauline.'

At some time that afternoon, a doctor is sent for as her contractions have stopped and it's to be a forceps birth. No sooner is he in the room than Pauline falls into a kind of stupor, unable to respond to commands or questions. It feels like a tortured hour passes before the doctor finishes and I hear an infant cry. The novice turns to me with a tense smile. 'God be praised. Your sister's had a boy.'

My sister, no. My friend, yes, whatever else has come

between us. The elder nun is chafing Pauline's hands, the younger one feeling for a pulse.

'Doctor?' She whispers something I don't catch. What is unmistakeable is the doctor's sudden change of demeanour. He feels for a pulse in Pauline's neck, grimaces and immediately asks for his bag. I am ordered out of the room. From the other side of the door, I listen to the sounds of professional panic.

The younger nun comes out, touches my hand as she flies past me down the stairs. I run after her. She's asking the farmer's wife where the priest lives.

The priest arrives within minutes, but too late for Pauline.

Her baby is placed against my breast. His face is wrinkled and faintly blue. He's alive, though, and writhes inside his cloth cocoon, his mouth emitting little growling cries.

Emotion pours into me like warm syrup from a jug, straight into my veins. One glance, and I know I will do anything to protect him. Anything. 'Welcome to the world, precious boy.'

Pauline's last words to me were that I must wait for Otto. 'He will come to the windmill one day and he must find his child. You will wait?'

'I will.' A vow, deep and binding.

'He must be baptised immediately,' says the senior nun. 'We'd better decide what is to be done with him, to give him the best chance in life. What is his name to be?'

I lower my face and drop the lightest kiss on his brow. He smells vaguely of the washcloths that cleaned him. Grey-blue eyes, the colour of the Seine on a moody day. The in-between tone of the German river his father wrote about. 'I will be his guardian, his foster mother,' I tell them. 'After all, I'm his aunt.'

Who can say that it isn't true?

I'm asked if I have a name. I nod. Pauline would want her boy to be named for his father. 'Otto.'

'Otto?' The doctor steps away from the bed, looking very grave. 'No, no, that will never do.'

The shock of witnessing life and death makes me forget to be cautious. 'His father is Otto Horst, the poet, pacifist and thinker.'

It means nothing to the doctor, except in the most basic sense. 'You cannot label the child a German's bastard.'

'What makes you think he's a bastard?' I am already battling for my boy, though of course his illegitimacy is indisputable, isn't it? I tell them again who Otto Horst is. 'He fled his homeland because they wanted to kill him. One day he will find me and I will put his child into his arms.'

The senior nun is more tactful but just as firm. 'A German name on the child's registration certificate will bring the worst kind of attention. Think, please. His wellbeing matters most, no? The *abbé* downstairs is Father Joseph. Will that name fit this little one, perhaps?'

I know when not to be stubborn. 'Very well. We'll name him Joseph Paul.' Paul is for Pauline, of course.

They nod, approving. It would be best also to register him under his mother's surname. I give way on this point too, knowing that one day, it can be changed.

My little boy. Welcome to this hard, hard world. I will do anything – *anything* – to keep you safe and let you thrive. The final time I touch Pauline is when I place a kiss on her ashen brow and unpin the Grey Eyed Dove from her blouse. A bird in flight is a messenger of love and this brooch is Joseph's inheritance. It is indelible proof of who he is. Who his father is.

53

HOPE

Hope had brought folding chairs along for their picnic on the pilgrims' path. They spent the morning sketching from a vantage point where Varsac's five windmills could be seen, stark shapes on their mounds. Afterwards, Yves made coffee with a spirit kettle, and Hope handed out lunch in brown paper bags. There was wine and bottled water.

They sat talking amicably, but Hope could not unlink her thoughts from the memoir, which she had read last night until her eyes blurred. Poor doomed Pauline. Had she gone with her Red Cross helpers to Vichy, she'd probably have survived childbirth. Lally would never have discovered Otto's betrayal. At least, not while the war went on. Afterwards, maybe. Otto Horst. At last, Hope had a name and could search for him. Had he ever come looking for Pauline, for Lally, for his child?

Yves was telling his audience about the pilgrims' path, how it wound towards the Pyrenees. He pointed to the mountains, their peaks snowy against the blue, like shredded white paper glued to the sky. 'At Saint-Jean-Pied-de-Port on the French–Spanish border, you join the Camino which goes all the way to Santiago de Compostela.'

'Are there wolves?' TJ wanted to know.

'There are wolves in Spain, and bears. And wild dogs. The point of doing the Camino is that it tests body and soul.'

It had been Otto's chosen route out.

When they'd finished eating and the paper bags were collected in, Hope strolled back in the direction of La Cachette and Yves caught up with her. When they reached the path that led down to the mill, they gazed on the strands of barbed wire.

'I can't help thinking about Pauline, having to get under a fence in the snow,' Hope said. 'Hours from giving birth, faced with a cross-country sprint. I see what you mean about this fence being a hostile act. They're guarding what – fifty paces of barren ground?'

Yves gave a snort. 'The Taubiers formed a vendetta against Lally after the war, as a smokescreen for their own actions.'

'Not Madame Taubier, Otto's friend?'

'No, not her. The male family members. The current generation are still at it, and I'm the target.'

'Have you ever sat down with them?' Hope had again almost called Taubier et fils that morning, before bottling out again.

'Come off it. You saw how Jonny Taubier looked at me at your place. You've seen how Manon behaves. What you haven't seen is how Jonny's father foams at the mouth when he sees me. Inherited quarrels are the worst, because people have forgotten why they started, but it's become a matter of honour.'

Hope changed the subject. 'What surname would my father have been registered under at birth – Granger, Horst or Ducasse?'

'Ducasse, I should think, as that was the name Pauline had assumed. It would seal his illegitimacy but would have raised no eyebrows.'

'He ended up as Joseph Granger because my great-grandparents got hold of him but did they know he had a German father?'

'I can't answer that if you can't,' Yves responded. 'Did you ever meet them?'

'My great-grandparents? No. They were long gone by the time I was born. Perhaps it isn't fair to judge their motives. I'd love to know how they discovered they had a grandson in France. Would Lally have told them? She might.'

'If she did, and the memoir is missing its last pages, we may never know.' Yves stepped over the barbed-wire fence and held his hands out to her. 'Let's trespass.'

She was worried about snagging her wide-leg trousers. He pushed down the top strand and let her use his shoulder to lean on as she swung over one leg, then the other. 'Into no-man's land,' she said.

They walked to a gate that led into Yves' property, where Hope asked how Lally had come to own La Cachette.

'Véronique Taubier sold it to her.'

'Véronique... Otto's admirer, she of the safe house?'

'That's right. She took Lally in at some point and, towards the end of her life, she offered La Cachette at a low price. That was about 1980, and I can tell you, it made the rest of the Taubier family spit nails.'

'What I don't understand is, why did Lally stay in a place where people mistreated her? Because she was waiting for Otto to come?'

'I suppose. Then maybe later for Joseph. Finish the book, Hope, so I can read the rest.'

They retraced their steps, and Hope detached a tag of cloth that had torn off her shirt. It was a favourite garment but that wasn't the cause of a niggling discomfort. She was Pauline's granddaughter, and while it neatly solved a mystery, it weighed heavy. Lally had died fifteen years ago, her life haunted by the conduct of the two people she loved most. Who *owed* her the most. Pauline and Otto had broken an honest, vulnerable heart. Yves was so protective of Lally, could he really look at Hope and not see the shadow of Pauline?

Instead of pursuing that line, she told Yves she was cooking duck for dinner. 'Trying to replicate the meal we had at Le Sentier.' She invited him to come back home with them. 'You can help again.'

He said he'd come along in a couple of hours. He was back to driving again, though Hope suspected it was probably not with his doctor's permission. 'I promised Claudia I'd check the oil in her car. She's collecting the twins tomorrow, then they're heading back home to the Netherlands.'

'Is she going to be OK?'

'I think so,' he said. 'A man she met on one of her bike rides invited her out. She turned him down, but seeing her ex living his best life in Bordeaux, she's having second thoughts.'

'Good for her,' said Hope.

They were greeted by the others with whistles. 'Where have you two been?'

'Checking the fencing,' Hope said.

Before she drove everyone home, Yves leaned into her car and kissed her on the cheek. '*À bientôt.*'

'*Ooh là là,*' said Goldie. 'What a tangled web we weave.'

Yves arrived as Hope was reducing a pan of *jus* with foaming butter. He put wine down and told her the food smelled delicious, but she couldn't block the suspicion that something had changed in the hours since they'd parted. Goldie's well-meaning reference to a 'tangled web' could have unnerved him. After dinner, when they were alone, she challenged him. 'Is there a problem? I've had all I can take of men giving me the silent treatment. You've been tense all evening.'

He looked aghast at her. 'Silent? I've done nothing but talk for two hours. Before I met you, I could go days without speaking to anyone. Give me a break, Hope.'

She apologised. Yves had steered the conversation and kept everyone enthralled with his stories of Thailand, but she didn't retract. 'I have a nose for resentment. Do you look at me now and see Pauline?'

'That would be pretty horrible, now we know that Pauline died more than seventy years ago. It's a sad, sad story. Poor girl. Why should I resent you?'

'She screwed Lally over, she and Otto.'

'It happens, doesn't it?' When she didn't answer, Yves made a gruff kind of noise. 'OK.'

'OK, as in, "There is something"?'

'Yes, and I'm embarrassed.'

'Please, just out with it.' She hadn't realised how fragile her tolerance for rejection had become.

'It's nothing to do with Pauline.' He took a breath. 'I looked up your ex. Rupert Ashton, in Brighton, his start-up company and that woman we saw on his Facebook page. DeeCee1988 is her Facebook profile and they've launched company, offering cyber security to high-tech firms and media companies. They're joint directors and have been since—' Another breath. Preparing for the killer strike. 'April of this year.'

'I know,' she said lightly.

'You do?'

'You're not the only one who knows how to use a search engine. I googled them last night, while chatting with a London friend of mine.' She'd called Katie at ten o'clock; they'd always been night owls in the past and Katie still was. 'You might say, I faced my worst fears.'

'I went one further. I called the phone number on his page.'

'Wow.'

'The woman answered. *Oh, Dieu*, this is awful. Her name is Dayna Cornwell. DeeCee to friends.'

'And?'

'And... we got talking. She likes to talk. I lapsed into French, a bit.'

'You mean, you flirted in a sexy French accent with the woman who took my man?'

'I might have done.' He screwed up his face. 'Pretty soon she was telling me that she and Rupert' – he said 'Rupert' with a rolling R – 'are not only partners in business but also in life. I'm sorry, Hope. I know it's crossing a line. I just saw the number, and—'

'Started dialling. The way you do.'

He looked wretched. 'I suppose you won't see me as a friend after this.'

'No. No I don't.'

From wretched, he looked ragged. 'I always screw up.'

'Oh, Yves.' She couldn't torment him any longer and put her arms around him. 'I don't see you as a friend because I feel more than that. It's outrageous, and crazy and embarrassing, but there is it.' She rested her chin against his. 'I've known about Dayna and Rupert for a whole twenty-four hours because Katie did the same. Called the number. Katie claimed she ran a casting agency in LA and there was so much hacking in the industry could she ask some advice... blah, blah, and DeeCee-Dayna took over the talking and overshared her personal life.'

'I'm glad you know.'

'I know something else too. Katie didn't want to tell me at first, but when I started going out with Ash, she knew people who knew him. Someone mentioned that before me, he was with a woman for two years, and before that, he was with another woman for two years.'

'You're saying he has a sell-by date?'

'I'm saying we girls get two years of the Ash love, then *ping!* He's out.'

'And when I so wanted to kiss you on your terrace...'

'He was coming to break up with me, but we handed him the opportunity to not be the bad guy. He doesn't like being the bad guy.'

A hank of hair that Yves' barber had somehow missed fell forward, tickling the bridge of Hope's nose. They kissed until Yves drew back. Cupping her face, he said, 'I have another confession. Before I went scrolling through Facebook, I looked up Otto Horst.'

'No!' Hope had wanted to do the same but getting dinner ready had taken up all her time. 'You found him?'

'After a hell of a search. It was the poem I found, in the end. "The Grey Eyed Dove", in German. It was on an obscure site, dedicated to German anti-Nazis.'

'Did he make it to freedom?'

A headshake prepared her. 'He died, Hope. In a concentration camp on the French–Spanish border. In 1940. I'm so sorry.'

For a while, she couldn't speak. It felt all so sad and futile. Otto and Pauline. 'Their lives just fell off a cliff. Did Lally ever know what became of Otto?'

'I don't know, but Victor, my grandfather, might have known. Or Julien might. He had influence, and friends in high places. One of them would have attempted to trace Otto.'

'And Lally would have too.' Hope said, 'After the war ended and the months went by, she'd have been desperate to know where he was.'

Yves agreed, adding, 'You need to read her memoir to the end.'

'Except there isn't an end, as you keep reminding me.'

'Have you got any Armagnac? We could both do with a pick-up.'

She fetched a bottle of the best Haut-Armagnac, bought from a local estate and poured two shots.

'*Santé*.' They tipped rims and he asked, 'Can I stay tonight?'

'I think you'd better.'

He went out to his car, coming back in with the charcoal-and-pastel portrait of Pauline. It was now in a clip-frame. Hope took down a so-so painting she'd bought on a whim and hung Pauline's portrait in its place. 'I'd love to have seen her when she was laughing, and wide awake. She looks empty with her eyes closed.'

'She was not well, Hope. Malnourished by that point, about to give birth. She must have been exhausted.'

Midnight found them side by side, doing the washing-up. Yves put the duck bones into a pot for stock and said, 'You have to remember, we get everything about Pauline from Lally's perspective. Let me tell you, Lally wasn't easy. I loved her with all my soul, but she could be an absolute nightmare. So damaged, so angry. She wrote the memoir when she was in her fifties and drinking quite a bit.'

'We know who damaged her, though, don't we?'

'No – it started before she even reached Paris. She was poor, and talented. A girl. I think she was seduced by a predatory tutor at Durham, from hints she dropped. In Paris, she struggled to be taken seriously. How many gifted male painters do you know who survived only because they sat for other artists?'

Hope returned a vague answer, thinking back to a conversation from earlier in the day. They'd all been in the windmill, painting, and during a break, Goldie and Paloma had gone to look at the portrait of Lally that still hung there. They obviously knew it depicted somebody special to Yves, because Goldie asked him, 'I know this is treading on history but what happened to her?'

Yves had returned a deliberately blank look. 'Happened? She had a bad hair day.'

'Drop the act, honey.' That wasn't going to wash with Goldie. 'You're always telling us to look into the soul of what we see. "Don't draw what you want to be there. If it's not there, don't add it."' Goldie had stood right next to the portrait, pointing a finger. 'I look into the soul of this painting and I don't have to be a retired psychotherapist to know the poor girl went through something godawful.'

Hope put down the glass she was drying. 'You swerved Goldie's question today, Yves. I don't blame you. I saw that photograph Inès was putting up, so I know Lally was attacked by a mob. But Goldie was right, the eyes don't lie. In her portrait, Lally looks like a woman who has glimpsed hell, then picked up a paintbrush.'

'Fancy a walk?' Yves glanced out of the window. 'Looks like a lovely night. Let's take candles.'

'OK,' Hope said cautiously. 'What's the event?'

'I'm going to answer your question.'

Within ten minutes, they were in the cathedral courtyard, with the slow-dripping fountain and ivy-covered walls. Yves once again uncovered the plaque with the men's names on. Leaning in to read it, with their flickering candles, Hope thought they must resemble a painting by a Dutch master.

Yves read what was on the stone. '"On August 5th, 1944, on this spot, twelve men of Lazurac were shot by the German SS. *Vive la Résistance*". It was in reprisal for their part in the Resistance uprising the previous day.'

He pointed out something Hope hadn't previously seen, that against the last of the twelve names was the addendum, 'Aged sixteen years'.

The lad was called Simon Royale.

'He was an uncle of the man Inès grew up to marry. She was a very little girl at the time of his death, but she would have known the story.'

'Then I understand why she is so angry, and if she blames Lally—'

'She *must* blame Lally, because otherwise, she would have to blame her own family,' Yves said fiercely. 'Inès was a Taubier. If you are going to hate somebody, hate the outcast, not your own tribe. Punish the unprotected woman and not your handsome well-to-do papa and uncle, particularly if there are rumours circulating about their conduct in the hours before the atrocity.'

Hope relived the moment Inès had set eyes on Lally's portrait. *Her.* Had Inès found, in Lally, a convenient scapegoat for her grief and trauma as well as a cover for something unpalatable in her own family? 'How did they get caught, the men of Lazurac's Resistance?'

Yves gave her the background. 'In the summer of 1944, the Americans, British and Allied forces were pushing their way up from the south. The Germans were fighting back, and the Resistance mobilised. Their aim was to hamper the Germans by attacking them, blowing up bridges and roads, cutting telephone wires. On August the third, the Lazurac cell was directed to sabotage the railway line. The one that runs below the town. It's the main spur from Brive-la-Gaillarde to Toulouse, and a key route down to the coast. Our Resistance planned to blow up part of Lazurac's ramparts, to bring tons of rubble onto the line. On the given night, eleven men and young Simon Royale gathered in a safe location. In fact, you've been there.'

'I have?' Hope immediately thought – Le Chat? She was wrong.

'The house they met in was a fortified manor, now a restaurant. Le Sentier.'

'Where we ate the Saturday my guests arrived.'

'It was a farmhouse then, owned by a family sympathetic to the Resistance, and the men met in their cellar. So – third of August was a Thursday night, and a day before the full moon.

That's not always a good thing. They smeared their faces with charred cork, pulled on their berets and set out. They were betrayed and shot in this courtyard.'

'And afterwards, Lally was literally dragged through the streets, accused of the betrayal, is that right?'

'As far as many were concerned, she was guilty without question.' Yves' candle stuttered out and he relit it from Hope's. Their eyes met, and without either of them speaking, both knew they needed each other that night.

54

BARBED WIRE AND FALSE NAMES: MEMOIR OF AN
ENGLISH GIRL IN OCCUPIED FRANCE

We bury Pauline in the grounds of the convent. The midwife-nuns have found Joseph a wet nurse, a local woman who has lost a baby and has milk to spare. I work long hours in return for my keep. Mopping, chopping, digging their vegetable beds once the freezing weather abates. Spring arrives, summer comes and goes. I help bring in the grape harvest of 1941, and little Joseph thrives. Part of me wishes to stay here forever. The other part cannot relinquish Otto, and my dream of being with him. There is my vow to Pauline, too, to find the safe place where, one day, he will come in search of his child.

In the end, fate gives me the nudge.

I am in the garden hoeing between rows and a nun approaches. 'Lally, the travel bag your dear sister had with her would be useful to one of our number who has to go to another convent. Would you be willing to part with it?'

Of course. I haven't enough possessions to need two bags.

'I'll empty it out,' I say. 'Time I did.' I've not wanted to gaze on Pauline's things, but I go straight to it.

I decide to keep Pauline's blouses, and a jumper. The rest, the nuns will find good use for. I find a canister of film, which I'm sure is the one Pauline took from her camera on our last night in Paris. One day, I'll get it developed. I'm not going to cry, I'm going to be orderly and resist hanging onto anything unless I think Joseph will treasure it one day.

I burn the letters from Pauline's family, thinking how ill-advised she was, before remembering that because she didn't go in person to the British Desk at the American embassy, as I had to, she didn't get the benefit of that nice chap's advice. 'Don't *even think* about writing a letter home, d'you hear?'

There is a sheet of fawn-coloured paper concealed under the false bottom of the holdall. Remember how I said that finding truth is like picking cake crumbs from the lining of a handbag? I find I'm reading a marriage certificate and the date is a punch to the throat. On the 12th of June, 1940, while I was scanning the surging crowd of refugees for Pauline, she was at the town hall. Pauline married Otto that morning, with two witnesses. One I think was the Marshalls' sewing woman she claimed she was visiting. The other was probably a stranger pulled off the street. It's why she wore her smartest suit and that wickedly expensive hat. Couture for her wedding day. The town hall in the fifth arrondissement is approached though an avenue of lime trees which in mid-June were in flower, explaining the petals on her shoulders. It all makes perfect sense. Instead of leaving Paris well ahead of the German advance, Otto lingered to marry his pregnant lover.

My heart tears from its anchorage and the ghosts of my dearest friends rip it to pieces in front of my eyes. Pauline was Madame Otto Horst. Had she not married that day, we would have got away from Paris an hour earlier and missed the bombing raid. Our driver might have lived, and we could have made it out of France.

The result is that I feel a driving need to be on my way. To be where Otto will come one day to find his son. Not to be reunited with him, but to ask him why.

Why Pauline, and not me?

I will go to Lazurac, to the safe house, before the weather turns. I write to Madame Taubier, whom I have never met nor spoken to, explaining who I am, informing her of my intentions, and enclose a little sketch of Joseph. On the picture I write, 'the grey eyed son', trusting she will understand the reference.

The nuns are sad to see me go. They adore Joseph. I am sorry to leave them and it's a tearful farewell.

We arrive in the département of the Gers on the last day of October and, after a night in a modest hotel, Joseph and I get a lift in a wine-merchants' truck to Lazurac, and a ride in a donkey-trap the last few kilometres to Varsac-les-Moulins. The Grey Eyed Dove is pinned to my coat. It feels strange to be throwing myself on the hospitality of a woman whose only connection to Otto is that she admired a poem of that name.

Joseph falls asleep in my arms as I trudge up a poplar-lined drive to Madame Taubier's front door. The crunch of my boots is the subdued finale of a harsh, eighteen-month-long concerto. I knock and the door is opened by a lean, tall lady with grey upswept hair. She wears black with a little lace and the instant impression is of discreet wealth. On cue, Joseph wakes and her expression changes from puzzlement to astonishment.

'*Mon Dieu*, you have come! This is Otto's boy?'

All I can do is nod.

She smiles radiantly. 'Oh, but you have a beautiful child, the two of you. Otto wrote to me from Bordeaux, saying I might expect you, that he was married. *Mon Dieu, mon Dieu,* I am so happy.'

She thinks I am Otto's wife, and this is our child. I know I should correct her, but I can't find the words. Do I want to find the words? The truth of Joseph's birth will never reach this remote place. Let Madame Taubier think I'm Joseph's mother. After all, I am the nearest thing to a mother that he has.

When Otto comes, I will confess it all.

55

My new friend's full name is Madame Véronique Taubier. She is a widow with no children. I was wrong in assuming her to be wealthy. True, she inherited property from her husband and the windmill next to her house provides her income, but grain supplies are sporadic and labour is unreliable. Also, Véronique gives away flour to her poorer neighbours when nobody is looking.

We fall into an easy friendship though at first, she wants to treat me as a guest. I am having none of that.

I tell her I will earn my keep. 'I like to work.' So long as I have Joseph with me and can do a little painting and sketching, I am content. Graciously, she gives in, admitting there is always too much for her to do. As the weeks pass, our days take on a rhythm. Along with myself, Joseph and Madame Taubier, the household consists of an elderly maid called Charlotte and her grandson, Aubin. Aubin is rather simple, but a kindly soul. Though the village is tiny, a hamlet really, it's not a lonely spot. Whenever I'm digging or planting in the garden, I hear the mill wheel grinding, and the shouts of the men who work it. I love that the shape of the sails against the sky tells a different story with each change of weather.

Winter comes. Christmas passes. New Year 1942 arrives and two months later, in March, we celebrate Joseph's first birthday. My darling boy is a constant source of delight and the seasons pass. Spring, summer, fading to autumn. In November that year, the Germans invade the Zone Libre, taking over the whole of France. Life, hard enough already, gets harder still. We know that the tide of the war is turning against the enemy, but a cornered dog is the most dangerous. Madame Taubier warns me to trust nobody, to say nothing to anyone that isn't either about the weather or the price of bread. Informants are like cockroaches, she says, everywhere but hidden. Still, we get by, growing our food, keeping chickens and goats and patching our clothes. When I am not being *la belle maman*, I draw and paint. My fatal mistake is to regain my health and looks. To wear colours other than brown, and to comb my hair in a becoming way.

Varsac-les-Moulins has five windmills, of which three belonged to Madame Taubier's late husband. On his death, she got the next-door one, and his two brothers inherited the others. The brothers resent Véronique, believing she got the best mill as well as the house. In short, they want what she has but Madame won't give it to them. It doesn't stop them visiting whenever it suits them and throwing their weight about. The older brother, Alain, is a blustering windbag with ambitions to be mayor of Lazurac. Étienne, the younger one, is handsome in a broad-faced, veiny-cheeked way and he boasts of being a member of the maquis, the Free Frenchmen who live out in the hills. He claims to have single-handedly formed a Resistance cell in Lazurac. Old Charlotte calls Étienne a 'Fireside Résistant', always to be found at home, toasting his toes, when the cell is active. She tells me that the brothers supply flour to bakeries that serve the Germans.

'Have their sons been sent to Germany for forced labour? *Non*. Favours come from somewhere.'

I give both brothers a wide berth, but occasionally, I'm not fast enough or Joseph, who loves everyone, runs up to them and I have to follow. They always ask me where I've come from, who my family are. Étienne mentally strips my clothes off me while he talks.

They know I'm a fugitive from something, they just can't work out what. The day Étienne puts his hand on my breast, holding my wrists in his meaty grip, is the day my happy life here comes to an end.

He is laughing as he gets a hand past the buttons of my blouse. *Rip!* When he pulls his fingers away, he's holding the Grey Eyed Dove.

'What is this?'

'A brooch,' I tell him. 'You know, one of those things women like to wear.' My cheeks angry-red, I do up my buttons.

'It doesn't look French to me.' He squints at it, trying to identify a hallmark.

'Could you give it back?' I'm trying to be calm, but my tolerance for being manhandled is non-existent.

He throws the brooch onto the carpet, and as I bend to pick it up, shoves his groin against the back of my skirt. As with Raton that time, something snaps. I retaliate, kicking his shins and he spits at me that I'm a frigid bitch. In return, I scratch his face with the brooch pin.

Just as with Raton at the prison, I pay for it later.

It is Christmas 1942. We are in the kitchen and Madame Taubier is making a compote of preserved fruits in Armagnac. I'm by the stove with Joseph on my knee. There's a heavy rap on the door. Charlotte's grandson, Aubin, goes up the steps, coming down a minute later followed by the local Milice chief. That is to say, the head enforcer in the district, a Frenchman required by reason of his rank to obey German rules.

He greets Madame Taubier before his eyes find me. 'You, Madame, may I see your papers.'

All who have felt existential threat know how a heart falls inside the chest, settling into a sharp, resounding beat. I hand Joseph to Madame Taubier, and leave the kitchen, returning with my *carte d'identité* and Joseph's ration book.

The Milice chief inspects the documents and hands them back, then explains his visit. Étienne Taubier alleges that I attacked him with a sharp object.

'Because he ripped my blouse,' I retort, 'having attacked me with something very small and blunt. Do you wish me to describe the offending object?'

Madame Taubier shakes her head. *Don't, Lally.*

Charlotte, in her usual corner, cackles delightedly. 'Small and blunt describes it. Very small and very blunt, I should say.'

The Milice chief doesn't wish to hear precise descriptions and apologises for bothering me. He is very respectful to Madame Taubier, whose husband was a leading citizen, and we end up drinking a glass of fiery Armagnac together. Next time I see Étienne Taubier, I receive a look of distilled loathing. I suspect that 'very small and blunt' has done the rounds. I should have kept my mouth shut.

A few days after Christmas, Étienne calls with his brother. Sidling up to me, he whispers, 'I know about the Grey Eyed Dove.'

'You mean the brooch I bought off a stall on the Rue des Rosiers, in Paris?'

'Not the brooch. The poem by Otto Horst. The one that got him on a death list.'

Ice hits my veins. I stammer that I don't know what he means.

'My sister-in-law tried to get me to read it. Huh,' he sneers, 'as if I have the time. Otto Horst and you, ha? The Germans would pay good money to have him.'

'Listen,' I say and manage a kind of simper. 'You and I have got off to a bad start—'

Madame Taubier comes in. She caught the end of the conversation and despite the way I widen my eyes, signalling to her to say nothing, she strides up to her brother-in-law. 'If you betray that man, by the blue eyes of Our Lady, I will burn my mill to the ground and this house too, with me in it, and you will get nothing.'

'Shut up, Véronique,' Étienne snarls. 'You like rotten poetry and you're a fool, taking in a woman who consorts with Germans.'

She orders him out of her house. 'Fight your imaginary wars against men your own size.'

He has his revenge when he induces Madame Taubier's workers to leave her mill for his. As so much of the male workforce is doing obligatory labour in Germany, those left are the old, the maimed or the simple ones like Aubin. Madame does her best to keep things going but every time she finds a hand to employ, Étienne offers more.

It's cat and mouse, they're the cats and we're the mice.

1943 arrives and on New Year's Day we listen to the BBC on the wireless, safe behind the kitchen shutters. We often tune in to Radio Londres, the Free French service, too, listening with delight to the coded messages, wondering what they mean.

'The Queen of the Night sends greetings to the Trumpet Player. Two down, not bad!'

It goes without saying, it's just as illegal here in the south-west as it was in the north, and clandestine wireless listening is bread-and-butter to informants and snitches.

Meanwhile, the Resistance recruits more men, those who prefer to live rough in the foothills than to be sent off to work for the Germans. Its tactics harden, feeding the neurosis of the Nazis in our midst. I should have predicted that Étienne Taubier would turn a profit in this febrile atmosphere and repay Madame Taubier for her taunt, and me for spurning his advances.

56

It is late January 1943, and I am hacking at frozen ground, trying to get the last of the turnips. What kind of God looks upon humanity writhing under the jackboot of war and says, 'I know, why don't I send three of the cruellest winters in living memory, one after the other?'

Madame Taubier, who is conventionally religious, insists it is to test us.

Test us it does. She shut the mill. Its sails are now a perch for birds of prey driven out of the Pyrenean mountains by the cold. Short-eared owls nest inside. I see them at dawn and dusk, hunting along the line of the pilgrims' path. We have no fuel, apart from the wood that I gather and cut with Aubin's help.

My poor little Joseph, coming up to his second birthday, suffers so badly from chilblains he howls. I rub balsam and goose fat into his swollen toes and take him into my bed, letting him lie against me. He spends his days on my knee or playing with wooden blocks under a blanket tent. I pin the Grey Eyed Dove to my belt, because he loves to close his small fist around it and now its provenance has been identified by

Étienne, there's no point hiding it. I play with the idea that Otto's energy and soul was captured in its silver. I let Joseph hold it.

'*Petit oiseau*,' he lisps. Little birdie.

Charlotte is wheezing dreadfully these days. We feed her broth – she has no teeth – but it's ever thinner broth and I see Aubin rocking on the balls of his feet as he watches her eat. If he loses his grandma... well, she's all he has.

I'm all that Joseph has and I'm in danger of failing in my sacred task. He is growing thin, no more plump cheeks or fat little hands.

Fate – or Étienne Taubier – hands me a way out of starvation, though as in Greek tragedy, it comes at a terrible price. It is a sleety February morning and I am carrying frosted turnips into the kitchen, finding my companions huddled around the stove. I'm the first to hear the approaching vehicle. As we wait, locked in a heart-pumping tableau, me with a turnip in my hand, the kitchen door blasts open and at least eight SS troops surge in. A moment's silence is broken as my turnip hits the floor.

'Seize her!' is shouted in German. I'm pinioned by two of them. The man in charge, who is probably around forty, wears a high-fronted cap bearing a death's head badge and silver eagle. He shouts for the house to be searched. I don't know why he feels he must shout.

Joseph, crying, wriggles off Madame Taubier's knee and runs to me, clutching my legs. I can't reach down to him, so I tell him it's all right, and to go back to Tante Véronique. I look at the man I assume to be in charge. 'What is this about?'

Madame Taubier picks up Joseph, who has huge tears bouncing off his cheeks. She also addresses the officer. 'Explain why you have burst into my home.'

A soldier comes down the kitchen steps, holding the wireless. He puts it on the table and the officer inspects it. We're not stupid. We haven't left the dial on the BBC's frequency but on one that pumps out pro-German propaganda.

'Clearly, you're looking for something,' Madame Taubier says.

The officer hasn't much French. He turns to another man who comes in and drops a bundle of my sketchbooks on the kitchen table. These are mostly drawings of Joseph, Madame Taubier, Charlotte and Aubin. There are some views of the turnip patch and of the windmill in varying moods. For the following twenty or so minutes we witness members of the elite German SS sifting through fifteen months' worth of my busy pencil. The dangerous sketches, with scenes of Paris and my fellow prisoners in Besançon, and the Ursuline nuns who housed me after Joseph was born – these are hidden behind a panel in the attic. These men won't poke around up there, in among the cobwebs.

Their officer comes to stand in front of me. His eyes are pale as a mountain spring, his features notably handsome. Heavens above. Am I finding men attractive again?

'Where are the pictures of Otto Horst?' he asks in uncomfortable French.

I make my face blank, and he repeats the name.

'*Horst*... that sounds German,' I say.

'We have information that you were involved with him.'

I shake my head. 'I have never been involved with a German, and never will be. Your information is bad. Who passed it to you?'

From the irritation that clouds his eyes it's evident he doesn't like to be cross-examined. He lets a silence build, an obvious technique, but effective all the same. Joseph grizzles and reaches out to me.

'Maman.'

'Who is the child's father?' The German lifts Joseph up, gazing into his face. 'He has grey eyes.'

'Grey-blue, like my father's,' I correct him. In truth, my Tynesider dad had eyes as blue as the glaze on a willow pattern plate.

'So – who is the father?' The officer looks down at my left hand, at the ring I wear. I took it from Pauline's hand. She claimed she'd worn it to make things easier at the YWCA, but I can assume it was the wedding band that Otto placed on her finger.

I tell the officer that Joseph's father was a French infantryman who died on the beaches of Normandy. His name was Joseph Ducasse and he originated from the Auvergne. I choose that location as it's the remotest, most underpopulated part of France. I add, 'From Puy-de-Dôme.' I once sat for a painter who came from there and, from him, I can throw in a few descriptions if need be.

It isn't needed. Puy-de-Dôme means as much to my inter-rogator as some town in Bavaria or Prussia means to me. Then he floors me. 'Where is the Grey Eyed Dove?'

I gape. I manage to stammer, 'I don't know what you mean.'

'It is a piece... a small...' His French gives up on him. He taps the SS runes on his tunic collar. 'Like this.'

I shake my head again. I'm still being gripped by his henchmen and the blood has stopped flowing to my fingers. 'I don't understand what you're asking.'

'The object, which Otto Horst is giving to you.'

I'm about to repeat that I don't know an Otto Horst when Joseph turns in the man's arms, points to the belt of my dress concealed under layers of outdoor clothing and says, 'Joseph wants it. *Petit oiseau.*' Little birdie.

57

HOPE

To be in her bed, the one she had shared with Ash, with another man felt both defiant and exhilarating.

Maybe there was an overlap between her and Pauline, Hope thought. An ability to embrace moral ambiguity because it felt good.

It felt *wonderful*. After blowing their candles out in the cathedral court, she and Yves had walked home in silence. At home, she'd led the way upstairs, her fingers laced with his. The erotic fuse lit many days ago made every touch more focussed and intense. For Hope, Ash's defection made the regaining of her feminine power all the sweeter, and as she blended her body with Yves', she found a freedom she'd never felt before. In his face she saw a kind of wonder, and fear that what they had created might just as quickly disappear. She had no intention of evaporating like morning mist; if this was dawn, then day was a short way behind and it would be fascinating.

Had she replaced Ash? She asked herself that as she lay with her bedclothes covering her as far as her hip bones, Yves' face against her shoulder. He was asleep, in an attitude of surrender. He had a great back. Muscular, broad and narrow in the right places, plus some pretty iffy tattoos. Probably done when young. No women's names, she noted.

She had not replaced Ash because Ash had gone. A page had turned. A different Hope had changed places with the old one.

What were her plans for today? She mused on it. First stop was the baker's and the grocery store for butter and coffee beans. Lally's memoir was on her bedside table but Hope wasn't tempted to pick it up. She wanted this euphoric moment to go on for as long as possible.

Little birdie, fly away. The pain can wait another day.

BARBED WIRE AND FALSE NAMES: MEMOIR OF AN ENGLISH GIRL IN OCCUPIED FRANCE

When the SS officer asks me why my son is pointing at my waist, I am faced with a choice: challenge him to search me or give in with dignity. I choose dignity, saying that if he'd ask his men to release me, we can clear up this matter.

He nods and my arms are dropped. Sensation rushes back, making me clumsy, but after shaking my hands and flexing my fingers, I'm able to hand over my Grey Eyed Dove.

He inspects it, turns it over, glances at me questioningly. 'It says here, "*Mit Liebe*".'

'Does it?'

'It is inscribed on the pin. Very small, but I have excellent eyesight.'

I don't know what to say. The brooch was a gift of love from Otto's sister. I took it from him, Pauline took it from me, and I got it back from her. It's an emblem of love entangled.

'Well?' The SS officer is an Obergruppenführer, I will

later learn. The senior rank around here. Not to be messed with.

I simply don't know what to say, except to ask if I may, please, pick up my little boy.

A nod allows it. Joseph bolts into my grasp.

'Maman.' His tears, my tears. If I'm arrested for aiding and abetting Otto's escape from France, I'll be killed or sent eastward into oblivion. What of Joseph? Because Madame Taubier will be implicated too. Étienne Taubier and Alain will profit from her downfall and the idea of my sweet, darling boy falling into their clutches makes me feel physically sick.

'You have to the count of three to answer.'

I'm starting to panic. Do I hold to my story of buying the brooch at a Parisian market stall? Or do I risk the truth?

'One. Two—'

I start talking, in German, and what comes out of my mouth astonishes even me. It is the only thing I have going for me, the only handhold as I tumble off the ledge. I grab it.

HOPE

Yves stirred and Hope twisted her head to the side to kiss his shoulder.

'Mm. Do we have to get up?'

'We do,' she said. 'I need to open the shutters and make breakfast. This is everyone's last day, so it needs to be a good one.'

'Then I will perform to my best. I want them to give you five-star ratings and for you to do well.' He rolled to face her. 'Then you won't have to sell up and go back to England.'

'What makes you think I'd go back? Like Lally, I've nobody to go back for.'

Not long after, showered and dressed, they were heading to the bakery. Passing Taubier's estate agency, Hope cast a glance at the desirable properties with their euro price tags. 'I will have to sell. There's no way out of that.'

'Has Ash replied, since you called him out on his ridiculous demands?'

'Not in any way I can repeat.'

'Don't ever send me a spreadsheet, Hope.'

'I won't. You need to give me your accounts so I can repay my side of the deal. Are they in a binbag, or was it a box?'

He made a kind of groan. 'I will, soon. Tonight, I want to cook for you all, *chez moi*.'

'We won't fit in your caravan.'

'Claudia has gone. The gîte is empty. Would you like to?'

'I would. I'll sell it to the others.' She laughed at his reaction. 'They'll love to. They adore you.'

It was decided that during the first part of that day, they would paint and draw in Hope's garden, then decamp to La Cachette after lunch. Hope found a moment to slip inside. Opening her laptop, she went into her business website and deleted all the pictures of her and Ash. She inserted a new image on the front page, and wrote the caption: *The studio with the best view in Gascony*

It was a picture she'd taken from the top floor of Yves' windmill, showing Goldie and Paloma at work at their easels, and the wide-open view towards the mountains. Yves had been on the balcony, turning to look back at her as she took the shot.

As a picture, it had everything. It was intimate, intense, sexy, dramatic. She saved the changes and sent a link to her mailing list.

BARBED WIRE AND FALSE NAMES: MEMOIR OF AN ENGLISH GIRL IN OCCUPIED FRANCE

'The brooch was given to me by an Austrian aristocrat named Herr von Salzach. I met him in Paris, before the war.' The art-loving second-in-command at Besançon had spoken of visiting Paris, and I could have met him without realising. In saying the first thing that jumps into my panicking brain, I am stepping across a line from which there is no retreat. Madame Taubier, poor lady, stares at me, aghast. I've never revealed to her my command of German.

The SS officer is flipping through another of my sketchbooks. Still using the weapon of silence, but I know I've piqued his interest. It emboldens me. 'Herr von Salzach liked my work. He liked me.' The alteration in my interrogator's expression reins me in. I refine what I'm saying. 'There was nothing improper. It was one artist to another.'

'"*Mit Liebe*"?'

I can't shrug with Joseph clinging to me. I sigh instead.

'Who knows? A different place, a different time... I admired him very much.'

'As you should! If it is Graf Sigmund von Salzach you are speaking of, he is a revered artist in Germany. Even the Führer admires his work and the Führer is an artist himself!' The man's voice throbs with veneration, though whether for von Salzach, Hitler or both, I cannot say.

I lower my eyes and make another precarious decision. 'Then I am doubly honoured that he said such flattering things about my work.'

'Where was this drawn?' He shows me a landscape.

'Er... from the old path that runs behind this house. There's a hill from where you can see our windmill and the tops of the others. To me, they look as though they are signalling to each other.'

'Signalling?'

'I mean, the wind was strong that day. So much so, the millers put the brakes on the sails.'

'What do you do with these sketches?'

I answer that I create far more views than I can ever turn into actual works. I have no paint, no canvas. 'To answer your question, nothing. I will do nothing with them.'

A few days later, a crate of art supplies arrives. Good-quality paper, tubes of oils, brushes, turpentine, a roll of canvas. The day after, the Obergruppenführer himself calls to see if the materials are to my liking. He tells me his name is Kristoff. He came expecting to arrest me, but now, those steely eyes glitter with admiration. In a region where people's colouring tends towards Spanish-dark, my blondeness perhaps makes me appear less foreign to him. And of course, I speak German. I won the battle and must now deal with the consequences.

One day, he asks me to accompany him for a nice walk. Of course, he has more than that in mind.

I have never in my life until this moment traded my body for material advantage but with this high-ranking German, I can see my escape from Étienne Taubier's treachery. From malnutrition. Becoming Kristoff's lover brings iron-clad protection as well as food, wood and coal. Joseph's cheeks fill out and old Charlotte regains her strength.

Kristoff is uncomfortable around Aubin at first, as his Nazi creed deems Charlotte's grandson to be 'defective', yet once he's got to know Aubin a bit, he says in awe, 'He has remarkable wisdom, locked in a child's mind.'

Madame Taubier keeps her feelings to herself. At first, she refuses to share in the rewards of my sin, but she can't hold out when I roast a chicken with garlic and wine. She accepts that this is a matter of survival for us all.

The winter and spring of 1943 play out far more comfortably than we feared.

If I have to describe Kristoff in three words they would be 'earnest, eager and predictable'. Being a German officer is, of course, his leading talent. A physical education instructor before the war, he has me doing daily exercises to create 'a corset of strength' in my waist and lower back, a legacy that benefits me to this day. He knows a lot about the great musical composers, of whom I am woefully ignorant. One evening, he arrives with a gramophone player attached to the back of his motorcycle. On subsequent visits, he brings records until I amass a collection. I can now never hear Wagner or Bach without his face appearing in front of me, those barely pigmented eyes, fair brows, stand-up collar with silver oak leaves. He enjoys teaching me better German, and I pretend to know less than I do because he has one great weakness. He underrates the intelligence of women, assuming I won't understand what he's saying when he instructs the driver who sometimes brings him and picks him up from the house.

When we're together, after we've made love, he will write his daily reports at the little table in my room, and he verbalises as he writes. I feign sleep, and this way, I discover the raids he is planning against the Resistance, and any individuals he has in his sights.

Whatever I hear, I pass on to Madame Taubier, and she feeds it to the Resistance. This way, my *collaboration horizontale* saves lives in and around Lazurac.

It doesn't mean I don't get spat at in town and called 'the Germans' whore'. And that is *Germans* plural. They assume I'm available to all of them. I stop taking Joseph about with me, as he's just old enough to know that people are baring their teeth at his *maman*. He likes Kristoff, who gives him a little pull-along dog on wheels. If asked, do I love Kristoff or hate him, I will answer that it's an unfair question. I hate what he does, yet to me in this moment, he is not a hateful man. When misgivings intrude, I draw or play with Joseph until they've gone.

In this fashion, another year passes, and the war moves towards its final act.

In March 1944, Joseph turns three. Old Charlotte dies and poor Aubin is inconsolable but will always have a home with Madame Taubier. People have started calling her house La Sanctuaire. The Sanctuary. I'm afraid it's meant unkindly, implying a safe haven for whores and idiots. Madame, who has a dignity as great as her courage, ignores them. I offer to leave; she taps me sternly. 'Where would you go, Lally?'

Besides, she loves Joseph too much to lose us. In an act of defiance, she has 'La Sanctuaire' carved on a board and jams it into the ground at the bottom of her drive.

I am now jumping to the summer of 1944.

Joseph, love of my life and child of my heart, has a precocious vocabulary and a delightful lisp. He looks like both his parents, depending on his mood. When he is chattering away,

I see and hear Otto. In repose, I see Pauline. His eyes are both Pauline's and Otto's. Greyish and bluish. That was what drew them together, I tell myself. Their smoky, understated sameness.

Have I forgiven them for falling in love and betraying me? Sometimes yes, sometimes no. I have the best of them in Joseph and have discovered that maternal love is the greatest, the fiercest, the cruellest love there is.

In June 1944, Allied forces land in Normandy and the slow destruction of German occupation begins. Kristoff's visits grow less frequent as the maquis, the Free French insurgency, engages his unit in skirmishes and battles that last for hours. The Germans are fighting for their lives against a Resistance that is well-armed and determined to free their country and avenge four years of oppression.

Kristoff drinks more red wine these days and is often too exhausted to make love. I keep his glass topped up. He's happy to just lie with me as I stroke his hair. I encourage him to relax and talk.

On the last day of July 1944, he lets slip that the Lazurac Resistance plans to dynamite part of the town's ramparts, blocking the railway line with tons of rock, putting it out of use for weeks.

I ask how he knows this. He gives a one-word reply.

'Informants.' He then adds, 'We need the line open in both directions or we'll find ourselves cut off and surrounded.'

I make soothing sounds. 'When's this act of sabotage planned for?'

'Friday.'

I presume he means this coming Friday, August fourth.

He confirms it by saying, 'It's the full moon, so the saboteurs won't need lights. But we'll be there.'

Has he forgotten he's talking to the enemy, or is he seeing

in me his imaginary Rhine Maiden, the one who speaks his
language and adores his music? He has drunk a great deal of
full-bodied Côtes de Gascogne, chased with nips of Armagnac. So, yes, he's seeing his Nordic love, not Lally Ducasse.

'How d'you mean, you'll be there?' I ask casually.

He rolls round to face me with dawning suspicion in his
eyes. I make love to him, and the danger passes. Next day,
Madame Taubier passes my warning on. 'Call off the mission.
Stay away from the ramparts. They know.'

That night, two men arrive. I don't need to be told they're
maquisards. Their lean faces and the hooded hardness of their
eyes give them away. They are professional soldiers, working
closely with our local Résistants. These men know that if
they're caught, they will be tortured or beaten to death. I'm
called down to the kitchen and find them at the table
wreathed in pungent cigarette smoke. Madame Taubier says,
'These men need to talk to you, Lally.'

They shake my hand, but they don't rise. The elder of the
two treats me with a sardonic gallantry, the fighting man to the
beautiful but fallen woman. The younger trains a look of deep
distrust on me. I'm asked about my relationship with Kristoff.
I speak the plain truth. Yes, it's sexual. Yes, he trusts me. He
revealed that he knows about the plan to block the railway
line. No, I have no idea who his informant is. How would I?

'He is expecting the action to take place this Friday,
Madame?'

'At the full moon, yes.'

'When do you expect to see him again?'

'He'll be here on Thursday, if he can get away. The day
before your mission.'

'How does he get here?'

'On a motorbike, usually. I never know for sure until I
hear it on the drive. He doesn't call as we have no telephone.'

So – am I with them or against them?

In a dramatic gesture, I unclip the Grey Eyed Dove from my dress. I tell them who gave it to me, what the giver meant to me. I tip back my head. 'If you ever have reason to believe I am false, Monsieur, you may come and cut my throat.'

'Believe me, Madame, if you betray us, we will.'

The younger of them addresses Madame Taubier. 'Your three nephews are part of our unit, Madame.'

She makes no answer, not even a nod.

The man persists. 'Your brother-in-law Étienne's boys will be with us, and his brother Alain's son too. You have skin in the game, Madame Taubier.'

She returns his gaze. 'If you are saying that to remind me to be loyal, shame on you, young man.'

We hatch a plan that will avert a German SS ambush. It is simplicity itself. The sabotage will be brought forward one night. It will be my job to signal to the Resistance that my lover is here with me and not lying in wait for them.

At around nine on Thursday night, I hear an approaching motorbike. I go to the side door and watch Kristoff turn off his engine and unbuckle his helmet. We go straight up to my room, and undress in silence. His lovemaking is, on this occasion, not particularly successful. My comment, 'Something's happened,' draws the hollowest of laughs.

'The Americans cut through our lines in Normandy. Our divisions abandoned their positions. The Wehrmacht couldn't hold. So yes, *Liebchen*, I'd say that something has happened.'

I pour him a large goblet of wine and put a Bach concerto on the gramophone. We lie on the bed, bolsters behind our heads and soon, his eyes droop. He doesn't sleep well in his lodgings, waking 'nine times a night' in his own words, so he's always tired. I wait, controlling my impatience and fear.

At around eleven, I take the glass from his loosening grip

and whisper, 'I'm just going to check on Joseph. Won't be long.'

Joseph's bedroom is between mine and Madame Taubier's. I open the door and peer inside, listening to my dear one's steady breathing. Leaving the door open a crack, I slip downstairs to the kitchen. Madame Taubier is there, with Aubin.

She asks questions with her eyes. I nod, then say, 'Go do your part, Aubin.'

As I said already, the plan could not be simpler. I will keep Kristoff with me until dawn. Meanwhile, Aubin will climb to the top of the windmill and hang a lantern from an outside bracket. Its light will be visible at the remote farm-house where the Resistance saboteurs will have gathered by now. As I walk outside with Aubin, I picture them round the table belonging to the widow who owns the farm, pickling themselves in cigarette smoke, fortifying themselves with local wine.

Waiting. Saying little.

Aubin exhibits no fear or tension. Certainly, he grasps the importance of his job. He knows that his lantern will signal to the Resistance that it is safe to move, with their boxes of TNT and their fuses. What he won't comprehend is the fearsome punishment that will befall him, and the rest of us, if he's caught. For a moment, I'm tempted to send him back inside and do the job myself. But what if Kristoff wakes and sees I'm gone?

'You know what to do, Aubin, you have matches?'

He turns to me, teeth bared in a grin, and pats his pocket. It's so bright tonight, one day shy of a full moon, I can make out the twill pattern of his jacket. The saboteurs won't need flashlights, which is safer for them.

As Aubin trudges off towards the fence that separates

house and windmill, I go back inside, pausing in the kitchen to ask Madame Taubier if she means to wait for him.

'Yes, till he's safe back. Lally?' She places her hand on top of mine. 'I know why you do what you do. I am grateful.'

'Most people round here think different. They think I shouldn't be allowed to be a mother, or your guest.'

'You are not my guest. You are my dearest friend. Now, off you go.'

I drop a kiss on Madame's brow and tiptoe upstairs, pausing by the landing window. From here I can make out the solid shape of the mill and a wavering light, moving erratically. It's Aubin, with his lantern.

The light disappears for a minute, before reappearing at the summit, shining into the empty countryside. *Well done, Aubin. Now come home.*

I don't go straight to my own room, but to Joseph's, gripped, in this moment of jeopardy, by an urgent need to see him. The door is wider open than I left it. The room is empty, the bed is empty. Terror sends me scuttling to my own room.

Kristoff is standing at my bedroom window with Joseph in his arms. They are looking out into the moonlight. Joseph is pointing and saying, 'Light in the sky. Light in the windmill.'

Kristoff can see the lantern shining at its summit. Did I not once say to him, how I imagined the windmills of Varsac signalling to each other?

He knows he has been duped. By me, by Madame Taubier, by Aubin. Whether he is inclined to show mercy will be revealed in a few heartbeats.

When, finally, Kristoff turns, I realise that he's fully dressed. Softly, he tells me to close the door. He's supporting Joseph with his right arm. In his left hand, I see the barrel of a service pistol.

I do as he says.

He tells me to put the record back on the gramophone. I'm

shaking and the needle scratches the record as I put it down. Bach's third Brandenburg Concerto in G major surges out. Kristoff talks with Joseph as if nothing is wrong, and he has all the time in the world.

The minutes roll off the cliff, and when the music ends and the needle makes that clicking, growling sound in the grooves at the inner edge, he passes Joseph to me.

'I wish you well, Lally. I advise you to leave this house tonight and do not go into town tomorrow.'

Minutes later, he's riding away without headlights. Perhaps he doesn't need them under the crystal-bright moon. That is the last I ever see of him.

Racing downstairs, I find Aubin and a frightened Madame Taubier. Leaving Joseph with them, I dash out to the windmill. Up the rickety steps, gasping at the wingbeat of an owl driven off its perch. At the top, I open the hatch where the sacks of grain were winched up before the mill stopped turning. Aubin closed the doors hard behind him, and I almost pitch out into nothingness when they fly open. Twisting, stretching, I prod the lantern off its hook, hearing it crash on the ground below. The flame winks for a few seconds, before going out.

I know it is too late. Kristoff bided his time, giving our saboteurs a good half-hour to get to the ramparts and begin laying their fuses. His informant was one step ahead of us and his men were primed to pounce. By lighting that lantern, Aubin sent our men into a trap, and I sent Aubin to carry out that task.

All I can do now is pray a miracle happens.

61

Friday arrives and drags by without news, until Madame Taubier can no longer bear it. She finds her priest and from him, learns that twelve Résistants were captured last night and are being held in the town hall, in Lazurac, under interrogation.

On Saturday at around midday, gunshots ring out across the open countryside. We do not have to ask what it means. Shortly after, smoke can be seen rising from the centre of Lazurac. Aubin stands at the bottom of the drive and asks everyone passing what has happened, until somebody gives him an answer. The Germans shot the prisoners in reprisal and torched the town hall.

All I can think is, did Kristoff give the order? Did he interrogate the Résistants and decide they should die? The answer pecks at me in a mocking voice. What do you think, Lally? What did you think he was?

On Sunday, I am washing Joseph's feet as he sits on the drainer. He is splashing his hands in the water, singing a song about a tiger. Madame Taubier hurries in.

'Lally, they're coming up the drive.'

'They?'

'Men from the town. My brothers-in-law, Étienne and Alain. I think—' She swallows. 'I fear they are going to blame you for the reprisals.'

A chill passes down my spine, though I'm expecting nothing less. 'I betrayed nobody. You know I did my best,' I whisper.

'I know.' Her hands, limp by her sides, display her power-lessness. The advancing men are close enough for us to hear whose name they are shouting.

'They should be baying for your brothers-in-law,' I say furiously. Of the twelve men shot, not one was called Taubier. Étienne's sons and his nephew, who were supposed to join the group, changed their plans at the last minute.

Madame pushes her purse at me. 'Run, Lally. Have you got your papers?'

They're in my room. There's no time and I can't flee with Joseph, or without him. I astonish myself by saying calmly, 'Madame, take Joseph along the pilgrims' path. They won't pursue you.'

'They might.'

'They won't. I'll make sure of it.'

I'm calm until the men are actually in the house. I'm sure they would have liked to beat down the door, but I spare them the trouble and they find me sitting on the first stair, in full view. I have taken off the Grey Eyed Dove and hidden it behind one of the banisters, the second one up from the bottom.

They seize me and carry me out like a trophy, face up, my head hanging so I begin to lose consciousness. I am only just aware of being thrown into the back of a truck, which has onion tops and cabbage leaves all over the floor. I brace my hands to stop my head striking the floor as I'm driven away.

I'm pulled out of the van in front of the cathedral. All the townsfolk are waiting. Women, old and young, scream at me. Toothless veterans of the last war spit at me. Little children on the shoulders of their parents repeat vile insults. Abbé Thomas comes out of his cathedral and to his credit, tries to intervene but I think they would tear him apart before they let me go.

I am the living embodiment of every atrocity committed against them: the blood-soaked courtyard where their menfolk were murdered, the smouldering town hall, the abuses they've endured since the Germans arrived. A chair is fetched from the café next door and I'm pushed onto it, my arms and ankles bound. Somebody brings the sort of shears used for cutting canvas, and one of the women, a war widow, goes to work, hacking my hair off at the roots. When she catches my scalp and draws blood, she gives a satisfied 'Ha!' that whips up the crowd.

Someone shouts, 'Take her eyes out while you're at it!'

I am begging them not to kill me. 'I have a child. Please, please, please, I have a child!'

When I am plucked to baldness like a hen for the pot, they paste my head with pine tar. It drips into my eyes and runs down into my mouth. I'm untied, but only so the women can rip off my blouse and underthings, baring my breasts to be painted with tar also. A feather pillow is slit and its contents tumble over me. I am hauled upright and driven at the head of a howling crowd to the place where the men of Lazurac were slaughtered by soldiers commanded by my German lover. I am forced down and my face is rubbed in the congealed blood on the flagstones.

Traitress. Harlot. She-devil.

Who fathered your bastard child?

German lover. Nazi whore.

A man growls close to my ear, 'I could kill you for what you did. I could do anything I want.'

I recognise Étienne Taubier's voice. I hear Abbé Thomas protesting, 'People, people, you have disgraced this woman enough and now for the love of God, cover her and leave her be.'

With tar clogging my eyes, its bitterness in my mouth, I realise all at once that these townspeople will let me live. Not through compassion but because they want my shame to stay with me until I draw my last breath. It will sit like a canker on the tongue, tasted in everything I eat and drink and every word I speak for the rest of my life.

I manage to sit up, lift my streaked face and roar something that, to this day, I believe to be true: 'I bedded a German to put food in my child's mouth. While he' – I point at Étienne Taubier – 'has been passing Resistance secrets to my lover for months. How do I know?' I pull sticky feathers off my brow and throw them at Taubier's feet. 'It's called "pillow talk".'

Étienne Taubier's boot cracks my ribs, and a second blow breaks my jaw. I don't speak again for many weeks.

62

HOPE

'Did they ever prove the case against Étienne Taubier?'

They were at Yves' place. He'd cooked dinner for them all, as promised, and their guests were strolling around the garden with candles, leaving Hope and Yves to sit alone by the fire pit.

Yves shook his head. 'Though his business suffered. His brother became a town councillor, but never got to be mayor and people kept asking why their sons failed to join the mission, at the last minute.'

'Why did those lads stay away?' Hope asked.

'God knows. One version says they were sent by their fathers to join the maquis, in the hills. You know, out of harm's way for a few weeks? It was an intense time, with the Germans fighting back with every savage tactic, the Resistance gathering momentum, and the Allies dropping in guns and ammunition. You probably know about this time from the British angle, the involvement of SOE agents and the female couriers taking messages between units. For us French, it was the end-piece of a long, vicious and deeply unbalanced struggle. The Taubiers played both sides, but so did many. Details get blurred in wartime and when the smoke settles and the bullets stop, nobody knows quite who did what.'

'You said yourself, to Inès and Manon, Lally was a convenient scapegoat.'

'I believe it, and Madame Taubier spoke up for her, as did Aubin. If anyone listened to him. And there were some who questioned the Taubiers' version but not enough.'

Feeling dispirited, Hope went to fetch dessert.

Yves followed her inside, saying, as she opened his fridge, 'Sorry. That was a downer.'

'Lally must have told you about the assault on her. You've been living with it for years.'

Yves didn't know if that was true. 'I got her story in occasional, wine-fuelled rambles but only by reading the memoir can I put it into any kind of chronology. I know that Abbé Thomas arranged for her to go into retreat at a convent.'

'The one where Pauline died?'

He shook his head. 'The one here, on the edge of town, where they hold the Thursday market. Madame Taubier looked after Joseph. Lally could hardly go back to the child with her hair shorn, covered in blood, tar and feathers.'

'It would have terrified him. Poor little boy.' Hope had to keep reminding herself that this 'poor little boy' was her father. By age three, Joseph had lost his mother and now his beloved Lally. His father was also dead by this point, though unbeknownst to his friends. Hope doubted her father had known anything about Otto's life and death.

'Grab the yoghurt and ice cream,' she said, putting a bowl of caramelised peaches on a tray. 'I can't believe this time tomorrow my group will be on a plane back to the United States. I've grown fond of them all.'

'Let's hope they give excellent reviews,' Yves said gruffly. 'I'm out of a job now.'

She laughed. 'Narcissist! I'm out of a job too.'

'What I mean is, I never realised I enjoy teaching. You'll be rattling around in that big house.'

Yes, and she wasn't looking forward to it.

Yves whispered into her ear, 'Maybe you'd like company.'

'You mean, move in with me?' Butterfly wings lifted in her stomach. 'First, I ought to inform Ash. If he turned up for any reason, it would be embarrassing.'

'Fine.' He pointed towards her phone, which was on the kitchen surface. 'Inform him.'

Their DNA test results arrived in the third week of July. Yves brought his with him when he returned to Hope's, having been to check all was well at La Cachette. By now, his presence was part of the flow of her life. They spent their days in her garden studio or at the windmill, she working on his accounts – which, as she told him, was akin to remaking a Roman mosaic from a tipper-truck of bits – and he editing his photographs. He'd been asked at short notice to do a gallery show in Toulouse and was nervous about it.

In the lazy time between breakfast and lunch, they took the DNA results and their laptops out to the terrace and sat side by side, each waiting for the other to make the first move. A bird hopped between the shrubs, flashing its yellow under-beak. 'I think it's a bee-eater,' Hope said. She suspected there must be a nest nearby. 'I hope they don't eat all the honeybees in the garden.'

'They won't. Are you putting off the moment?'

'Yes. Let's do it.'

On their laptops, they each signed into the ancestry website, created their accounts and entered the activation code that had come through the post. 'Click for results'. Hope glanced at Yves' screen. 'Ready?'

'Ready.'

They clicked. 'I won't look at yours till you invite me.'

Yves groaned. 'What if we are related? I know we're not, but what if we are?'

'It just isn't possible, stop catastrophising.' Even so, her heart was pounding like an amp with the bass turned up. She read her results and laughed. 'I have a third cousin. Name of Tom Hershall, so that's a relation from my mum's side. And... Oh, my God.'

Yves turned to her. She shifted her laptop so he could see.

He caught a breath. 'More third cousins and all called *Horst*. Find out where they live,' he said.

'I can't. I'll have to "friend" them on the site and invite them to contact me. I'm not sure I'm ready for that.' She counted the names. 'Six third cousins I never knew I had. It's amazing. What about you?'

For a moment, he said nothing. Then: 'What is that phrase, having no friends?'

'Er... Billy No Mates?'

'Then that is me.' Yves turned his laptop. There were no links for him to click, no relations to connect with.

'Doesn't mean you don't have any, just that they haven't got round to taking DNA tests. One day, one of them will.'

He nodded. 'My grandfather, Victor, had nieces and nephews. I could try finding them.'

'Your grandfather had a sister too,' Hope reminded him. 'Dorienne, owner of a knocking shop on Rue du Maine.'

His shoulders shook, and with relief, she realised he was laughing. 'I had forgotten about Dorienne. Lally had no discretion, did she? Another person would have changed names in her autobiography. Not my grandmother.'

'Not surprising it triggered a libel action and got pulled. Was it the Taubiers who took out the lawsuit?'

Yves didn't know. 'Have you finished the memoir yet?'

'You know I haven't. I only read in bed, and somebody keeps interrupting me.'

'That is reprehensible of whoever.'

They were still at the turbulent, chemical stage of love where, whenever their eyes met, they kissed. They kissed now, as a bee-eater hopped through a red-flowered escallonia, picking off an easy meal. Why, on this glorious July day, under a big, blue sky, should she suddenly say, 'Do you think the convent where Pauline was buried still exists?'

'The one outside Lons-le-Saunier?' Yves considered it probable that the building was still there, though whether any nuns remained was less likely.

'I'd like to visit her grave, even so,' said Hope. She asked where Lally was buried. The answer was, 'Nowhere.' Yves had her ashes but had never decided what to do with them.

'Should I scatter them in the Seine, or plant a tree in my garden?'

'At La Cachette,' Hope said after a moment. 'Because she chose to stay there.'

'She did not choose,' Yves contradicted. 'She had to stay.'

'Waiting endlessly for Otto?'

He looked at her fiercely. 'You know what I am going to say.'

'Finish the memoir. All right, I will. You can make lunch.'

BARBED WIRE AND FALSE NAMES: MEMOIR OF AN ENGLISH GIRL IN OCCUPIED FRANCE

Madame Taubier writes to me at the convent every day and tells me how Joseph is doing. I suspect she sugars things because he would not be singing as he helps Aubin pick the late raspberries, not with me suddenly absent. I'm sure he asks about Kristoff too, because he liked him. I must trust that Madame knows what to tell him.

From my convent bedroom, between the chiming of the bells, I hear planes and muffled explosions. British and American bombers are striking the docks along the Atlantic coast, and though it's several hundred kilometres away, the dull boom of each detonation reaches us. The Germans are in retreat. I know it is a cliché to talk about a long row of dominoes falling, but it does honestly feel like this, and the Germans are the dominoes. That is my amateur account of the liberation of France, but I am living it from the inside, as a hare in the field experiences the farmer's scythe.

On the first day of September 1944, I steel myself to look

in the mirror. I almost gag. I am so thin! My eyes by comparison are huge, and I look more frog than human. My hair has grown a bit, but arguably looks worse than when it was first cut. Being thick, it has sprouted in uneven tufts. My expression is frozen in a moment of unearthly shock. Just as Samson's strength was cut away with his hair, my poise and confidence fell beneath those hateful shears. Still, I want to go home.

A letter from Madame Taubier, reporting that Joseph fell trying to find me at the top of the windmill, is the push I need. I take my leave of the nuns and walk back to Varsac-les-Moulins. Trudging up the driveway under the poplars' shade, I relive being carried out above the shoulders of vengeful men, a witch for burning. I have to force myself to keep moving.

Joseph only fell down the first three steps of the windmill. Aubin had seen him heading that way and had the sense to follow. My little boy has a bump on his head. Madame tells me all this at the door – Joseph is in the garden.

'Oh, Lally, we'd better tidy you up.' She finds a silk headscarf, a pretty one from Paris in the 1920s, and ties it in such a way that I resemble the girl by Vermeer. The one with the pearl earring.

My Grey Eyed Dove has gone from where I left it, but Madame quickly assures me that Joseph found it. 'You'll have a job getting it off him. It's his comfort, since you went.'

She boils water, fills a bathtub and takes an old, but pretty, frock from the wardrobe. 'You must dress as though you mean to live, Lally. It's the only way.' She gives me a stub of pre-war lipstick. Cherry red, and after I apply it, I'm reminded of Norma-Rose. I blot most of it off again.

'Better,' Madame says. 'Let's go out and find Joseph. No tears, agreed?'

Joseph peers at me as if he's not sure who is walking

towards him. I stop, crouch, hold out my arms and he runs to me.

'Maman! Maman!'

It is the most beautiful sound I have ever heard.

He is perfectly content to see the Grey Eyed Dove once again on my breast. In the following days, I paint a self-portrait. I do it with the door locked so I can take my headscarf off. A mirror placed on top of a chest of drawers allows me to see myself from the head down to the fourth button of my dress. Into those brushstrokes I pour my shame and mortification. I enter into dialogue with my reflection. I will live. I must survive, for Otto should he ever come this way. But most of all, so I can watch Joseph grow and become a man.

I paint the Grey Eyed Dove in quick, loose strokes then go over it with a brush that's just four bristles thick, to get the detail right. I want to get its colours and jaunty tail feathers exactly as they are. Working helps me reclaim myself. I will never be what I was, but the two parts of me, former Lally and new Lally, can co-exist. It's many months before I realise I have signed my self-portrait 'L.L. Shepherd'.

I jump now to the following summer, to June 1945. On the day when peace finally comes, Madame Taubier and I hug, before dancing in a circle with Aubin and Joseph. Later, as we drink a celebratory glass of champagne which she's kept for the whole of the war, I confide something that has started to trouble me.

I can't live in her house as a guest for ever. I will never be able to get work locally, and so I must plan my future. I don't say as much, but I'm conscious that Madame Taubier is nearly sixty and when she dies, her property will go to the brothers-in-law, or their sons, minus a small bequest for Aubin. At that point, my fate will be stark. I broach the subject that night, after dinner.

'But Lally, why must you go?'

'I need to find a way of living here, and not off you.'

'You've worked harder than any of us! And if you go and your husband comes back...'

I open my mouth, a confession on my tongue. Otto is not my husband. It doesn't get said, because she pours us a glass of Armagnac, and I cannot bear to spoil the moment. The upshot of our little talk is that I remain. Just as all those years ago in Paris, it is easier to stay and paint, and tend the garden and the chickens, teach Joseph his lessons, than to face the unknown. I should have listened to my instincts, though.

Why do I never do that?

HOPE

Hope put down the memoir, jolted from Lally's world by the arrival of a text.

'Ugh.' It was from Ash. Having informed him that she was in a relationship with somebody else, she'd invited him to name the items he would like from the house. She would have them couriered to whichever address he provided. Reading his reply, she felt her blood come to the boil:

> *Quick work, Hope. Wd prefer if your person-of-interest does not stay over in a house I still have a financial interest in. Nick has offered to drive to Lazurac to pick up my clothes and my bike. This is likely to be on the 30th or 31st of July.*

Hope answered at once, because those dates wouldn't work. And the last person she wanted to see, other than Ash, was his smug elder brother. She didn't mention that from the 29th to the 31st of the month, she and Yves were taking a trip to Lons-le-Saunier.

No need for you to come in person but if you must, make it after 1st August

She pressed send. 'Now get out of my hair, Ash. I have a memoir to read.'

BARBED WIRE AND FALSE NAMES: MEMOIR OF AN ENGLISH GIRL IN OCCUPIED FRANCE

In February 1946, a month before Joseph's fifth birthday, on a raw, dank day, a car comes up the drive. Cars are a rarity out here. The last engine I heard up close was that of the van, the day the mob fetched me from the house.

I open the door and peer out. The car is a Renault, rather battered as most cars are these days. I recognise the man at the wheel. It's Madame's elder brother-in-law, Alain. He was recently elected to the council in Lazurac.

Madame Taubier comes out, and greets Alain politely, inviting him into the drawing room. I follow. I think I know why he's here.

Joseph ought to have started at the *école maternelle* two years ago, but as it meant going into Lazurac, I didn't send him. Madame Taubier and I have taught him but now he's rising five, he'll have to start primary school. I'm marshalling explanations, so when Alain tells me that an English couple, a

Mr and Mrs Granger, have travelled from their home to find the child of their daughter, Pauline, I'm knocked for six.

Madame Taubier looks flabbergasted. 'What on earth are you talking about, Alain? Who is Pauline? What have her parents to do with Lally and Joseph?'

I am seeing white lights in my head. I don't understand how anyone living in England could possibly know that Pauline had a child.

Joseph runs in. He's been helping Aubin pull up onions and his knees are patched with soil. Being well-brought-up, he offers his hand to the visitor and I note how reluctantly Alain Taubier accepts it. I assume it's because Joseph hasn't washed the oniony soil off his fingers, until Taubier says, 'The Grangers believe this child's father is German.'

I exchange a glance with Madame. She opens her mouth, then shuts it. Alain continues: 'They're claiming that his mother is their daughter.'

Véronique Taubier bursts out, 'Lally is Joseph's mother. You can see the resemblance quite clearly.'

'I can't,' Alain retorts. 'Can't see a trace of her. I do see a Germanic look to him, though.'

'Lally?' Madame Taubier waits for me to contradict. 'Explain that you are Joseph's mother and tell Alain who your husband is.'

'I... can't.' I'm too bewildered and frightened to come up with a story and so my friend does it for me.

'This boy's father is the distinguished German pacifist Otto Horst.'

'If you say so, Véronique,' Alain replies. 'The point is, is this woman the boy's mother?'

'Lally?' There is a pleading note in Madame Taubier's voice because I haven't leapt in with a contradiction.

I end my silence by shaking my head. I then confess. I'm

not his mother. I lied. Because I love him so much, I let the world believe he was mine.

Madame is appalled, and her confusion – her sudden mistrust – is horrible to witness.

Alain Taubier asks sternly if I falsely registered Joseph as my child.

I assure him that his birth was registered under his real mother's name, Pauline's name. Only not her actual name as we were using false documents to get across the demarcation line – we pretended to be sisters.

'Let me understand… your surname is not Ducasse?' Madame puts her hand to her brow, trying to pull facts into a semblance of sense. 'It's all false?'

'Joseph's surname is Horst, because Pauline and Otto were married. My surname is something else, but who cares? I had to change it when the Germans came.' I know I sound like a desperate imposter but how many people in France went by fake names, and codenames, during the occupation? Thousands. 'Joseph's mother was Pauline Granger, who went under the name of Ducasse, like me. Even when she married. She couldn't use Otto's name, because he was a wanted man.'

'What is real, Lally?' Madame Taubier is close to tears. 'If you are not Joseph's mother, nor his legal guardian, and if these people Alain speaks of can prove they are his grandparents, they can take him.'

'But they can't. He has a father.'

'He doesn't.' Alain Taubier makes a face, preparing himself to impart bad news. 'At the grandparents' request, I had enquiries made about this man, Horst. It seems he was arrested in Spain in October 1940, as he crossed the mountains. He was sent back to France, to Gurs, to the holding camp, and there he died.' Alain adds, as if somehow it will help, 'Of typhoid fever.'

This awful news has a strange effect on me. I run upstairs

and frantically push clothes into a bag. I've spent months and months waiting for a man who cannot come to me and reeling from the violence of this news, my instinct is simply to go, to take Joseph. To run where nobody can find us.

I'm packing his clothes as another car arrives. Looking out from the front of the house, I see it's a police car. Two gendarmes alight, along with a woman in a suit. Two more people, a man and woman, get out of the rear of Alain Taubier's vehicle.

I didn't notice them when he pulled up but they must have been waiting all this time.

English. You can tell by the clothes: the utility shape, his brown-grey hat plonked centrally, her cream gloves and stout ankles in brown worsted stockings. These can't be Pauline's parents. They can't be. I repeat it as I run downstairs. Alain Taubier has opened the door and has Joseph by the hand. I shout, 'Let him go!'

The woman with the stout ankles screams as she sees him. 'It's Pauline to the life. It's Pauline's child.'

I'm barely aware of them being introduced to me. They hardly look at me either, all their focus on Joseph. They call themselves Granger, and have papers to prove it, and can prove also that their daughter came to France to work and never came home.

The woman comes to stand in front of me. 'Where is she?' she demands. 'Where is Pauline?'

I tell her, in the sparest words, the circumstances of Pauline's death. The cry that comes from the woman's throat is terrible to hear and Joseph starts to whimper, then scream as Pauline's mother begins hitting me, around the face, the shoulders and breasts, shouting, 'You killed her! You killed her! She would have come home. We wrote and told her to come home, but someone stopped her. It was you. You made her stay too long and now she's dead.'

I never stopped her; we were equals in foolishness, both as blind as each other. When the attack is over, I tell the woman why Pauline remained in Paris. 'She was in love.'

'Love? She was hoodwinked. Seduced. As if our girl would ever fall for a Nazi.'

'He was no Nazi.' I'm angry now. Not only does this woman not know me, or Otto, I don't even think she knew her own daughter. 'He was a fine man. A poet.'

'He corrupted our beautiful girl. And you did your bit. We've been told about you.'

Her husband, Pauline's father, tries to intervene. 'Mary, you're making the little lad cry.'

'You heard what she did, consorting with a German here in front of the town.' Mary Granger is beyond the reach of calm persuasion and pokes me in the ribs. 'We have words for women like you in England, but I won't say them.'

There's nothing I can say either. Again, I am convicted. Tarred and feathered.

The woman accompanying the gendarmes now pushes forward. She is a child welfare officer and takes Joseph, but not before he has attempted his own escape out into the wintry garden. A gendarme catches him easily, and when he's brought back, he has a small sprig of lavender in one fist. I planted the lavender three years ago, to lure bees into the vegetable patch. I catch him to my waist, knowing they will take him and I can't bear this to be his last memory of me.

I unpin the Grey Eyed Dove with fingers that are a shuddering blur. I secure it to his jumper and say, 'Your father loved this little bird. Always keep it, and never forget me. Come back when you can, Joseph. Come back to the windmill. I will wait for you here for ever.'

66

HOPE

It was early morning, July 29. Hope and Yves had spent the previous night in a hotel which might – if their research was on target – have been the one where Pauline and Lally stayed before crossing the demarcation line. In a compact room where the bed was scaled to match, they finished Lally's memoir.

It was a hot night and they'd thrown off the bedcovers. After reading the final sentence, after which the pages were missing, they lay in silence, holding each other. They had no words to summarise the entwined tragedies of Lally, Pauline and Otto. What cut deep was the realisation that, while Lally and Pauline had been wondering constantly how far Otto had got on his journey, if he'd made it to Lisbon, he was already dead. Captured by pro-German Spanish guards. Sent to a concentration camp on the French side of the border, where death from an infection in the hideous conditions quickly followed.

After breakfast in a café which might, at a push, have been the site of the Café Suisse where the 'Old Man' had acted as go-between for escapees, they hired bicycles. Cycling through the straggling suburbs of Lons-le-Saunier, they reached open countryside by mid-morning on their mission to find Pauline's grave.

To stand beside it and bear witness was all they could hope for. There would be no grave for Otto.

A single-track road wound through quaint villages. With all the time in the world, water and nectarines in their bicycle baskets, they didn't attempt to put themselves into Lally and Pauline's shoes on that winter trudge through the same country. Reaching the village that would have been the first settlement on the 'free' side of the demarcation line, they parked their bikes by a church.

The convent where Lally had come with newborn Joseph and where Pauline's body had been brought for burial was a short walk on: they found an abandoned shell of broken windows and crumbling pediments. They stood, numbed by disappointment.

'You were right,' Hope said.

'Still, let's go in.'

Ignoring the 'Dangerous Structure' notices, they forced their way through a gate and prowled around until they found a graveyard that resembled an overgrown meadow. Its wall was low enough for them to scale. A groundsman must occasionally visit, as roughly mowed paths ran between rows of vaults and monuments. These bore the names of deceased Ursuline nuns, the most recent from the 1970s.

After an hour of searching, almost ready to give up, they found a small, stone cross tucked in the lee of a wall.

Pauline Ducasse, died March 6th, 1941

Hope pulled away the grass encroaching over the base of the cross and read, *Mother of Joseph, wife of Otto.*

She glanced up at Yves. 'Lally must have done this.'

'She respected truth,' he said. 'But yes, I'm sure she commissioned the stone because Pauline's parents wouldn't have. They wouldn't have allowed Otto's name next to their daughter's.'

'Do you think Lally forgave Pauline in the end?'

'I believe she did right from the beginning. One thing about my grandmother, she knew she was human and she forgave other people their faults and flaws because, as she said, "If I can't understand them, how will they ever understand me?"'

Placing their hands on the lichen-encrusted cross, they stood silently until Hope returned to a question Lally's curtailed memoir had failed to answer.

'How did the Grangers know their daughter had a child, and where to find him?'

'Pauline wrote home,' Yves replied after a long moment's consideration.

Of course. Pauline wrote to her parents when letters could still travel between France and England, and later, via the Red Cross. 'If that's what she did,' Hope said, 'she lacked some crucial faculties.'

'Is that a posh way of calling your grandmother stupid?'

'Reckless. Thoughtless.'

'Sure you're not seeing her through your twenty-first-century lens? We have the benefit of hindsight. All those films where spies and SOE agents outwit the Nazis. They go on the run, helped by good-hearted folk or betrayed by collaborators. Pauline knew none of that. She was a nineteen-year-old caught out in a terrifying situation. It explains why she clung to Lally, and probably to Otto in the same way. He fell for her, got her pregnant and felt he should marry her.'

It made sense to Hope, almost. 'A letter reached her parents, telling them about her marriage. But how did they know to look in Lazurac?'

Yves suggested that Otto gave Pauline the safe house address when they were together in Bordeaux, without Lally. 'It's what Pauline said to Lally, wasn't it? She must have told someone.'

'Crazy.'

'If she hadn't,' Yves said, 'your father would have grown up in France. He wouldn't have met your mother, and I wouldn't have met you.'

Hope crouched down and flattened her hand against the base of the cross, feeling the chiselled letters beneath her palm. 'Oh, Granny. You walk for hours on a winter's night, nine months pregnant, and get under the barbed wire to freedom. Only, childbirth defeats you. It's so bloody unfair.'

Tears worked their way free. Yves stroked the back of her neck, smoothing the hair that now reached to her collar. 'Can you say, hand on heart, that you don't share some of Pauline's attributes?'

Hope stood up. 'I don't think so.' It was Lally's no-holds-barred attitude that resonated with her.

'I see it different. Like Pauline, you live out your illogical dreams. She left an English town and came to Paris aged seventeen, with a little bit of schoolgirl French.'

'Hm. She didn't succeed, but then, neither have I. I'm losing my home. So maybe we are alike.'

'You haven't lost your business, nor your dream. To dare is to live. Everything else is mere existence.' Yves put an arm around her. 'We will start again, I will do my exhibition, and you will paint.'

The pressure of his touch restored her and she found a smile. 'No – *we* will paint. I'm told you have talent, Yves Ducasse. No more hiding it.'

Arriving back at Hope's that night, Yves driving them from the railway station, they saw a black Transit van parked outside the house. Its nose was right up against the back bumper of her car. Yves squeezed his Land Rover in behind, then reversed a couple of car-lengths. 'Otherwise, whoever owns the van will be knocking on the door, asking me to move.' He stretched in his seat. 'I want a bath, a drink and dinner in that order.'

'It has British plates,' Hope said. A nasty thought trickled in. She'd told Ash not to come until at least the beginning of August. There'd been no response, which had suited her fine. Putting her key in the lock, her front door swung open. Light flooded from the hall.

'Someone's here,' she said.

67

There were half a dozen bulging black sacks in the hall. Ash's clothes were inside one. In another were some vintage cushions they'd bought together at Saint-Sever. Male voices from the lounge took Hope straight there. Opening the door, she was greeted by the sight of Ash, looking lean and tanned in a white sweatshirt, gripping one side of her flatscreen TV. Supporting the other end was a bulkier figure in a Rolling Stones tour-date tee-shirt.

'Nick,' Hope said through gritted teeth. 'Ash. Is it a coincidence you're here? Don't answer that. Were you hoping we wouldn't be back until morning?'

Nick Ashton turned his head, completely unabashed. 'I hope it's a nice surprise.' He pronounced 'hope' with the vocal underlining that so riled her.

'Why are you taking my TV?' Where was Yves? She heard a Land Rover's throaty roar. He wasn't abandoning her, surely?

'We're reclaiming Ash's things.' An edge to Nick's voice suggested she shouldn't to try to prevent them.

A month ago, she'd have found the scenario intimidating and maybe backed off. Now, having dealt with rejection, faced her fears and come out the other side with Yves on her team, she discovered that anger was uppermost. 'Ash, can you speak or has your big brother taken your batteries out?'

'I'm getting my stuff, that's all,' Ash muttered. From the twitching of his cheek muscle, she suspected he'd wanted to be gone before she turned up, and that his brother had spun the proceedings out. Nick liked conflict, Ash didn't. 'You can't stop me,' he added.

'Put the TV down,' she said. 'I paid for it. Where's the DVD player?' The black glass stand was empty. You could see where she'd missed some patches with her duster.

'Packed,' Nick told her.

'Unpack them, then. If you don't, I'm calling the police. You have no right to break in while I'm out.'

'I used my key,' Ash said wearily. 'You have no concept of security, Hope. You haven't blocked me on my social media either or changed the passwords on your website. I could have gone in and changed your prices. Ten euros per week, just for fun. I could have put rude words under the picture of your boyfriend.'

'Yes,' she agreed, 'and surrendered your last shred of digni-ty.' Where was Yves? She really could use some backup.

'Let's get this baby into the van,' Nick said. The TV was heavy. Hope closed the lounge door and stood in front of it.

'Don't be boring, sweetie,' Nick said.

Hope told Ash to put it back on its stand. 'You and your brother look like a pair of bookends.'

Ash had either run out of strength, or his hands were hurt-ing, because he lowered his end of the TV abruptly, breaking his brother's grip. Its corner landed on Nick's foot then fell on its back with a thump.

'Jeepers, Ash!' Now she'd have to have it serviced. 'You total pair of clowns.'

Ash's response was to come closer and speak in the tone of a reasonable man pushed to the limit. 'I've tried to get you to talk, tried to open the doors to communication.' His eyes were oddly cold. He sounded the same as when he'd caught her with Yves, on the terrace. Suddenly, it felt a teeny bit like an act. 'It's always about you, and your needs, isn't it, Hope.'

Hope felt unreasonably sad. Did relationships always come to this? One person holding the stick, the other person waiting to be struck? She thought of Lally, standing up to Raton at Besançon, stabbing the groping trustee with a panhandle, later walking out under the noses of the guards in a stolen nurse's uniform. Making her last verbal dagger-thrust at Étienne Taubier as she lay beaten, tarred and feathered, at his feet. Lally's blood did not run in her veins, but her spirit had entered Hope's soul.

'Actually, Ash, you ignored my many calls. Even pretended to lose your phone so you didn't have to speak to me after you ran away so let's cut to the chase. I have to sell this place, but it'll take months. I was serious when I sent my account of what you owe me. Everything I laid out on your living expenses will be set against the money you paid towards the business. We can go through lawyers or we can do the low-cost option and talk. Up to you.'

Feeling the door opening behind her, she stepped aside and Yves walked in. He took in the situation, seeming to assess whether Nick or Ash was most likely to cause him trouble. Hope couldn't help a tremor of pride at the way he faced beefy Nick Ashton without a flicker either of aggression or surrender. 'It's been a long day,' he said, as if it were the most natural thing in the world to arrive home and find two strangers removing electrical goods. 'I'm tired, Hope's tired and it's time for you to go.' His gaze moved from Nick to Ash then back again. 'First, return everything that doesn't belong personally to you. And apologise to Hope.'

'I don't see why.' Ash still had some fight in him.

'Apologise and offload everything from the van that doesn't have your name stitched into the back,' Yves said.

'That's not happening, mate,' Nick put in. 'You can't make us put anything back if we don't want to.'

'No? Then enjoy sleeping in your van.' Yves went to the chrome-framed recliner that was his favourite piece of furniture in the house, lay down and closed his eyes.

Nick strode out, and came back saying, 'OK. The twat's blocked us in. Ash?'

So that's what Yves was doing outside. Double parking. Hope said in a voice that bubbled with amusement, 'It's about one-and-a-half tons.'

'What, the TV?' Ash's lip curled as if Hope had finally lost the plot.

'No, the weight of a Land Rover. I'm pointing out that you can't push it out of the way and my car's parked directly in front of you. You're stuck.'

Nick swore. 'Bro? I've got to be in London by lunchtime tomorrow.'

After releasing a volley of F-words, and hurling the TV remote at the bookcase, Ash gave in.

The following hour was spent 'adjusting the inventory' as Nick put it. Things were put back in place, while Hope went around the house collecting items Ash had bought and others she no longer wanted. She watched them load the last bin bag.

Nick gave her a wink as he climbed behind the wheel of his van. 'See you when I see you.'

'I doubt it.' She guessed that for Nick, this escapade had been a bit of fun, which had run out when he realised he might not get home in time. Ash's motives were probably darker, but he was leaving, and the slamming of the passenger door signalled his clean break from her and Lazurac. She was thankful she hadn't come home alone. First thing tomorrow, she'd change her online privacy settings. Ditto the locks on the doors.

When the Transit's lights had disappeared and its engine was the faintest hum, she and Yves went back inside. He reassembled the DVD player's plugs and cables, and Hope picked up the remote Ash had chucked and reinserted its batteries. Her parents' wedding photograph had fallen off the bookcase. Its glass was broken.

'I wonder if Ash wanted me to feel insecure in my home?' she mused as she came back with a box to put the broken pieces in. 'You know, showing me he can disrupt my life whenever he wants.'

Yves was pushing in a SCART plug. He pointed to something that had fallen from the back of the wedding photo.

It was a small envelope, buff-white, the kind people used when paper was a restricted commodity. Hope switched on the centre light, to see it better. There was a French stamp on the front and a smudged postmark. October 1940. The address was written in a back-slanting hand.

Mr and Mrs G.A. Granger, Palmerston Road, Fareham, Hampshire, Angleterre

A second postmark from a sorting office in Southampton was dated February 1945, stating, 'Delayed in transit'. Delayed in transit *for five years*.

Hope began to tremble. 'I think it's the last letter Pauline wrote home.'

68

Rue Sainte Catherine, Bordeaux, France

Dearest Mummy and Daddy,

Thank you for your last letter, received ages ago I'm afraid, though I know you posted it even earlier. I fear we will now be writing to each other through the Red Cross, but I wanted to send you my wonderful news. Your daughter is married! I am no longer Miss Pauline Granger, I am, wait for it, Frau Horst.

Don't be alarmed, he is a wonderful man, and not at all like the Germans you read and hear about. In fact, he had to leave Germany because they wanted to put him on trial. I know you will love him every bit as much as I do. And I have more news. We are expecting a baby.

The rest of the letter dealt with Pauline's plans to find a safe place in which to have her child.

Outside Lazurac, a house by a windmill, and doesn't that sound blissful?

Her husband had already made a break for safety, she said, and would travel through neutral countries. In her condition, it wasn't possible for her to go with him, though one day they would be reunited. She finished:

I can't wait to see you both again, and to place your new grand-child in your arms.

Your loving daughter,

Pauline

'"Your new grandchild",' Yves echoed. 'She must have imagined the war would end in a matter of months.'

'I try to give Pauline the benefit of the doubt,' Hope said, 'but honestly, she was away with the fairies. And her parents only got the letter after the war ended. Imagine their emotions, hearing from their daughter after so long. Realising she'd married, shock, horror, a German and that they had a grandchild old enough to go to school. What would they do?' She answered her own question. 'Contact someone in authority and set about finding them.'

She read the letter again, and as the dates impinged, a frown slipped across her face. 'Bordeaux, October 1940. Didn't Pauline leave Lally behind in Paris in July?'

Yves nodded. 'Though she insisted that Otto sent her straight back.'

'Then she told yet another lie.' The date suggested they'd spent weeks together on Rue Sainte Catherine, just the two of them, before Otto made his second attempt to get across the mountains.

'Having a honeymoon,' Yves said. 'I know, poor Lally, but I don't entirely blame them. They wanted to be happy, is all.'

'Poor Lally, for sure,' Hope said angrily. 'And what the hell was Pauline up to, putting such sensitive information in a letter to her parents? Otto may have felt he had to divulge the safe house address to her but why didn't he say, "Don't, for heaven's sake, write home about it"?'

'He probably did.' Yves suggested that in Pauline's nicely-brought-up English mind, 'You post a letter and it is delivered unopened to whoever's name is on the front. And if the Red Cross was involved, she'd trust them. She certainly wouldn't expect German intelligence to intercept mail.'

'Otto would expect it! I can't believe how stupid she was! To infer Madame Taubier's address and write that she'd married a German "who wasn't like other Germans". God. She even states that Otto is heading for a neutral country. Any mildly astute postal clerk could have worked out that she meant Spain and passed the information to the enemy.'

'You believe Pauline's letter triggered Otto's arrest?' Yves asked.

'He didn't make it, did he?'

'He was recognised in Paris, remember. He had to escape through the park. Hope, honestly? I would stop thinking that Pauline accidentally sabotaged the man she loved. It's too painful.'

'Not sure I can. Lally spent her life at Varsac-les-Moulins, waiting.'

'For Joseph,' Yves said. 'She knew that Otto had died but I don't think she ever gave up believing Joseph would come back to find her.'

'Thank goodness she had you.' Hope kissed his shoulder. She loved his smell. Healthy skin and pheromones. 'It would be unbearable, otherwise.'

He pulled her against him. 'I was there when she died, then

I ran away for years. Sometimes I think I'm trapped at La Cachette too.'

'If we could find the end pages of Lally's memoir, it might release you. If she found peace, would you find it too?'

'Not while the Taubiers put up barbed wire and while Manon lives off the proceeds of my grandmother's work. I ought to sell up, but I can't bear to. That is my tragedy.' He began stroking her arm. 'What is yours?'

'That my dad never knew who his mother was, and it's too late to tell him.'

'What would he have done with the information? From what you've said, meeting Lally, learning what happened to his parents, might have been too much. Better that it's you who found out, not him.'

'You are very clever, Yves Ducasse. You know exactly what to say to make me feel wise.'

They went to bed and made love and afterwards, Hope thought how it might feel if this man who took her to the height of pleasure, and held her there for a breathless time, one day wrote a poem, or presented something deeply precious to him – to another woman.

I would lose my faith in life. I would become Lally, bitter, waiting in vain for love to return and prove itself to me.

We have to fix this, she thought, and as she nestled against Yves under the covers, an idea floated in.

69

Yves was at Saint-Sever. There was a particular view he wanted to capture and he had set off with his camera for the hilltop *bastide* before sunrise. As Hope sipped her morning coffee at the kitchen table, she fished out Manon Taubier's business card and called the number.

'*Ouais?*' Manon sounded as if she'd just rolled in from a heavy night. Hope said who was calling.

Ignoring Manon's unflattering groan, she added, 'I have a business proposition.'

'Fine. I'm listening.'

They met at Le Chat, Hope arriving first, which gave her a chance to study Inès's exhibition. Lazurac and the Résistance, Seventy Years On.

Jeanne came up and asked how Yves was.

'His hand is healed, if that's what you're asking. Is he still banned?'

'Yes. No. Maybe not. That fight was awful, though. It took me hours to get the blood out of my tablecloth.' Jeanne smiled at Hope's expression. 'Well, it did. But that wasn't why I was angry.'

'Angry with Yves?'

'With Inès. With Manon, with the ones who can't let go of the past but don't have the courage to face it either. There were collaborators and informants in Lazurac and all around the countryside in the war.' Jeanne lowered her voice as the café was busy. 'Yves' grandmother made no secret of sleeping with her German. Others did it behind closed curtains.' Jeanne leaned closer. 'I know at least two people in this town who did a DNA test and discovered they had German relations. They shouldn't have any.'

The door swung open and Manon ambled in, saying, 'I hope you've got decaf today, Jeanne.'

'*Ah, pht!*' Jeanne was unimpressed. 'You need caffeine, Manon. A sloth would beat you up a tree.' She turned back to Hope. 'Find a table and forget what I just said. Nobody can know who betrayed our Resistance. It's too long ago.'

'Still with Yves?' Manon asked as they sat down. She immediately answered her own question. 'Thought so. He always wants sex in the morning, even if you have errands to run.'

'This morning' – Hope smiled – 'he drove to Saint-Sever before the sun was up.'

'Then he's getting sick of you. What is your proposition?'

Manon's over-sharing about morning sex empowered Hope to do some straight-talking of her own. Once Jeanne had brought their drinks, she got started. 'You've profited selling Lally Shepherd's work. I want Yves to have back whatever you still have. Drawings, paintings, sketches, doodles.'

'Does he know you are here, saying this?'

'He doesn't, yet.' Hope spooned frothy milk off her coffee into her mouth. 'I'm giving you the chance to put things right.'

'Uh. Sure. I can put out a call for her stuff, say I'll pay a decent price. I'll give you first refusal and add on a commission.'

'That's very generous.' Hope's tone could have stripped nail varnish.

'A place to start is with the Taubier family.'

OK, progress. 'They have some of her work?'

'They've been collecting it for years.'

'What?' Surely, they hated Lally, as people always hate their victims. 'Why would they buy it?'

'They didn't.' Manon sniffed her coffee. 'Damn sure Jeanne has given me caffeine.'

She is beautiful, Hope thought, exotic eyes and a bone structure that would keep the years at bay, if she lived cleanly. A beauty spot nestled beside a mouth with a cruel tilt. This woman had spent years depriving Yves of his property.

'I'm confused,' Hope said. 'You said the Taubiers had Lally's work. Are you meaning Jonny Taubier?'

'The family. His old aunt bought it all. Véronique. The one who was Lally's... whatever. Friend. Protector. She sold La Cachette to Lally for a few thousand francs before she died. Before that, she'd buy Lally's work. The only person who would. Lally and Yves' mother would have starved otherwise. When Véronique died – and she lived into her nineties – her nephew and great-nephews inherited everything and thought they were sitting on a gold mine, with the art. Do you like irony?'

'When it's not directed at me.'

'Lally had an exhibition in Paris, in the 1970s.'

Hope knew that. 'Julien Marshall staged it.'

'Whatever. It was supposed to relaunch her as an important artist. But news leaked out and some of the old cats from Lazurac went to Paris on the train, and stood outside with plac-ards, denouncing her as a Nazi collaborator. The exhibition was pulled, she sank back into obscurity. The pictures Véronique Taubier had stockpiled became all but worthless. War ruins lives, into the next generation and the next.'

'Yes, and Manon, it needs to stop. I care about Yves.'

Manon sniffed. 'I used to care for him too. Things change.'

'Your son still does. I've watched Noah and it hurts him when Yves is hurt.'

'I don't know how you'd see that,' Manon snapped back. 'Noah always has his head buried in his Game Boy.'

'It's my opinion, that an act of kindness towards Yves will play well with your son. By the way, I'm calling on a relation of yours later. Shall I extend your best wishes?'

'Who, Aunt Inès?'

'No. Somebody else I've been meaning to contact for a while.' Hope didn't say who. Petty, but holding out on Manon was her revenge for the last time they were in this café and she'd been left with the bill.

Yves was cooking for her at his place that evening. Hope bought wine and chocolate- covered almonds and set off in good time, turning off a hundred metres short of his property, into a long driveway. It was a perfect summer's night, the moon a quarter slice through the rustling poplar branches. She hadn't lied when she'd told Manon she was going to pay a visit to a relation of hers. This was a decision she'd been... not exactly putting off. Just pushing along in front, like dead leaves on the head of a broom.

There was a single car outside the house, and light between the slats of the shutters. Hope walked up to the front door and pulled the bell.

70

Jonny Taubier answered, a glass of what looked like vodka or gin and tonic in his hand. His first words were, 'Sorry, my wife's out. It's her Pilates night.'

'Actually, I've come to see you. Hope Granger, the Lazurac house?'

'Oh.' He looked closer. 'Course. Come in.' He lifted his glass. 'Fancy a drink?'

'Er, water would be good.'

He led her to a large, modern kitchen. The house was old, but somebody had updated the interior. As she passed the staircase, Hope glanced at the lower banisters where Lally had hidden the Grey Eyed Dove.

Jonny Taubier put ice and lime in a glass and filled it with sparkling water from the fridge. He waved Hope to the granite-topped centre island, and a long-legged stool.

'I suppose you've come to demand an apology?' He added a lop-sided grin she supposed some women would find irresistible.

'No,' she said, 'but don't let that stop you.'

He laughed, raising his glass in a toast. 'I apologise for

coming to your house when you weren't expecting me. I swear, I had no idea you had not agreed to sell. Your partner told me different.'

'Ex-partner.'

'Ah. OK. So?'

'I have changed my mind.' She took a breath and the words came out on the exhale. 'I want to put the house on the market in September. Hopefully get a buyer before winter.'

'You would like me to sell it? There are three other estate agents in Lazurac who haven't offended you.'

She sipped her water. Ice cubes clinked against her teeth. 'I'm offering you a sole agency mandate but it comes with a condition.'

'All agency mandates come with conditions,' Jonny Taubier pointed out.

'Outside the business of selling.'

'Go on.'

'I want you to remove that horrible barbed-wire fence that stops people on the pilgrims' path from accessing Yves Ducasse's café. It's the most mean-spirited abomination I've ever encountered.'

Her host jerked his head, taken aback. 'The fence my father put up? I thought it had been taken down.'

'How, unless you did that?'

Jonny Taubier explained that his father had recently retired from the estate agency and moved to the coast. 'He had a handyman put up the fence before he moved out. It wasn't my decision. Please understand, that for his generation, a grudge was a grudge and nothing shifted it. *His* father, Étienne Taubier, really couldn't stand Lally Ducasse.'

'It was mutual.'

Jonny surprised her with his next words, which were a question. 'You know something about French inheritance law?'

'I'm getting to understand,' she said.

'Widows get a share when their husbands die but the family of the deceased also gets their cut.'

'How does this end up with a barbed-wire fence, Monsieur Taubier?'

'Jonny, please. My grandfather had a widowed sister-in-law, Véronique.'

'Yes, she sold the windmill and the land that became La Cachette to Yves' grandmother. To Lally.'

'At a giveaway price,' Jonny added. 'The English were arriving in force, snapping up old properties like that. By the time it was sold, Étienne had passed away, but his son, my father, felt he'd been robbed.'

'Surely, under the rules, members of your family would be given alternate assets, as compensation.'

'And so they were.' Jonny lifted his glass, clinking the ice. 'But you know what grudges are? Grudges are the opposite of sweet reason. My father grew up having his youth stolen by war. He died with that anger and shame inside him, like many of his generation.'

'Will you take that fence down?'

'No.'

'Oh, Monsieur Taubier!'

'*Jonny*. I won't take it down because I am not very good at that kind of thing, but if your friend Yves Ducasse wishes to pull it out, he's free to do so.'

'You won't come for him for trespass?'

'*Non*. That wedge of land between him and the path is not ours. It's not his either.'

'Whose is it?'

Jonny shrugged. 'Nobody's. If he fancies buying it, I'm happy to help. My brother Lucien is a *notaire*.'

'It's hard to escape Taubiers in Lazurac.'

Jonny frowned and Hope wondered if she'd offended him, then realised he hadn't actually heard the last comment. He said, 'I tried to make friends with Yves, you know? When he came home, only he was so angry, so...' He was trying to find the word.

'Defensive? Mistrustful?'

'Yes, but with an edge. Not one I wanted to test, so I backed off. To him, the Taubiers are the sworn enemy. I don't blame him. If half the stories are true, my grandfather and his brother were vile to Lally, so I excuse Yves' hatred. We need to find a way to set things right.'

It was a relief. She'd arrived bristling for battle and, instead, had drunk sparkling water and discovered a man with a rational side to his character. She ought to go – Yves would be looking at his watch. One last thing: 'Do you have any of Lally Ducasse's work? Lally Shepherd, that is. She signed her paintings "L.L. Shepherd". I heard that your great-aunt Véronique bought virtually everything Lally created.'

'Tante Véronique certainly collected a lot of it, to my grandfather's disgust. But when Véronique died in the 1980s—'

'You sold it?'

'My father gave everything back. He left several van loads on Lally's drive. Did Yves not tell you?'

'He might not have known that detail, but Yves certainly grew up with Lally's work all around him. Your cousin Manon seems to have misdirected me. It comes back to the fact that she, basically, stole it all.'

'Yves should call the police. Manon may be a cousin, but I'm not blind to her tactics.'

'She has a son Yves is very fond of. He won't get the police involved, even if he could prove it. I suppose we'll never get Lally's work back.'

'You'll pick up the odd piece, if you try. I'll keep an eye out, but you know what? Yves should stop chasing the past. If you are part of his future, all the more reason he should raise his eyes to the horizon.'

'I'll tell him.' Hope smiled.

'No, I'm serious. The day I met him, after he came home from wherever, he was painting. In his windmill, at an easel, like a man possessed. I interrupted him, and he cast his canvas to the floor as if he couldn't bear anyone seeing.'

'He's afraid he's not good enough.' Hope spoke from sudden insight. 'With Lally as his grandmother and his grandfather being Victor Ponsard, he's got too much to prove. I'm lucky, one set of grandparents were shopkeepers and the others—' She stopped. The others were Pauline and Otto. 'I'm the first-generation artist, such as I am. It makes it easier.'

Jonny Taubier reached across the table and took her hand in a hard grip. 'Make him paint. It doesn't matter how bad he thinks he is. If he can break the bonds of the past, he not only frees himself, he frees us all.'

Hope told Jonny Taubier about Lally's memoir. A lawsuit had seen the book withdrawn from sale. 'Was that your family's work?'

Jonny shook his head. 'I never heard of it. Can you imagine my father or grandfather taking out a court action in London? They thought Paris was the end of the earth. Who brought that action, I have no idea.' He gave her a thoughtful look. 'Would you like to see upstairs?'

Hope got down from her stool. 'Er, you're fine. I'd better go.'

'Don't be alarmed. Let me show you something.'

Reluctantly, Hope followed her host up the stairs that Lally and her father as a little boy had trod in their time, into a narrow room on the first floor.

'This, according to my father, is where Lally entertained her German lover.' Jonny opened the window and pushed the shutters outward. 'It's a pretty moon tonight.'

Joining him at the window, Hope saw the ghostly silhouette of Yves' windmill. 'What are you showing me?'

'Just look.'

She saw a figure walking towards the mill. Yves, who had probably come outside to get a better signal on his phone, to call her. She felt mean, spying on him.

'From here,' Taubier said, 'Lally's German lover could easily have seen a lantern being taken up to the top of the mill, seen its glow through the window slits as its bearer walked up the steps.' He turned to her. 'I know the story of the betrayal of the Resistance fighters. Her lover could have watched the light being lit, to send a signal across the terrain.'

'It was a man called Aubin who hung the lantern. Lally describes him as simple-minded.'

'We would say now that he had learning difficulties, *non*? There were informants everywhere. There were active collaborators, the ones who were pro-Nazi, but the Resistance was leaky as a sieve too, and you know why? Because it was composed of human beings, some of whom drank, some of whom gossiped. Some of whom went to bed with unreliable people. A German unit commander knew exactly where to go to for his intelligence.' Jonny gestured into the moonlight. 'The lover got out of bed and came to the window to look at the moon and sees a wavering lantern. He knows it is a signal being placed. That tonight is the night.'

'You're saying, it was bad luck? Bad timing?'

'That is a plausible explanation, Madame.' Jonny put out his hand to shake hers. 'I'll be in touch about doing a valuation on your house.'

Hope drove the few hundred metres to La Cachette and met Yves walking down his drive. She stopped her car, getting out. 'Sorry.'

'I kept phoning you, Hope.'

'I'll explain. Jump in.' But he didn't move and she sensed he was agitated.

'I thought La Cachette had gone and done it again,' he said. Taken his dream, strangled it.

'No, the opposite. Quite the opposite.' Abandoning her car, she walked with him up the rutted driveway thinking, When I've sold my place, I'll help him finish this place. Make a home and business of it. This was rushing ahead, so she kept it to herself and, instead, asked him if he had a pair of heavy-duty wire cutters.

'I have bolt cutters. Why?'

'To tear down a barbed-wire fence.'

'They'll only put it up again,' Yves said gloomily.

'No. I have lots to tell you. Oh, blast.'

'What is it?'

'I've left wine and chocolates in the car.'

He chuckled. 'Lucky I have plenty, then.'

By noon the next day, the barbed-wire fence was down, its strands rolled up for disposal. As they walked back towards the windmill, Hope and Yves heard the sustained hoot of a car horn. She'd left her Renault blocking the track.

A minute later, Manon stumped into sight. 'Stupid place to park,' she shouted at them. Noah walked a few paces behind.

'Good morning to you too,' Yves replied. 'How can I help?' His voice was straight out of the deep freeze. Hope had recounted her conversation with Jonny Taubier.

Manon launched an accusation. 'You promised Noah a job, I've just discovered. He's too young. That's illegal.'

'Only until his birthday. But sure, I did. In the café.'

'Which nobody comes to.' Manon stared contemptuously at the windmill.

'It will be a soft take-off for him, then. There are things he can help me with. It's my intention to get as much of Lally's work back as I can and display it here.'

'For nobody to see.'

'Or everybody to see. Like the legend, I rise.' Yves pulled up the hem of his shirt and displayed a lustrous phoenix tattoo, its wings outspread on his belly.

Noah came up and presented a wad of dry, mouldy paper to Hope. 'It was under the leg of our bath,' he explained. 'The bath's wonky, so Mum shoved this underneath to straighten it.'

'They don't need to know,' Manon snapped.

What on earth was being given? Hope separated the compressed layers. 'Oh, my God,' she breathed. 'Yves, look.' It was the cover of a paperback book, with a few pages attached back and front. It had an ink sketch of a windmill on a hill, and fighter planes dark against the sky. The silhouette of a woman with very short hair filled the foreground.

Its title was—

BARBED WIRE AND FALSE NAMES: MEMOIR OF AN
ENGLISH GIRL IN OCCUPIED FRANCE

Epilogue, August 1994

I published this memoir, in its first imprint, fifteen years ago. I
felt ready to tell my story. Not in the hope of being forgiven,
but to be understood. That's all I ever wish for. For the
judgers and the finger-pointers, the spitters-into-the-gutter, to
know where I came from and why I ended up here. And why
I stay, the lonely lady in the windmill, painting the hours,
moving painfully to the music of life.

But, like a hare out of the traps, my little book was brought
down and murdered by a vicious dog. Strangely, not the dog I
predicted would go after it. Not the Taubiers, though I
libelled them without mercy. Life is strange. I gave up on my
memoir.

Not long ago, having turned eighty-one, I unearthed the
typed pages and penned this epilogue. I took the whole lot to a

printers in Auch, our region's capital, and said, 'How much to turn this into a book?'

They said, 'How many copies do you wish for, Madame?'

'One.'

'One thousand, Madame?'

'No. Just one.'

They goggled at me. 'But, Madame, your single book will cost hundreds of euros.'

'No, it won't,' I answered, 'because I am an old woman who has survived much, and you will cut me a deal that brings down the price to something I can afford.' Haggling while looking hard done by gets results. I have my one book, to be left to my darling motherless boy should he ever wish to read it. My Yves, named for the singer whose tender voice calms me as I paint. I have stayed at La Cachette for more than fifty years, waiting for the other boy who never came.

I will live as long as I can, to allow Yves to thrive and survive. I have something else to add, which makes this a true epilogue. Something strange and magical.

It is August the fifth. I am painting in my bird's nest studio. It is a beautiful day, a breeze bringing me the scents of ripening vines and my view is the golden grins of a million sunflowers and the mountains beyond. Some way off, a public address system pumps out music, warped by distance and heat. It comes from Lazurac, where they're having a parade and a street party for the fiftieth anniversary of the night the Resistance was broken by the Germans. Why would anyone wish to remember?

To my dismay, a car noses from the overgrown drive and stops in front of my gîte. I recognise the local taxi. It's one I use if I need to go anywhere.

Visitors rarely bode well. Since dear Véronique died, and Aubin, and lastly my daughter, I have lived only with Yves for company. He is somewhere around, I suppose, though unlike me, he has friends in Lazurac. Muttering, I wipe my brush and put it into its turpentine jar and begin the slow climb down.

I'm old, I shouldn't be going up and down windmill steps for no good reason.

My visitor is a woman. She has a child with her, a girl of about nine. Pretty little thing, brown hair and big eyes. Blue-grey eyes. The past races up and almost knocks me off my feet.

The woman introduces herself as Tina Granger. 'Mrs Joseph Granger.' She asks if I understand English. I nod, mutely, my eyes on the child.

The lady says, 'This is my daughter, Hope.'

'Hope.' The blessing that ferries us between misfortunes. The child smiles, uncertainly.

She is the image of Pauline. I see Otto too, and Joseph. Tearing my gaze from her, I look at the taxi, thinking – Joseph has come. At last, at long last.

'My husband couldn't come,' says the woman.

'Couldn't?'

Tina Granger, who has a neat, sensible face, makes an apologetic noise. 'To be honest, he wouldn't. He hasn't got a passport and nothing I can say will persuade him to apply for one. May I ask, are you his mother?'

I don't answer. She continues, 'He's scared of meeting her because it was all so traumatic, how they took him away. He still has nightmares about it.'

Him too, then. I will never forget the policeman bringing him back after he tried to run away from the English couple who came to take him. A sprig of lavender in his little fist, all he had of me. *Maman, Maman!*

His cries fly about my head at night, like the owls who nest in the rafters of my windmill. I have a choice, whether or not to tell this good lady and her shy child the truth about Joseph's birth.

I walk over to the taxi and ask the driver to come back in two hours. Then I hold out my hand to the little girl and say, 'Well, Hope, would you like to look inside a real French windmill?'

HOPE'S EPILOGUE

AUGUST 2015

The terrace table and chairs looked good on the paving stones outside the windmill. Yves had put up umbrellas because the summer weather had broken records. August heat wasn't diminishing the energy of the children playing swing ball on the lawn. Yves had moved the post into the shade.

Claudia's twins were still going for their personal goal of one thousand uninterrupted thwacks. Claudia's new partner was keeping count. Four hundred so far. They'd appreciate the lunch Yves was putting together in the gîte, helped by Claudia, who now lived in the Gers.

Hope was catching a quick, private chat with Jonny Taubier, who had become a surprise friend to both her and Yves. He and his wife had attended Hope and Yves' wedding two days before. Goldie, Paloma, TJ and Elkie had sent flowers, and were coming back in September, to stay. La Cachette was now the home of Eat-Sleep-Paint-Gascony.

'So go on, tell me what you found.' She refilled their glasses. Wine for Jonny, elderflower fizz for her. A few weeks ago, she'd asked him if his brother, the *notaire*, might do some cross-Channel sleuthing for her. She wanted to know who had taken a lawsuit against Lally's memoir, as a surprise wedding present to Yves. Jonny's brother had studied in London, and a friend there had obligingly searched records at the Royal Courts of Justice.

'I have your answer,' Jonny said, batting away a fly. 'Do you want the big reveal?'

'I do.'

He took a card from his pocket and read what was scribbled on the back. 'The person who took the libel suit out against L.L. Shepherd, otherwise known as Lally Ducasse, in the summer of 1979, leading to the book being withdrawn and Lally having to pay costs and compensation was...'

'Get on with it.'

'Mrs Horace Blackshaw.'

Who the hell was she?

'A respectable lady, resident in... not sure how to pronounce this, in Dulwich, London. Which according to my brother's friend was and still is very chic.'

'Your brother must have given out the wrong name.'

'Lucien never gets things wrong. Trust me. The records were searched and gave up their secrets. I can tell you that before she married in 1948, Mrs Horace Blackshaw was a Miss Norma-Rose Foster.'

Hope smacked her palms on the table. 'A working girl in a Parisian brothel.'

'*Mon Dieu*, then I doubt she liked having the world told of it in a memoir. She had married well and took out a lawsuit. My brother says her barrister squashed your Lally like this—' Jonny caught the irritating fly in his palm.

Yves came out, bringing hors d'oeuvres, sliced baguette and olive oil for dipping.

'Not too much of the new man act, Yves,' Jonny said. 'My wife will start to get ideas.'

Putting down the plate, Yves draped his arms around Hope's shoulders, lowering his lips to her hair, which was still blonde but had grown thicker and longer. 'I do all the heavy lifting for now.'

'When's it due again?' Jonny asked. 'When do I get to be godfather?'

'Christmas.' Hope and Yves already knew their baby was going to be a boy. Her hands made a protective shield across her swollen stomach. A little boy would arrive and grow up in the shelter of a windmill, secure in his parents' love, free to thrive.

Hope pinned on the Grey Eyed Dove every morning, to whatever top she chose that day. She did it to remember the one whose battle to survive had given them life. Had Lally surrendered in ice-cold solitary at Besançon, Yves would not be here. Had she abandoned Pauline by the fence at Lons-le-Saunier, Pauline's baby might not have lived and Hope wouldn't have come into the world.

Mit Liebe, with love.

Otto, poet, thinker, hunted man, had tried his best to survive. The dedication etched on the brooch pin belonged to him and Pauline. But Hope wore it for Lally.

A LETTER FROM NATALIE

Thank you for reading *The Paris Inheritance* and following the intertwined stories of Lally and Hope. I do hope you enjoyed it, and perhaps glimpsed a time that is gradually fading from living memory. If you enjoyed it and want to keep up to date with all my latest releases, just sign up at the following link. Your email address will never be shared and you can unsubscribe at any time.

www.bookouture.com/natalie-meg-evans

I have set many of my novels in the Paris of the 1920s, 30s and 40s. This one has been a little different: it's about *leaving* Paris and how that separation changes the lives of Lally, Pauline, Otto and their friends.

I am not always aware of themes in my stories while I'm planning them. As I wove Lally's narrative alongside Hope's, the idea that our lives can heal the pain of the past emerged. Whatever darkness exists in this world, there is always the gift of hope. Each new life brings the opportunity for each of us to do better, *be* better, and hope is born afresh.

In my research, I delved into an aspect of wartime history I touched on in an earlier novel, that of the internment of British (and later, American) women living in occupied France. I did not know much about the prison at Besançon, until I turned up some first-hand accounts. I have to say, what I read horrified me.

As a historical writer, I am drawn to less-exposed aspects of the past. Not always with pleasure, as it makes for hard reading, but my aim is to humanise history. To present it through the eyes of brave people, the ones wearing worn-out shoes and patched dresses, who have nothing to fight with other than their wits and determination.

For my next novels, I'm heading back to London where I lived in my early twenties. I've rarely met anyone who was blissfully at ease at that point in their lives and while I loved the freedom the capital city offered, there were scary times too. Like all big cities, London has a toughness behind the handsome façades. My upcoming books are set in 1940, in the traumatic months of the Blitz with the bombs falling and the skies burning. Despite mining some difficult stories and memories, I can't wait to get going and hope to meet you again on the page. If you'd like to get in touch, my contact details are below.

Thank you for reading my story.

Natalie Meg Evans

www.nataliemegevans.uk

 facebook.com/nataliemegevans

 x.com/natmegevans

 instagram.com/natalie.meg.evans

PUBLISHING TEAM

Turning a manuscript into a book requires the efforts of many people. The publishing team at Bookouture would like to acknowledge everyone who contributed to this publication.

Audio
Alba Proko
Melissa Tran
Sinead O'Connor

Commercial
Lauren Morrissette
Hannah Richmond
Imogen Allport

Cover design
Emma Graves

Data and analysis
Mark Alder
Mohamed Bussuri

Editorial
Natalie Edwards
Charlotte Hegley

Printed in Great Britain
by Amazon

54544489R00223